A Soul to Touch

Duskwalker Brides

Book Three

Opal Reyne

ISBN: 978-0-6455104-7-8

Cover art: Sam Griffin

Trigger Warning
Major spoiler below

Please only read further if you have triggers, otherwise you will seriously spoil the book for yourself.

Firstly, I will list what triggers **AREN'T** in the book so you can stop reading in order not to spoil it: No rape, non-con, purposeful harm done to the FMC by the MMC, torture, suicide/self-harm, depression, ow/om drama, abortion, mental/emotion abuse, incest, drug/alcohol abuse, or child harm.

Please consider stopping here if your trigger has been detailed above as the rest are major spoilers.

There is no pregnancy in the main story, however there is an epilogue pregnancy which is skippable. We delve into a wide variety of kinks in this book, such as: breeding kink, dp, minor bite/blood play, minor strangulation play, tail play.

This book does have detailed descriptions of wound and wound care, such as: stitching, blood, gaping wounds. As always, my books have gore.

There are descriptions of death, mourning before death, discussions of a possible upcoming death, and grief. A HEA is always guaranteed in my books.

The FMC is a hunter and Demonslayer who uses animals to bait Demons. There are descriptions of wild animal deaths, although there is no maliciousness or torture. She tries to do so painlessly.

Author's note on language

I'm from AUSTRALIA.

My English is not the same as American English.
I love my American English spoken readers to bits. You're cute, you all make me giggle, and I just wanna give you a big 'ol hug. However, there are many of you who don't seem to realise that your English was born from British English, which is what I use (although a bastardised version since Australians like to take all language and strangle it until it's a ruined carcass of slang, missing letters, and randomly added o's).

We don't seem to like the letter z.

We write colour instead of color. Recognise instead of recognize. Travelling instead of traveling. Skilful instead of skillfull. Mum instead of mom. Smelt is a past participle of smell. We omit the full-stop in Mr. Name, so it's Mr Name. Aussies cradle the word cunt like it's a sweet little puppy, rather than an insult to be launched at your face.

Anyway, happy reading!

To all the *horny* MonsterFuckers out there,

this book is for you.

For the people that the monster would be more afraid of you than you are of it. Where you'd grab that big badass by the horns and direct them between your thighs – doesn't matter if it's their other-worldly face, or their strange, fancy cock.

Embrace your MonsterFucker heart, you know you want to.

I would like to give a big shoutout to the wonderful **sensitivity readers** who helped to make this book a safe place for those I am trying to positively represent. As you all know, representation is a big part of what I want to do, but I want to do so in a way that isn't harmful.

Thank you to Amanda, Careen, Charna, Emily, Marcella, PollyAné, Sue, Susan, Tracy, and Veluz for your contribution regarding Asian sensitivity.

I would also like to thank Crystal for your contribution towards POC sensitivity.

I appreciate all the time and effort you put into helping me with this book. You will forever have a place in my heart.

ONE

The snow pressed against her flesh, causing goosebumps to flare up her bare legs until they assaulted her spine. Mayumi shivered, her little four-year-old legs sinking so far into the cold, dry powder that it came all the way above her wobbly knees.

She didn't have far to fall, constantly having to steady herself with her hands to dig herself out so she could press forward through the forest.

It was dark.

But she'd been marching through the night for so long that her eyes had adjusted to it. She could tell the difference between shadowy tree trunks, their leafy branches reaching down, and the shrubs on the ground. The sky was blue-black, helping her to know where darker obstacles were so she could avoid them.

The glow of the moon bounced off the snow, aiding her vision as she searched.

Should she, a child, be walking through the dangerous forest by herself? Definitely not, especially since her family resided outside of a village and its towering, protective walls.

They were one of the rare families to live in the potentially Demon-filled forests, but her father guaranteed them they were safe – even more so when she was scared and in need of comfort.

Did her parents know where she was? She sincerely hoped not – otherwise her father would give her a stern talking to. He was comforting and yet very scary. He was strict; he had to be with such a curious girl as his daughter.

So, what was she doing outside in the forest by herself on one of the darkest nights of winter when she very much knew she'd be in trouble for it?

Her tiny breaths came out as fogging huffs in front of her face. They tickled her freezing nose, giving it a moment of warmth before fading. One nostril was dripping, and she constantly sniffled it.

Her feet were freezing in her night boots, and they ached with a numb kind of pain. It was the same in her hands and fingers. She pulled the jacket she'd thrown over herself taut with one of her hands, while the other steadied her so she could, once again, dig herself out of the snow.

Luckily, she was small and light. She'd seen both her parents struggle to walk through such thick, fresh powder.

"Shadow!" she called, her young voice echoing. "Shadow! Here, kitty!"

She received no answer.

Her thick black hair fell across her brow as she searched. As they had many times during her stubborn march, tears welled in her eyes.

"Please! I'm-I'm sorry for pulling your tail!"

Her cat, which was nearly black other than a white mask across its face, had been missing for most of the day. Usually, she'd come home after running off, but she hadn't returned for dinner.

She was gone, and Mayumi was heartbroken.

Since Mayumi always stayed home with her mother, as she was too young to travel through the forest safely, she hadn't met any other humans her own age. Shadow was her only friend. They'd known each other all their lives.

Mayumi skilfully stemmed her tears and furrowed her brow with determination. She even pursed her lips, more so on the left than on the right side – she hated it when her mother made fun of her pout.

But it was Mayumi's big girl brave face.

She was going to find her kitty, and then she would return home before either of her parents knew she was gone.

Yet as the night drew later and somehow became colder – the wind soft but biting with frozen teeth – she slowed. Although her *teeth were clacking from her jaw jittering, eventually she started to feel... warm.*

So warm, in fact, that sweat beaded on her forehead.

The trees began to split in two, as did the bushes. The ground became wavy, and she found herself stumbling.

"Here, K-kitty, K-kitty, K-k-kitty."

No matter how far she wandered, Shadow never came.

Mayumi didn't know how far from home she was now, but she knew she needed to return if she didn't want anyone to notice she was missing.

She turned around, foolishly believing home was directly behind her, too young to take into consideration she'd been swerving around trees, bushes, and the odd boulder.

A cracking, crunching sound caught her attention.

Her heart raced with delirious hope, and she headed straight for the noise. It's Shadow. It has to be Shadow. *Of course, it was her cat – nothing else could* possibly *be lurking in the dark.*

Unwittingly, Mayumi sprinted straight into danger, her mind foggy and her fever getting worse by the second.

A creature, so black it made it near impossible to see how big it was in the dark, turned its head to her. Yellow eyes caught her attention, big, just like Shadow's. Mayumi smiled brightly. Like Shadow's mask, their face was white, and with how blurry her vision had become, it was easy to mistake what it really was.

Yay! I found her! *Mayumi tripped in the snow in excitement. It distracted her enough that she didn't notice the reflective slick of the snow revealed the yellow glow had turned red.*

Their maw was opening as a growl echoed, but she took that bass as a rumbling purr. They were coming to greet her.

A black paw landed right in front of her as she got to her feet. Mayumi leapt blindly with her hands reaching.

"Kitty!" she squealed joyfully, wrapping her arms around their thick neck.

All rumbling sounds suddenly went quiet.

Mayumi rubbed her face into the familiar soft fur she was used to. They were warm, and she lost herself in it, her body seeking the heat.

"D-don't," she started, her voice raspy and growing softer.

"Don't l-leave me again. I missed you."

Mayumi grew weak. All her determination faded now that she'd found her pet, and eventually her arms loosened their tight, hugging hold. She fell to the side, knocking into a fluffy limb, as though the creature had been standing on all fours.

Out in the open, thinking she was laying in front of her cat, Mayumi fainted as her fever took hold...

"Fuck!" Mayumi yelled, the blanket falling from her chest to her hips as she quickly sat upright on her bed.

Her long black hair swayed forward. The ends settled against her chest while the length of it framed her face.

She panted, breaths sawing in and out of her rapidly heaving chest as sweat dotted her brow. She looked around, making sure she knew where she was before bringing her legs up.

She placed her left elbow on her bent knees so she could cup her forehead, ignoring the perspiration there as she stared at her blanket with wide eyes.

It's that dream again. A dream... or a memory?

Mayumi didn't actually know. She had been too young to remember what she'd seen, too sick to really believe what her eyes took in that night.

All she knew... all she knew was that she'd never actually found her cat. Shadow never returned; she never saw her again.

But whatever her four-year-old self had stumbled upon... whatever the fuck it was, it hadn't eaten her. At least, she didn't think it had tried to.

After collapsing in the snow when she was four, she'd woken in bed, fever-stricken, to her parents panicking – mostly her mother. Someone or *something* had taken her home.

They didn't knock, didn't yell for her parents, didn't stay around to explain anything.

Her parents had found her in front of the porch steps laying in the snow after they'd been *searching* for her. Of course, her parents had realised she was gone in the middle of the night.

They thought she was dead, most likely eaten by a Demon that attacked her while she was stupidly walking around. One would have stumbled across her frozen corpse and eaten her eventually.

With the help of Priests coming to their home to aid her, they'd healed her fever over the course of many days.

The scolding and punishment she'd received from her father after she'd gotten better had been brutal enough that she never left their home after dark again.

"Fuck," she cursed again quietly. "What the hell did I see that night?"

It was a question she'd asked herself many times over her life. She'd often had this reoccurring memory-like dream.

There were only two options available: a Demon or a Duskwalker.

Blindly, Mayumi reached out beside her roll-out futon bed. She patted the ground before her fingertips grazed a cool ceramic bottle that tried to roll away. She grasped it.

"I really need to stop drinking," she muttered, lifting the bottle above her head so the remaining drops of alcohol would coat her tongue. "I always have weird, vivid dreams when I drink."

She'd been hoping there were more than a few drops in the bottle, but as she turned her gaze to the side, she realised she'd knocked it over and spilled its contents. Before or after she had fallen asleep, she wasn't sure. At least it fell the other way and didn't ruin her futon.

Dropping the bottle to the side, she got to her hands and knees to crawl over to the last dry log. She threw it in the fireplace, knowing the remaining coals would eventually set it alight and rewarm the house.

Completely and utterly naked, since there was no one else in this empty house besides herself, she dragged her sorry, hungover ass to the kitchen counter.

She unlocked the wooden blinds and pushed them to the sides to reveal the long, plain, gridded window behind them. It was snowing lightly, the world a sea of white. With drowsy eyes, she paid the outside world no mind. It was warm enough within her house, and that's all she cared about.

She reached across the well-maintained wooden counter for the ceramic jar she wanted, removed the lid, then *immediately* sighed and rolled her eyes.

"I forgot I was out of my morning tea."

She reached for another jar, one she rarely opened because its contents were precious and extremely difficult to obtain – and costly. She opened it.

"What the hell?" she growled, tipping the empty jar upside down to see a few brown speckles fall from it. "The coffee too?"

She stamped her foot, leaned over the counter while resting her elbows onto it, and groaned into her hands. *I don't want to go to town today!*

She'd been saying that for three days.

However, she was now officially out of everything decent in this house. No tea, no coffee, and she was well aware she was out of booze.

Nope. No. Not doing it. She leaned back so she could stand straight, rolling her shoulders back defiantly to no one but herself. *I can survive without that shit. I've been doing it for years.*

Her eyes drifted to the front door.

"There's only one option left."

TWO

A The snow rendered a gasp from Mayumi the moment her entire, bare-ass naked body landed in it. She'd thrown herself off her porch and into the thick powder right in front of her stairs, basically salmon diving into it.

All her grogginess dissipated within an instant.

"Woo!" she squealed, sitting up and throwing both her fists into the air. She blinked at the brightness surrounding her in the late morning sun, as falling snowflakes slowly collected in her hair. "That never ceases to hit the spot."

Her light, fawny skin began to pinken in some areas, the air frigid and cruel to her complexion.

She quickly got to her feet, incidentally sinking to her calves in the fresh snow and having to steady herself. She yanked them free and grabbed the metal bucket she'd brought with her so she could start shovelling snow into it.

By the time she was done, her nipples were tight and uncomfortably hard, almost pinching. They pointed the way as she sprinted inside her cottage house to escape the wintery elements, making sure to clean her feet before entering her home.

She placed the metal bucket over a heating rack within her fireplace before kneeling in front of it to warm her body and blue-tinged fingertips.

It wasn't long before she had fresh water, and she used a ladle as a cup to moisten her tongue. Then she let the water heat for long enough that she could use it to wipe her body clean with a dampened cloth.

She had little else to occupy her thoughts and couldn't help but look around her home while she waited.

Most would say it was modest. It bore only one additional room and was made mostly of wood, but it was sturdy and had stood the test of time. Her family had resided in this medium-sized cottage for centuries.

On the left wall behind her, there was a wide kitchen with a rack nestled between its countertop and the door. There were no cupboards above the counters, but many spanned underneath, and there was a rack behind the door hiding her dwindling fruits and vegetables. On the right-hand side of the counters was a dining table that had been pushed longways against the wall to save space, but could be pulled out to sit four comfortably.

Currently, there was only one chair available. The other three were being stored outside in a wooden shed.

Next to the table at the far-left corner was a door that led into a storage room, where Mayumi mainly kept her clothes. It was designed to be a space for everyone living within the house to store personal items. Clothing, toys, *weapons.*

It was where her futon currently was. She'd rolled it up and put it away with all her bedding before she'd gone outside. Most of those who lived outside of protected villages used futons to save space, especially since the number of people within the house could frequently change.

She usually slept next to the fireplace, as it often had the freest space – her parents had done this as well. It was also warmer in winter.

To her left, which was also the back of the house, was a sort of seating area. There were two bags filled with sheep wool; thankfully, they were light and easy to move around. One of them was on the floor, as she often sat in it, while the other rested in an unused armchair made from leather and wood.

The last seat was a rocking chair, and she eyed it, knowing it was her mother's favourite before she passed away.

She sighed, turning her eyes away from the rocking chair that filled her with longing... to bring them back to the fireplace. It was made completely from brick, and above the mantle were various Demon-warding ornaments they'd discovered over the centuries – whether they actually worked, she wasn't sure.

Her father's personal sword rested above it like a reminder and a warning.

Lastly, between the fireplace and the door to the right, was a full-length mirror that ran from floor to ceiling with a coat rack next to it. The mirror was there so they could check their outfits before they left the house. If one didn't like looking at their own reflection, it would be difficult to avoid doing so because of its placement.

It often reflected Mayumi's bored and tired expression.

Despite the lack of furniture, leaning against or nailed to every wall was personal décor collected by her family over the centuries. An old painting of a meadow and river drawn with black ink on a cream canvas. An ornate lantern that had never been used because it was too precious. A picture a child had painted, displayed above the kitchen counter.

Nailed to the back of the front door there was a flower ribbon Mayumi had made, which was a rainbow because every petal was a different colour.

There were so many memories collected here. If anyone came here and found it vacant, she was sure it would be heart-aching. Too often in her life, Mayumi had walked into a stranger's home to find it stained in blood but with evidence of a mostly humble and happy home.

Sometimes those memories lingered, and she turned away from her darkening thoughts to concentrate on her task.

I can't change the past.

Once she was done cleaning herself, Mayumi dressed in tight brown leather breeches, hooking the button clasps at her right hip. Then she donned an undershirt before placing a thick grey cotton tunic over her torso. Lastly, she threw on a white wolf-pelt jacket – something that was invaluable, as only hunters could obtain a pelt of such a colour.

Mayumi stepped in front of the full-length mirror situated permanently against the wall. It had a few aged spots but otherwise was mostly clear – except for the frosted top right corner.

Her gaze barely registered her frowzy appearance. It didn't

linger on her brown eyes that appeared black in shadows but shone nearly tawny in the light. It also didn't linger on her small, pointed chin, her ears, or her cupid's-bow lips. Her body was hidden by the thick jacket, making it easy to mistake her slender body frame – which was deceptive to her strength.

What she really cared to look upon was her thick, waist-length black hair. After debating on whether or not to brush the tangled mess that looked more like a bird's nest than hair, she realised she didn't give a damn. She just threw it up in her usual high ponytail so it wouldn't obscure her vision.

She poked her finger through the bars of her messenger pigeon's cage to scratch the back of his neck. He cooed delightfully in response.

Before she left her house, she wrapped her sword belt around her waist, checking to make sure her dagger was secure as well. Then she slung her quiver and bow across her back.

Mayumi had spent many afternoons hand-making her arrows. The arrowheads were forged from steel in the small rudimentary smithing station she had at the back of her home. The feathers were odd colours because she used any bird she managed to shoot down for her fletching feathers.

Dressed for the weather and the dangers that could be lurking, she opened the door to step onto the wooden porch. The area spanned two sides of her cottage, wrapping around the front and right side from the front entrance.

She leaned down and shook her leather and fur boots of any snow that may have collected inside them overnight before shoving them on her feet. There were many other shoes on the rack next to the front door, from working boots to slip-on flats.

Now that she was ready in what she wore most days, she walked along each corner of the porch to check the *omamori*. Her ancestors believed the omamori protected them from the Demons and bad spirits. Dating back centuries before they became stuck in this part of the world after the Demons came to Earth, her family had continued the tradition of hanging them up.

Alongside them were wooden charm plates given to her by the Priests and Priestesses from the closest town. These didn't create any sort of barrier but were apparently more of a deterrent.

Her home had never been entered by Demons, and that's all she truly gave a shit about.

Doesn't look like I'll need to obtain new plates anytime soon, she thought as she roughly grabbed at them.

Mayumi then reached up to touch the brocade silk bag of the omamori that had some kind of wood inside of it – no one knew what kind, as it was customary to never open them. They were old and so frayed that she made sure she touched them gingerly. *These will not last too much longer.*

They had a few years left before the threaded silk rope holding them snapped. She believed they worked, but she also knew that could be false hope, as they hadn't been blessed for hundreds of years.

Sometimes it was just easier to believe.

She cupped her hands together, bowed her head, and prayed to them that her ancestors would continue to look over her. Then she stepped back while lowering her hands, giving them a small glare.

They better be watching over me. I'm the last one left. At least on her father's side.

She had no idea about her mother's origins, as her mother hadn't either. Her family had been killed by Demons when she was young, leaving her orphaned.

On the other hand, Mayumi knew all about her father's side of the family.

She rolled her eyes. *I'm not going to give myself a history lesson. My father gave me* plenty *of those.*

No, she had far more important things to do.

Adjusting her bow so it sat better across her mostly flat chest, she walked down the porch steps. The moment her boots were crunching in the snow, she headed to the right towards the back of her home.

Pressed against the back of the house was a wooden shed. She pushed up the long, heavy wooden latch that spanned it completely to open it. Fetching a long rope, she slung it over her shoulder before grabbing an axe and clipping it to her weapons belt.

After she closed the shed and secured it, she walked under the canopy attached to the back wall that provided shelter the entire way. This is where her smithing station was. There was a spring bath that had been made by someone from her family years ago. It connected to the stream nearby, which could be manipulated by terracotta pipes and dam points to block or release water flow directly to it.

But a bath outside in the middle of winter sucked. It took far too long to warm with the outside furnace.

Once she passed it, she began her descent down the mountain. She didn't even bother to look back; there was no point.

The surrounding forest was filled with tall, spindly trees, most of which were cedar or fir. They created just enough shadow to make any human feel wary. Mayumi scanned her environment carefully as she hiked.

The snow was thick upon the ground with more falling slowly every second, but she traversed it with ease. She was creating a trail behind her, and she knew she'd be able to follow it home.

Mayumi knew where she was going and would always find her way back. She'd grown up in this forest. She knew it better than anyone. It didn't matter that it had grown in the few years she'd been away from it.

A sound in the distance caused her head to lift in its direction, but she didn't pause. She just placed one hand firmly around her bow and the other on her short sword in preparation.

Nothing approached, and it was quiet once more other than her footfalls and her steady breaths.

There was a fallen tree she'd started cutting up a few days ago for her firewood, and she eventually spotted it down the long hill. Her reserves were empty since she'd thrown the last piece in the fireplace that very morning. If she didn't want to freeze for the next few nights, she needed more.

A severe snowstorm could also happen upon her at any time.

All the more reason to go to town, I guess. If I get stranded for more than two days, I'll have no food. She groaned out loud as she came upon the tree she wanted. *I'm going to have to go tomorrow, no question about it.*

She released her axe from its clip on her belt and rotated it in a circle to prepare her wrist. She also stretched her arms, back, and neck as she drew closer.

With the axe resting over her shoulder, she eyed the last long branch remaining since she'd already removed the rest. Then she grabbed the axe handle with both hands and slammed it into the thick base of it.

A snorting squeal sounded off to the side of her in a bush, Mayumi's first strike spooking whatever was inside it. Only a tree's distance away from her, it rustled wildly.

She immediately dropped her axe and unslung her bow from her back while reaching for an arrow. She lifted both, pulling back the string until her body locked into position, and aimed it in the shrub's direction. Something small, black, and hairy sprinted from it.

A Demon? No.

A Demon lure? Yes, and she was absolutely taking it home.

With a skill that took years to hone, she released her arrow, her exhaled breath following it straight into a young boar. It gave a piggish squeal when the arrow lodged in its shoulder, making it stumble. She was already running for it.

Just as it was about to get up and start running again, Mayumi leapt. With her weight pressing down on it, she tied its mouth shut to keep it quiet before hogtying it.

With it squirming to free itself to no avail, she hoisted it over her back. It was heavy, as boars were usually quite dense. She was lucky it was relatively small, and that she was unusually strong.

All that training did me wonders.

She dropped it onto the ground next to the tree. She needed it alive for what she wanted to do with it, needed it fresh, but she still needed firewood as well.

Palming her forehead before brushing a few strands of loose hair from her face, her cowlick curls unable to be tamed, she wondered what she was supposed to do.

She'd used the rope she'd been intending to carry her firewood back with. Somehow, she grew impossibly tired despite the adrenaline running through her.

With her warm breaths fogging in the cold air, the boar received a glare.

"*You*. You just couldn't be in a bush near the house, could you?" She yanked her axe from the snow and hacked at the branch again. "Now I'm going to have to carry you and this branch back at the same time. Do you know how hard that's going to be?! And I don't have any booze to reward myself with!"

She'd originally planned to cut this branch into pieces and carry it all on her back like a backpack with the rope wrapped around the edges. Now she would have to grab the thin end of the branch and drag it across the ground while carting the animal on her back.

Her words were strained, often following with a grunt when she used the axe, when she said, "Then again, this will give me something to do tonight."

It was better than drinking and staring at the flames, or out the window, or at the damn ceiling.

I need a boyfriend or something. She paused and scrunched up her nose at herself. *Ew. No, I don't. Men are too complicated.*

Girlfriend then? She thought about it for a long while, her eyes scanning the canopy of leaves above... and then she shook her head. *Same problem. Too complicated.*

Regardless, she was feeling a smidge lonely. *I'd rather just fuck and forget their face.*

Another reason to go to the town, she supposed.

Once she was done with cutting the branch free from the cedar tree lying half-buried in the snow, she hoisted the boar onto her back. Then she walked around to grab the tip of the tree branch, pulling on it to start her treacherous climb back up the mountain.

She created a noticeable track in the snow behind her, but she was more focused on not tripping while carrying her heavy load. Her heart raced with exertion, her breaths growing more rapid as seconds passed with every strained leg lift.

This is going to take forever, she thought after five minutes, finding she'd barely covered any distance. *Damnit.*

THREE

After returning home and waiting for nightfall to begin, Mayumi securely tied the boar's back feet and pulled on the long length of rope connected to it so she could hang it upside down. In the middle of the small clearing in front of her house was a nine-foot-tall wooden stake. At the top of the stake was a carved slit to guide the rope through without it slipping to the side as she pulled.

When her bait was chest height, she temporarily looped the rope around a metal spike that had been pounded into the ground.

The boar made noises of distress. She was sure it was uncomfortable or in pain, but she'd long ago become desensitised to this kind of cruelty. Its suffering would end shortly.

That didn't mean earlier in the day she hadn't nursed the injured boar. She'd cleaned its wound inflicted by her arrow and bandaged it while giving it herbal medicine in the hopes of removing its pain.

She hated doing this to a defenceless animal, but it was a necessity in the reality of the Demon-age the world was currently in.

Removing the cutting blade from between her teeth and the lip-curling grin that prevented her face from being sliced, Mayumi gripped the handle tightly with one fist. Then she stabbed the blade into the boar's gut just below its pelvis.

She stepped back slightly as she cut downwards, letting its blood and entrails fall to the ground to make sure very little, or hopefully none, touched her.

Knowing she needed to discard it so as not to carry around the smell of fresh blood, she dropped the knife to the ground and then eyed the sky.

Dusk was settling, and the shadows were already long. A few more minutes and the sun would fully finish dropping beyond the horizon.

Mayumi grabbed the rope and hoisted the boar carcass higher up the wooden stake to make it difficult to reach. Her movements were quick, rushed, but not panicked.

Once it was tied permanently, she sprinted inside.

She didn't remove her boots, although she usually would, so she could be swift. Her hands had a few crimson droplets, and she washed them in a shallow bowl.

The mirror was her next stop to check that she didn't have blood anywhere else before doing a final look over her boots with her own eyes.

The clothing she wore was black from head to toe.

Her boots felt more like socks as they were flexible and durable, moulding between her big toes so she had dexterity with them. Her leather breeches had been soaked in black dye, as had her skin-tight shirt and leather jacket. Her gloves were thin, not designed to keep out the cold, but rather, to hide the skin.

Over her head was a specialised hood with a button on the inside so she could hook a mask over her face that hid everything but her eyes.

And those eyes, that had been bored and tired earlier, now looked back at her from the mirror with a distinct sharpness they only ever held when she wore this outfit.

The last detail on her otherwise plain clothing was a silver insignia pressed into the upper chest at her sternum. A sword stabbing all the way through a circle that tapered off at the end before it could finish completing.

It was the symbol of the Demonslayer guild.

This outfit was a perfect replica of hundreds that were worn by the guild, from the hood and pants to the very shoes.

All of it was uniform, all of it was the same, except for one major detail – the colour of the insignia revealed the person's status within the Demonslayer guild.

The highest colour was gold, the lowest was black.

Her left nostril twitched in irritation at the silver insignia on her chest that designated the second-highest ranking in the guild. She twisted away from her reflection.

Mayumi left the main area of her house to enter the only other room.

She ignored the array of personal items that belonged to various ancestors. Dust-covered clothing, shoes that weren't of use because they didn't fit her, a doll belonging to her great-grandmother. The area was packed to the ceiling with items that no one had the heart to discard.

Not even her.

She always noticed the old, slightly mouldy smell in this room, and it occasionally set off her mild hay fever if she disturbed anything too much.

The mask covering her face was thin. It was meant only to hide her skin but not cause her breaths to become deepened and loud, and did little to shelter her from the uncomfortable, history-drenched smell.

She pulled on the rope attached to the ceiling in the middle of the room to unlatch a door hatch. Stairs tilted down, and she pulled on the rope beneath the first section to unfold it so she could climb up.

She ducked her body forward, nearly hugging the stairs to keep her bow, quiver, and arrows from preventing her ascension into the attic.

The area here was dusty but showed evidence of recent and frequent use. She struck a match once she was kneeling on the level, lighting a candle she knew was right next to the opening.

Very little was tucked away up here.

It was mostly empty aside from a few scattered weapons that remained here purposefully, just in case of an emergency.

The attic provided an escape in two different directions. Up if Demons entered from the lower level, or down if she needed to get off the roof – which was where she was currently headed.

The moment she opened the door leading outside from within the attic, the cold night air assaulted her. She ducked down, quickly placing a brown cloak over her body that would camouflage her.

Mayumi hoisted herself outside onto the roof, crawling on her hands and knees until she was where she wanted to be. She lay flat on the slanted roof and observed the clearing where the boar currently hung as she pulled her bow and quiver off her shoulders.

She nocked the end of an arrow to her bowstring but laid it flat against the roof in a relaxed position and waited.

She was used to being outside in the dark of night hunting the monsters that often hunted her back. With her practiced eyes, she could clearly see everything.

The boar was her bait. She'd needed to wait until it was almost dark before she could utilise it, needing its freshly spilled blood to lead Demons here. Dried blood was only useful when the animal was larger, such as a deer or wolf.

She'd had to kill it where she did, in the way she did, in order to lead them to that specific location. The last thing she wanted was to lure the Demons to multiple places, making it disorientating for her to hunt from her sniping spot. It also meant they wouldn't be sniffing around in search of more blood, which could reveal her instead.

Mayumi's clothing was saturated in strong-smelling herbs, and her skin was coated in an oil that had already started soaking in. This was enough to dilute her human smell, but not enough to erase it.

It helped that fresh snow slowly covered her, but she was warm enough under her cloak. She was used to the harsh elements from her training.

Since her home was well-thought-out in terms of location, the wait was long.

Her ancestors had built the house between two large villages north of the Veil's forest, both of which were filled with hundreds of people. The villages cloaked Mayumi's family home under the overwhelming mass of humankind.

Small homes like hers were often safe because the Demons were drawn to the larger populations.

Although the villages were far from the Demon's home in the Veil, they were, unfortunately, close to the mountains. Many

Demons liked to build their nests outside the Veil in the mountainsides' dark caves and old mines.

This was how all those who lived outside of villages remained safe. It was odd for their forest homes to be attacked, and it generally happened when a wandering Demon caught a thread of their presence in the distance.

Luring them was a game of patience, one Mayumi had played many times in her life – not so much here, but for the guild.

From a pouch at her hip, she pulled bread or fruit to eat, never leaving her position.

Roughly after midnight, she heard it – the first sounds of ugly life.

The swallowing shadows gave it the perfect shelter to hide from sight until it was in the clearing, but the snarls coming from the left notified her where she needed to look.

She pulled back her arrow, extending the string of her bow to a medium placement as she lined it up. She'd eventually pull back harder when she knew how big it was and where to shoot. There was no point in tiring out her arms when she didn't need to.

Mayumi gave no smile of triumph when it burst into the clearing and headed straight for the boar. It was medium in size, a difficult opponent to fight on her own, but if she shot it in the right spot, she could kill it near instantly.

Since the carcass was so high in the air, the Demon's black, void-like body jumped up and down to reach it. It clawed at the stake as it tried to get purchase to climb, adding to the many marks already on the distressed timber.

It had a lizard-like shape with a long tail behind its thin arse, and it made snarling hisses as it struggled for its prey.

"Come here, come here!" it wheezed, froth beginning to build at its mouth.

Mayumi's eyes only narrowed, having heard many Demons speak in the past. She didn't release her arrow, even when the Demon paused its frantic jumping to sniff around the base of the stake to figure out another way to get to the carcass.

There was only one way up, and it was too stupid to realise that cutting the rope tied to the metal spike in the ground would release it.

Come on, she thought, readying herself even further by bringing the feathers of her arrow up to brush her cheek. *Hurry up!*

Finally, it managed to get purchase and dug its claws in to climb. The Demon was moving swiftly. She waited for it to grab the boar with its teeth and start tugging before she truly lined up her shot.

Got you.

Right before she released her arrow, a shiver-inducing roar sounded from the left.

Mayumi paused, knowing that roar could only be created by a larger Demon, and aimed her shot in that direction instead.

I'll need to wait. The Demons would fight for their meal.

It would be pointless for the smaller Demon, as the larger one would likely win, but it meant the latter would be weakened before she tried to kill it herself.

Loud, crunching, thumping footsteps came from the left of the house, slightly behind her, making it difficult to catch its face. The speed at which it sprinted was faster than anything she'd ever seen, showing the creature as nothing but a black blur with the dark of night shadowing it.

What she thought would be a battle ended up being a barrage of swiping claws as the bigger Demon broke into the clearing. It slaughtered the small one before it even finished lifting its head from the boar it'd managed to rip to the ground.

That was so fast! Thankfully she didn't gasp and give away her hiding spot, but she'd started from surprise, and usually nothing surprised Mayumi.

The smaller Demon was forgotten, barely moving, as the larger one ate what remained of the boar. It was so big that it just threw the carcass into the air and swallowed it whole.

Then her upper lip twisted with a disgusted sneer when it turned for the smaller Demon. *Fucking cannibals.*

The bigger Demon kept its back to her as it ate the smaller one. From this angle, she could only see it shaking its head from side to side until it had torn it in half.

Without hesitation, she lined up her shot and waited.

I have to get it between the eyes.

It was... it was massive from what she could tell, bigger than any other Demon she'd ever faced. One of this size would be classified as a suicide mission for a lone Demonslayer – unless they shot it between the eyes.

The back of the head wasn't enough. The arrow could go through its throat with the downward angle she was shooting from.

On all fours, it continued to messily eat, never turning around for her to get a clear shot.

Turn, damn you!

Mayumi was a sitting duck like this. The moment it finished its meal, it would likely start investigating the human smell that wafted from her house. It was currently seeking fresh blood, a free meal, but soon it would grow interested in *her*.

The masking incense she'd lit on the porch railing wouldn't be enough, not once the carcass was gone.

TURN!

Then it did. It wasn't finished eating its own kind like a freaking savage, but it turned its head to the side to look off into the forest.

Glowing red orbs came into view.

She had been expecting red eyes, but these were odd. Her own widened when she realised it wasn't a Demon at all, and the waxing moon highlighted the side of a white skull.

Shit! Mayumi ducked down and laid her arms flat to hide. *A Duskwalker?*

She pursed her lips together as her brows knotted tightly. Her eyes traced over the reflective snow next to her as she thought.

I can't fight a Duskwalker on my own.

Still, she perked her head up just slightly so she could watch it eat the last of the Demon it had killed. It was only now that she realised she'd been able to see the back of a skull the entire time.

I've never fought a Duskwalker before. How different could it really be? Nothing could survive an arrow between the eyes, right in the forehead where their brain was. She doubted a Duskwalker would be any different.

Hmm. But I have heard their skulls are basically

impenetrable.

A mental debate warred heavily within her.

She didn't know how many Duskwalkers there were in the world, but the guild knew for certain of five of them.

There was an Impala-horned one with a wolf skull for a face – one many had tracked and lost their lives to. A deer-antlered one with a fox skull. A bear-skulled one with bull horns spiking on its head like the devil himself – it was ruthless. Every Demonslayer within the guild had been told never to engage it.

There was a new one that had only been sighted once in the last two or so weeks. She'd received a pigeon message about it, as had most towns and villages.

The new Duskwalker had antlers on its head and a rabbit skull. It was larger than any they'd ever heard of and was rabid, attacking anything and everything within earshot. Another *'do not engage'* warning had been given by now-dead Demonslayers who'd released a messenger bird before their demise.

There had been sightings of a fifth one, but so far, no one had managed to get a good look at it before retreating to safety.

Many guild members died at the hands of both Duskwalkers and Demons. She was sure there were many more of both. Information was often lost due to the constant high frequency of death.

Mayumi rose up on her haunches, once more aiming her weapon.

But if I kill a Duskwalker and obtain their skull as proof... She pulled the bow string as far as it could go, hoping for a blow powerful enough to shoot through its skull. *They might let me back into the guild.*

Mayumi had been discharged for violating an order.

It was an order she would never follow, even if it meant she could never be a part of the guild and could only hunt Demons as she did now – at her home or in her wanderings.

She was no longer allowed to fight alongside guild members, hunt with them, or be within ten miles of a Demonslayer stronghold. She wasn't even allowed to wear her uniform, but it was the safest thing to wear. It hid her in the shadows, just like the Demons themselves.

I'll kill it. I have to.

A malicious grin formed as her upper lip twitched, her eyes bowing with it. The Duskwalker turned around, finally finished with its meal.

If not, I'll die trying.

She found its glowing red orbs and then got a full-frontal view of its skulled face.

All the fire in her veins, all the determined heat, instantly deflated out of her. So much so that a surprised gasp tore from her.

Thankfully, it didn't hear her. It just shook its head as if trying to clear its thoughts before darting it to the right, then to the left, then pausing to stare at the house.

The colour white snuffed out the red in its orbs, its body frozen like it was in the clutches of fear—like it'd seen a Ghost.

The Duskwalker darted off to the side and disappeared into the forest.

Apparently, it never saw a now-shocked Mayumi on top of it, who began slouching forward over her legs as she knelt there. Her bow and arrow fell to either side of her to rest against the roof as realisation blew through her, clearing away the fog of her memories.

A cat skull... It had a cat skull.

She let her wide, disbelieving eyes fall onto the snow-covered roof. She'd never hesitated before, never shied away from a foe once she'd made up her mind on killing it – even if it was a risk. She'd even had a perfect shot of it when it had stared at the porch as still as stone.

Instead, she'd completely lost all her will.

I saw a Duskwalker that night. That's what she'd seen when she was little. That's what had brought her home.

It was hard to mistake that skull when she'd briefly seen it in the past. She'd been trying for *years* to clear away the blurry haze of her memory, to piece it together, but she'd never had anything real to place it next to. Until now.

It saved me.

Why?

FOUR

Mayumi sat cross-legged on her bed and rested the points of her elbows on her thighs. Hunched forward with her thick hair curtaining around both sides of her head and the blanket wrapped around her hips, she blinked lazily.

She shut one eye before the other and then opened both to find her vision momentarily murky. *I'm so tired.*

After the feline-skulled Duskwalker vanished into the trees, Mayumi waited until the sun rose and not a single Demon came to the clearing. Once that bright light finished chasing everything away, she crawled towards the attic to go inside.

Although she'd rolled out her futon, she couldn't remember how long she'd sat with the covers over her legs as she stared into the fireplace.

What were once murky visions of her past, were now clearer. Her little mind had mistaken the Duskwalker's cattish skull for Shadow's white mask. She'd been too dizzy and childish to realise the gigantic thing in front of her wasn't normal.

But upon seeing him again, she knew that was the truth.

Mayumi had so many questions, and those questions she'd had all her life now resurfaced tenfold, making falling asleep nearly impossible. Instead, she'd remained hypnotised by the flames.

As usual, she woke midmorning – no matter that she'd barely had two or three hours of *restless* sleep. It was a deeply ingrained habit from being a Demonslayer. Most were on duty during the night when Demons usually roamed.

Being a Demonslayer often made them feel nocturnal.

Of course, her first waking thought was of the Duskwalker.

A small smile curled her lips. *I kind of wish he'd come to say hello.* Mayumi tossed her head back and let out a deep laugh. *Foolish! He'd probably eat me within a heartbeat.*

But she couldn't help feeling this way. He'd saved her life, and she'd never, *ever*, forgotten that.

Perhaps I wasn't enough of an enticing snack as a kid.

Though if he tried to kill her now, she wouldn't show him a shred of mercy and would return the sentiment.

Knowing she was out of both tea and coffee, Mayumi collected her metal wash bucket and carted it outside under her arm. Naked in the frigid air, her skin instantly broke out in goosebumps.

She salmon dived into the snow so she could freeze-shock the tiredness out of herself. Then she collected the snow in the bucket like the day before, melted it over the fire, and wiped down her body before getting dressed.

Since she'd gotten home later than she wanted to the previous day, she hadn't completely cut up the tree branch into logs. She'd only made herself enough for the night.

She headed to the back of the house next to the spring bath where she'd left her branch. It took Mayumi longer than it should have to realise her neck was prickling with awareness. Before she even started chopping, she stopped and darted her gaze to the forest around her.

She had the remarkable inkling that she was being... watched.

She heard and saw nothing.

Despite that, the feeling of being watched never dissipated as she continued her task. Perhaps the person that could be watching her was wary of coming close to her while she had weapons. She was wearing her sword belt, after all, and swinging a sharp axe around like it was nothing.

Damnit. I was going to go into town today.

Mayumi wasn't a foolish person.

If someone or *something* – which was always a possibility since Demons lingered, even in the shade – was spying on her, leaving her safest environment would only serve to endanger herself.

She wouldn't go waltzing through the forest to have something sneak up from behind. Here she had weapons. Here she had protection charms.

Her eyes lifted to look at the mostly cloudless sky. *It doesn't seem like there will be snowstorms any time soon.* She could go another day without leaving.

There was also the possibility she was just making up excuses again. *I guess it's potatoes for dinner.* She didn't have much else.

It was quiet, other than her own grunting sounds, which made the sound of a large stick breaking in the distance even more discernible.

Sitting on the long length of a strong, sturdy branch, Kitty – his self-proclaimed name – watched the tiny Demonslayer woman go about her day. His yellow orbs followed her every movement, from swinging the axe high above her head, to the way her shoulders heaved when she wiggled the blade up and down to free it. He even noticed her occasional little cold tremors.

She'd already cut a dozen sizeable logs, and once she was done, she took the larger ones to a tree stump where she cracked them in half with her axe.

It doesn't appear that she saw me.

When Kitty had been crawling up the mountainside on all fours in his monstrous form last night, he hadn't expected to be greeted by the scent of blood on the wind. Boar's blood, to be exact.

As much as he'd tried to not fall into a craze and hunt for it, he'd eventually lost the battle the closer he travelled. It was always difficult to clearly remember his hazy, disconcerting memories whenever his mind switched over.

Bloodthirsty, mindless, and always hungry, he vaguely remembered destroying a Demon who had already fallen onto his prey, who he'd then consumed after eating the boar.

Once the threat and his meat were gone, it didn't take long for

Kitty to come to his senses – in front of the very house he'd been seeking. He'd never thought it would lead him here.

Worried about being seen by the female occupant, and perhaps her family, his first thought had been to flee and hide within the shadows of the forest. He now realised he needn't have worried.

I didn't expect her to actually be here... or be alone.

The last time Kitty had felt... compelled to come to this very house, Mayumi, the human he was watching, hadn't been here. Only her father had remained.

He'd been weathered by time and many years of hard work, supporting himself with a cane from some injury he'd received in the past.

Kitty had been disappointed to find Mayumi was absent.

She had occupied this house almost every other time Kitty had come to check on the little human he'd saved, and he'd witnessed her grow into the strong woman he saw now.

I don't know how many years it's been. Had it been twenty-three, perhaps even twenty-five years since he'd first seen her?

She had been horribly sick with a fever when he'd rescued her. He'd grown concerned for her life, but once she was better, Kitty remained until he knew for certain she was well.

He always came back.

He watched her as an older child being trained by her father to wield a wooden sword, while her mother taught her how to cook and clean.

He saw Mayumi as a teenager, training in the forest by herself. She often looked awkward, her body at an odd stage of growth with all these red dots on her face that he saw many other humans at similar ages possessed. Some were scolded for touching them, whereas Mayumi always showed discipline.

He found her pretty then, but nothing prepared Kitty for his breathtaking first glimpse of her as an adult. Even though he was a Duskwalker, he wasn't able to stop himself from thinking she looked beautiful.

Unfortunately, his visit was brief since she was leaving.

He followed her and her father as they both made their way to the Demonslayer stronghold. He only knew they were headed that way because they were in their black uniforms. He stopped following part way, knowing the direction they were going wasn't safe for him, but he stared at the space they disappeared into long after they were gone.

He never expected to see her the next time he was compelled to come here, but she showed up while he was watching her parents. From what he overheard, her mother was dying. Kitty witnessed Mayumi hold back her emotions, just like her father, until the frail woman passed, and she left proudly in her uniform – leaving her father by himself.

Nearly half a day's walk from this house, Mayumi eventually let her emotions overtake her in the forest.

Although she didn't know he was there, he acted as her eyes and ears to make sure she remained unharmed until she composed herself. It was a memory he cherished, witnessing this woman's pain that was only meant for herself. Especially since it was the middle of spring and she fell onto her hands and knees in a sea of colourful flowers to scream and weep her grief.

He grew amused and interested in the sudden way she then buried her emotions and headed to the stronghold with her head held high. She stomped her feet the entire time he followed her until he couldn't go any further.

He'd always admired that part of her; he'd seen her chin lifted superiorly many times.

She was even doing it now while she completed her task.

It seems she hasn't changed.

Kitty leaned back against the tree trunk and crossed his arms behind his head to use them like a pillow. He winced when he overlapped his feline, paw-like feet and accidentally broke another stick. It was the second time now.

Mayumi perked her head up, but she only ever looked towards the horizon, never high up in the trees. He paused the swish of his long black tail to avoid catching her attention, then let it finish its curl when she stopped searching.

Her senses are keener than before. The yellow of his orbs brightened in colour. *Dangerous tiny thing.* She had a stare that he thought could turn a Demon into flames with enough concentration.

He thought he would like to see a Demon suddenly combust – it'd be awfully hilarious.

Once she was done cutting, what he assumed was her firewood, she left to go inside.

That gave him time to himself. Kitty carefully climbed down from his perch and circled the entire house in a large radius, so as not to be seen from the windows.

He made sure no Demons had crawled close by, using the shadows to travel in the daytime. Even when he confirmed there were none, he continued to walk on all fours in his most monstrous form while he thought.

He was double, no, *triple* checking since his nose holes were currently plugged with dirt. He'd clogged his nose to snuff his ability to smell anything that would send him into a frenzy again, such as blood or the scent of fear.

Although Kitty didn't plan to leave Mayumi's side ever again – unless she went to the Demonslayer stronghold – he also didn't intend to reveal himself.

I will be her guard until one of us dies.

It was anyone's guess whether it would be her or him first.

Kitty lifted a hand to brush over the crack spanning the left side of his skull. The blue of sadness entered his vision as his heart shrivelled in his chest, but he eventually shook his head of any negative thoughts.

As long as I survive all her years, that is fine.

He hoped Mayumi would reach an old, frail state, but he was also sure she would soon go back to battle more Demons.

And he would be there, waiting outside of her team's notice, to protect her. That or they'd discover him and finally have a Duskwalker kill under their great guild name.

He tried to let out a snort through his clogged feline nose hole.

I'd let them kill me so as not to harm her myself.

Part of him hoped it would be Mayumi that ended his life. She was the only human he deemed worthy to do so.

When she emerged from the house once more, Kitty was already back up in the same tree as earlier. It gave him the best vantage point of her home from above, while also having a blanket of leaves to cover him from beneath so she couldn't see him.

He watched her sweep her porch of the snow that had collected on it.

Although Kitty scratched at the irritating cloth covering his snout, agitated by both it and the dried mud in his nose, his orbs brightened again in their normal yellow hue.

I do hope she walks out naked tomorrow like she did today. Completely bared to the world, and unwittingly to him, she'd thrown herself in the snow.

Kitty's cock had tingled behind his seam at the glimpse he'd received the other day. And just like then, he experienced the same feeling now, his cock giving an enthusiastic jerk behind his seam. He had to suppress the urge to chuckle, especially since her eyes were suspicious as she looked at her surroundings.

This dangerous woman would be quicker to stab me in the seam than let me touch her. Still, Kitty didn't mind his one-sided, dark fantasies.

He'd come here to protect her and nothing more.

A pleasant vibration rumbled in his chest, something he only ever experienced when she was near. His long, thin tail swished under the branch he sat upon.

Hereeeee, Mayumi, Mayumi, Mayumi, he mentally called, just like how she'd once called for her precious kitty.

FIVE

Mayumi knew exactly why she had the urge to cover herself in a silk robe before she threw herself into the snow today. Either she was still being watched a day later, or she was growing paranoid.

The nagging intensified as she lay belly up in the cold white powder. Stretching the long column of her throat, she leaned her head back to look behind her into the forest.

She *swore* she saw a flicker of yellow between the trees, but when she turned her gaze there, it was no longer present.

A human would have made themselves known by now. She looked up to the blue sky, the snow finally ceasing its gentle, frozen tears for a short while. *And a Demon would have attacked by now.*

She knew a Duskwalker was no better than a Demon.

But this feeling just won't go away.

With a sigh, she got to her feet and stared down at the metal bucket in the snow. Her life had become a boring, mundane cycle of the same habits.

It was the same each morning, tea, coffee, or a snow dip, then a body rinse before she decided on collecting firewood first or cleaning her already spotless house. What she discovered on her trip into the woods would determine if she would set up a Demon trap or not, often letting the bait come to her rather than the other way around.

And always constant, incessant thoughts.

Her mind was like a non-stop chatterbox. Which was often irritating as she liked complete and utter silence – only to be thwarted by herself.

Look, Mayumi. You're either being watched or you're not, but you need to go into town today regardless. With an aggressive hint to her jarring movements, she swiped up her bucket. *No more excuses.*

There were many more excuses she did come up with, but not an hour later Mayumi was geared up and deep within the forest.

She heard no traces of life as she travelled to Colt's Outpost, one of the largest villages north of the Veil's border canyon. Given its name because it'd been a military outpost before the scourge of Demons arrived on Earth in the early 1700s, it eventually turned into one of the most overpopulated, but safest, villages.

It was also relatively close to Hawthorne Keep, Mayumi's Demonslayer sector head base.

She had to tread carefully, as she wasn't allowed within ten miles of Hawthorne Keep as a forcibly discharged guildmember, and Colt's Outpost was just outside of this distance.

She wore a hunter's outfit, the same one she'd been wearing the last few days, though she had washed it. She gripped the hilt of her sword tightly as she walked across the empty meadow that spanned in front of the village.

At the start of the wooden drawbridge, two soldiers stood guard. Their arms and legs were clad in leather armour, but their torsos were polished steel. She narrowed her eyes at them, knowing exactly who they were and that they would probably get on her nerves.

"Open the gate," she demanded once she was standing before them.

"I'm sorry," one of them said before eyeing the other through their metal helmet, "but we don't allow forest trolls into our city."

"Yoshida," Mayumi grumbled as she rubbed her temples, "I swear if you give me trouble today, I'll climb the tower wall and drop cow dung on you again."

Henry, the dark-skinned soldier next to Yoshida, threw his head back and let out a bellowing laugh into his helmet.

"I told you not to do it. I could tell she was in a foul mood today by how she walked across the meadow!" Henry began stomping his legs with exaggerated movements, causing the armour he wore to clink and chime. "You walk like you're an angry bear when something's got your back up."

Yoshida, who had similar Asian features to her but of a different origin, narrowed his light-brown eyes at her. "You wouldn't."

"I knew you two were going to give me issues just by seeing you across the meadow." She pointed the way she had come. "I can tell it's you two idiots because you're always leaning against the wall rather than watching out for danger like you're supposed to."

"It's daytime," Yoshida quickly argued back. "There's never been a Demon attack in the middle of the day."

"I bet you guys messed up something to get this shift *again*."

Being assigned to guard the gate during the day was considered a punishment. No matter if they were baking in the heat of the summer sun or freezing in the middle of a snowstorm, they couldn't leave their post. It was always boring and uneventful, except for the odd traveller like herself.

"Oh, just go inside," Yoshida sighed, bashing the bottom of his fist against the drawbridge so the soldiers on the other side would lower it. "I just wanted to have a little fun and you had to be in a shitty mood. Becoming a high-ranking Demonslayer made you a hard arse."

Both Henry and Yoshida moved to the side when they heard the whirring of gears and the clink of chains.

"We're not children anymore," Mayumi answered sternly. "It doesn't matter your post; every position has its importance. Just because there aren't Demons throughout the day doesn't mean there aren't bandits."

Henry lifted his gauntlet to push a finger under his helmet and scratch at his ear hole.

"We're getting another ear pulling, and we already received one yesterday. You've never had jurisdiction to tell us what to do since we're Colt soldiers, and you lost any authority you had when you were expunged from the guild."

"I'd listen to a Demonslayer Novice over you," Yoshida chimed in. "Not that I would listen to one of them anyway."

"Anyone who is exiled from the guild is considered a traitor."
She lowered her eyelids to portray a lack of care.

"I was honourably discharged," Mayumi stated with a careless tone, tilting her nose up in their direction. "And the Elder ranks informed all the nearby villages of that."

Henry waved his hand up and down dismissively. "Yeah, yeah, so we've been told."

Thankfully, saving her from this darkening conversation, the gate finished lowering between the two Colt soldiers. The loud sounds of whirling gears and chains finally stopped when the gate bashed against the ground.

Before she could enter, Yoshida grasped her wrist in his gauntlet. "You never did tell us what happened for you to be expunged from the guild, Yumi."

Yumi. She hadn't heard that nickname since she was a teenager hanging out with the boys of this village. She'd trained with a few of them that became soldiers, like Yoshida and Henry, or Demonslayers, who were all dead now. Some went into different trades, like blacksmithing or carpentry.

She twisted as she wrenched her arm free. "I don't have to tell you anything. What happened is my own personal business."

"Only those who are incapable of fighting after an injury are honourably discharged. You, however, are stronger than ever."

Mayumi didn't look away, even when she felt the urge to avert her gaze. Instead, she bored it inside his helmet, making Yoshida narrow his eyes at her with suspicion.

"I'm under an oath that forbids me from speaking of it." She rubbed her wrist in annoyance rather than pain. Her fur jacket prevented her from being abraded by his grasp. "Is that a good enough answer for you, Yoshi?"

"What he's trying to say," Henry butted in, giving Yoshida a glare from the side, almost shaking his head in disbelief at his behaviour, "is that we care about you. We used to be friends."

"We still are," Mayumi conceded while rolling her eyes to the side. She couldn't believe the strength of their friendship was so paper thin. "I'm fine. I don't need anyone's help."

"Never have," Henry added.

Then Yoshida chuckled. "Never will?"

Mayumi snorted a mild laugh, hearing her own stubborn chant from when she'd been a teenager repeated back to her.

That was no longer the case for Mayumi. Although she didn't often need assistance, nor want it, only a *fool* would reject an offer of help when needed.

As a Demonslayer, they had to work as a closely knit team within their regiments. A lack of teamwork caused death, and anyone who rejected help in these trying times was an arrogant moron.

"Yeah, something like that," she grumbled.

Mayumi headed inside, but not before Henry yelled for her to buy them an apple each. Deciding to humour them both for putting up with her foul mood, she gave them each a middle finger without looking back.

She never heard their response, but she was sure there had been one.

Colt's Outpost was odd in comparison to many other villages on Earth. It was broken up into four parts of human living, with an additional section at the very back that was a small farmland.

What used to be a military castle keep for training army soldiers in preparation of invading another human city, was now the centre point of this refuge.

The keep in the centre was where all the soldiers lived together and trained ferociously every day.

They also allowed civilians to enter during allocated times throughout the day for basic defence classes in order to protect themselves from bandits and Demons outside the walls. The latter was often a laughable attempt at just surviving for a longer period before being inevitably eaten.

Unless they were a high-ranking soldier or there was more than one of them, killing a Demon alone was unlikely.

The keep was rectangular in shape, with the furthest end containing the sleeping quarters. The closest end was the entry point, and people had to walk through that section of the castle keep to gain access to the open dirt area inside it.

In the middle was nothing but a training ground with an assortment of different weapons. There were targets for bow and arrow training and bigger ones for spear throwing. Straw dummies for sword fighting were on one side, while the other side had more dummies for axes.

Hand-to-hand combat was a basic requirement before anyone was allowed to handle a weapon of any kind. Civilians were often only taught how to wield an axe or sword, depending on their preference, and officials would help them select their weapon based on their physical strength and mobility.

There was very little point in giving a tall, yet skinny, man a claymore when he would be far more proficient with a short sword. She preferred the lightness of a short weapon herself.

Many villages north of the Veil instructed their own soldiers to travel here to receive the best possible training.

The keep had been here long before the Demons arrived, and it became a refuge before they built the surrounding areas.

Each area was walled off from the other by stone, and people required certain passes or invitation letters to go deeper within the Colt's Outpost without being chaperoned by guards. There were gates that were constantly staffed, although freely opened unlike the entry gate into the large city.

As the keep was the centre point, only soldiers and their guests were allowed free access. Civilians had to be escorted within by soldiers for training.

The walled rectangular area outward from the central keep was considered the noble sector. They were closest to the soldiers who could protect them and furthest from the dangers presented to those on the outer ring.

It was clean, mostly rat free, and spacious, as the rich tended to hate living on top of each other. Most of those that lived here worked directly towards the maintenance of Colt's Outpost's functionality, including trading with other villages or directing the soldiers as one of the military commanders, or were one of their relatives.

To have unguarded free rein of the noble sector, a person was required to have a special plaque or a soldier's coin. Both were difficult to replicate.

The next ring out was the shopping district that anyone could access. It was pretty self-explanatory as to what it was designed to be.

Lastly, the furthest ring from the central keep was the peasant sector.

Although this sector was the largest, it was horribly overpopulated. Everyone was poor, mostly struggling, and worked as labourers or maids for the inner sectors.

They were often afraid. Not just because there was a higher likelihood of becoming infected with disease because of the close living quarters – houses were filled to the brim with people who weren't all related – but because Demons had been seen within this sector.

The stone walls could be climbed or even flown over for Demons to snatch their prey.

It was an extremely rare occurrence, but almost every village faced this same problem – no matter how strong or vigilant their army was.

Mayumi knew too well that Demons could be cunning.

I hate coming here, she thought as she looked around.

The sad reality of society always reminded her why she preferred living in Hawthorne Keep or her cottage in the forest.

She ignored the thin woman sitting against the wall, taking a quick break from her walk – or whatever she'd been doing – to cough into her hand. She also ignored the man with a horrible limp who led a goat by a rope and offered its milk, trying to get anyone's attention to buy his wares, probably so he could afford medicine.

Although she kept her features cool and neutral, her heart especially ached for the young boy holding up a broken ceramic plate in hopes someone would be kind enough to give him coin.

There was nothing she could do for them.

The moment Mayumi tried to help one person, even if it was that little boy, others would flock to her in desperation. Adults were especially cruel since they would attempt to pick her pockets or share stories in hopes of manipulating her into giving them money. They may even follow her into a secluded area and try to beat her for it – which would only cause them injury since she'd win any fight she was faced with.

She also wasn't interested in fighting with poor, struggling, sick, desperate civilians. She understood their motives. It was hard to hate them for it.

As much as she wanted to help, the coin she had wouldn't last her so long if she gave it away. She'd been expunged from the Demonslayer guild, and her finances, although rather large, were also finite.

Dust kicked up under her boots, since workers shovelled any snow that collected each day, placing it outside the walls to melt in spring. It was always dirty here, always shaded, as the buildings were tall to compensate for the number of people living in Colt's Outpost. It lacked any kind of greenery.

Houses were made from clay and brick with straw tops. Windows had no glass in the peasant sector and instead had wooden shutters. Much of the outer ring looked worn down, whereas further in towards the keep was better maintained with more access to structural materials like glass windows.

Mayumi passed through the gates that led into the shopping district and straight into a large crowd of passing pedestrians. The sound of chatter and general pedestrian activity was loud, but there was very little joy or laughter.

The people within the shopping sector were made up of peasants, nobles, and a handful of travellers from other relatively close-by towns, villages, or cities.

Mayumi completed her usual tasks, trading pressed gold, silver, and bronze pieces at different stalls for food, such as fruit, vegetables, and a small amount of meat. She also procured tea. There had been no coffee as they were out of stock, and she doubted she'd get any in the near future.

She also bought incense herbs and bath oils that would help to shelter her smell – though not hide it completely.

Some of the places she went were temporary box stalls, while others were inside multi-level, permanent buildings.

Mayumi didn't linger in any location. She'd been coming to this town all her life and knew where every shop was – aside from the odd and rare changes that happened over time.

She exchanged her bow from resting across her torso to swinging over one shoulder, feeling it tap against the back of her left knee when she walked. It allowed her freedom to be weighed down comfortably by the pack she had on her back filled with all her food ingredients and the two satchels she had on both sides of her body.

Although the village was a steady three-hour walk here and another three hours back, if not more since she was ferrying much, she always overbought so she didn't have to return often.

There was a small garden at her cottage, but it was buried under snow and barely grew in the current winter climate.

Her gaze drifted above her to the clouds that were forming. She narrowed her eyes at them.

Winter was one of the most dangerous times of the year.

Not only was the frost deadly to those who weren't used to exposing themselves to the elements, but the days were shorter, and there were often clouds.

Demons travelled above the surface on cloudy days.

Mayumi glared at the sky. *Night will begin to fall in a few hours.*

She headed off to the side of the path she was on to avoid being shoulder barged by pedestrians. She opened all three of her bags and took a mental note of everything she'd bought to make sure she was satisfied.

Alright. Only one place left to go. It was the most important place, after all.

The saloon-style doors opened with a distinctive low squeaking noise as she made her way inside one of the many taverns within Colt's Outpost. She often visited this tavern since it was the one most soldiers and mercenaries frequented to drown their sorrows in bitter, yet strong, alcohol.

The vibe was solemn to the point it felt almost physical, weighing heavily on all. She imagined the lighting was dim on purpose to hide the tired, depressed looks on everyone's faces.

Many eyed her entrance as she approached a lonely edge of the bar, but none truly cared to pay her any more attention than that.

Other than the bar, most patrons sat at mismatched round or square tables, with one large, rectangular one in the middle that allowed more to converse. There was little décor, and it often smelt of armour-cleaning oils, metal and leather, hay, and body odour.

Mayumi tucked her bags in between and around her legs as she sat in the available stool.

The tavern attendant stood in front of her, slapped her bar rag over her shoulder, then leaned an elbow on the table. When Mayumi caught her blue eyes, she cocked a blonde brow at her.

Marianna had two pigtail braids that swayed down both sides of her head to rest past her medium-sized bosom. Her face was freckled, although tanned from too much sunlight, with thin lips. Her frame was thin underneath her plain brown dress – it was hard to be plump in this city unless you were rich – but she took absolutely no shit from any drunkard inside her establishment.

Her two brothers also worked within the business, mostly as muscle and waiters.

"One mug of Honeybrew Mead and three bottles of Marianna's Sleeper," Mayumi demanded. "I'd also like the day's special stew."

"Cheap, and still not sleeping well, huh?" Marianna snorted, immediately reaching under the counter to obtain a wooden mug. Then she turned away to grab the Honeybrew Mead in a green glass bottle from the shelf behind her.

"I sleep fine," Mayumi grumbled, watching her fill up the mug before placing it on the sticky counter where Mayumi rested her forearms. "It's just *getting* to sleep that's the problem."

"There are demons in all of us." Marianna placed three tall, round glass bottles on the table for Mayumi to put inside one of her bags. "That's why I specially made this."

Mayumi tossed one bronze piece on the counter followed by three silver ones, then nodded her head upwards in a way that told Marianna to leave her alone until her food was ready.

She didn't need nor want a therapist, and she only came in here for a hearty meal to fill her belly and to obtain liquid warmth before she set back out into the bitter cold.

SIX

Trudging through nearly knee-high snow, Mayumi paused to stretch her neck one way and then the other before cringing when she accidentally made one side crack. Then she readjusted one satchel strap that was cutting directly into the tender arch where her neck and shoulder met.

She continued her gruelling walk home.

She hadn't long ago crossed the meadow that spanned the front of Colt's Outpost, the city having long ago deliberately cut the surrounding trees, before she started traversing through the forest. Within minutes, she heard noises.

A deep huff of breath there, a *shhh* and the sound of crunching snow over here.

Damnit. She turned her head up to the sky, silently cursing some unknown, unmerciful deity. *I'm tired and just wanted to go home.*

Mayumi craned her head to the side so she could unloop one satchel bag from her neck and carefully place it on the ground before she bent it the other way to do the other. Her backpack was heavy, but otherwise fine for her to leave on – for now.

She placed her bow on top of her satchels.

"There is no point in hiding," she said with a sigh underlying her tone. "I've already heard you."

Two men, one wielding a dagger and the other a long sword, reared their heads over a mound of snow before standing to fully reveal themselves. Another man brandishing an axe came out from behind a tree.

The first thing she noticed was that the sword was dull and partially rusted from disuse. The axe was also nothing more than a small crude wood-chopping blade designed for small branches. The axe and sword holders were older, both sporting messy, unkempt beards, while the third man was young. The younger man was holding the dagger so tightly with both hands that the blade trembled slightly, like it was too heavy for his twig arms.

All their clothing was thin, dirty, filled with holes, and most likely smelly. The sword holder didn't have two shoes on his feet. The left shoe he did wear had a hole in the big toe, and it stuck out as if the boot he wore was too small for him.

"If you want money," Mayumi started as she unbuckled her coin pouch, "I don't have much left. Maybe a silver and a couple pieces of bronze."

"Give us the bags," the man with the axe demanded. He wore a beanie on his head in a desperate attempt to keep warm. Then, thinking better of his singular demand, he added, "The coins too."

Mayumi cocked one of her brows at that.

"Take the pieces I'm offering and leave," she warned, finally removing her backpack. "Be thankful I'm offering them at all, since I can see you're poor and desperate. I don't want to hurt you."

"Listen here, girlie," Mr Axe warned. She was calling him that for now, since he seemed to be the most inclined to talk. "I don't care that you're some silly ex-Demonslayer. There are three of us and one of you."

"P-please just give us the bags, Miss Mayumi," the trembling dagger holder begged. She wasn't sure if he was shaking from the cold or fear. His eyes were open so fully she thought they might fall from his face. "We have families to feed."

"Okay, you can have them."

In her peripheral, she watched Mr Axe lower his weapon. It appeared they didn't actually want to hurt her.

They weren't truly malicious people. They weren't going out of their way to rob her because they were arrogant bandits.

"R-really miss?" the dagger holder asked with hope in his voice.

"Yeah, sure," she answered, before she darted her right hand to her sword hilt and pulled her blade out of its scabbard. A silver, glinting, and sharp short sword rang out as it was freed, and she brought it into position in front of her torso. She lifted her head with her bottom jaw jutting forward, twisting her lips into a sneer. "If you can take them from me."

Since they'd obviously come to corner her specifically, there was no point in trying to persuade them otherwise. Desperate people couldn't be bargained with, not when their bellies were empty, and they would do anything just to survive another pitiful day.

This also wasn't the first time something like this had happened to her, and it sure as shit wouldn't be the last.

Mr Axe roared as he sprinted forward, crossing his arm over his torso to give a downward strike with his cutting axe.

Mayumi stepped back while lowering herself and raised the flat edge of her sword. She hooked it behind the axe's shoulder and pushed it, and the man's arm, to the side. The sword wielder charged while holding it with both hands above his head, the blunt blade like a sail fin through the air.

She lifted her leg and booted him in the gut.

"Blergh," he gasped, holding his stomach as he keeled forward. She knew she'd hit his diaphragm when he heaved out a choke.

Unfortunately, that put her in a position where Mr Axe was right in front of her with his arm raised to slam his blade into either her skull or shoulder. Either way, he was pointing the blade at her rather than the blunt pole, which meant he truly aimed to kill her. The weapon came for her swiftly.

Mayumi dropped to her stomach, narrowly missing the arc of his blade's swing. The axe continued between his spread legs, luckily avoiding cutting his own body.

Leaving her sword for the moment, she pushed her hands against the ground to lift herself up on her arms and twisted her body. She slipped across the ground and swiped both her legs against his.

He fell to his hip in one swift move, his axe twirling through the air before landing in the snow.

On her back, she placed her hands behind her head, brought

her knees up to her chest, then pushed off while kicking. The momentum tossed her to her feet, and she landed in a crouch.

As she stood, she stepped back swiftly as the dagger holder, who was still foolishly gripping it with both hands, ran at her with it pointing forward. She easily dodged him by stepping back because his eyes had been fucking closed while he'd been running for her. *Idiot!* He stumbled and nearly slipped face-first into the snow.

Just as dagger boy was steadying himself on his feet, Mr Axe was getting back to his own.

She dived and rolled forward to be closer to her weapon so she could reach for it if the need arose. She landed on her feet and turned. Mayumi expected to see the sword holder, but as she spun in a quick circle, stomping her right foot around to help her turn, he was... gone.

Where'd he go?

She kept searching until her eyes brought her back to Mr Axe, who was digging in the snow in search of his weapon.

Dagger boy, or man – she couldn't tell how old he was – finally put his weapon in one hand. He swiped it sporadically through the air.

Mayumi just backed up, darting her head one way and then the other as she shot it back to avoid being struck in the face.

"Stop this foolishness!" she yelled, using both hands to messily capture his arm.

Once she had a good grip of it, she pushed his hand back, twisted his arm, and overextended his wrist.

"AH!" He winced as he dropped his dagger to the snow with a plop. "Please! That hurts."

She pulled him forward as she lunged back, forcing Mr Axe, who never found his weapon, to punch his own comrade in the face with his mighty fist.

She threw the crying dagger boy to the side and swiftly faced Mr Axe.

She brought her leg up to kick him in the head with the front of her foot. He backed up to dodge before coming forward to hit her while she was slightly turned away. Mayumi merely bounced her foot off the ground and kicked him with the back of her heel as she rotated to be forward-facing again.

Constantly eyeing her surroundings, she'd thought the one holding the sword would reappear, but he never did. Dagger boy backed off, his trembling seeming to worsen now that he no longer had his weapon.

His dagger was somewhere underneath her and Mr Axe's feet as they fought over the top of it.

He did eye her sword.

"I wouldn't touch that if I were you," she warned, as she rained punches against Mr Axe.

She first hit him on the right side of his gut, aiming for his kidney, then used her left fist to catch him in the diaphragm.

He keeled forward just like the sword wielder had and incidentally brought himself down to her level. Mayumi grabbed his hair through his beanie and shoved his head down while bringing her knee up. The crunch of his nose breaking was drowned out by his yell.

A glance upwards told her dagger boy had picked up her sword and was pointing it at her. Mayumi gave him little of her attention, since he looked uncertain.

Instead, she wasted no time with Mr Axe, who was on his back. She straddled his torso and used both hands to punch him across the face, tossing his head left and right.

Because of her short and slim stature, nobody ever suspected that she would have such a weighty punch to her.

Mr Axe passed out when she hit him in the temple.

As soon as he did, she looked up to face dagger boy, her eyes narrowing on him. With blood coating her knuckles, she stood.

As she positioned herself over the unconscious man below her, she glared at her final attacker and rolled her shoulders back, preparing to engage. Mayumi only paused when she noticed his trousers were wet, and yellow was beginning to stain the snow at his feet.

"You're joking. You're really pissing yourself?"

She thought she'd put on a good show, but she wasn't actually scary. She was only five feet and one inch tall, for heaven's sake. Swift and strong she may be, but she never truly compelled fear.

"Oh. Ha. Ah." He couldn't even formulate a word, only

sounds fell from him. It took her far longer than it should have to realise that he hadn't been looking at her.

"Ahhhhhhh!" he screamed, tossing her sword to the ground and sprinting for Colt's Outpost.

Mayumi looked behind her but found nothing there.

She sprinted to her bow that rested on top of her satchel bags, slipped an arrow from her quiver, nocked it against her string, and pulled back as she aimed for the back of his leg.

Her chest heaved, her lungs compressing and expanding on heavy breaths. Mayumi considered it. She considered unleashing her arrow into the back of his thigh.

With a light gust of wind wrapping around her body, billowing her tied hair forward across her shoulder to tickle her cheek, she hesitated.

She didn't truly want to hurt him. He'd been no fight at all, and she was sure his family would miss him terribly. *Those people in the poor sector of Colt's Outpost are suffering.* He could have a wife, even children, who may be sick or starving.

To never see their father again would be even more devastating.

Mayumi loosened the tension she had on her bow string.

It wasn't in the nature of a Demonslayer to kill anything other than monsters. Humans, although cruel and just as beastly at times, weren't deserving of death unless they were truly vile.

They were told to incapacitate bandits rather than kill if they could. Humankind was a dying breed. They needed to keep their numbers if they didn't want to go extinct.

With her decision made, Mayumi placed her arrow back in her quiver.

The sword wielder disappeared out of nowhere, she thought while she walked over to her sword. She picked it up as she looked around, scanning the forest warily. *I doubt he would have run away. The one with the dagger was more afraid.*

She shoved her sword into its scabbard and turned her gaze up to where dagger boy had been staring. She squinted her eyes at the disturbed snow.

Nothing was there now, but *something* had been.

Mayumi crouched down and leaned her forearm across one

knee to balance herself. She lowered her hand to touch the footprint tracks she could see. The imprint was four times the size of her hand, which wasn't hard to do, considering hers were so tiny.

But the footprint was barely human shaped, massive, and didn't belong to any normal creature she'd ever seen.

Two possibilities came to mind, Demon or Duskwalker, but she knew without needing to think about it.

A Demon would have made itself known by either the clicking sounds they made, or by hissing, snarling, or growling. This creature had been silent, hadn't attacked her, and seemed to have gone out of its way to assist her.

The sword wielder didn't just disappear into thin air, and dagger boy didn't pee himself over nothing.

That's who has been watching me. While still crouching, Mayumi let her eyes drift over the forest once more, this time searching for any sign of the feline-skulled Duskwalker. *He never left. He's protecting me.*

Once more she asked herself, *why?*

It was a pointless question.

She stood and curled her bloodied hands into fists, ignoring the sting the back of her knuckles gave.

"Come out! I know you're there!" she yelled, hearing her voice reverberate off the snow as an echo.

She got no response.

Maybe he ran after the man who fled?

"I hope you didn't kill that man," Mayumi yelled. "He didn't deserve to die just because he was hungry. If you had left him to me, I would have knocked him out so he could return home to his loved ones."

She only received more silence.

Even the wind was calm and barely moving. No sticks snapped, no snow crunched underneath footsteps. It was quiet, *too* quiet.

Suddenly the area grew darker, telling her the sun had dropped past the trees and was beginning its final descent over the horizon.

Damnit. I don't have time for this.

She walked over to Mr Axe and dropped into a crouch in front of him.

"Oi, you." She tapped him against the cheek a few times until he stirred.

His eyes flung open, albeit barely as one was bruised and nearly swollen shut. Mr Axe sat up, bewildered and likely concussed.

"You!" He looked around hastily while backing up on his arse. "Where are—"

"Go home," she told him. "Go back to your family, or whatever. There's something in the forest, and it spooked the piss out of your friend."

"A Demon?" he squeaked.

"Not sure. Maybe it was just a bear, but you need to go back to the city before the sun finishes dropping."

She rolled back onto her heels and stood as he got to his feet. His knees appeared wobbly, but he managed to get to a slouching position while holding his gut.

"Why would you wake me? We tried to rob you."

Mayumi walked over to her belongings and criss-crossed her satchels over her torso.

"Because it's inhumane to leave you unconscious in the snow for either the frost to clutch you or for a Demon to eat you."

Mayumi saw his axe on the ground close to where her bags had been. She picked it up and then offered the handle out to him, holding the blade.

He looked so unsure as he slowly reached to grab it. Mayumi had a feeling it was one of the few belongings he owned, and he probably used it to work for the little coin he could gain.

"Thank you?" he awkwardly asked when he took hold of it.

Mayumi nodded and stepped back. "Now, if I turn around and you try to attack me again, I'll slice your throat open and use you as Demon bait tonight. I don't give second chances easily."

She couldn't tell if his partially blackened, blood-stained face paled, but he stepped back from her.

They parted ways.

The entire way back to her home, Mayumi tried with all her might to listen for the Duskwalker that might be following her.

SEVEN

decision had been made on her walk home, and Mayumi planned to enact it now. Her food had been put away, she'd gotten the fireplace going, and she'd washed the sweat from the day off her body – as well as the dried blood from her knuckles.

Night had fallen before she managed to get back to her home, and she exited the cottage now into darkness.

There was no hesitation as she crossed the porch, her boots loudly thumping against the steps, then she walked into the clearing. In the middle of it, she knelt and sat back on her feet. She had to shuffle her body so her sword sat comfortably. Her bow could be unwieldy over her body as well because of its length.

Then she yanked her dagger out of her weapons belt and sliced at the back of her arm. It was a place she could still handle fighting with a wound.

It was mostly superficial and stopped bleeding relatively quickly, but considering the Duskwalker didn't go rabid and feral when she'd beat Mr Axe to a pulp, splattering crimson liquid over her knuckles – now tender, pink, and swollen – she didn't think she had anything to worry about.

With her own blood dripping on the snow, Mayumi waited.

"You have two options," she yelled into the cold night air. The wind had a terrible bite to it, and she stifled a shiver when it coursed down her spine. "You can come out, or you can wait until a Demon picks up my scent and comes for me instead."

Her ears twitched when she thought a snarling growl echoed

back, but it was so low that it was hard to truly distinguish.

Nothing emerged.

Fine. Mayumi gripped the handle of her dagger again and pressed the tip to her forearm.

She flinched when something *landed* directly in front of her – she'd been expecting something to sprint at her from within the brush. The wrist holding the dagger was swallowed by an impossibly large hand that *yanked* her until her knees unbent and barely touched the ground.

Mayumi was forced to rest most of her weight on the backs of her ankles.

"Are you insane?" the Duskwalker snarled, his voice so dark, vibrating, and rich that it almost sounded as though he'd eaten gravel.

The floating orbs in front of his empty eye sockets were a flaring red colour, warning those who saw them of imminent danger.

"Finally, you show yourself," Mayumi bit out with a slight sneer.

However, her heart, usually so quiet and calm, was near stammering in her chest. Her cheeks and chest heated from the blood in her veins pulsing more rapidly.

He has ram horns. I didn't know he had ram horns.

They were tan in colour and curled forward down the sides of his white skull. His face appeared to be that of a larger feline predator – perhaps a mountain lion or panther, rather than a cat's.

She could just make out in the dark that he had exceptionally long fur covering his torso, back, shoulders, and legs, but she thought she also saw spikes jutting out from his back underneath a long black cloak he wore.

Before she could take in anymore details, the Duskwalker threw her sideways. She landed on her side and sunk into the snow.

On all fours, his spine arched like that of a feline, he put space between them. The end of his long tail curled in obvious agitation as it poked out from his cloak.

"Why is it you were so desperate to force me out that you would do something so foolish?" he asked, waving one of his

clawed, human-like hands in her direction. She noticed his legs were feline in shape, with paws for feet to match. *"Why is it you wanted to see me?"*

While he was speaking and beginning to pace, his steps slow and calculated, Mayumi made her way to her feet.

"If you seek a confrontation, you will not receive it from me. I have no interest in fighting you." There was some form of black cloth covering the end of his snout, and she wondered if it was from the noticeably missing corner of his cloak. *"Especially since you would not win."*

Mayumi pulled a bandage roll from a pocket of her weapons belt and casually wrapped it over her arm.

"I don't want to fight you," she answered truthfully, taking her eyes off him so she could see what she was doing. It was a test, and she was ready to stop her bandaging at any second to grab her sword. "You've been watching me, following me. I wanted to know why."

He stopped pacing and darted his head in her direction.

"Can I not? As long as I am not causing any harm, what does it matter what I do?"

"Of course, it matters. What you're doing is odd." Once her arm was covered, she tucked the tail of her bandage beneath the wrapping to secure it. "Duskwalkers kill and eat humans. Why would you go out of your way to protect one?"

He had the damn audacity to lift his head up and point his cloth covered snout higher... almost dismissively!

"Who says I've been protecting you? Perhaps I've just been waiting for you to lower your guard."

Mayumi burst out a laugh. "The man holding the sword today didn't just disappear into thin air, and the other one didn't piss himself because he saw a fluttering leaf. If you wanted to kill me, you've had ample time to do so."

He let out a snorting double huff.

"Fine. I'm protecting you." His floating orbs morphed into a neutral yellow, but his stance was utterly aggressive with the way his hands and paws were spread, resting on the ground. *"What of it?"*

"If I told you to leave, would you?" Mayumi asked, raising a singular brow and folding her arms.

"No," he answered, his orbs flashing red momentarily before fading back to yellow. The single word had been uttered with a deep and defining tone, ensuring she understood he wouldn't be moved on this matter.

The hairs on her arms stood on end at the menace she heard, but not because she was frightened or put off by it, but because she found it oddly... titillating.

"You still haven't told me why." His lack of answer informed her she wouldn't be receiving one. "Is... is it because of what happened when I was a child?"

The Duskwalker's head lowered, and he took a step back. *"You remember?"*

Mayumi shrugged, but her heart skipped at the confirmation. She hadn't been completely sure. To finally have her answer reduced some of the many questions she had about that night.

"Vaguely." She palmed the side of her forehead to brush back a few stubborn curling cowlicks of hair from her face. "All I remember is that I thought I found my cat, Shadow, but that's not what really happened, is it?"

"No."

"I mistook your skull as her white mask and then collapsed in front of you. That's what happened." When she realised she'd averted her gaze, which she *never* would have usually done with an opponent in front of her, she brought her eyes back to him. "Were you the one that brought me home?"

She took a step forward, her eyes bowing as she beseeched him for the truth.

Mayumi had been waiting all her life, not only to find out the truth, but to meet the... creature that had saved her. She thought she'd be waiting until the day she died – whether that was of old age or by a Demon's claws.

Yet here he was, right in front of her, and emotions Mayumi usually bottled up inside of her threatened to bubble over and spill in front of him.

Even if he lied right now, Mayumi knew what the truth was. But she desperately wanted him to say it. She wanted confirmation that he'd truly become Mayumi's saviour. That instead of eating her like a monster, he'd brought her home.

She was a four-year-old girl lost in the forest in the middle of the night. No one would have known it was him. He could have freely gotten away with it without any consequences, and she doubted he would have had a moral conscience about it.

So why didn't he eat her?

Kitty shuffled all four of his limbs nervously at the expression she gave him. It was like something rested heavily on the next words he projected beyond his skull.

The cold press of snow against his hands and paws meant little to him, and the frigid wind did nothing more than disturb his cloak and fur. Still, his skin tightened in tension.

His breaths were scattered through the torn bit of cloak he'd wrapped around his muzzle, but they fogged out due to the immense heat his body always provided – even more so in his current monstrous form.

If he wanted to, he could have revealed to her that he didn't always walk on all fours – though he was most comfortable doing so – but he didn't, so he could have the best mobility and strength. Mayumi had cut herself purposely, and the scent of her blood would likely bring Demons here.

Thankfully, he couldn't smell anything, as he'd shoved mud into his nose and further covered his snout with a barrier. If he hadn't, Mayumi's foolishness would have caused him to attack her in a blind hunger.

And Kitty would have been *furious* had she caused him to kill her. The guilt he would have felt after he'd eaten her would have churned his insides.

He looked into the forest in the direction of the Veil. *I need to get her inside.*

It was too late. Her blood scent would already be fluttering on the wind, but it would provide shelter and a barrier so that Kitty could fight those that came.

Yet, Kitty had the undeniable urge to draw this conversation out. *When will I ever get a chance to just... speak with her again?*

He knew enough about Mayumi to be sure that she wouldn't hesitate to draw her sword and point it at him, at which he would then slowly retreat to protect her from himself.

He'd never hoped for this moment because he'd thought it was an impossibility. Kitty had been content with watching over her like an unknown shadow, but of course, her senses were far too keen for him.

Mayumi was smart. He should have known from the beginning he'd be discovered. But this soon? He'd only been here a mere few days.

She'd always been out of reach for him, but his palm now burned in memory of holding her wrist through her thick fur jacket. What would it have felt like if he'd touched her flesh directly?

She was right there, only a few metres away. So close, *so near*, yet still too far away.

I wish I could smell her.

From afar, there was always the undertone of sweet pumpkin, sleep, and the leather she often wore littered in the air. He wondered how strong that would be with their proximity to each other.

He wondered how it would affect him.

His heart was already beating frantically. From nervousness? It felt shy within his chest. Maybe it was anxiety? He worried this conversation would end horribly at any moment. Kitty even thought there might be a heat in his heartbeats, informing him of the tenderness he felt in her presence.

His long feline tail curled at the end when her face appeared crestfallen.

She was still waiting for his answer.

He felt no desire to lie.

"Yes. I am the one that brought you home," he answered, his voice distorted due to being in this monstrous state.

This woman before him had almost lost her life to his stomach.

Years ago, Kitty had smelt the scent of a human on the wind and stalked it with every intention of eating what he found. His orbs had turned red that night, signalling his hunger, when a small child had appeared before him.

Kitty knew the little humans were easy food.

However, when he lowered his head to strike, Mayumi threw her tiny, weak, little arms around his neck and hugged him. He was so shocked. He'd never been hugged by anyone before.

Then she pleaded for *him* to never leave her again. She also said she missed him.

Just those words were enough to stir his heart.

When she collapsed in the snow, Kitty noted how cold her body was and scooped her into his arms. She fit perfectly across one forearm, and he held her to his chest to feed her freezing body his warmth.

Limp and almost lifeless, it was obvious she was unwell.

He considered stealing the sweet child for himself, this child that showed him more kindness in less than a minute than he'd received his entire life, but he knew very little about how to care for a human. Especially one that was young.

So instead, he followed her light scent and tracks back to her home.

Then, sitting in the middle of the clearing and holding her to ensure she stayed warm, Kitty waited until he heard human life returning. He laid her in the snow, retreated until he knew he wouldn't be seen, and watched from within the forest.

Although he remained out of sight, Kitty watched over the house until he saw that child emerge on her own two legs. He needed to know she had survived. That she was well. That she didn't... *perish.*

He could never remember how long he remained to watch the child with her family afterwards. Days? Weeks? It was only when her father returned from hunting with a bleeding deer carcass, almost causing Kitty to attack, that he left.

As much as he'd longed to, he couldn't remain.

Every few years, he returned. Just as he had now.

After his answer, he thought she would ask him why he'd saved her, which he would have refused to tell her. Instead, he watched her features soften and her lips curl upwards ever so slightly.

"Thank you," she said, almost breathlessly, causing him to

cock his head in surprise. "I know I would have died if it weren't for you. Do you have a name? Mine's Mayumi Tanaka, if that helps."

He *almost* chuckled. He'd known her name for years.

She'd also incidentally given him his name. He wore it with pride since it'd been this human that had given it to him. He knew it was a childish name that didn't invoke fear or ruthlessness. It wasn't compelling, but he didn't care.

Not when she had given him his first, and only, taste of affection.

"It is..." He paused. Suddenly he was embarrassed to speak his name to the person who had originally bestowed it upon him. His orbs changed to a reddish pink, and he looked to the side, though that would have done very little to hide them. *"It is Kitty."*

"Kitty?" Her head reared back with her nose crinkling tight to form little wrinkles over the bridge of it. "That's an odd name."

"Says the one who gave it to me," he grumbled, his sight brightening with its reddish-pink colour.

"Me?" Her brows drew together before they shot up her forehead. "Wait... you named yourself Kitty because that's what I said when I found you?"

The growl that rumbled from his throat was in reaction to the outrage in her voice. Her younger self had finally given him something to be called, and he wouldn't allow this version of her to mock it.

Mayumi's head lifted slightly while the end of one of her brows twitched at his growl.

"Well, that won't do." She brought a hand up so she could curl her index finger and tap the side of her knuckle against her lips. "Give me a day or so. I'll come up with something better for you."

Kitty thought his heart had ceased beating. *She wants to better name me?*

Such an idea caused his orbs to turn a bright yellow, one that signalled his absolute and utter joy.

He merely lifted his own snout dismissively.

"If that is what you wish." He kept his tone as neutral as possible to hide his reaction.

"Alright. So, where have you been sleeping?"

Kitty couldn't help giving a quizzical head tilt. *"What do you mean?"*

"You've been here a couple of days, correct? I saw you the other night when you killed the Demon and ate my boar."

His orbs flashed white, and he gave a surprised step back. He couldn't believe he'd been seen! *I thought her senses were just keen, but instead, I showed myself to her as soon as I arrived.*

He gave a sigh, shaking his feline skull at himself. Then he brought his sight back to her.

"I sleep wherever I see fit." He bounced the end of his snout at the treetops. *"Sometimes in the trees. Sometimes on the ground. It depends on how I wish to rest."*

"Well, that's no good." His hackles rose when she placed her left hand on the hilt of her sword, but she never pulled it free. It appeared she was just holding it to keep it steady as she turned towards the house. "You're welcome to sleep on the porch. I'm sure it'll be warmer and more comfortable."

His head tilted the other way in bewilderment. It was hard not to when he was completely dumbfounded by her words.

"Sleep on your porch?"

He took a hesitant step after her when she reached the steps and began to climb them. When she was at the top, she turned to him.

"You already said you weren't going to leave, even if I asked you to. Since that's the case, you might as well just sleep where I can see you. There's no point in going back into hiding. I'd feel more comfortable knowing where you are." Then Mayumi gave him a large grin – one he didn't particularly trust. "I'm going to make you regret coming here."

He was curious as to what she meant. Nothing could make him regret coming to be her protector... unless, of course, he failed her.

"I cannot enter your premises. Your ward won't allow me access without pain."

Her expression fell. "What do you mean 'without pain'?"

Kitty came closer on all fours. He climbed the steps and then tried to put his hand through the archway that connected the outside world to her porch.

His hand could pass through, it wasn't completely foolproof, but pain tingled up his arm. There was also a shimmer of magic that looked remarkably like the translucency of a bubble when he agitated the ward by trying to pass through.

With an annoyed huff, he pulled his arm back.

"See? I'm sure if I was to rush my way through, I would be able to gain access. But if I do so, it'll hurt my entire body."

"I see." Mayumi walked over to the left corner of her house and unhooked a hanging wooden plate that had black painted symbols on it. "How about now?"

Kitty tried again, but this time he gave a soft growl as he pulled his arm back.

"I will admit, it isn't as painful as when you were little. That's why I laid you in the snow rather than on the porch. I was unable to do so."

She only nodded and lifted the plate back on its hook. Then she removed a material covered plate and told him to try again.

Kitty did, and this time he felt no pain. She figured the same when he was able to walk up the stairs, each one creaking under his weight.

"You're joking," she laughed, bouncing it up and down in the air. "After all these years, these still work? You know what? It doesn't matter." She looked over her shoulder as she said, "I won't need these since you'll be here, right?"

The immediate confidence she had in him was both alarming and heart-warming. His orbs flashed a brighter yellow.

"Yes. I will protect you far better than these charms, but you should keep them safe in case I am no longer here."

"Are you planning to leave so soon?"

He didn't know if he heard the hint of disappointment in her tone correctly, but he chose to ignore it.

"No. I plan to remain." Unless something out of his control happened – for instance, and most likely the only cause, his death.

"Alright. I'll take these down for now."

Mayumi walked around the outside of her house to remove them, going down the porch stairs at one point to reach the ones at the back.

This only brought on a question of his own.

"Why are you allowing me to stay?" he asked when she finally made her way back to him.

"Because you obviously don't intend to harm me, and the idea of having a big guard dog sounds far safer than some charms."

"But you Demonslayers hunt Mavka." Although rather unsuccessfully.

Mayumi halted before her cottage's front door.

"Okay, I have two questions," she said, her brows furrowing deeply. "Firstly, what is a Mavka? And how did you know I was a Demonslayer?"

"Mavka is what the Demons call my kind."

He purposely didn't answer her second question.

She waved her hands in the air, crossing them and then uncrossing them.

"No. Never. I don't give a shit what those foul Demons call you. I'm a human, and to me you're a Duskwalker. I'll expect you to call yourself what I do."

Since his jaws were parted in order to breathe because of his blocked nose, his teeth shut with a chomp. He hadn't expected that from her, but he would follow her demand.

"Fair enough. You still haven't answered as to why you are allowing me to stay when you Demonslayers usually hunt my kind. I am surprised to have your trust, which is why I ask."

"And you chose not to answer my second question. So fair is fair." His teeth chomped again, this time in irritation. "Also, I've been meaning to ask. Why the hell do you have that cloth wrapped around your face?"

His orbs flashed red.

"Because you keep doing shit that makes me want to attack you!" he shouted in outrage. *"First you baited me into attacking your boar and then the Demon, then those humans in the forest, and now your arm! Do you know what would have happened if I were not wearing it tonight when you cut yourself?"*

"No?" she answered with a hand raised, as if to shrug.

"I would have tried to attack you. One thing you must be aware of, now that we have come to an understanding, is that Mav-Duskwalkers are often brought into a blind hunger by the

smell of blood from any creature... or by the smell of fear."

Mayumi folded her arms with a bored expression.

"As you so clearly pointed out earlier, I'm a Demonslayer. You'll never have to worry about the smell of fear from me." She butted her chin higher. "However, I *am* a woman. What are you going to do when I bleed once a month or if I accidentally harm myself?"

"You're a strong woman," Kitty stated with absolute confidence. *"Just cut off my fucking head if I ever try to harm you."*

"Excuse me?"

"You cannot permanently kill a Duskwalker this way. The only way to stop us, although temporarily, is to remove our head. In a day, I will regrow the rest of my body and continue to protect you." Then Kitty came closer, standing slightly taller than her despite being on all fours. *"And, Mayumi, I am **expecting** you to do this. If my eyes are ever red and I am coming for you, you are to do this because there will be very little else you can do to defeat me. You may be a Demonslayer, but you are still human. And I will be very, **very** angry with myself if I am the one to harm you."*

Kitty heard the familiar sound of a snarling Demon in the distance making its way here. He nodded his head to the front door as he stepped back.

"Now go inside. There are Demons approaching because of your foolish actions."

She placed a single hand on her hip. "I want you to know that I don't actually need your protection. I've been hunting Demons ever since I was a teenager."

"I don't give a damn what you've been doing. I may be inclined to believe you're capable, but that doesn't mean I will allow you to endanger yourself while I am here."

With an adorable little huff from the *tiny* human woman, she placed her hand on the round doorknob of her home, opened the door, and went inside.

He expected her to slam it. She didn't, and he wasn't sure if it was truly a sideways smile she had given him before she closed it.

Within minutes, Kitty was nothing but a moving blur as he charged into the forest, planning to meet the Demon head-on for an easily won battle.

EIGHT

Curled up in a ball in his monstrous form in a corner of the porch, Kitty lifted his head slightly when he heard movement. He was alert but groggy, as he'd been watching the house all night, even after the sun rose.

Duskwalkers usually went to sleep just as the sun rose, but he'd stayed awake to wait for the lingering shadows to move out of reach of her home.

With just a few drops of her human blood, Mayumi had attracted two Demons during the night. He'd killed both, but he'd gained a handful of wounds from one who had been a strong opponent.

The sun was only moderately higher than when he'd fallen asleep.

He watched Mayumi cross the porch of her home dressed in some sort of shiny brown robe before she tossed herself into the snow.

He was no longer shocked by her behaviour. He'd seen her do this over the past few days he'd lingered here. She didn't suddenly sit up and shout into the air this time though. Instead, face down in the snow, he watched her body tense before she gave a groan.

Kitty chose to ignore it. He just tucked his head back underneath one of his forearms while resting his snout on top of the other and went back to sleep.

Mayumi would be in little danger close to the house in the daylight. When she planned to leave the vicinity, she'd stomp across the timber porch in her big boots and wake him.

That's exactly what happened.

However, her heavy stomps didn't lead into the clearing; they came to his pawed back feet.

Just as he was lifting his head, already alert before she'd gotten close, she kicked him – although rather gently.

"Hey, you, wake up."

He gave a soft, half-hearted growl. *"Stay near the house so I can sleep."*

He covered his face again, only because it warmed his skull, before his sight went black. She hooked the front of her boot around his back leg and lifted it. He pulled it against himself to get it away from her.

"Wake up. You can't live here rent-free. It's time to put you to work."

"Wouldn't protecting the house all night be enough to trade for my nap on your porch?"

"Up, Duskwalker!"

She booted him in the arse this time!

With a snarl, Kitty got to his hands and paws. Then he lifted just to his paws to stand, bringing his height higher and higher above her until the fur at the back of his neck scraped against the porch roof.

He was forced to stop raising himself despite being a few inches away from standing fully. He remained partially curled forward due to the height of the roof, which would only appear more towering and menacing as he looked down at the human woman with his orbs reddening.

Mayumi had to crane her neck. Otherwise, she would have been staring at the bottom of his sternum.

"You can pretend you can control me, but that isn't the case. I will happily be your 'guard dog' as you so crudely put it, but I am the one who is in control. If I tell you to sit, you are to sit. If I tell you stay, you are to stay. And if I tell you to come, you are to come like a good, obedient Demonslayer. Understood?"

Her brows shot up her forehead in disbelief, but she showed not an ounce of fear in his presence.

"There was a reason I became a Silver-rank Demonslayer,"

she said while glaring up at him bravely. "And it's because I'm terrible at taking orders. I'm much better at giving them."

"That sounds like a flaw you should work on."

"I've heard that before." She surprised him by smirking. "Now, are you going to help me or not?"

Falling to the side because his upright position was uncomfortable in this form, he landed on his hands with a double thud.

"Fine. I will assist you if I must."

He was awake anyway, and although he'd warned her, he didn't want her to know the actual truth. He'd do whatever Mayumi wanted him to, even if it was to roll onto his back with his belly up.

"Good, because you look like you're strong, and I'm tired of walking back and forth into the forest."

Since he'd blindly follow Mayumi wherever she wanted to go, he didn't question her as she led the way. She was geared up as she normally was, which made it feel as though she didn't fully trust him, but he was thankful for it. If something went astray, she had weapons to protect herself – especially from him.

It felt... odd walking side by side with her. In all his life, he never thought he'd ever stroll *with* a human, and he definitely hadn't thought it was a possibility to do so with this one.

He resisted the urge to brush his elbow against the side of her leg just for a meagre chance at contact with her, but the idea gnawed at him the entire time.

"Are you able to remove that cloth yet?" she asked, speaking loudly to be heard over the crunching sounds of their movements through the thick snow. "I'm not bleeding anymore, and I doubt I'll do anything to cause you to go crazy, or whatever it is will happen if you smell blood."

Kitty thought about it for a few long moments.

He eventually reached up and pawed the cloth off his face. Then he dug into the hollow nose hole of his bony snout and flicked out the dried mud. He snorted to get rid of what remained.

"There's your face."

He looked sideways to find she was already staring upon him.

"Thank you," he said, catching just a flicker of sunlight in her

near-black eyes that now appeared like a liquid hazel. It was an absolutely mesmerising sight that had his stomach clenching against his will. *"It was remarkably uncomfortable."*

"But you did it in order to keep me safe?"

"Yes. My goal is to protect you, even if it is from myself."

She stretched her arms above her and walked a few steps with them crossed behind her head. Her gaze drifted to the canopy of leaves and branches above them that hid away the angry grey clouds above.

He could tell by the temperature and the feel of the wind that no snow would fall for quite some time today.

"I didn't know you had a crack in your skull. I don't remember that from when I was a child since I was dizzy at the time, but have you always had it?"

"No," he answered, before turning his sight and head forward to watch where they were going. *"I obtained it recently."*

He wouldn't reveal the significance of his cracked skull, and he didn't want to talk about it.

"Does it hurt? I can't imagine how I'd feel if my skull was broken. Humans would probably be screaming in pain."

Oh, I screamed alright, he thought with a growl.

He'd never experienced anything as excruciating as his skull being penetrated by a thumb claw and cracking from the pressure.

"It hurts a little, but it is mostly fine," he answered truthfully, although with a hint of nonchalance to hide its significance. *"I barely notice it anymore."*

Kitty had gotten used to his new pain as it just mildly tingled. It was a constant reminder, though, like an ominous black cloud that refused to dissipate.

He felt... trapped by it.

Especially since this cloud would never go away but would continue to become more noticeable and prominent. At any point, it could strike him down permanently with a bolt of lightning and end him.

Kitty turned his head away when the shift of his sight began turning blue, pretending to search the area. Only once he'd managed to stifle the emotion did he bring his head forward.

Mayumi hadn't noticed.

Before they'd left, she'd stopped to obtain a large wood-chopping axe from a shed at the back of her home. She handed it to him when they approached a fallen tree laying half-buried in the snow.

It had no branches and was only the central trunk.

She pointed to a tree upright and rooted to the ground.

"Cut that down. It'll be much faster if you do it than me."

Really? She brought me here just to cut down a tree?

If it were anyone else but her, Kitty would have been annoyed he was being used in such a way. He probably also would have said no and walked off.

Kitty stood and reverted to his humanoid appearance. He wouldn't be able to do this task properly in his more animalistic form.

His fur began to shorten. His legs, although rather thick in the thighs due to muscle and slightly bowed, became more like hers as partial feet formed. The tips of his toes were like fat paws with claws that could retract.

There had been bones covering much of his flesh when he'd been beastly. They mostly sunk underneath his body except for his hand knuckles and upper ribcage. His skull and ram horns remained the same throughout the transformation.

The clothing that rose from beneath his flesh was a pair of trousers that had managed to remain mostly unscathed and a long button-up shirt with a handful of claw marks. His cloak was tattered at the ends, not that he cared.

Once the transformation was complete, Kitty began chopping into the tree Mayumi had pointed to in order to cut it down. She sat on the one lying on its side and watched him with her expression neutral.

"I didn't realise you could change or that you were wearing clothing."

"There are many things I can do that you wouldn't know of," he answered, his voice finally back to its normal depth.

I am thankful I have seen many humans do this. Otherwise, he would have needed to go through the embarrassing conversation of figuring out what she wanted him to do.

The blow from his first chop was deep, and the sound spooked nearby birds into taking flight while squawking. His muscles tensed as he wiggled the blade free before he brought the axe diagonally from his shoulder and then swiped it through the air.

The blow was just as damaging.

Mayumi was right. He was much faster at doing this from what he'd seen of humans. On his third chop, he could tell he'd blunted the blade and had to put additional force into his swings to give them a more violent blow.

Within a matter of seconds, he was halfway through the trunk, before it began swaying. Creaking and cracking noises came from where he'd been chopping.

"I figured out your new name," Mayumi chirped from the side as he cut into the tree again.

"Have you now?" he remarked as he went to strike again. There was no need. Under its own weight, the tree fell in the opposite direction. "And what might that be?"

Although his tone was sarcastic, his orbs brightened from their usual yellow, and his heart began a strange dance in anticipation.

Whatever it was, he'd accept it.

He turned towards her suddenly, revealing that she'd been *biting* at her bottom lip while leaning her hands back on the dead tree she was sitting upon.

He had no idea what her expression meant, but she quickly stopped and darted her gaze around. It was almost as if she'd been caught red-handed doing something she wasn't supposed to.

There was no redness in her cheeks from embarrassment, but she did clear her throat.

"Well, *Faunus*, you did a wonderful job of cutting that down. In what? Only a minute or two?" She clapped her hands in a way that appeared... mocking, her palms never parting and only her fingers tapping.

He walked over, flipped the axe until he was holding the back of the blade, and offered her the handle's side.

"Faunus? That is your name for me?"

"Yes."

She took the axe as she stood and clipped it to her weapons belt.

She never asked him if he liked it, which he did, but he appreciated the lack of need for thanks or even appreciation. The name was given without a requirement from him.

"Now, you and I are going to strip the tree of its remaining leaves."

The tree had been mostly barren to begin with, considering its leaves had wilted due to winter. A few stubborn dead leaves had fallen over him and the ground when he'd been cutting it.

Mayumi looked up with her hands on her small hips. Then, like she wasn't some tiny creature standing in front of an omen of death that she had just witnessed destroy a tree in a matter of minutes, she *fucking* grinned at him.

Faunus growled in satisfaction at her when a desirous spark speared him in the gut, but thankfully he *did* manage to control his damn lusty purr before it burst from him.

His tail curled behind him before it swayed to the left.

Never, in all his imaginings, had he thought Mayumi would befriend him so easily. That she would be comfortable with him within the span of a day. That she would give him that wicked face that immediately had his body heating.

And Faunus wanted to share that heat with her.

Her light, fawny flesh looked delicately smooth. It was difficult to resist reaching closer and touching the only exposed parts of her body he could see – like her face, her softly shaped jaw, the delicate column of her neck.

Her eyes were hidden gems; two nearly black pools that, when hit with light, morphed to such an alluring molten brown it was easy to be sucked into them. They tried to do that to him now, although muted because of the lack of sun, but there was enough light pouring through the clouds to transform them.

Her thin but plush-looking lips were pale in their pinkish colour, but they stood out as feminine against her more sharpened features, such as her high eyebrow arches and cheekbones.

Faunus had noticed there were many kinds of humans in the world, varying in their shapes, colours, and features.

He'd rarely seen others, besides her parents, that shared traits similar to hers – especially her monolidded eyes. He was sure there were many, but they seemed to be more uncommon in comparison to those of darker or pinker skin in this region.

But it was her he deemed the most beautiful creature he'd ever seen on Earth, and he'd seen hundreds. Her features, every single one of them, from her feet to her hair, deserved the silent praise he was currently giving them.

Had been giving them for years.

From her thick, unruly black hair that she had in a ponytail to her small, rounded ears that were pink on the top edges due to the cold.

He'd seen just enough of a glimpse of her body when she'd tossed herself into the snow naked a few mornings ago to know she was slim but strong. Under her thick and bulky clothing, Mayumi was hiding a leanly muscled physique that had instantly appeared delectable to him.

It was as though the world had decided she be short of height, even in comparison to most humans, so it could be deceitful as to how staunch she truly was.

"After we remove its leaves, I'm really going to test what that strength of yours can do," she said almost impishly, as if she thought he wouldn't be able to complete any task she gave him.

Her words weren't enough to distract him from gazing upon her. No, he fell deeper into his trance when her eyes almost squinted to be spiteful and then grew rapt in the way her long, straight eyelashes became more prominent.

He found himself wanting to draw one of his foreknuckles across them to know if they were as lush and soft as they appeared.

I am doomed. He'd been attracted to this female long before he'd returned here. *I should not have allowed myself to be found out by her.*

Faunus, as she had renamed him, already couldn't contain his ravenous thoughts for this human woman now that she was so close to him – just within reaching distance.

Just within *licking* distance.

NINE

How did I end up in this position? Faunus thought as he gently gripped Mayumi's thighs that were wrapped around his neck from behind.

The task she was unsure if he'd be unable to complete? That was Faunus dragging the already pruned dead tree on the ground – and the one he'd freshly chopped down – back to her home. She wanted her firewood closer to where she could obtain it.

When he'd asked why she didn't just chop down a tree near the cottage, she said it was because the forest acted as a barrier of sound and scent. She believed if they cut more of it down around her home, it would make them easier to find.

He thought perhaps that might be true.

The task had been strenuous, and she'd offered not a single ounce of help, but he'd completed it. All the while, she rudely told him to hurry up, and that he was being too slow when he lagged because the branches snagged.

Once they'd returned to her cottage, she demanded he start cutting up the dead tree for her firewood. Mayumi had disappeared while he did this, but he knew by the scent covering her that she'd eaten something.

She was rather bossy and commanding, but he kind of liked this. It was just strange that she was bossing him around, a Duskwalker, but he preferred this over her trying to shoot him in the face with an arrow – which is what he'd expected from her.

Then, just when he thought he could catch a break, she'd asked him a question that had his head cocking. Not because of the question itself, but because he hadn't understood why she was asking him.

Mayumi wanted to know if she could trust him.

Faunus had shrugged and confirmed that she could, then she demanded that he allow her to sit on his shoulders.

So here he was, holding her thighs to the point his hands were completely wrapped around them. Mayumi was careful not to press on the injured, cracked side of his skull since he'd asked her not to. She didn't need to steady herself; Faunus kept a nice firm grip on her.

The task they were completing together was her cleaning out the wooden gutters of her cottage. The leaves had collected inside and clogged them during autumn.

Although that wasn't a problem now, she said it would be when the snow melted, or the rain started falling in spring.

Not a single complaint was uttered by him, especially since he couldn't stop himself from licking at his snout.

The smell of pumpkin, sleep, and the constant stain of leather infiltrated his senses so completely that he found it difficult to swallow the copious amount of drool that collected in his mouth. Her thighs were moulded around his neck and the bottom of his jaw like they were a comfortable, warm pillow. He tilted his head slightly to the side and sniffed.

He caught a delicious whiff of her scent. Unfortunately, she also had this strange, lingering smell he only ever found on those who were wobbly on their feet – a scent he wasn't particularly fond of.

Mayumi, who had been straining and wiggling, paused. She looked down, causing him to look up through the valley of her body to meet her gaze.

"Did you just sniff my thigh?"

"No?" he lied.

She huffed at him, so he huffed back to mimic her. She continued her task.

"Could you step to the side again?" Faunus took a wide step to the left so she could dig into the copious amount of snow to get to the gutter beneath it. "You know, this is much easier than doing it on my own."

Snow fell on the tip of his snout when she pushed it out. He had to huff through his nose to rid himself of most of it, but then he accidentally inhaled a small amount and had to bite back his choke.

"How else were you planning on doing it?"

Mayumi had been leaning forward slightly, and she bounced back to sit firmly across his shoulders. It seemed she was deep in thought for a few moments before she started scraping leaves out again. One mouldy and decaying leaf fell through his glowing orb to cover an empty eye socket. He left it there, as it wasn't bothering him.

He barely felt her weight resting on him, and her thighs were crushing the back of his thick neck as it didn't quite fit between them. At least... not in the position they were in. He was sure Mayumi could spread her thighs further if he tried to make them.

Faunus licked at the outside of his snout in interest at the wicked mental image that assaulted him.

"Well... my family usually used a step ladder that we have in the shed, but then I would've needed to constantly step down and move it over to reach a different section. You being able to move without me needing to stop makes this a lot faster."

"Would you have even been able to reach?"

In answer to his question, a large number of leaves and snow fell on his face. He looked up just in time for more to fall to the point it created a mound on top of his face, and he could no longer see.

Instead of wiping it away with a hand, he shook his head instead.

"Eeep!" she squealed when she swayed side to side before she steadied herself by placing one of her hands on his snout.

Faunus internally cringed when she accidentally shoved two fingers inside his nose hole knuckle deep. He could feel his wet breaths around them.

"Ew! Gross!" She pulled her fingers out, looked at the mucus on them, then wiped her hand on her pant leg. "I didn't expect it to be wet inside your, uh... nose?"

"Shove your fingers into my nose hole again, and I'll return the favour by shoving my own into any holes you have," he warned with a growl.

Despite his aggressive rumble, his threat had been laced with a hidden undertone of a tease. There was one hole currently pressed to the back of his neck that Faunus was *very* curious about.

Expecting Mayumi to be horrified, or at least disgusted, he looked up. She was biting at her bottom lip again and appeared to be stifling the urge to speak a retort. Her eyes were bowed in a way that made her gaze appear inviting.

The wind picked up for a fraction of a second, blowing a leaf down to slap against the side of his snout before falling wet and heavy to the ground. It broke the strange moment they shared, reminding them both of her task.

Mayumi dug into the gutter again, careful not to cause anything else to fall on his face before she eventually sighed.

"There's another way I could have done this. I could have climbed through the attic door and crawled on top of the roof, but that would've been really unsafe with this much fresh snow. There's a chance I could have slipped off and broken my neck."

"Then don't do that," he quickly said. "You humans don't survive an injury such as that."

"Yeah, yeah, I know. I've seen plenty of people getting their necks snapped in my line of work. I'll be honest, though. It's probably what I would have done without you since it would have been quicker and required less effort."

"Am I not only going to have to protect you from Demons but from yourself as well?"

"I already told you I don't really need your protection. I just wanted you to stick around so you could help me with chores I can't do on my own. As well as..."

She never finished what she was going to say, her words trailing off before silence fell between them.

"As well as?" he tried to continue.

He looked up to see her lips had pursed tightly.

"People have expectations I refuse to conform to. A part of the reason why I live here is because it's my family's home, and I wish to preserve it, but another is because living in a town just seems too tiresome." Her movements seemed more jarring as she dug. "It's kind of lonely, in its own way. I get bored easily."

Mayumi chose her words carefully, as they weren't the complete truth.

Yes. She was somewhat lonely.

Humans weren't supposed to live by themselves for long periods of time, and she'd been living in this cottage for six months with no one to talk to.

That was six months of having nothing else to think about other than her life with her now-dead parents. Six months of thinking about her life as a Demonslayer and everything she'd done wrong and right in that regard.

She'd been a Silver-rank Demonslayer Master.

There were only two ranks above hers. Gold, which was the Elder rank and the council of each stronghold. Then the medallion wearers who were considered Elders as well, but there was only one for each district surrounding the Veil – north, south, east, and west. They invoked the rules and held the guild's most sacred secrets.

As a Master rank, it meant she'd often overseen others. She'd saved many lives, but her decisions as mission leader often meant she'd been the cause of a lot of death.

Those deaths were on her hands, and there were *hundreds.*

She knew the name of every single one. She knew their faces. She was also the one to travel to their families to inform them that their loved one wouldn't be returning home – it was her punishment. She'd failed them, and the consequence of that was to witness the agony in their eyes.

Sometimes she'd see their hatred like it was her fault the Demons existed.

It was designed this way so that those who oversaw lower members didn't become complacent. It was to teach them that their teammates weren't pawns to be used as Demon fodder.

But even though she was lonely and isolated, she could no longer live inside of towns. Rent was expensive, for one. People were struggling, and she couldn't bear to witness it when there was little she could do to help.

She'd have to work.

The idea of Mayumi cleaning houses or cooking for stuck-up rich people was ludicrous. She'd have to work as a soldier, taking orders from some arrogant idiot who had rarely stepped outside their protective walls.

Her pinkie toe had more experience than most of them had in their entire lives, but she'd have to bite her tongue and listen to orders she'd want to disregard.

She'd have to watch over civilians, speak with them, listen to their problems, and keep them safe. She'd have to discipline them, and she'd seen not all guards were kind to those that were struggling.

In her eyes, it was easier to constantly be in potential danger living here than to deal with the sad reality of life inside those walls. Her father had once told her he felt the same way.

Colt's Outpost was one of many towns just like it. Slater Town, which was relatively close by, had no keep but was sectioned in a similar way. For some stupid reason, the rich still got rich even in this apocalyptic world they currently lived in. There was still a ridiculous distinction within the societal hierarchy.

Humankind no longer cared about race or gender stereotypes. They didn't care who loved whom.

What they cared about was how many people they could fucking step on to not go hungry and be as safe as possible. Greed was the true monster in this world, and it was just as prevalent as it'd been before the world was overrun by Demons.

Mayumi refused to be a part of it.

She'd rather die out here alone in the forest. She didn't care if someone made her a gravestone like she'd made for her parents. She didn't care if no one grieved for her.

Mayumi didn't care if no one missed her.

She just *wouldn't* take the home of someone that needed it when she had one available here. She wouldn't shove herself into an already overpopulated town.

When the frost melted in spring, she'd have a small selection of home-grown food. She could hunt for herself.

That meant more food for another.

She was mostly self-sufficient. Winter made it difficult, but she only returned to Colt's Outpost once a month before it came, whereas currently it was once a week – *if* she didn't try to push it to a fortnight.

But the reason as to *why* Mayumi was careful with the words she chose when speaking with the Duskwalker was... because she was also lonely in other ways.

He wasn't human, making her requirement to conform to human social etiquette null and void. Mayumi had always been bossy and brash. She knew she could just be herself since she highly doubted he'd spoken to many humans, if any at all.

The ideal companion.

However – and this was where Mayumi really had to be careful – she *desperately* wanted to jump his bones.

Perhaps it was foolish of her, but the fact he'd been her saviour as a child and was now here just to protect her, Mayumi trusted him without a single shred of doubt. He would have already tried to eat her if he wasn't trustworthy.

She wouldn't be straddling his shoulders and cleaning the roof of her home. They wouldn't be having a back-and-forth conversation.

The moment he'd revealed himself in the clearing and confirmed he had been there that night, she'd instantly wanted to sink her nails and teeth into him.

A grin formed on her features, one filled with immoral and reprehensible thoughts.

I hope my big forest God has a cock. If not, she'd ride his face, fingers, and perhaps even that cute kitty tail he had.

Although Mayumi had killed every Demon she came across, there were a few who looked... rather human-like but completely otherworldly. It was an odd concept, but she'd sometimes found them alluring.

She wondered if the reason she'd always been attracted to non-human beings was because of the night Faunus had saved her.

It had also created some arguments with her father when

she'd been growing up. At first, before she really understood that Demons on the surface above the Veil were truly dangerous, she'd thought she could befriend them. Mayumi had some silly notion that they could be 'changed' – like she was a chosen human who was destined to fix the world.

Now, as an adult, she knew that would never be possible.

That didn't stop her from thinking their claws made them look devilish, or their teeth sinfully dangerous.

The number of times she'd aimed an arrow right between their red eyes and unleashed her bow while thinking she would have adored pinning them down and riding whatever cock they may or may not have had been countless.

She would have preferred them to pin her down, but her fantasies always ended with her being eaten, and that was a massive turn-*off.*

So was the foul, nose-tingling, bile-rising, gut-churning smell of decay most produced. Not all smelt horrible. Mayumi knew some of the Demons were becoming so human-like that they grew skin, the transformation reducing their scent.

She was a Demonslayer who had seen much, and a Master rank who was privy to information most didn't have.

But the creature between her thighs wasn't a Demon; he was something else entirely. A Duskwalker, one with a face she found more compelling than any other she'd ever seen – even more than a human's.

He smells so damn nice. Like lemongrass and freshly cut limes.

Her eyelids wanted to flicker in bliss every time she caught a good whiff of him, and she'd only just discovered his nipple-pearling scent this morning on the porch!

When he'd tried to tower over her menacingly, she'd almost buried her head against his chest so she could rub her face over his fur to cover herself in it.

The desire to tease him had nearly been too much.

He'd told her she would be required to sit when he told her to, and she'd happily sit anywhere on top of him. To stay? She was sure she could work out something sexual with that. Maybe if he were buried deep, coming, and needed her to be still while he filled her? Of course, that required him to have a cock, but her naughty, hair-twirling *fantasies* could be whatever she wanted.

Oh, and when he'd said she would have to come when he told her to... Mayumi had stifled the desire to ask if that was a fucking promise or not.

She never would have truly entertained the real possibility of these thoughts with any other Duskwalker. It was only Faunus she could have trusted, her unlikely saviour.

But... how do I go about instigating this with him?

She doubted she could just come out and ask him about it. *He may not know what sex is.* He might run off, thinking she was a completely unhinged, crazy human, and then she'd be alone again.

I need to see if I can get him to start this. With Mayumi trying her absolute hardest to get him started.

It took her a while to realise she hadn't told him to move over. While she'd been deep in thought, Faunus had noticed she'd been leaning to dig out more leaf litter. He'd moved according to her actions.

Now that's a good, smart Duskwalker. She resisted petting him on the head.

She was thankful they'd ceased speaking so she could come up with some kind of foolproof plan.

How about... Here, kitty, kitty, kitty. I've got a pussy that needs licking? She scrunched up her nose. *No, that's way too forward.*

She let out a sigh.

Once they were finished with this lengthy task – they had gone around the entire house – Mayumi still hadn't come up with a suitable idea.

I have to be subtle but brash. She wasn't the greatest at being subtle. Her friends, Henry, Yoshida, and a red-headed man named Klaus, always said she was as subtle as a thunderclap.

She tapped him on the forehead, avoiding the crack in it. "Hey, you can let me down now."

Faunus lowered until he was on his hands and knees and allowed her to slip off. When he stood in front of her, she lifted her gaze to his mesmerising yellow orbs.

I guess... I guess I just don't want to do anything he wouldn't want.

She wanted him to remain here. She wanted him to be comfortable around her, which she knew would take time. Invoking sexual contact could make him *very* comfortable or cause strain between them.

Hell, they'd only just started talking less than a day ago.

I don't know him at all. She was willing to be patient.

She already knew what she felt, and she had no qualms about her attraction to him. In some ways, she'd been dreaming of this very Duskwalker all her adult life. He'd been some faceless black entity that had given her troubling yet body-aching dreams.

Now she knew that faceless entity had a cat skull and ram horns.

I feel like I've been waiting for him my whole life. She didn't want him to leave because of her desires. *I'll be happy even if he just remains here with me as my friend.* Sex would just be one heck of a pleasurable bonus.

"You're staring at me," he stated, his guttural, gravel voice rumbling between them. Her eyelids lowered in satisfaction at being able to hear it. "It makes me worry what task you plan to give me next."

"I think you deserve a break," Mayumi said, before turning her gaze up to the sky. "It's also going to be getting dark soon, and it's easier if I start cooking now."

Although he didn't respond verbally, he gave a snorting huff.

She didn't know what that meant, but he didn't immediately step away from her. Actually, she thought she may have seen his right hand twitch in her peripheral as though he wanted to lift it in her direction.

He stepped back, putting space between them, with a nod. Faunus then changed his shape, reverting to the monstrous form where he stood on all fours.

To her surprise, he didn't roam around the house. Faunus climbed the porch stairs, and she followed him so she could go inside. He laid down to curl up in the corner she'd woken him up in this morning.

"I am going to have a nap so I can be more alert for when

night comes since someone so rudely woke me." He tucked his head between his arms. *"And then they didn't even thank me for all the work they made me do."*

She bit the inside of her bottom lip.

I guess he really was tired after all.

Now she felt bad for making him work all day.

Mayumi still didn't thank him. She wasn't the kind of person to fold and give someone gratitude just because they manipulated her for it. She'd rather give it naturally, and if he had just waited, she would have.

TEN

The next morning, with a humorous expression hidden behind the cup of peppermint tea she held with both hands, Mayumi leant against her kitchen counter. She was fully dressed, but she'd been groggy the entire time she put her clothes on since she hadn't made her tea yet.

After being kind enough to let him sleep a little later than she had the previous morning, she'd put Faunus to work again.

He's so tall. He easily reached up to the ceiling.

Actually, the poor Duskwalker had to curl his enormous height forward and awkwardly lean his hips to the side while dipping his shoulders the other way just so he could see what he was doing. His face was only centimetres away, making it extremely difficult for him.

Which was hilarious for Mayumi to witness.

What is he? Seven feet and three inches? Either a little less or a little more, but she knew her house could only fit the height of a six-foot human. Anyone taller struggled to stand upright.

He's lucky he doesn't have long horns or antlers on top of his head like the reports I've seen of other Duskwalkers.

It would have been impossible for him to be inside her home at all if that were the case.

She'd convinced him to remove his cloak, and it was now draped over her coat rack right next to the door. It revealed that he had long lizard-like protrusions coming from his back, which had ripped through his shirt. They mostly pointed down his spine to be almost streamlined. He also had them down the back of his calves and forearms.

Mayumi took a refreshing and waking sip of her hot peppermint tea and watched as Faunus pushed a loose bit of timber up until it was flush with the others. Then he reached for a nail he had clamped between his fangs.

She'd offered him a hammer, but he told her he doubted he'd need one. Now she understood why.

He used his thumb to press on the back of the nail and just *pushed* until it was flush. He grabbed another nail and did it again to the same piece of flat timber.

For the last few minutes, Faunus had been fixing some of the normal wear and tear of her ceiling. It was something she'd been planning on doing in the future with a ladder, but it was a hell of a lot easier just to have him do it since he was already here.

I wonder if he could fit inside the crawl space of the attic and fix in there too.

There was a lot of damage to her home.

Before he passed away, her father had a leg injury that prevented him from safely doing any repairs himself. Over the last few years, the house had begun to wither.

Mayumi had been working through a list of tasks to fix it. She'd already repaired the top of the roof as soon as she arrived because of multiple leaks, then there were the shattered windows she'd replaced, the door blinds that were falling apart, and the front door that had been squeaky.

Much of what was left required either two people or someone tall.

Since Faunus was done with that section, he moved to another slab of timber that was beginning to fall. He pushed it up and then held his hand out to her.

She gave him a handful of nails, which he put between his fangs, and he slowly got to work making sure it was secure.

Faunus had made no complaint. The moment she'd emerged outside, she'd turned her head to the side to find he was already awake. He'd been leaning back with his arms folded behind his head, one leg crossed over the bent knee of the other, with his tail tapping against the ground.

He'd immediately asked what she wanted him to do today,

giving her the impression he wanted to be helpful.

"What is it you are drinking?" he asked, randomly striking up a conversation when he'd mostly been quiet. "I've never smelt that scent before."

"Oh, this?" She gestured her mug forward. "It's peppermint tea. It helps me wake up."

Mayumi wasn't a morning person.

Tea was her first preference, coffee second. She'd take tossing herself into the snow when it was available and she had no other resources. If it was any other season of the year, she'd dunk her head into water and nearly drown herself awake.

Yesterday morning had been more challenging.

She'd tried using tea, but it had done very little to ease her hungover and tired mind. Throwing herself into the snow hadn't really been of much help either.

After drawing him into the clearing with her wound and then speaking with him, she'd been restless afterwards. Marianna's Sleeper had taken longer than she would have preferred to slip her under, and she'd drank way too much.

She didn't make that same mistake last night.

Mayumi looked down into the yellowy contents of her mug. "Would you... perhaps like some?"

"No," he quickly stated, moving to another spot. "It just smells nice. Yesterday there was a horrible scent on you, but it was one I've noticed humans have when they are unstable on their feet."

Her back went ramrod straight defensively. "Are you talking about alcohol?"

"Is that what you call it?" he asked casually, pushing a nail in. "Then yes, alcohol. I don't know what it is, but it wasn't pleasant."

"I'm surprised you could even smell it, considering I hadn't drunk another drop since the night before and washed myself in the morning."

Just how good is his nose? Mayumi bit at her bottom lip only enough to slip it between her teeth. *I wonder what else he'd be able to smell.*

Hell, Mayumi could only just perceive the contents of her steaming tea, and it was swirling right below her nose.

Would he be able to smell if I'm turned on?

The bigger question was if that made him react to her.

But watching him awkwardly bent inside her home right now wasn't enticing at all. She just felt pity for him. It was probably straining his body and would be painful.

Would it be weird if I offered him a massage afterwards? The idea of digging her fingers into his body, preferably shirtless so she could discover what was beneath it, sounded delightful.

She opened her mouth, but her lips only opened and closed, the desire to ask him on the tip of her tongue. Her hesitancy caused her to remain quiet.

Just as Faunus had his thumb below a nail head to drive it upwards, he paused.

"There are humans approaching your home," he said as he calmly pushed.

Mayumi nearly choked on the sip of tea she'd been sucking in.

"Pardon? There are people approaching?" She turned her head in the direction of the front door. "How do you know?"

"I can hear them." He lowered his arms and turned to face her. "I can't quite make out what they're saying, but they aren't being quiet."

Mayumi's eyes widened as she looked at him standing inside her home. "Well, then you need to get out. They'll probably want to come inside."

"It's too late for that. They'll most likely see me leaving. They aren't far." He came forward so he could offer her the two nails he had left, and she had to crane her neck to look into his yellow orbs. "Do you have another exit?"

One side of her face scrunched up before she dug her fingers into her hair to scratch the side of her head.

"Not really. None of the windows open very far, for obvious safety reasons, and you wouldn't be able to fit through the attic trap door from the inside, only from the outside. You're too big." She lowered her hand and then drifted her eyes over him, from his bony head to his paw-like feet. "Look, just stay inside. I'll figure out who they are and what they want, then get rid of them."

Faunus crouched, bringing himself just above her height, then stepped back to allow her to pass. She pulled her fur jacket from the coat rack next to the door to slip it on.

When she was reaching for her weapons belt, she heard a muffled back-and-forth conversation from the people who were approaching.

"I want you to know," Faunus stated as he followed her to the door on all fours but remained in his more humanoid form, "that if you are at risk of being in danger, I don't care that they are human. I will kill them."

Mayumi cocked her head over her shoulder and raised both her brows at him. "I'd prefer you didn't kill my kind, to be quite honest."

"And I'd prefer you didn't come to harm whatsoever, no matter who or what has provoked me." The threat was made even darker by the unnatural grit he had in his voice.

"And what if one of your own kind tried to kill me? I doubt you'd harm one of them."

When he didn't respond, Mayumi gave a snide and mocking snort.

That's what I figured. With anger burning in her chest, she gripped the door handle tightly to go outside. He'd blatantly threatened her kind but wouldn't be willing to harm his own.

"You are angry with me." He reached around her to slam his hand against the door to prevent her from opening it. "Why?"

She didn't turn around, instead glaring at his impossibly large, dark-grey hand. Her glare deepened at the razor-sharp claws tipping his fingers.

"I became a Demonslayer to protect my fellow humankind. It goes against the oath I took to hear something I'm supposed to *kill* threatening that I would be the cause of human death when you wouldn't give the same courtesy to your own kind if they were to try to harm me. It shows that your 'promise' is half empty."

Warm breath enveloped the left side of her neck and face when he leaned over her shoulder, brushing over her exposed flesh. She *swore* that heat also wrapped around her from everywhere as he drew closer, even though he never touched her.

His lemongrass and lime aroma made it hard to remember

why she was angry the moment it invaded her senses.

"I hadn't considered this, as it is highly unlikely we'd come into contact with another Duskwalker," he said right next to her ear. "But I'd tear them apart as well if they were a danger to you."

She had mistaken his original lack of answer when he'd only been thinking heavily on the subject.

Her lips fell open in a stupefied expression. She turned her head to him, putting her less than an inch from his short, feline snout.

"What, really?"

His orbs changed from what she now knew to be their usual yellow to a flaring red. It was anger, an obvious show of it.

He was so deliciously close that it made him appear even more menacing when he quietly uttered, "No creature is safe from me if it wishes to harm you, Mayumi, and I will make sure it suffers for ever touching you."

Goosebumps rose on her flesh at his declaration, and her nipples hardened. She probably shouldn't have found his threat so titillating or the red colour of his orbs enticing, but they both had her gut clenching with want.

"Mayumi?" someone shouted, causing her to avert her gaze from him.

"I have to go," she muttered, stepping back, despite her desire to lean into him. "If I don't, they could try to come inside."

"Be smart," he told her while lowering his hand so she could freely open the door. The way the points of his claws scraped against the hardness of the wooden door had her ears tingling. "Anything that comes into contact with you from now on has its life in your hands."

She didn't know what to say to that.

"Mayumi, are you there?" she heard, even closer than before.

Faunus backed up so she could open the door, and she went outside hastily.

Three men were in the middle of the clearing. They wore armour belonging to Colt's Outpost soldiers with long swords belted to their hips. They each also had a satchel crossing their torsos.

"Mayumi!" Henry shouted, removing his helmet to reveal a

large, relieved smile.

Yoshida and Klaus did the same, removing their helmets to reveal who they were, each of them wearing a similar expression.

Klaus was another boy she'd been friends with when she'd trained in Colt's Outpost in preparation to become a Demonslayer.

He was a pale man with freckles that seemed more prominent the older he became. It might be because of his orange hair that showed he was more sensitive to the sun than others. His hazel eyes sat above a thin and crooked nose, which had been broken far too many times, and she always noticed his pale lips pulled to one side in a permanent scowl.

Yoshida unveiled his thick, but short, straight black hair when he removed his helmet last. His face was clean shaven, which highlighted his high cheekbones and sharp jaw. His nose was a little wider than her own, and he had dark, fawny skin. His black brows were furrowed deeply in concern, like they always were in her direction.

Henry's dark-brown hair was closely shaven on the sides but longer at the top of his head. It was cut similarly to Yoshida, but when they were younger, she'd known him to wear locs. He seemed to have changed styles after becoming a soldier, perhaps due to their tight-fitting helmets. However, his warm smile and inviting brown eyes hadn't changed in all the years she'd known him.

Most soldiers kept their hair short, if they could, for comfort, or they had it long and never cut it, so they could wear a low ponytail at their nape, out of the way.

Klaus' hair was tied back like this, long enough to hang down over the front of his chest when it was released.

"What are you guys doing here?" she answered from her porch, folding her arms and widening her stance. "You never come to my home."

Braving the forest was unusual for them.

"We thought you were fucking dead," Klaus shouted, pushing his empty satchel behind him.

Her brows drew together tightly. "Why would I be dead?"

"Two people came back to the village, Mayumi," Yoshida

stated, his own brows furrowing in disbelief in her direction. "One said they were with you when they saw a Demon in the forest, and the other was so beat up he could barely see! He said you heard something."

"The least you could have done was come back and tell us if you were alive or not," Henry added in, scratching at the nape of his neck. "Do you know how worried we were?!"

A sense of ease washed over Mayumi. *I thought Faunus may have killed those men.* Maybe he'd let them go because she had. She'd disengaged her bow, after all, and woken the other one and told him to go home.

He may have also been too worried about leaving her alone in the forest to exact revenge against them. It'd been growing late, the night falling and bringing potential Demons.

However... it didn't escape her notice that they said only *two* returned. He must have plucked the sword holder from the fight and killed him. She tried not to be angry over it since it was too late, but she'd have to inform him of her new 'no killing humans' policy.

"No?" she answered, raising a hand to shrug. "And if you were so worried about me, why did you come today and not yesterday?"

"We had to wait for the shift roster," Yoshida grumbled, turning his gaze to the side. "We can't just abandon our duties because we were worried about you, even if we wanted to."

Mayumi sighed. "Fair enough."

She couldn't stop her gaze from trailing across all three of them – specifically their bags. *Empty* bags.

"Are you going to let us in?" Klaus asked while stepping forwards. "Or are you just going to let us freeze our dicks off? Do you know how cold it is in this armour?"

Mayumi stood her ground and refolded her arms.

"No. I don't particularly want to let three robbers into my home."

"Excuse me?" Klaus cried. "What kind of response is–"

"You had two reasons for coming here," she stated casually, before unfurling an arm just enough to point at them. "I'm sure you were truly concerned for my wellbeing."

Mayumi knew these men. Had known them for years. They were truly good people, and if it wasn't for the Duskwalker currently hiding within her home, she would have welcomed them inside and offered them tea to warm up before sending them home.

They were no danger.

"However," she continued, tapping her index finger in the air in the direction of each of their bags. "If I were not here, presumed dead, you three had every intention of robbing my home of anything of value."

Klaus' lips tightened as his brows narrowed, whereas Yoshida and Henry averted their eyes in shame.

"We would never hurt you, Yumi," Henry grumbled before he bravely brought his gaze to her. "But–"

Mayumi chuckled lightly.

"Don't worry. I know, and I get it." She forced a smile upon her face. "It's trying times, right? Everyone is struggling, and when there is free money here, it's hard not to want it. Honestly, if I *were* dead, it'd be you three I'd want to rob my home."

Henry winced.

"You could have pretended not to know," Yoshida said with a slight sneer. "Do you understand how humiliating this is?"

"We don't want you to think we don't care for you," Henry continued, his eyes beseeching and showing the depth of his kindness. He even stepped forward. "Our first hope was that you were here."

She had no doubt Yoshida felt the same way, but he hated being caught doing something he thought was wrong. This had probably been a difficult decision to make, and he'd probably been pushed into it by Klaus and Henry.

Yoshida had some uptight issue with being honourable. Henry was in a difficult situation Mayumi was well aware of. Klaus, on the other hand, was the kind of man you wanted on your side, because he had no qualms about screwing anyone over if it benefited him – unless it was his friends.

"I'm sure it was," she admitted. "But did any of you consider that I could have been alive and just not... home? I often go into the forest to chop down firewood or hunt or collect roots for food.

What if I had been gone and returned to my home to find it'd been ransacked?"

"We would have given it all back," Klaus argued.

"Would it have been too late by that point?" she asked as she brought her eyes to his blue ones. "I would have returned home late and wouldn't have been able to travel with night falling. You lot would have sold everything of value before most likely drinking your sorrows away in Marianna's Tavern, thinking I was dead."

"We're sorry, Yumi," Henry said with sincerity.

"And I forgive you, and I really appreciate you three coming here to check on my wellbeing." Her eyes crinkled with humour as she gave them the biggest, most malicious grin she could. "But as punishment, you three can turn around and walk home with your tails between your legs."

A small chuckle flittered past Henry's lips. "I half expected you to try and kick our arses, but you're just going to hang this over our heads for the rest of our lives. Aren't you?"

"Rest of our lives?" Yoshida shook his head. "She'll most likely hang this over our heads in the afterlife too."

It was a desperate attempt to lessen the weight of their conversation. She usually would have worsened it, but she decided against it.

Just as she opened her mouth to give a teasing retort, the air pressure dropped significantly, and a chilly gust of wind blew her hair wildly around her face.

They all turned their heads to the sky to see the clouds were dark and angry.

"Go home, boys," she said while staring at the sky. "Otherwise, the next person who will be doing a wellbeing check-up will be me, wondering if you three died in the blizzard that's coming."

"Fuck. *Of course,* a blizzard is happening right now, of all days," Yoshida bit, lifting his helmet so he could shove it on his head.

"The gods are punishing us for our actions today," Klaus added while shoving his own on. "They always side with her."

They turned to start walking away while waving goodbye,

rushing to beat the incoming storm. Henry remained, his intense expression boring into hers.

"Stay safe, okay?" he pleaded. "There are only a few people in the world I care about deeply enough to not want them to wind up dead, and you're one of them."

"Oh, *pssh*," she said while waving her hand through the air in a singular dismissive stroke. "Such gentlemanly words like that will make a girl blush, Henry. How is it you still don't have a wife?"

He gave a snorting chuckle. "You, of all people, should know that not everyone is interested in getting married."

"You're a terrible role model for your son," she retorted playfully when he turned away with his helmet under his arm. "I hope he doesn't turn out like you."

Henry shook his head as he walked away. "Better me than his cheating whore of a mother. Charlotte's the reason I know love *doesn't* exist."

Her eyes crinkled in sympathy for her friend. Henry just couldn't catch a break, and she was sure the money he would have made from robbing her home would have gone to pampering his precious and very much beloved child.

Charlotte was Klaus' sister. They'd met each other through Klaus and formed a relationship, only for Charlotte to become smitten with every man she could find who had coin.

Mayumi slipped back inside her house once she knew Klaus, Henry, and Yoshida were truly gone.

She was surprised to find Faunus standing but hunched forward to account for his daunting height, his orbs bright red as he waited for her to return. His fingertips twitched, causing his claws to glint in the light coming from her fireplace.

"You let them go freely when they intended to steal from you?" Faunus growled out.

Since it was safe, Mayumi unclasped the loop of her weapons belt and put it away. She also removed her fur jacket and went to hang it up.

"Did you not hear the rest of the conversation? They never intended to harm me, and they're actually..." She scratched at the side of her neck awkwardly. "I guess they're my friends, although distantly these days."

She heard his heavy footsteps – hard not to be heavy with his massive, bulky size – as he crossed the room.

"But you were right, Mayumi. What if you had not been here and came home to discover your home had been stolen from?" Her name coming from him, in that gravel voice like he'd swallowed bits of rock, made her shiver. "You're alone here. What if they return upon knowing you often vacate your cottage?"

"But I'm not alone, am I?" She turned and placed her hands on her hips while meeting his towering gaze head-on. "And they won't. Those are good men. They're smart and brave and kind, and if someone ever did come here to steal from me, they'd be the first to start an investigation so they could mete out retribution."

For a moment, a flicker of green flashed in his orbs. He stepped back with a deep huff and a curt growl.

"It's not for you to understand." Mayumi gave a solemn sigh as she made her way to the kitchen counter. "If they were any other people, I would have been wary, but I don't need to worry about those three."

She picked up her mug and downed the rest of her now cold tea. She then reached beneath her counters and opened their doors, pulling out flour, yeast, salt, and some grains. She had a little water left, snow an easy and abundant source, and poured all five ingredients into a bowl.

Mayumi had no issue giving Faunus her back for an extended period. She knew he must be watching her, considering she hadn't heard him move.

"A blizzard is approaching," she said as she kneaded the ingredients together to make herself a fresh loaf of bread.

"I know," he answered darkly, the presence of anger deepening his tone. "I can feel it."

"What will you do during it?"

"What do you mean?"

"From what we've gathered, it makes it impossible for Demons to sniff out humans during rain and snowstorms. If you don't need to guard the house, and I can't give you any tasks because of it, what will you do?"

"I will... sit outside and watch the storm, just in case then. What else would I be able to do?"

She kept her movements casual and at ease, but a grin curled her lips and grew so large that it bowed the bottom of her eyes.

"Do you know how to play board games?" She kept her tone nondescript. "My family's been collecting them since we came to this land."

He gave an agitated huff. "I don't know what that is."

Mayumi grabbed the dough she'd kneaded into a decently sized, sticky blob, and placed it inside of a rectangular bread tray. Her cooking stove, which was made of metal and bulbous in shape, had a section to cook on top of and a door she could open to expose the flaming insides.

She planned to let the bread rest for two or so hours to let the yeast and gluten work into the dough, but she doubted it would be as nice as what the bakers within the village could make. This kind of cooking hearth also wasn't suitable for what she was doing.

She didn't care so long as it was edible.

"That's fine. I can teach you how to play. We have plenty of them since it helps to pass the time when you're stuck with no one else but each other. I'm sure we can find something easy for you to learn."

"You want me to remain inside with you?"

Mayumi turned around to find he was standing idle, like he was unsure of what to do. He had his hand to his chest with his head tilted.

"Sure, why not? I'll be bored brainless inside by myself for however long it takes for the storm to blow over."

It could be days, or worst-case scenario – or best case for Mayumi since that could put them in close proximity for a longer period – a week.

"You're a Duskwalker. Do you know what the guild would pay just to have a conversation with you?"

Faunus huffed and crossed his arms, lowering himself until he was no longer standing bent so he could be comfortable. He appeared to have no issues crouching.

"You Demonslayers would want to do more than have a

conversation. I know you examine Demons."

Her lips pursed into a cruel smirk. "And how would you know that?"

"Humans in the past, those who have tried to capture me, have often shouted demands to each other. 'Take the Duskwalker alive so we can find out what it looks like on the inside.' Or, 'I bet it looks like a Demon once we cut it open.' It doesn't take a genius to figure out what you've been doing."

"Do you?" Mayumi asked with bright curiosity. "If we were to finally cut open a Duskwalker, would you be exactly like a Demon?"

"No. We are vastly different to everything living on Earth."

"How so?"

Faunus slowly turned his head away, and she couldn't stop the way her heart shrivelled a little inside her chest at him doing so. *Does he think I'm only allowing him here so I can find out more about his kind so we can kill them?*

It was a smart move, and something she *should* have considered doing right from the start, but it hadn't even crossed her mind until this very moment.

I just... wanted to know more about him.

She could tell him she was no longer a part of the guild, but then she'd have to tell him why. She wasn't particularly ashamed of the reason, but it was a heavy conversation to have with someone she barely knew.

He was also some*thing* that might not understand.

Since it didn't appear as though he was going to respond, Mayumi walked to the storage room to start searching for a board game, or any game, that would be suitable.

What would be the easiest game to get what I want? She needed one that could be quick, easy to learn, and wouldn't look suspicious if she kept... losing.

Mayumi hadn't asked him to play just to be cute. The snowstorm gave her an idea.

Chess? she asked herself, before immediately shaking her head. *No, that's too complicated. Shogi?* She almost snorted a laugh. *That's even more complicated.*

Her father had been a big fan of playing shogi. It was a game like chess but also vastly different in the fact that once an opponent's piece was taken, it could be re-entered into the game by the person who obtained it.

The original antique her ancestors brought to these lands was packed away in a special box to preserve it, and her great-grandfather had commissioned someone to make a new one for them to be careless with.

What about checkers then? she thought when she was crouching and came across it in the pile. She dumped it to the side when she realised that she'd never really found checkers any fun as a child.

Ah ha! Perfect. She picked up the game she wanted and headed back to the main area of the house.

Mayumi paused.

Faunus was standing off to the side, staring at the fireplace with his orbs a startling colour of white. Blue momentarily shifted in before they faded back to white, but she could see his breathing appeared laboured and heavy by the way his shoulders lifted and fell.

"Faunus?" she asked warily.

His orbs turned yellow like she'd brought him out of a trance, and he turned his face to her.

"Yes?" His snout tilted down slightly, showing he was looking at the box in her hands. "Found something you wanted to play? You were taking a while."

"Yeah. I thought backgammon would be simple enough to show you. I loved playing it when I was young."

And if she could play it when she was eight, she was sure he'd have no issues, considering he was more intelligent than what she'd thought a Duskwalker would be.

She placed it on the ground next to the fireplace and walked over to where there was an assortment of chairs. Behind the unused leather chair, which had a wool-filled bag seat resting in it, was a small coffee table leaning on its side up against the wall.

"Do you want some assistance?" Faunus asked when she picked it up by herself. She slammed it on its four legs in the middle of the house and gave him a glare. "It appears not."

"Come, sit here." She gestured to the opposite side of the table while she sat on the ground.

Obediently following her command, Faunus approached while she placed the game on the table. She unclipped the metal lock on the side of the wooden box to reveal fifteen round sandy-coloured pieces of oak, and fifteen round reddish-brown walnut wood pieces. There were also two sets of matching dice.

Mayumi explained how to play the game as she set it up, giving him the oak pieces to be in control of while she took the walnut ones.

"...and once you've rolled the dice, you just choose if you want to add the number you've rolled together to move a singular piece, or you can split the two die numbers and move two different pieces. I'll help you in the beginning if you roll a double."

For a long while, Faunus stared at the game before him. He was seated cross-legged, his limbs so long and large that his knees easily poked up higher than the table, whereas her knees fit underneath it.

She couldn't help smiling when he appeared far too big within her home. He dwarfed everything – from the table, to the die he examined between his thumb and middle finger, to herself.

She'd been surprised he could sheath his claws, but that only made her focus on how thick and long his fingers were. *Kitty can hide his claws, huh?* That was *very* handy to know.

His hand was covered in dark-grey flesh with white knuckle bones protruding so that they appeared to be sinking under his skin. It was so taut around them that in the light she could see a few thick veins crisscrossing over the back of his hand.

She nibbled her bottom lip as she examined them. She didn't know why, but she'd always found strong, veined hands attractive. The fact he had a large pair with those features was even hotter, and they were so big that she knew two of her own could easily be held within one of his.

I've seen dicks smaller than just his middle finger.

Being so distracted, it took her a while to notice Faunus was turning a die within the pads of his thumb and middle finger, looking at each surface of it.

"Is something wrong?"

"I don't know how well I will be able to play this game of *backgammon*. The pieces seem rather small, and I have never done anything like this before. It seems rather complex."

Complex? She thought while looking down at the game.

"Are you saying you don't want to?" That'd toss her plan right out the damn window.

"That isn't what I said," Faunus said in that deep voice while tossing the die onto the game board. "I learn fast. Then I will try everything within my power to defeat you in this little human game of yours."

His orbs changed into a brighter hue of their yellow.

She was still trying to figure out what the colours meant, but Mayumi thought perhaps the brighter colour meant either happiness or determination.

Regardless, she found herself smiling.

"Bring it on, bone man." She wiggled her arse against the ground, knowing she may be sitting here for the long haul. "I'm pretty competitive, so I'll make you eat those words with those sharp fangs of yours."

ELEVEN

Bone... man? Faunus thought with a quizzical head tilt.

He was not made of bones, although he was aware he had a skull for a head, nor was he a man, even though he knew for certain he was male.

I never expected Mayumi to be this odd.

He never expected to be sitting inside her home conversing with her or learning how to play a human game. He was sure this was strange, and if either of their kinds were to walk through the door and witness them, both would be confused.

However, Faunus felt joy fluttering around his heart that he was doing so.

She re-explained how to play the game after she set up all the little round pieces, and he now had some vague understanding. The *dice*, as she called them, felt odd in his large hand.

They were so small, the equivalent of a human holding a pea in their palm. Juggling to rock them in his hand in order to stir them had taken him time to master.

Holding them too tightly meant he couldn't shake them properly, but holding them loosely meant Mayumi was forced to rush around on her hands and knees to chase them when they slipped between the large gaps of his curled fist. He'd also tossed them onto the game board too hard the first couple of times, and they'd bounced away.

Faunus was battling to learn new information while also needing to wield his inhuman body for something designed for her size, forcing him to control his overbearing strength.

By the time they'd managed to get through a whole game without him fumbling in some way, the snow outside pelted against the windows. The blizzard had come in full force, and the sound of it was high-pitched, screeching, and distracting against his sensitive hearing.

The wind whistled and howled like a ferocious creature, and even he could tell the temperature within the house had dropped significantly.

Mayumi eventually dragged the table closer to the fireplace, seeking its warmth after throwing more fuel onto it. Faunus was hesitant about getting any closer than he'd already been, but he complied without complaint for her sake.

I could keep her warmer than any fire. He quickly pushed that thought to the side.

Although Mayumi was allowing him within her home, seeking some form of companionship with him, he doubted she'd ever be willing to crawl into his lap for Faunus to shelter her in his arms.

But he would sincerely like her to.

Currently, Faunus was reserved, and almost... skittish, simply because he had no idea how things would turn out between them. What they were currently doing was more than he had ever hoped for.

When he'd managed to win his first game of *backgammon*, his orbs flashed a bright yellow, this time in delight.

"There you go," he chuckled lightly. "I have defeated you."

Finally.

"Beginner's luck," she quickly retorted with her own chuckle, making him feel as though his win was utterly invalidated.

Faunus gave a growling huff, which only seemed to deepen her humour. He'd thought he'd won the game by skill, not by 'beginner's luck.'

Her stomach chose then to remind them she hadn't eaten anything for quite some time. She'd pulled a baking tray from her cooking hearth at one point, but she hadn't eaten the brown, lumpy food, claiming it was too hot.

"Give me a little bit," she said, placing her hands on the edge of the table so she could stand. "I'll make myself some dinner, then we can play seriously now that you've got the hang of it."

Faunus, with nothing to do in this house he knew he didn't fit inside of, nodded and looked down at the game. He stared at it for a time before the fireplace eventually drew his attention.

He grew lost and hypnotised by the flickering flames that danced before his orbs, billowing mild heat in his direction.

A heaviness, a deep burden, sank inside his chest, causing his heart to quicken. His hearing rang as the sounds around him dampened. His fur even puffed when his skin tightened as disquietude trickled down his spine. Within moments, his orbs shifted to white.

As much as the fire disturbed him, he found it near impossible to look away.

Fire was hot. And Faunus knew it *burned.*

He hadn't realised his breathing had become strangled until Mayumi startled him as she sat in front of him once more. Her sudden appearance out of nowhere caught him off-guard, making him choke on a panicked pant.

Thankfully, she didn't notice his change of behaviour as she shoved some white fluffy substance into her mouth. He thought it might be mashed potato. He knew there was carrot on her plate simply because it was still whole, but he couldn't quite name the other vegetables she had on offer for herself. Everything was steaming as if she'd boiled it.

She'd also brought a chunk of the bread and dipped it into some sort of sweet, possibly berry, sauce she'd drizzled over everything.

"That appears to be a lot of food for one human," he commented, noting her plate was rather full.

She shovelled it into her face, licking messily at her lips with smacking noises. He grew wildly fascinated by her doing so, that cute, stubbly, little tongue dabbling out. He wondered what it felt like, if it was softer or firmer than his own, since it appeared shorter and fatter.

"I'm hungry," she answered around a mouth full of food. "And this is nothing. You should have seen how much I ate back at the stronghold. Everyone used to make fun of how much I ate and never gained weight except in muscle."

He didn't understand why someone would pick on another for eating well, especially since he was rather envious of a human's capability to feel full. Even now, his stomach gave the tiniest grumble, always empty and never satisfied, no matter how much he gorged.

He'd given up on sating it.

"You asked me how Duskwalkers differ from Demons and everything else living," Faunus casually started. "One way is that our stomachs are never filled, and we absorb our food no matter how large it is as soon as we eat it."

Her pretty, dark eyes lifted from her plate to him as she paused.

"Another is that, although we have a heart, stomach, and lungs, they are not made of the same muscle as all other creatures." He laid his hands in his folded lap and ignored her dumbfounded expression. "We may bleed, but if you are to puncture any organ within our body, we will reform around the wound or weapon so we can continue normal functionality. Our insides are soft, mouldable, which makes it near impossible to stop us. Whereas our outsides are much firmer and harder to pierce. An attack that would cause a deep cut on a Demon would only hit the surface of our bodies. We can still come to harm in that we are slowed, and blood loss will make us dizzy, but we will never cease moving."

Blood would draw from deeper within, sucking their strength to replace what was lost. They would attack anything moving, even if it was a blur – such as a person or even a shaking bush.

"I thought you didn't want to share this with me," she said with furrowed brows.

"When did I say that?" he asked while cocking his head.

"Well, you didn't answer me when I asked you about it."

"That was because I was unsure of where to start."

She pursed her lips before squinting her eyes with what he gathered was either suspicion or annoyance. Then she lifted a forkful of food and blew on the steaming green vegetable to cool it.

He wasn't sure if she was waiting for him to continue or not, but he took her lack of response as an invitation.

"You mentioned you were able to consume as much food as you wished and only gain muscle – that appears to be a trait in which we share. We start out almost hollow in body and begin building muscle over time. However, we also absorb our food so completely we start taking on its characteristics." He waved his hand to the side. "This is similar for Demons, but they produce waste whereas we do not."

"So, you're similar, but different." Her eyes glinted with a mischievous hint when she added, "Does that mean you're just a big softie deep down inside?"

"I already stated that," he remarked with his head leaning to the side in confusion. "And you just... never mind."

"There's a question we've always wanted to know the answer to." Mayumi looked away from him to her food, but her eyelids lowered as if she was attempting to be blasé. "Why are the Demons growing human skin? Those who do are able to speak intelligently, although they refuse to tell us anything no matter what we do to them."

"They are becoming human. I am unsure of how deep the transformation will go for them, but they gain humanity with each human they eat. They grow skin and mimic your kind's way of life." He tilted his head down to look at his claws. "Although Duskwalkers gain humanity in the same way, it has already been shown that we will never become human, nor begin taking on your characteristics no matter how much we try. Our forms are mostly permanent."

"Have you tried?" she asked, and he was unsure of why there was a hint of concern in her tone.

"In the beginning, when I realised my mind was changing, yes. I didn't want to remain in this form. But I met another who is much older than me and has gone to greater lengths. He has informed me that there is simply no point."

"What about Demons, then? Do you take on their characteristics?"

"No," he answered plainly. "We only steal their strength."

"Thank goodness for that." Mayumi chuckled, placing her plate on the ground now that she was finished with it. "Thank you for sharing with me."

"Why wouldn't I?"

Mayumi moved to lean back on one hand, but she nibbled at the corner of her lips, a contradiction to the casual position she'd placed herself in. It was hard to understand her, as her body language often made it difficult to decipher what she was truly feeling.

"I originally thought you didn't want to tell me because you were worried I would give the information to the guild."

That was something he'd considered.

"All I have just told you is useless for a Demonslayer. I revealed nothing which could aid you in killing my own kind, and have explained that your efforts are futile."

"You don't trust me enough to tell me, is that it?"

Although Faunus didn't want to give Mayumi any information that could help her murder his *brothers,* or any other family tie that came from them through the brides they'd obtained, that wasn't why he didn't tell her.

If I tell her the truth, she will understand what the crack in my skull means.

He was sure she wouldn't truly care if he were to perish, but he didn't want to give her the knowledge of how to kill him. His wish was to protect her, and he couldn't do so if he were dead.

"Perhaps we should continue?" Faunus asked while directing one of his hands towards the game board.

He needed her to set up the game; the round, button-like pieces were far too small for him to pick up with the tips of his fingers. Even sheathing his claws did little to help, and his attempts to do so had him fumbling with a single piece for so long his orbs had turned a reddish pink in embarrassment.

She gave a huff at his redirection of the conversation.

He thought she would remain irritated, yet the way she leaned forward almost giddily to set up the pieces was once more evidence of just how hard it was for him to gauge her.

She was a conundrum. One which was beginning to annoy him because he felt as though he was one wrong move away from Mayumi attempting to stab him in the chest like the vicious little Demonslayer he knew her to be.

Could it be one wrong move, one wrong word, that caused

her to have a change of mind?

I would allow her to stab me in the heart as much as she contents.

He'd known for a long time it already belonged to her. She could do what she wanted with it; he'd just rather not have it come to that.

"So, I was thinking we could change the playing field and make it more serious," she said once she finished setting up the pieces.

"Sure." The game had been easy enough to learn. He didn't see any issue with an increase in difficulty.

"You're agreeing to something you haven't even heard the rules for yet."

She looked up with a sly little smirk curling her lips, one that almost caused him to lick at the outside of his snout to signify his want and interest in her.

He shrugged in answer.

"Fine. You can't back out now. It's pretty simple, actually. Whoever loses has to remove a piece of clothing."

Faunus' head reared back to the point he had to quickly place his hand on the ground behind him, or he would have fallen over.

"Pardon? How is this a wise addition to the game?"

"Pssh, don't be shy. I have more to lose than you do since you're covered in fur, and I'm not." She picked up a singular die and rolled it so they could determine who would go first. "It makes the game more fun as there are higher stakes involved. It means you'll choose your moves more wisely since there are consequences. The person who is completely unclothed by the end of it is the ultimate loser and must deal with the embarrassment of being naked. Humans play games like this all the time. I've had my share of wins and losses at strip poker."

Faunus had no qualms about being 'naked' since she was correct. He had fur, and anything... private was hidden behind a seam at the centre of his groin.

That wasn't the problem.

The problem was Mayumi removing her clothing to expose her delicate yet beguiling body to him. He'd already gotten a glimpse of it, and he *knew* he'd be tortured by it.

"I don't think—"

"You can't back out now," she quickly interjected before he could finish. "You already agreed, and I'll even make it fair, since you're only wearing a pair of pants and a shirt. Since I'm wearing three items, you can unbutton your shirt as a loss."

She will be the victor. He picked up one of the two dice and gently let it roll from his palm onto the board to see who would be first to move their pieces. *She has beaten me every other game except the last.*

Faunus wasn't concerned about showing his body to her. She knew what he was. She'd seen him in his more monstrous form, which was far worse than his humanoid one.

She will do everything in her power to defeat me. She did say she was competitive.

She was only doing this because of her own curiosity about his kind and to study a Duskwalker. She'd made that perfectly clear with her questions.

Of course, Faunus lost the first round.

While she was setting up the board again, he blindly began undoing the small buttons of his shirt. It took him the same amount of time, as it was a difficult task.

He'd always wished the buttons were larger.

Only allowing it to gape a little, he revealed the centre of his torso. His sternum was completely sunken beneath his flesh, as were his bottom ribs, but the rest of his ribcage was still on the outside of his body – a stark white against the black of the long fur of his chest. His stomach was covered in short black fur.

Mayumi lost the second round.

She'd grumbled about losing as she raised to her knees and unclasped her leather trousers.

He thought she was too bold in her removal, but became thankful for her choice when he saw she had a strip of cloth between her legs.

Still, he couldn't stop his sight from drifting over her shapely thighs, her flesh reflecting an orange glow from the flames behind her. How could just a pair of bare legs be so damn enticing that he wanted to draw his tongue from the arch of her foot all the way up until he found her centre?

He lost the third round and was forced to remove his shirt.

Short fur covered him from the back of his hands up to his biceps until it became much longer around his shoulders, back, and chest. Lizard spikes, perhaps three inches long, ran down the sides of his forearms and down his back like the sailfin of a fish. They also spanned down the back of his calf muscles, but he had yet to reveal that.

Faunus thought he'd lose the next round, ending their game, but Mayumi was the one who hadn't managed to get her pieces in their home.

The slow removal of her long-sleeved grey shirt was gruelling, making his fur stand on end in nervous anticipation.

The glide of it up her sides to reveal her cute little navel, her stomach hollowing as she dipped her body so she could draw it higher, had his hands clenching. The moment just the very bottom of her small breast mounds started to show, a light purr rumbled in his chest.

He had to stifle it quickly before she noticed.

Her breasts were so small they almost appeared flat when she was stretching higher to pull the material up and over her head, but they settled into little mounds when she was relaxed. They were perky and tipped with pale-brown nipples.

Faunus dug his claws into his calf muscles when he felt violent movement behind the seam of his groin. He wasn't doing it hard – he just needed a minor distraction.

He also darkened his orbs to black and took in a large breath to stop them from turning purple.

It was difficult to control the emotional response of his orbs with sheer will, especially when he needed to ease the chaotic beating of his large heart. His body grew warm, rushing the liquid fire of need and desire into his muscles to make them feel as though they were swelling.

When he opened his sight again, he caught her gaze already upon him, staring at him, witnessing the reaction that he was desperately trying to hide.

He lifted his snout just enough to hide her breasts from his view, but it didn't prevent him from seeing the flat plane of her upper chest, her pretty shoulder joints, or even the enchanting view of her sharp collarbones.

Faunus knew he would have enjoyed burying his face between the crook of her shoulder and neck, feeling the soft flesh covering it as he took in deep draws of her sleepy pumpkin scent.

He let out a thankful sigh when she seemed to think nothing of his reaction and leaned forward to reset the board.

"This is the last round," she stated. "We both have one item of clothing left, so this will determine the winner."

The game was very slow, each one calculating their moves carefully. He wasn't very adept in the game to see the potential of his next moves, nor hers.

The fire dwindled over time, lessening its light and heat as though it was faster than they were.

And when the game ended, Faunus' orbs flashed white for just a second as he stared down at it.

How did I win? He'd tried to lose!

Luck had not been on his side, and he'd rolled a double in the end. It wouldn't have mattered. She'd lagged behind somehow.

His orbs had already shifted to purple during the game since moving his pieces required that he look down, forcing him to catch more and more glimpses of her body. At one point, he'd just blatantly stared at it, hypnotised by the way the light danced against her skin. The way it twisted or bowed when she moved. How a muscle gave a twitch, or an artery pulsed.

Fuck, he thought when Mayumi scooted back and started slipping her underwear down.

She kept her legs shut, probably to preserve some semblance of modesty, but nothing could stop him from taking in that this female was *naked* in front of him.

With little effort, he could easily reach across the table and part her pretty thighs for himself. There was nothing stopping him from seeing what he longed to, what he *ached* to.

What colour was she down there? Did the lips of her pussy match the pale pink colour of her facial lips or her pale-brown nipples?

Faunus had only learnt what desire was in the past nine years, a few years after she'd become an adult. Before then, he'd known nothing about the significance of a human's naked body or even a certain place of his own.

He'd stumbled upon *sex* by complete and utter accident.

With the intention of entering a lonely house in the woods to eat the humans living within it, Faunus had witnessed something. He'd grown curious of the strong scents that seeped from within, the strange sounds he heard.

His confusion and curiosity had gotten the better of him, and instead of rampaging inside to eat them, he watched. They'd fornicated the following night and then, for some reason, in the middle of the day while also completing other intimate and raunchy acts.

He'd enjoyed the smells, the sounds, and the sight enough that it had caused his cock to unfurl involuntarily from the seam at his groin for the first time.

Having watched the human male tug on his shaft in preparation for the female he was with, Faunus had mimicked him simply because he'd gathered they were similar by shape alone. *Although*, Faunus *did* have additional appendages that liked to squirm at the base of his cock, and his came from within him rather than swinging like some fleshy pendulum.

He'd scared the absolute shit out of the humans when he roared upon his first release, but *damn...* it had felt phenomenal.

After fleeing to a safe distance, Faunus had gotten to know his own cock rather intimately until he collapsed. He attempted to drain it of seed, brutalising his cock until it ached.

He learned much about himself.

After that, whenever he'd travelled on the surface belonging to the humans, Faunus sought out houses and watched to see what else he could learn. It was mostly nothing other than boring human customs and chores, but he'd seen many of them fucking – and sometimes not just two on their own or a male and female pairing.

At first, he'd touched himself with the memory of what he'd witnessed. It was only after he'd learned all this, then felt compelled to check on Mayumi's wellbeing again, that a new desire had birthed within him.

One in which he touched her... in the same way those human males had touched their females.

What he wouldn't give to reach across the table and just run his palm over her thigh. What he wouldn't give to be able to follow it with his tongue. What he wouldn't give to learn what it felt like rather than watch from a distance.

To no longer be an unwanted voyeur to unseemly acts.

The females had created this sweet scent whenever they were aroused, and he wanted to know what hers smelt like, what it tasted like. He wanted to eat it, hoping it would quell the hunger in his gut.

He knew it had to be just his imagination, that he desired it so deeply, but he thought he could smell that ripening arousal scent coming from her now.

If it was just his imagination, he didn't care.

He lightly panted, but he made sure to keep his fangs shut so it wasn't noticeable. That meant he could only breathe through his nose hole, which just made it easier for him to grow hotter and greedier for that scent.

She is naked before me.

His tentacles swirled around his cock when he began to extrude. He placed his hand against his seam to prevent it, and clutched his abdomen on purpose to help his tentacles win the battle of preventing his cock from slipping any further forward.

I need to leave.

He couldn't do that. The moment he tried to get to his feet, he knew he'd lose the battle within him. He didn't want Mayumi to know he was having this kind of reaction to her.

He wanted her to be comfortable with him. He also thought she would probably try to cut it off if she knew he was growing hard and aroused by her.

He could picture her horrifyingly waving it in his face.

Mayumi was staring at him, and she leaned her head to the side to place her ear against her shoulder, giving him a strange but assessing look. Her eyes were on his while she rested back on both hands, her knees up and in front of her, with her feet against the ground.

Then she did something that had him digging his claws into his thigh so deeply he knew he'd sunk them halfway down into his flesh. Blood welled instantly.

Her left leg fell to the side.

Purple brightened in his orbs as they grew fixated on the puffy mound and slit between her thighs that she'd just revealed to him.

She's both. Her folds were a pale brown, while the rest revealed a gentle pink. *Fuck!*

He quaked when he was unable to hold back his cock, and it forced his hand back. He couldn't push down on it without making it obvious, so he allowed it to reach the length of his tentacles, which held it back from extruding the entire way.

But he was hard, unbearably so.

Faunus couldn't stop his purr, but he hoped she couldn't hear it. The growl he had to bite back.

The consuming impulse to *flip* the only barrier between them, the wretched table, gripped him by the throat. He wanted to remove his obstacle so he could have the freedom to grab her foot and drag her across the ground to him.

I want to taste her, fuck her, put my fingers in her, my cock, my tongue. What would she feel like?

All he knew was how it felt to release in his own hand, but she looked wet, and even if she wasn't, his cock had a lubricant on it. He knew she would be warm just because her body was, but would she feel smouldering around him?

He liked squeezing his cock; it felt good since it was like it was stroking him all the way to the core. Would she give him that same feeling?

I want to make her come. He gave a light shudder.

The scent of a female's orgasm was highly intoxicating, but what if it was *hers?* He already adored her natural aroma, but what if it was spiced like this?

And to know he made her feel so good that she gave it to him? That he pleasured her?

She will never accept me.

Why would she when she had human men less than a few hours' walk from her home?

There was no reason for her to desire him, want him, as he did her. He was considered a monster – an ugly one, he'd heard. His face was an omen of death to her kind.

Yet, her baring herself like this to him, her left leg still parted, felt like an invitation.

He wanted it to be, but he'd had almost no contact with humans. He didn't know their customs; he didn't know what her actions meant.

This could just be a part of the game they'd just played.

Mayumi gave a little shiver, and she looked over her shoulder. The flames of the fireplace were dying, as they hadn't been fed additional fuel for quite some time.

She turned so she could obtain more timber. On her fucking hands and knees before him, her arse was high while she dipped her chest forward. He saw... everything.

Her arse cheeks were spread, her pussy lips partially spread to reveal the little slit of her cunt, the little ring of her arse.

Take her. His heart quickened in its pace until it was a deadly drum. *Fuck her until she screams the very name she gave you.*

Faunus leaned forward and licked at his snout.

Fill her until she swells with your youngling.

His own thought made him pause.

That wasn't possible. Mayumi was human, and he was a Duskwalker; they weren't compatible, and he knew this. But he *could* make them compatible... if he were to take her soul.

She will never *want to bond with me.* His heart stuttered in his chest as a lonely coldness stabbed it.

As she was stabbing the fireplace with a poker, Faunus took this chance to flee. He didn't know if she heard his footsteps, but he cared naught, and didn't even bother to grab his cloak.

He needed outside. He needed away from her before he did something foolish and ruined whatever companionship they currently had. One they had only just started.

The blizzard wasn't pleasant. It was near impossible for even him to see three feet into it, and it was chilly.

It was too cold outside to ease his ache. He worried his lubricant would begin to freeze the moment he freed his cock. Also... Mayumi catching him tugging it desperately on her porch was the last thing he wanted to experience.

Faunus changed into his monstrous form, thankful his tentacles still sheltered him, and curled into a ball around it to keep it warm.

As a panting, needy, shuddering form, Faunus watched the storm, his sight flickering between a deep purple and a swallowing colour of blue.

I want her so badly it hurts.

TWELVE

Mayumi heard Faunus' heavy footsteps thudding across the timber floor, she looked over her shoulder. A chilly billow of air sent a flurry of snowflakes inside when he opened the door, but she said nothing, nor tried to stop him as he left.

Disappointing, she thought, leaning back to sit on her feet and watch the fresh kindling she'd put on the fire come to life.

The amount of effort she'd needed to put into losing that last game had almost failed her. Thankfully, she was a better player than him, which meant she was also a better loser.

If he were human, he would have known exactly what I was trying to do. But he wasn't human, was he? That was exactly why she liked him so damn much.

Despite her disappointment, her lips curled back so she could grin at the flames.

There could only be two reasons why he left. One being that he was repulsed by her body. The other being that he desired her, but was running away from his feelings.

She was hoping it was the latter.

Her grin died as she drifted her gaze down her body. She gripped what she could of her right breast while pinching her hard nipple with her thumb and the side of her index finger, stifling a moan at how sensitive it'd grown.

I guess I never took into consideration he might find me unattractive because I'm human. What if he found her too small? Too delicate? Too... fleshy?

Mayumi had *never* been insecure about her body. She didn't

care if people made fun of her stout height. She'd often been harassed because her body was muscular when she wore a singlet or tube when training.

Men had told her she wasn't feminine. That her small, nearly flat chest didn't entice desire. They wanted someone with curves rather than her slim, manly frame – as they so rudely put it.

Mayumi had never been insecure about her body... until this very moment, facing the possibility that Faunus had left as a rejection.

Could it be because she was human? Or because he was like the human men who wanted something more feminine?

Mayumi fell back to lie against the ground, throwing her arm across her face. *Imagine how humiliating it would be if I got rejected by a Duskwalker.*

She raised her hand to stare at it above her face. *But I really want to fuck him. What the hell am I supposed to do now?*

That hand descended her body so she could run the tips of her fingers through her folds, finding them slick and swollen with need. She brought her fingers up to look at them hovering above her face, examining the liquid she'd collected.

He has an impeccable sense of smell. She rubbed her thumb over her index and middle fingers to move her slick around. *Maybe the smell of me being turned on was off-putting to him?*

She brought them down and sniffed, concluding that she smelt just fine – like any other horny woman.

Having him looking at her body while she'd been naked before him had been exceptionally arousing. She'd almost considered touching herself right in front of him just to see what he'd do.

She let her hand fall to the side to hit the floor.

I need a fucking drink.

She eyed the bottles of Marianna's Sleeper she had on the dining table.

Getting to her hands and knees, she shoved herself to her feet. She didn't grab a bottle, only because Faunus said he hadn't liked the smell of alcohol on her. She was trying to entice him, so that would obviously go against everything she was trying to do.

Mayumi entered the storage room and collected her futon.

She rolled it out before grabbing her winter blankets and two pillows, one to rest her head on, and the other to cuddle.

Then she stared at the flames on her side, wishing for sleep but knowing it was going to be a battle. She was horny, disappointed, and a little saddened because of her own whirling thoughts.

I'm scared to get close to anyone, but I hate being alone. Faunus being here eased her desire for a companion, but it was also making her realise just how lonely she felt.

For the past six months, drinking and keeping herself busy had been her only real friends. *But I can't drown my demons; they know how to swim.*

Mayumi had regrets in her past. Regrets that refused to allow her a good night of sleep. *I'm so tired.*

The storm was oddly calming to her senses, but it did little to help her have a full sleep. Instead, it was fitful, and she gave up by the time it was late morning.

She groaned as she sat up and held her forehead.

I feel hungover. Her head was pounding.

She put her arms over her head and stretched before twisting her neck one way and then the other. She turned her gaze to the window to see the snowstorm was still as prevalent as the day before.

I'm going to have to do so much snow shovelling once it's done. She wasn't looking forward to that. She hated doing it. *I'll just get Faunus to do it.*

Perfect.

For today, though, I'll get him to help me fix the attic.

Slow to get up and moving, Mayumi dressed in her brown robe and went outside to fill a bucket with snow so she could melt it for her drinking and bathing water.

Faunus was curled up in the corner, and by the blackness of his orbs, she knew he was asleep. She was surprised he didn't wake upon hearing her movements, but she figured he'd been awake all night to watch out for Demons.

Maybe that's why he left?

She took that string of thought and tugged on it to save herself from further dark thoughts that may want to persist.

A soft whine from him had her brows knotting and her body stepping just a fraction closer. His limbs twitched wildly, as though he was trying to run from whatever was chasing him in his dreams.

Is he... having a nightmare? Mayumi shook her head. *Of course not. He's a Duskwalker. What could he be afraid of?*

She went back inside without disturbing him. Her little clothing was making her tremble with the icy chill, and she wanted to escape it.

As her tea was boiling, she did her usual routine of cleaning her body and dressing for the weather.

The storm made it impossible to truly know what time of day it was, but she figured it was midday. Once she finished her peppermint tea while eating brunch, she made her way outside so she could annoy the Duskwalker into giving her attention.

He wasn't on the porch anymore, and when she investigated the yard, she couldn't find him.

"Faunus?" she called.

Don't tell me he left...

A sigh of relief slipped past her lips when he emerged off to the side.

"What is it, Mayumi?" he asked from the middle of the clearing. He didn't come any closer.

"Was just wondering where you were. I need help with something."

He didn't answer straight away. She thought his orbs flashed white momentarily, but that might have been a trick of her eyes because of the fluffy powder falling around him.

"I think I heard a Demon nearby," he said. *"It is hard to hear and smell through the storm. I will remain outside until I know for certain it is safe."*

Mayumi opened her mouth to argue, then promptly shut her lips. Without responding, she went inside to put on her thicker jacket.

Then she came back out and entered the storm.

"What are you doing?" he asked as he followed a large distance away. Surprisingly, his orbs remained their normal yellow, as if he wasn't worried. *"I said there may be a Demon."*

She shrugged, watching her footing as her legs sunk almost all the way to her lower thighs. There was no reason not to believe that there might be a Demon, but she didn't particularly care.

"I'm not going to be able to sit still inside. The worst of the blizzard has faded, but we'll probably have a continuous snowstorm that will linger. They're boring." She made her way to the shed and opened it to retrieve a hammer and more nails. "The attic needs fixing, and I might as well do it today."

She also took a few planks of timber that had been stored for this very reason. She'd obtained them during one of her trips to Colt's Outpost, but just hadn't done anything with them yet.

She went back the way she came in order to have an easier time sloshing through the snow. All the while, Faunus followed.

"You're welcome to come inside when you know it's safe," Mayumi offered when she'd climbed the porch.

She did the best she could to wipe the snow from her clothing before removing her boots and going inside.

Faunus never did.

What remained of the day was spent coated in dust and sneezing as she cleaned the attic. Then she set to work nailing down timber or pulling away boards that were too damaged. She replaced what she could before inspecting the roof from the inside.

There was an area that was caving in. She was sure the weight on top of her home was worsening it, but there was nothing she could do to repair it until the snow stopped.

She'd need Faunus' help with that. She may even need to create a new support beam, which would require one of the longer and thicker branches from the trees she'd asked to be brought here.

It was late in the evening when she was done.

She cleaned her home to keep herself occupied – except for the overfilled storage room. She had no desire to go digging through the past to figure out what needed to be thrown away or not.

She also cooked a large soup that would last her a few days, wishing she'd hunted before the storm came so she could have meat. Winter made for a good ice box.

By the time it was deep into the night, she found herself overtired, overworked, and still very much alone.

Demon, my ass, she grumbled with a pout, bashing at the fireplace with her poker. *He just didn't want to spend time with me today.*

She'd been hoping since he picked up backgammon so easily that she could teach him chess. It was a popular strategy game often played back at Hawthorne Keep, since no one knew what shogi was. *Uncultured swine.*

If he'd picked up chess well, she'd planned to make him learn how to play it. Her father was the last person she'd played with, and it was one of the few fond memories she had with him.

Come play with me, kitty cat. She stabbed the burning log in annoyance.

Then her eyes fell on the empty space next to the fireplace. She'd forgotten to get more firewood to burn, but that meant she would have needed to go outside and cut it up herself while battling the storm. The trees were probably partially buried now too, and it was late into the night. It would be impossible to do now, as she wouldn't be able to see.

Faunus hadn't been around for her to ask him to do it. Or maybe he had been, but she'd refused to call out to him.

She wasn't going to act like a sniffling child demanding attention. She could play by herself – she had been doing so for months, even longer when she'd been young.

I hope this storm goes away soon, she thought as she rolled out her bedding and lay down.

She fell asleep easily since she was exhausted, but she ended up waking in the middle of the night shivering. The last of the fire had died down enough that it was no longer warming the house.

Mayumi wrapped herself as best as she could to endure it. Pointless, really. Her blankets eventually made her feel even colder. She fought against the chill but found it futile.

Screw this.

She threw the blanket off and used a match to light her indoor lantern. With the dim light, she went to the storage room in search of her long-sleeved tunic and some underwear. She also threw on her robe and a jacket, but nothing she wore was going to protect her from the bitter subzero temperature she was about to expose herself to.

Not wearing any pants, her legs prickling with terrible goosebumps, she headed straight for the Duskwalker she could see curled up in the corner.

Her shivers were violent, and they made her wobbly and unsteady on her feet.

His orbs flashed yellow right before she gently kicked him. It was obvious he hadn't been deeply asleep – if he'd even been asleep at all.

"H-hey y-y-you," she stuttered through chattering teeth. "W-wake up,"

Fuck. It's so freaking cold out here! She folded the arm not holding her lantern so she could shove her freezing hand under her armpit.

"What's wrong?" he asked before pawing at his face. Then his orbs turned white before he lifted his head. *"Has something happened? Why are you outside in the middle of the night?"*

"I-I don't have a-a-any firewood. I'm fre-eezing."

Faunus immediately got to all fours, revealing he was in his more animalistic form. His voice should have given him away, but it'd been too dark see properly, and she wasn't paying attention.

"I will cut you some more," he said, his orbs remaining white as though with worry. *"You will become sick if you stay cold."*

"That w-will take too long," she argued. "C-can you just c-come inside and k-keep me w-warm?"

Mayumi knew from when they'd been cleaning out the gutters together that he was deliciously warm. She'd been able to feel his overwhelming body heat even through her leather trousers when she'd been sitting on his shoulders.

Faunus took a wary step back.

"Come inside and warm you?" He lowered his head while twisting it slightly. *"You mean... hold you?"*

"Please?" she begged. "I w-w-wouldn't be out here a-asking you if it weren't s-serious."

Sure, there was a sense of ulterior motives. She could be patient and wait for him to quickly obtain her some firewood, but this seemed like a faster option.

She also *very* much wanted to snuggle with him.

She wanted to be showered in his heat, covered in his soft-looking fur in the form he was in, holding him while taking in his yummy lemongrass and lime scent. It sounded like heaven.

What better way to stay warm?

Thank goodness he didn't come here in the summer. She loved the heat, but the idea of sweating all over him didn't sound compelling or sexy.

Faunus took far too long to answer, and her knees knocked together the entire time. She thought he was going to reject her. Just when her feet were becoming painful, he stepped forward and gently bumped her shoulder with one of his ram horns – the good side.

"Inside, human. I will do as you have asked." He bumped her again to direct her. *"Quickly, before you freeze."*

Mayumi ran into her house.

She pulled her blanket from the bed as he slowly came inside, having to shove his large body through the doorway while twisting. She gestured at her futon mattress to encourage him to lay down on it. It was way too small for him, but she thought it was better that he lay on it, so no part of her body touched the bitter ground.

The ground underneath the house would be cold, making the flooring feel like ice.

"How do you want me to lie?" he asked as he came over and tilted his head at the futon with his orbs a dark yellow.

"I-In a ball, I g-guess?" she asked as she removed her robe and jacket, leaving herself only in her shirt and underwear so he could warm her more easily.

Faunus curled up with his shoulder resting against her pillow. Mayumi didn't hesitate to crawl straight on top of him to lay with her back resting against his hind legs, so she was facing him. Heat enveloped her on three sides, and she drew the blanket on top of her to help shield her further.

It took a while for her trembling to stop, for Mayumi to regain feeling in her extremities, but when she did, she gave a blissful sigh.

"Thank you. That's so much better," she said with every bit of gratitude and an undertone of humour in her voice. "I really should have just gotten more wood when I knew I was running low."

"Why didn't you?" There was no suspicion in his tone.

"Got tired after doing the attic and didn't really want to face the storm."

The truth was... she was stubborn as an ox when something got her back up. It was a flaw she was aware she needed to work on but refused to. No one was perfect, and as long as she wasn't hurting anyone, she didn't see why it mattered so much that she changed.

Mayumi was aware this was a stubborn mind frame to have. She preferred to call herself headstrong since it was a far more positive attribute.

"You could have asked me to do it." This time his voice was darker, deeper, and filled with a hint of displeasure.

His voice always sinfully rumbled and grated, but when he was in this more beastly form, it was criminal to her depraved senses.

He could tell her a bedtime story, and she thought she'd be sopping wet by the end.

In answer, Mayumi shrugged before turning onto her side. She curled into him and blatantly snuggled into his partially exposed abdomen.

"Your fur is really soft," she mumbled groggily, her energy waning swiftly from being soothingly heated. "And you smell really nice."

Why do I have to like everything about him?

His unholy face that was like a deity of death. His glowing orbs that were swirling and prettier in the night. His daunting height that made her truly feel small and feminine when usually she felt like a stomping ogre. His bulky, muscular body that she could feel now like a big pillow.

His scent. His rich voice. Even the sound of his huffing breath had her ears tingling.

He was too beautiful to be kept hidden in the dark.

"I do?" There was a hint of curiosity and surprise in his tone. She thought he may have moved to sniff at his own arm, but her eyes were already shut. She was drifting off. *"You like the way I smell?"* he asked, like he really wanted a confirmation. *"Mayumi?"*

Despite her tiredness, she could feel arousal softening her muscles while forcing other parts of her to become swollen or hard – like her pussy and nipples.

She only confirmed his questions mentally when she meant to verbally. Mayumi passed out before she knew it.

THIRTEEN

umi moaned as she buried her face against the scent that was currently setting her body on fire.

She knew when her eyelids fluttered open that she was lying face down on her mattress by herself. It also wasn't as warm as *he* had been.

Where'd he go? Faunus was gone from her bed.

She rubbed her face against his lingering lemongrass and lime scent before she just bit at her sheet, hopelessly wanting to taste it. Her nipples scraped inside her shirt as her breasts slipped against the mattress when she lifted her hips. She slid her hand down her body.

Resting on one cheek, she checked around the dimly lit room, the morning so early that it was only just brightening. There was no Faunus within her home either.

She didn't think she would have cared if he were there to watch what she was about to do.

She did notice there was a barbaric, broken bit of branch in the fireplace and that he'd managed to get it going. The flames were small, but they spared her just enough warmth to stop her from shivering.

Her skin was too flushed anyway. She felt heated and uncomfortable in her own flesh, and just a mere touch to her pounding clit informed her she was overflowing with wetness.

Mayumi had no memory of what she'd been dreaming about, but it wasn't hard to guess. Her brows crinkled in anguish. *I want him to touch me so badly.*

She hadn't masturbated in days – since his arrival, to be exact. Before, it had been a daily ritual, but she'd been building up her own anticipation in the hope that he'd ease it.

I can't wait anymore. She needed release.

Still biting at her sheet, Mayumi lowered her fingers and slipped two inside herself. She gave a deep groan before she took them away so she could use her drenched fingers to glide over her sensitive clit with ease.

Her vision split in two the moment she circled it with a firm press.

Shaking with need, Mayumi's insides quivered when she pressed just right, making one of her legs kick before she ground against her hand.

His fingers are so long and thick. I bet they'd feel so good inside me. She would adore holding the back of his veiny hand as he pumped them inside her.

His tongue was a soft violet colour. She wondered what it would feel like petting her clit or sinking inside her. A human's couldn't reach far, but she imagined he'd be able to reach a wonderful depth with it.

Fuck, Faunus. Mayumi rolled onto her back when she needed more freedom to move. *What do I have to do to get you to play with me?*

Mayumi dipped her free hand down to her pussy and slammed two fingers inside her pooling core. Then she brought it up and exposed one of her breasts so she could slip her wetted fingers against an aching nipple. She pictured it was his tongue.

This time, her right hand slipped inside so she could start pumping it. Her back bowed as her head tilted, a moan falling from her lips.

I need to come. I want to so badly.

She pulled her blanket closer and buried her face against it so she could breathe in the intoxicating smell captured on it.

Smells so good. Why does he have to smell like lemongrass? Why does he have to smell like my favourite herb? She'd been caught eating it from the garden when she was younger. She'd been caught *sleeping* in it.

She was like a damn cat meowing at catnip.

Arousal had been building within Mayumi from the moment she'd first laid eyes on him – the night she'd almost shot him with her arrow. She ached for that Duskwalker.

She didn't care why. She didn't care that it would be wrong. He was beautiful exactly how he was... with his unholy, forest-God skull and curling horns. His big, long, muscular, fur-covered body.

And those fangs and claws. Mayumi shivered, her orgasm long overdue and impending.

She was down to get a little clawed and bitten, and she wasn't shy about returning the favour. *Would he like it if I bit him?*

She'd sink her teeth into him so he couldn't get away.

Mayumi bit harder at the blanket, her jaw aching to feel pressure from her own bite.

Just a little more, her mind whispered, her pussy clamping down on her fingers in preparation. Her eyelids flickered right when she was on the cusp, and her cheeks flushed. Her insides clenched. *Almost... there.*

A cold wind brushed over her heated skin, instantly causing goosebumps to prickle.

Get fucked, she mentally cursed when she saw through her wide, parted knees that the door had been opened. *I didn't think he'd come back inside.*

Because there she now was... caught red-fucking-handed with the index and middle finger of her right hand sunk knuckles deep inside her own pussy, while the other gripped her breast.

In his more humanoid form, Faunus had been ducking down through the doorframe to clear his height, holding multiple timber logs in his arms. When he saw her, he froze.

His mouth rarely ever parted since he didn't use it to speak, but she watched his bottom jaw drop like it was threatening to fall off.

Mayumi had two choices.

Self-preservation was to tell him to leave and cover herself, but she doubted she'd be able to finish if she did. It would make getting caught embarrassing. It would also give him the wrong impression: that she didn't desire him.

She went with her second option.

Biting at her tongue, Mayumi kept her eyes firmly on his yellow glowing orbs, pulled her fingers back... and then slowly pushed them back inside.

His orbs morphed into bright purple so fast that it had her clenching. *Do they mean something good? Is it desire?* Was she enticing him?

They'd been that colour the other night when she'd been naked before him.

When Mayumi grazed her most tender and pleasurable spot, a part of her inhibitions died. Her uncertainty and worry dissipated as she dug harder against it.

She was masturbating in front of him and being watched was making her even wetter. She wasn't even bothered that he was in the way of the door shutting and letting in the cold air.

He isn't leaving. He wasn't running away even though her fingers were moving, even though she was fucking herself with them right before his very eyes. *He'd flee if he didn't want to witness this... right?*

The lack of flesh on his face made it impossible to know what he was feeling.

"Do you know what sex is, Faunus?" she asked, her voice so croaked and raspy she worried he might not have heard it. Gods, it sounded so pathetically lewd to her *own* ears.

"Yes," he grated back, his voice even more gravelly than usual.

Her breath hitched as her inner walls clamped around her fingers.

"So, you know what I'm doing?" She pumped her fingers a little slower but more sensually, making it obvious to him.

He gripped the logs in his arms tighter to the point bark flaked off them from his claws.

"Yes," he grated even deeper, his orbs growing brighter.

She drifted her gaze over him, from curling horns down to his paw toes and human feet. It settled on his curling tail for only a moment before she shot her focus back up to his feline skull.

Her heart rate picked up. She was about to go bold and learn whether Faunus was interested or not. She was tired of playing cat and mouse – with her being the chasing predator.

She'd always been impatient, and even just these few days of waiting had been... tiresome.

"Would you like to help me, Faunus?" Mayumi slipped her fingers out so he could see her pussy, see that it was wet and that she'd stretched it a little. She even opened her entrance slightly with her fingertips. "I'd like you to."

Faunus *dropped* the logs he was holding, and they clattered against the ground as he stepped over them. There was no hesitation, not even a second of it. He headed straight for her, almost stumbling over his feet in his haste, like he thought she'd change her mind if he wasn't fast enough.

She watched the door close gently behind him before giving him a beckoning smile.

FOURTEEN

Mayumi was on her back, legs spread, her fingers deep inside her cunt, and asking *Faunus* to come take over. He couldn't get his feet to move fast enough, despite crossing the room in only a few long strides.

His heart had never beat this erratically before, and he swore it sped up even faster when she smirked at him. Her lips had a mischievous curl to them, and the glint in her eyes promised unspoken, wicked things.

And those naughty fingers were still moving like she was beckoning him closer by thrusting them into herself.

Even if this was a trick or some kind of dangerous ploy, Faunus knew he would have done anything to get to her right then.

He would have taken an arrow, any blade, or even been threatened with fire, and Faunus would have ignored it. He would have mauled whatever was in his way to do so – a human, a Demon, another Duskwalker, even a poor unsuspecting table.

Like she was his destruction, he fell before her on his knees, both of them thudding against the timber before his hands *slammed* down around her shoulders. He pierced the mattress she was lying on with his claws.

The aroma in the air had been strong all the way from the doorway, but now it was choking. Faunus panted at her, his fangs parting as he struggled to breathe, being so close to that sweet scent of arousal.

With her eyes glued to his orbs, she bit at her bottom lip. He could tell by the sound of the squelching that came from between them that her fingers had picked up their pace.

Her face and chest were flushed a *cute* pink. She looked so heated, like she was burning from the inside out.

Shit, he cursed when his tentacles writhed quickly to capture his cock and prevent it from extruding. *I don't think I can do this while remaining calm.*

Already he was fighting his own body, and he hadn't even started touching her.

That was *not* going to stop him.

She was offering him something he'd always wanted and never thought possible. He would touch this little human even if it was the last thing he did.

An unhidden moan fell from her lips. It caused his orbs to blacken momentarily so he could savour that melodious sound.

When he noticed her fingers had ceased moving and they were slipping from her, he couldn't contain the threatening growl that burst from him.

"Don't stop," he demanded.

Her brows drew together. "But I thought you were going to touch me."

He was so turned on by what he'd just been witnessing that he didn't even have the decency to feel embarrassed about his next words.

"I have never done this before," he admitted, his voice husky and strained. "I want you to show me where you like to be touched first."

"You said you knew what sex was, what I was doing." Her frown deepened. "How is that possible if you've never done this before?"

Unable to resist the tantalising creature below him, Faunus lifted a hand so he could run the backs of his fingers and claws under her jaw. Just the minor skinship felt wonderful. All the while, he gave a deep chuckle.

"Because I have been watching you humans tasting, touching, and fucking for years."

When she gave a shiver and tilted her head to the side under his mostly innocent touch, Faunus turned his hand over and drew his index claw down the side of her neck. Goosebumps broke out on her skin this time as she gave him a little cry.

The fact he'd been the one to elicit such a wonderful sound made his stomach clench.

"So I'll be your first?" The way she asked it all soft and breathy made him think she might be excited by that prospect.

"Yes, you'll be my first."

And my last, he thought.

Because Faunus knew there would be no other female for him beyond Mayumi. Even if she convinced him to leave, to stop his self-proclaimed duty of protecting her, he had chosen her.

She was the bride he wanted – although utterly unattainable.

"*Fuck,* Faunus," she rasped before her hand started moving again.

He looked down to blatantly watch her.

He was thankful he'd asked her to continue because he'd never been this close before. He'd seen the basics. He'd witnessed men moving their hands around a woman's pussy, but he'd never truly seen what they were doing.

Mayumi showed him everything.

She showed him how to pet her little clit, going up and down, then pressing while going in a circle. When her fingers dipped back inside, he noted she didn't just thrust in and out. She sometimes stayed deep, and he could tell by her knuckle joints she was moving them inside. Sometimes together, sometimes individually.

"I wanted you to touch me the other night."

She did? He'd never been more irritated with himself in his entire life!

"I thought you may not want to when you left."

"How was I supposed to know you wanted this from me?" he grumbled in answer, his sight never leaving her moving fingers or her folds.

"I was pretty obvious," she teased, her eyelids flickering in what he thought might be nervousness.

She needed to give him some leeway here. How was he supposed to know when a human woman was trying to get a male to touch them? *Him,* a Duskwalker, no less?

However, something was making him curious enough that he didn't respond. The scent coming from between her thighs was strong, but he *swore* it was right in front of his nose, just millimetres away – which should have been impossible.

With quick sniffs, he followed the thread and came to her left breast.

It's wet. Her left nipple glistened when he could see the other was dry, although both were hard. *Did... she touch herself and then coat her breast with it?*

Although he'd intended to wait to touch her until she came, he couldn't stop himself from sniffing even closer, twisting his head. Then he parted his fangs further and slipped his tongue across her small breast.

What touched his tongue was tangible, edible heaven.

"Oh!" she moaned, her chest bowing like she wanted him to press harder.

His fur stood on end from neck to tail, as did his spikes.

Faunus messily licked at her breast, trying everything in his might to taste that sweet nectar upon his tongue again. *More. I need more of it.*

Instead, he just drooled all over her skin, his saliva dripping down the side of her. Still, he hunted and searched for more with long, flat licks.

"I expected your tongue to be rougher," she mumbled.

He didn't know why she thought that, but he was too consumed by what he was doing to answer.

Now that he'd finally instigated real contact, he lifted his right hand and wrapped it around the side of her head and neck. His thumb brushed over her cheek before he caressed down to rub her shoulder, her arm, even her sexy, pointed *elbow*.

Then he twisted his head so he could go to her other breast, but he didn't lick this one. He'd seen men suck on them to entice their woman. He'd never been more upset about not having any sort of lips to play with.

He carefully nibbled at it with his smaller front fangs. Her breath hitched multiple times, and he wondered if she liked the sharpness of them flicking over the flat bud. He lightly bit around one to pinch it.

"Please, Faunus." Mayumi placed both her hands on the sides of his head and stroked downwards so she could lift it. She made his gaze meet hers. "I want you to touch me."

One side of his skull had been wetted, and her arousal marking his face had his heart beating quicker in feral thumps. He licked across his fangs, desperately trying to steal it, to taste it.

"I want you to make yourself come."

She narrowed her eyes at him. "No."

"No?" he questioned in disbelief.

He brushed his exploring hand over her chest, from the left all the way to the right, petting both of her nipples. Her back bowed sharply.

"I didn't expect your *hands* to be so rough!"

Thinking he'd hurt her, he pulled it away and looked down at the callouses he had from walking on his hands for most of his life.

With her lips parted from shallow pants, she sternly demanded, "Do it again."

His orbs flashed a bright yellow in utter joy, showing the depth of his delight before they returned to purple. Starting from her stomach, he palmed up her chest and over her left breast.

Her back bowed again, this time her head tilted along with it. Her breath hitched like he'd stolen it from her very chest. He couldn't believe she had such an intense reaction to him palming her!

"Why will you not make yourself come for me?"

He swiped downward, feeling her little left nipple move under his touch. He also lowered his head so he could tongue the right nipple he wasn't caressing.

He wanted to watch her come while she was staring at him. *I have never been the object of a human's desire.* She'd been the centre point of many of his own self-touches, and he, for once, wanted to be just not any human's, but hers.

"Because I've spent enough time doing it by myself," she moaned, leaning her head forward to look upon him, the monster caging her in.

She gave a full-body shiver at his different playful touches.

It didn't take a lot of convincing. Not when Faunus licked at his snout and pointed it downwards so he could see down the valley of their separated bodies.

Seeing her spread open for him, legs that gave no resistance when he brought his hand down so he could palm her pretty thigh further to the side, he knew he wanted his tongue on those glistening folds.

"Only if you let me taste you, Mayumi."

If she wanted him to be the one to make her orgasm, then he wouldn't give her an inch in this argument. He would have it on his tongue. He was *dying* to.

What had been on her breast was just a tease, a meagre taste. He wanted to gorge on her juices like they would quench his thirst for the rest of his life.

A lasting drink.

"Okay. On one condition." The teasing, mischievous, almost *titter* in her voice had him looking up in concern. "I want you to lie back."

He tilted his head slightly. "Why?"

From what he gathered, him being on all fours with her on her back would be much easier.

"I want to sit on your face."

Faunus reared back and then brushed his hand over his short snout. "I don't have a face on which one sits, Mayumi."

It was made of hard bone. It wouldn't be comfortable.

"Sure you do." She leaned up and began pressing on one side of his torso. "And I've been wanting to from the first moment I saw it."

The first moment?

He let himself fall to the side, trusting in Mayumi and honestly just giving her whatever she wanted if it meant he could taste her.

She pulled the shirt that had been sitting around her neck up and over her head to remove it, leaving herself completely bare to him.

Faunus had no idea what he was supposed to do when she flipped her leg over his head and straddled him high on his chest, right below his throat. Her thick hair fell around her shoulders and framed her face when she placed her hands on the ground around his head. He had the nagging urge to touch those delicate strands.

"Let's see how far those big, scary fangs of yours part."

Oh. Understanding dawned on him, and his cock gave a powerful jerk behind his seam. He almost extruded, but he managed to clench his groin muscles in time to prevent it – barely.

What she meant by sitting on his face was to actually sit *inside* his mouth.

He placed his large hands over her thighs to grip them tightly, then he lowered his jaw as far as he could.

Before she could do anything, Faunus was already lifting her forward on her knees. His snout was feline, so it was shorter than most other Duskwalkers' skulls he'd seen.

He was thankful for that.

Even though her thighs hugged the sides of his skull, he was able to fit beneath her so he had room and could see since he didn't bring her all the way in.

He was hesitant about doing so. His fangs were sharp, and the four longer ones meant she was in danger of being nicked if he wasn't careful.

What if I cause her to bleed? Anxiety warred with his choking desire. *I... just need to be careful.* Because now that the source of her sweet, aroused scent was just a tongue touch away, he knew nothing was going to stop him from sampling her completely.

While slightly twisting his head, he rolled his tongue the same way so he could slip the top of it, where his tastebuds were, from that pretty little slit she'd opened for him all the way up to the hard nub of her clit encased inside her folds.

"Ngnhh!" he violently groaned upon the delicious slick that coated his tongue.

She let out a quivering moan, and his mind went blank.

One of his hands slipped to her round arse so he could grip it, knead it, just fucking hold the perfect thing, as he brought the other to her waist to make sure she couldn't escape him. He foolishly drew her deeper within his mouth as his sight darkened under the sheer euphoria he was experiencing with just his disastrous first foray.

Faunus didn't even care that his cock had slipped past his seam to the length of his tentacles sheltering him. Or that a heavy, thick bubble of precum spread on the inside of them. Or that bringing her closer could be dangerous with his sharp feline fangs.

Not when he lowered her at the same time he penetrated her tight hole with his entire tongue just so she could saturate it completely, warm it completely, and feel it completely.

His mind melted underneath her.

Fuuuck.

Her sleepy pumpkin scent made him feel groggy, to the point he wondered if this was what humans experienced when they were 'drunk.' His body grew hotter, his mind so dazed that he thrust his tongue without thought inside her tight, plump channel. Its movements were languid, lapping at her slowly.

His flesh tightened.

My tongue is inside her. A vigorous groan scratched his mouth, filled with Mayumi's slick. *Fuck, my tongue is inside her!*

Her small but warm hands pressed against the cool bone of his face, and he opened his sight just enough to see her head had fallen back. She let out a haunting cry, one that had Faunus shuddering, lost beneath her.

It had sounded blissful. *She likes it.*

It was difficult to remove his tongue from her because of how deep she was inside his mouth. When he did, he accidentally flicked her clit.

Her head fell forward with her lips parted and her eyes open wide. He winced when her hands moved against his face, palming the injured crack on it. She was too busy moaning – with her hips twitching like they wanted to move – to notice he'd grabbed her hand and placed it on the top of his snout for her to hold on to. He also redirected her other hand to his ram horn on his good side.

He twisted his tongue against her folds, slipping between them and around them. It was messy, there was no pattern or reason to his movements, but it was obvious she enjoyed them by the way her breath turned higher pitched with each one. Her body dipped. Her thighs moulded around his face like they wanted to finish cracking it.

He would have let her. He would have died a happy Duskwalker with his head between her thighs.

"I'm going to come," she whispered so quietly that even he had difficulty hearing it. "I'm going to come so hard."

Not without his damn tongue in her.

He lifted her when he found it difficult to slip it back in. The moment he speared her with it, her inner walls snuggly clamped down on it.

"Faunus!"

He answered her scream with a snarl when liquid flooded his mouth. She twitched and shuddered, and he moved his tongue back and forth, trying to get her to gift him more.

Her orgasm was sweet, so damn tangy, and he wanted to fucking drown in it. *Mayumi,* he mentally groaned beneath her.

Faunus swallowed when the pool of it mixing with his drool nearly overflowed the crevice of his mouth. He wasn't going to waste any of it. It was his to drink.

More, he quietly begged when she stopped coming inside his hungry maw. *I want every drop she has.*

It seemed she wanted the same because she started bouncing slightly, riding his tongue herself, fucking his face. When he realised there was a tender spot she reacted to more, he curled his tongue in that direction.

"Yes." She closed her eyes and bent forward, leaning more firmly against his skull to steady herself through her movements. "Right there."

Her bouncing up and down on his tongue quickened, and he couldn't have been happier.

Neither cared about his fangs.

If she was bleeding, he couldn't smell it over her arousal. If she was in pain, she couldn't feel it over her pleasure.

And it was far too much for him.

His cock swelled at witnessing this, experiencing it, and that was the last punch that his tentacles couldn't hold back. It extruded completely and was immediately abraded by the roughness of his trousers.

I can't. His claws dug into her arse, needing her to centre him as he removed his other hand from her waist. *I can't take it.*

He originally wasn't going to touch his cock, but he needed to. Could any male go through this and not have their cock jerking wildly for attention? He'd lose his mind if he didn't ease the prevalent throb. He was already a panting, needy ache beneath her, and every second longer caused him to squirm, his hips lifting with the desire to thrust into something, *anything.*

Faunus was used to handling the buttons of his trousers; he'd opened them plenty of times. He was able to undo the three buttons with ease by coming at them from the side.

The groan he released was the loudest and most agonised one he'd ever made when he grasped the throbbing, solid, and slick rod. His hips tried to dip downwards when he stroked up, then he thrust into his hold, *hard.*

"Fuck, Mayumi," he grunted, violently quaking beneath her as she rode his tongue, his face, his damn mind. "You have no idea what this is doing to me."

Her eyes opened just halfway so she could stare down at him. Her one-sided smile made him pulsate and swell, forcing a drop of precum to well.

"Yeah?" She stayed deep momentarily, then just wiggled her hips.

I want to feel her do that *on my cock.* To have her be seated as deep as possible and then play with it by grinding.

His strokes became shorter so he could twist his fist over the rim of his cockhead, focusing on the most sensitive part of his shaft.

I want her to fuck my face again. He'd never thought it was fuckable before, yet here he was, gaining a new fantasy while experiencing it for the first time. Just imagining her doing this again while she was already doing it was hurtling him even deeper.

Faunus released another deep groan against her, trying to get his fist and tongue to match a rhythm. Back when he stroked downwards on his cock, and forwards when he drew up.

Because... what he really wanted was for her to slam this sweet little cunt on his big cock until she'd claimed it for herself.

Her movements halted.

"Wait..." She started to turn. "Are you–"

Shit. White flashed in his orbs, and he let go of her wonderful arse so he could grip her jaw. He forced her head forward.

"Don't."

He didn't want her to look. Faunus knew what it looked like, how different it was. He didn't want to see her be repulsed by his body or for her to stop because of it.

Humans didn't have the four long tentacles he had at the base of his cock. Theirs generally matched the colour of their bodies, but his was a light purple. Theirs were smooth, whereas Faunus could feel soft spikes in his palm that spanned all around his shaft. They weren't uniform but dotted everywhere, including the bulbous, slightly pointed head.

"But I want to see it," Mayumi whispered, her pussy clamping around his tongue as if she was excited just by the idea. "I want to see your cock, Faunus."

His lungs compressed and decompressed rapidly in anxiety as he flickered his gaze over her face, trying to read her expression.

It was her soothing hands brushing over his fangs – that were pressed against the lower part of her abdomen – then running down his snout and all the way to his forehead, that made him hesitantly release her.

She knew what he was. That he wasn't human, and here she was doing this to him. Allowing him to feel her cunt fluttering her fragile heartbeat around his tongue.

She'd even asked him for this.

More of his self-lubricant seeped between the gaps of his fingers when he gripped his cock tighter – just as she turned to look.

Her inner walls spasmed, and her panting seemed to worsen. She stared, examining this part of him, and it felt like minutes rather than the few short seconds it truly was.

He tried to control his tentacles from squirming, but he could feel them twitching with the nagging need to move, to hold on to something, to just be their wiggling, seeking selves.

Only because he worried he'd start drying out, which stung terribly, he bobbed his hand down and then up, smearing his lubricant from base to tip. Just when he was about to let go so she could see better, Faunus let out a choke.

Her inner walls had clamped down so hard that it felt like she had tried to suck his tongue from his own mouth!

Did... she like me doing that?

Just to confirm, he did it again. He fisted his cock and squeezed as he stroked down all the way to the sacs embedded in the base of his cock before he drew up. He didn't even make it to the flaring rim before she tried to steal his tongue again.

He even felt and heard the squelch of more liquid forming from her.

She may not be saying anything, but her body was speaking to him. *She's enjoying it.* To know that, to know she was enjoying watching him stroke his own cock...

Screw this! She could do what she wanted, but now his body was growing overheated. He'd never been this turned on before.

A breathless pant fell from him as he started masturbating his cock with fast and short strokes, just as he wrapped his arm around her waist to keep her steady while he moved his tongue in and out of her.

She could watch all she wanted, but he was not done feasting.

His sight went dark, no longer able to keep it open under the onslaught of sensations brushing over him. Her scent, her taste, her grinding against his tongue. The way her thighs warmed his cool skull or how his sensitive tastebuds explored the texture within her. His fist was tight, squeezing to the core, and he found himself unconsciously thrusting into it.

The only thing he was conscious of doing was sheathing his claws when he knew his movements everywhere were causing him to dig his fingers into her soft skin.

Her scream was the only warning he got before she came. He answered it with an aggressive, demanding snarl, twisting and moving his tongue faster.

He didn't swallow, letting her juices sit in his mouth so he could savour them, could taste them for longer. All he did was make sure they didn't overflow by sipping remnants down his thirsty, Mayumi's-slick-covered throat.

"Oh, God! Oh, my God!" Her hands slapped against the mattress before she leaned over him to move her hips back and forth. Her movements were minute – he bet she felt his fangs stabbing into her – but her ecstasy-filled cry was the most beautiful song he'd ever heard. "Inside me. Put it inside me."

When he opened his sight, just as her orgasm started to wane, he saw she was curling forward around his head. Her face was blistering red, her eyes a little wetter than normal, and her lips were swollen, red, and parted.

He looked at her through a purple, lust-filled hue.

"Please," she begged, her voice so broken and hoarse that it was sinful. Nothing should sound that erotic.

Mayumi didn't seem like a begging type of woman. She was a bossy, commanding, demanding one, yet her word had been uttered with a plea. It twisted his thoughts into knots.

"What do you want me to put inside you?" he asked, refusing to relent his prodding tongue.

He had many things he could put inside this hole. His fingers, his tail, a candlestick. She was going to have to be more specific if she wanted to give him any direction.

He'd already told her he had never done this, any of this, before.

The smile she gave him was a little broken, only lifting up on one side. "Your cock."

He strangled it in his fist when it swelled to the point he thought it was threatening to come.

He never thought he'd ever hear her utter those words. Even if it was just the heat of the moment for her, Faunus didn't care. He'd fantasised about mounting this woman for so long it felt like eons.

Taking his mouth away, so he didn't harm her, Mayumi squealed when he rolled them over. Her back slammed against the mattress, but she didn't get a chance to say or do anything before he shoved his middle finger inside her pussy.

I want that. I want to put my cock inside her.

Since his tongue had stretched her, he quickly added his index finger, *knowing* he needed to prepare her. She was tight, small, and breakable.

What greeted both his fingers was a snugness.

He'd released his shaft so he could hold himself above her,

and he pumped his two digits inside her.

Mayumi spread her thighs for him, parting everything, including her pussy lips, to help him reach deeper. She was soaking wet from both his saliva and her own arousal, everything swollen and hot.

Her hips undulated, lifting up and down to greet his movements. Her eyes were closed as she buried her face sideways into her blanket before she bit at it. She released sweet cry after sweet cry, lost to her pleasure.

She's so tight, he thought, his head twisting slightly as he watched her. Then he looked down when he tried to split his fingers to stretch her further.

She gasped, one of her hands shooting down to grasp the back of his hand.

When he wasn't able to split them completely, he tried again. Then he tried to slip a third inside to fit into the gap he'd made. He couldn't.

Faunus groaned, this time in dismay, as he lowered his head to press his forehead against her dipping abdomen. She was trying to grind on his fingers as he moved them.

I won't fit. He slipped his entire face against her in need. *I won't fit inside her.*

His fingers were long and thick, but as he leaned on his elbows and gripped his cock again with his free hand, he knew the girth he was holding was even thicker.

He removed his fingers so he could replace them with his tongue, wanting to pacify himself with his newfound addiction. He pumped his fist around his shaft to bring himself to release, knowing he wouldn't be able to do it within her.

I can't fuck her. She's too small for me. Or he was too big for her. Either way, it was impossible.

"Faunus?" she whispered when he licked at her clit, probably wondering why he wasn't trying to mount her now that he'd removed his fingers. "I said I want you. That I want your cock."

Unwilling to look at her, Faunus closed his sight. He didn't want to see the disappointment on her face that he could hear in her voice.

"I *can't,*" he tried to explain, quaking in unanswered longing and deep pleasure as he pumped his fist. "Just... let me do it like this. Let me taste you as I come." He tongued her clit sideways as he let out a whimper when his cock swelled. He was close, so, so close. "Please, Mayumi."

He slipped his free hand up her side so he could palm at her chest, wanting to abrade her nipples with his rough callouses.

"Come for me again," he pleaded, his knees parting in preparation to steady himself for his oncoming release. His groin spasmed. "You taste so good."

He even brought his tongue away for a moment so he could rub his entire face against her glistening, drenched folds, smearing it all over his skull. He was trying to show her how much he adored it.

He didn't know if it was his obvious desperation for it, his palm stroking her nipples just right, the fact he was on his knees masturbating over her, or his tongue, but one or all of them pushed her over the edge.

He only licked up enough of it to stop it from dripping so he could smear it over his face again, using the bone to pet her.

I want to fuck her. She asked for it. She wanted it.

He slipped the side of his face over her pubic mound and gave a shuddering groan against her hip. The end of his tail curled in tension as his tentacles curled into themselves, wanting to grip something as his seed rose.

I want to make this cunt mine. Stretch her so only I can take her, make her beg for it. Make her need me. I want to claim it. I want to fill her with my seed. I... nhnn... fuck.

His trembling jaw parted as a loud groan fell from him, right as his cock swelled and then stayed thicker. He had to stop moving his hand when his spikes hardened right before he released his first mind-numbing, body-shuddering, bliss-filled burst.

He heard it *splatter* against the ground under the force and volume of his first rope of semen.

His expires were heavily panted and shaken when he released a second spurt, then a third. It went on and on as Faunus released against the ground when he wanted to be sheltered by her heat instead.

He was too far gone to roar, too lost.

He had no idea what he was doing to her. If he was crushing her small body under the weight of his head against her abdomen. If his hand was loose or tight around the side of her ribcage.

If he was hurting her...

The bliss was too profound for him to think of anything other than the way his cock pulsated and jerked. He was coming so hard he thought he was going to drain his semen sacs completely by the end of it.

When he was done trying to steady himself through one of the most intense orgasms of his entire life, he could do nothing else but pin her. Every bit of energy had been sapped from him for a few seconds as aftershocks assaulted odd and strange parts of his body.

The crack in his skull thumped with a slightly more noticeable ache than usual from how hard his heart pumped, but it was mostly fine.

Then he finally looked up to find Mayumi was limp against the mattress. Her chest was rising and falling at a rapid rate, but it seemed her last orgasm had weakened her.

Faunus didn't care that his softening cock hadn't gone inside his seam yet. Nothing in that moment would have stopped him from scooping Mayumi up into his arms, not even her. On his knees, he sat back onto his calves so he could hold her naked, languid form on top of his spread bulky thighs.

Tenderness surged when she freely let him.

She is too beautiful, too perfect, to be real.

He worried this was just another one of his dreams. If it was, he hoped he never woke up.

FIFTEEN

Faunus held Mayumi's light weight with just his left arm by cradling her across his forearm with his hand splayed under both arse cheeks. Her folded knees locked her in by pressing against the crease of his groin and thigh.

He adored how she curled into him, her gentle, soft, hot breaths fanning over his abdomen. Her hands were laying over her stomach like she was limp – making her appear docile.

He should get his shirt back from her since he'd left it behind last time in his haste, but he also liked that her face was pressed against the side of his bare chest. She didn't seem to mind the hard bone of his ribcage as she rubbed against his long black fur.

The moment was peaceful.

And for him, it was blissfully serene. Especially when he reached his right hand up so he could brush the backs of his claws against the side of her cheekbone.

For so long, he'd fantasised about having this tiny Demonslayer relaxed in his arms. He'd longed to gaze down at her and brush his fingers into her hair to become intimate with its texture.

He did so now, pushing his claws into her hair so he could greet each strand with his fingers. They were glossy but also coarse in their own way. That didn't make them any less soft or tantalising as he tangled himself into them.

Her droopy, half-cast lids only grew wider so she could look up at his face. She was still catching her breath, but it was easing with each intake.

She looks tired. There was an additional crease in the lower inner corners of her eyes.

Faunus knew it was still early morning by the dim light that was fighting its way through the dark cloud cover.

She was never awake this early, and he doubted she'd slept well since she'd woken in the middle of the night. Faunus had wanted to touch her then, to stroke her face while she slept, pet her hair, but he hadn't wanted to be caught doing something she may not have wanted, nor had consented to.

After what they'd just done together, he felt his more innocent but adoring touches were acceptable, even if they made him feel vulnerable.

He was trying to show her it wasn't just her body he desired, but all of her.

The little mewl she gave when his claw tips drifted over the back of her neck was enthralling. When he did it again, wanting to soothe her, she gave him another mewl as she buried her face against him more.

The fireplace was in full force now. He was uncomfortable so close to it, but he was thankful he'd added that bit of log. Otherwise, her home would still be as cold as ice, like when he'd gone back outside to cut some more properly. He hadn't been able to sleep since he'd been experiencing an intense, pestering need to touch the pretty female who had been using him as her bed.

He never expected to walk inside to the scene that played out before him, but he was ever thankful for it. He wondered if any of this would have happened today if she'd woken still on top of him.

She'd been alone, doing something he'd mostly seen humans do privately.

"Don't think I'm not mad at you," she mumbled. Yet she tilted her head forward so he could have more room to play with the nape of her neck.

"And what could you be mad at me for?" he asked with a quirk of humour in his voice.

If he recounted everything correctly, she'd not only consented to his touch, but had asked for it. Then he'd done everything he could to make her scream multiple times for him, forcing her to come over and under his tongue. From what he'd seen, this was sometimes a difficult task for a human man to achieve, and when they did so, the woman generally seemed to be happier afterwards.

The longer he played with her neck, occasionally scraping his claws into her hair to dance along her scalp, the droopier her eyes became.

She even gave a small yawn.

He knew there had to be a level of deep trust for her to fall asleep like this. He was petting her while she was naked against him. He was supporting all of her weight on one arm, sheltering her with his body and giving her his heat.

"You didn't give me what I asked for," she mumbled, her voice even softer than before. Then her eyes shut completely. "Next time, you better give it to me. Or *else*."

Before he could even respond, she was out.

It seemed her lack of sleep and their busy morning had tuckered her out. She snored lightly against him with her lips parted.

Faunus would have chuckled if her words didn't weigh heavily on him.

He should be rejoicing that there was a possibility of more. He should be filled with satisfaction and triumph that she wanted his body to sink into hers until they were joined.

But he wasn't. *I won't fit.*

Those words were now becoming a sad mantra.

He could try to fit, but Faunus knew the girth of his cock and now the snugness of her channel. They weren't compatible at all.

I'll break her if I try. His tail swished and flicked in unease against the timber flooring.

Although he'd love it if she tried to fuck him to death, he wasn't willing to cause grievous harm to her just so he could fulfil his fantasies.

He curled his arms around her and brushed the side of his feline jaw against her. *I would give anything to be closer to you, Mayumi.*

He pulled back and turned his head over his shoulder so he

could peer out her kitchen window.

Is there a way?

Beyond this house and the northlands belonging to the humans... if he were to go back to the Veil that he promised himself he would never return to, would he find the answer?

Faunus knew of at least one other Duskwalker who had a human companion that had not only become his bride but had given him a child.

He'd been studying humans long enough to know children were born through sex.

Magnar had managed to be intimate with his bride.

Sure, Delora, the antler Duskwalker's female, was taller than Mayumi, but Magnar was slightly bigger than Faunus – yet somehow they'd managed to succeed in this.

How did he do it? Faunus cursed himself for not accepting their offer to remain a little longer to speak with them when he'd been given the opportunity. He may have had the answers he now sought.

Instead, he'd rushed to come to Mayumi, travelling over a great distance so he could see her. All he'd thought about at the time was protecting her while also fleeing the Veil.

He'd never thought he'd ever need to know these answers.

Faunus carefully laid Mayumi against her mattress, which was completely dry of any mess because he'd cleaned her himself. His seed was a large puddle between his knees, but it was on the ground just at the foot of it.

Being careful not to make much noise, Faunus found a cloth on her kitchen counter and cleaned up the mess that had come from his body. He had no idea what to do with it once he'd wiped up his seed, so he just... threw the drenched cloth in the fire to get rid of the evidence.

Then he walked over to the firewood he'd cut and dropped near the door. His fur puffed when he bent down to grab the first log, the memory of him walking in on Mayumi sending a thrill throughout his entire body.

Was she thinking of me while she was fingering herself?

He still couldn't believe this! Couldn't believe what they'd just done, and that he could still smell her arousal all over his face.

If he could, he'd never remove it. He wanted that scent permanently on his face. Forever. Mayumi eternally claiming his feline skull as hers. Marking it.

With a shudder as his cock stirred behind his seam, he finished collecting the wood and placed it where he'd seen her stack others up against the wall.

He couldn't find his shirt when he looked for it, but he took his cloak off the rack and placed it around his shoulders. He covered his head, easy to do so since his ram horns curled around the sides of his face.

When he went outside to leave, a lingering doubt passed over his thoughts. *What if she gets cold again?*

He stared at the tree he'd dug out of the fresh snow earlier.

With a huff, he picked up the axe he'd placed on her shoe rack outside and began cutting up more. Much more. A few days' worth – he was hoping. Especially since Faunus had every intention of being gone that long.

I will go to the Veil, he told himself as he chopped. *I will find the answers* – whether they be elating or disheartening.

He wouldn't sit here and contemplate. He didn't know if he had enough time in this world to be hesitant. Faunus didn't want to deny her again if there was a possibility that they could be intimate like this.

He also worried he'd get caught up in the heat of the moment and *try* like an idiot.

Mayumi's struggle to awaken was a tough battle, as it often was.

The way her body thrummed in satisfaction but also throbbed in mild soreness had her sighing contentedly into her pillow. She would have stayed in bed if she'd been wrapped in heat, the smell of lemongrass, and the feeling of fur, but she rose when she felt none of those things.

She didn't know how long she'd been asleep, but the fireplace was dying of heat, and the sun had gone, thrusting her into dimness.

I should let him know he can stay inside with me. That he could enter whenever he wished to.

Mayumi begrudgingly threw a fresh log on the fire and then worked her way into getting dressed. She was hungry and thirsty, and she wanted to find Faunus.

It's been so long since I slept that well, she thought with a smile curling her lips. *I don't even need tea today.*

She was bright-eyed, bushy-tailed, and... happy.

Mayumi was rarely happy.

I also haven't come that hard in... Actually, I don't think I've ever been that excited. She bit her bottom lip as she fetched herself a pear from her kitchen rack.

Just as she was about to take a bite, she pulled her mouth away so she could throw her head back and laugh. *And his cock!*

It was so fucking weird, and she wanted every part of it.

She'd only seen it from the top, but she knew it was thick and so long that it'd probably only fit about a third of the way inside her. She didn't mind that. If she was filled to the brim with as much as she could take, she knew she'd be sighing around it.

He looked a bit... big, though. His girth had been shocking, but she didn't mind a bit of pain.

Hell, she'd lived in pain. She had a nasty scar marring her entire back and another on her left biceps – evidence of the dangers she'd faced as a Demonslayer. There was also a shallow one on her left thigh.

As she finally sunk her teeth into the pear, the sweet juices of it filling her mouth after a distinct crunch, her eyes bowed in humour.

I didn't expect the tentacles though. She didn't really know what she was expecting, but it definitely wasn't *that.*

The backs of them had been a smooth dark purple, while the insides had been much lighter in colour. She'd noticed small thorn-like spikes on the insides that also covered his cock. Despite its oddness, there was a similar phallic shape to what she'd seen in humans. His shaft may have been purple, but it had a flared head like a man's – although a little more pointed than normal.

She'd never managed to see the underside of him, so she wondered what his sac looked like.

Hopefully, she'd find out soon enough. Tonight, even.

Once she drank a small amount of water, she pulled her fur coat from the rack stand and went outside.

The storm was, annoyingly, still going. Ignoring the frigid, blustery air, she stepped onto the porch. She immediately looked to where Faunus usually curled up in his more monstrous form to sleep. He wasn't there.

What she did notice was a massive pile of timber logs on the porch behind the open door. She frowned at them before searching as far as the falling snow would allow her to see.

"Faunus?" When she got no response, nor did he come, she shouted again, "Faunus!"

Nothing.

Mayumi eyed the logs before she walked to the front of them and placed her hands on her hips. Her lips pursed together tightly.

There was a lot there. Too much, if she was being honest. It was stacked in a triangle against the wall to a height that reached all the way to her bottom ribcage. This was more than a few days' worth.

"Faunus!" Mayumi yelled even louder, turning her head towards the clearing while her eyes remained on the logs.

She wasn't expecting a response this time; she knew she wasn't going to get one. As she had expected, all she received was silence.

He left.

It didn't take much to put it together, considering he didn't come when called and had collected all this for her. He was ensuring she wasn't cold while he was gone, or at least until the storm was over.

Mayumi took in a large, deep breath, grappling for calm. It came out shaken.

It also didn't calm her whatsoever.

With the bottom of her bare, freezing foot, she kicked the neatly stacked pile with the heel.

"How dare he fucking leave!"

Her angry, spiteful side wanted to start throwing the logs into the snow, but the logical side told her not to. Instead, she watched them roll and scatter across her porch with her hands curling into tight fists.

Anger boiled in her blood, forcing heat to the surface of her flesh. She knew she'd be flushed red with it.

"How dare he leave without saying goodbye or telling me if he is even coming back," she growled to herself. "He didn't even talk to me."

He just went *poof.*

Men don't leave me. I leave them!

Mayumi never put down roots. She always promised sweet nothings while nailing some man, watching him fall asleep after having his balls drained before she quietly picked up her boots and tiptoed her way out their front door – or through the window if she had to.

It was the same with all the women she'd conquered too.

Not once had she ever done the walk of shame. It was always the deviant whistled strut of a well-satisfied woman getting what they wanted before disappearing, mostly forever.

Sometimes she'd see them again and had to have the awkward conversation of 'why did you leave?' But she often managed to get away from the conversation with an excuse. Other times she just hid to avoid them if she entered their town and saw them on the street.

With a bristling exhale, Mayumi stomped her way back inside and slammed the door shut behind her with a loud *bang.* Her eyes drifted along all the walls of her home with a glare.

She couldn't believe a Duskwalker had nailed and bailed on her without even giving her the courtesy of actually feeling that strange cock. She had wanted it, asked for it!

Mayumi had practically laid herself out on a silver platter, and this is the thanks she got?

If he comes back here...

That thought made her pause.

She had no idea what she'd do *if* he came back here.

He said he was here to protect her, and he couldn't very well do that being gone. Did that mean he intended to come back?

Some of her anger cooled, but only by a small degree.

When he comes back...

The urge to kick his arse for this was strong, but if or when he came back, which was hopefully soon, would he touch her again?

Mayumi had spent her whole life avoiding playing with the same person twice. She hadn't wanted to be misleading or toy too much with a person's feelings.

But... she *really* wanted that big Duskwalker to come back, more than she was willing to admit.

She wanted to play with him until her heart and body were content. She also didn't know how long that would take. Could it be days, weeks, months... years?

Mayumi had a deep well of lust that only he could tap into – one that a human could never, ever satisfy. Her desire was based purely on curiosity, and the taboo allure of exploring a creature most considered a monster.

Would she be the first or only human to fuck a Duskwalker?

A shiver of desire tingled down her spine. She was well aware she was a monsterfucker, or monsterlover... a monster-enthusiast? She didn't know the right name for it – since it was an unknown lustful desire for most of humanity.

Most didn't want to rail what went bump in the night, but she'd always found the darkness... arousing. People were often afraid of the dark because they feared they weren't alone in it, which is why she often found herself biting her lip at a shadow or even a haunted-looking coat.

However, Mayumi was also very interested in just getting to know him. She wanted to learn everything there was to know about Faunus.

Currently, she knew basically nothing.

She wanted to know where he came from, where he lived, and what he'd been doing all his life. She wanted to know his hopes and dreams and if they were different to what a human would seek.

Eventually, a sigh left her lips.

I hope he comes back.

She'd try not to be mad. She really would. She'd ask him

where he went, and hopefully, that would reveal more about him.

It better be soon, though. Mayumi had never been a patient person.

SIXTEEN

Faunus stalked his way deeper inside the Veil's forest with hesitant, careful, and calculated steps.

He tried not to lift his head too much, hoping to shadow the white of his skull with the hood of his cloak. It was dark even though it was the middle of the day, the constant foreboding gloom and haunting trees creating shade, but he knew the eyes of Demons were superior to those of humans.

Every noise caused him to spook and redirect his path slightly, just to avoid whatever had made it. Since he was travelling on all fours, he lowered himself if he smelt a Demon nearby.

He had to evade being noticed by the one creature he dearly wished to avoid at all costs. Unfortunately, that person could see all the Veil through their magic and could show up within the blink of an eye.

I never wanted to come back here.

He never wanted to see the mixing black and white mist nor hear the eery silence of a place that was afraid to have life. There were no bugs, no birds.

Stomachs were living, moving graveyards – that's what lived within the Veil, death. The malodorous rot of it never escaped his notice.

It had taken a single day and night of solid running on all fours to reach the edge of the Veil, which would have taken a human at least four, if not five. He'd slept at the border, knowing he needed to rest and recover before the rest of his treacherous journey.

He'd been walking inside it cautiously for five days.

Entering north of the forest's canyon, he'd been slowly making his way southeast the entire time. He avoided the middle altogether, but he'd been walking as direct a path to his destination as he could.

A destination he came upon now.

Faunus let out a sighing breath of relief when his left hand pressed inside the magical green ward belonging to the Duskwalker he planned to visit. There had been no Demons loitering on this side of the ward, but he heard them in the distance on the other side.

He imagined there were only a few, as it was difficult to see the house and its occupants through the swaying trees.

When a Demon approached the side he was entering, he picked up his feet and sprinted for the middle to shamefully hide.

He'd done well to snuff his apprehension of wandering through the Veil. His fear was not unfounded; he had every reason to be cautious, but he hated how it felt. The blanket of emotion was cold within his chest and so heavy it was impossible to remove – no matter how much he wished to shed it and be his usual free-spirited, warm-hearted self.

In the middle of the forest sat a log cabin. The trees this close to the building had scarcely been cleared away, as if those that lived here never wanted to be able to see the Demons that lurked – to pretend they didn't exist, that they weren't inside the Veil.

The house was tall enough to accommodate one taller than him by at least a foot, and it was rectangular in shape. At the back, he knew there was a large garden with an apple tree nearby. He could faintly smell all those pleasant scents, and they helped to ease his senses. He felt safer near them.

The long logs that made up this house were fairly new, and the porch was mostly free of any kind of weather damage.

He paused when he neared the house and found two sets of glowing orbs already facing him. *There is another here.* Faunus was not the only Duskwalker visiting.

One set of green orbs remained their colour. The other set, which had initially been blue, turned a threatening red. Faunus' own remained yellow. He held no worry for the tetchy

Duskwalker, as he intended no harm.

When Faunus broke through the trees on his hands and paws, the white wolven skull and Impala antelope horns he saw brought to light who it was.

Orpheus, he lightly growled within his mind.

He'd been less than friendly when he'd found Faunus investigating his home out of curiosity. The male was very territorial, just as Faunus had been when he had a home.

Unfortunately, his own home had been destroyed years ago. It had upended him and caused him to find a residence in the middle of the Veil with the Demons. A poor choice, one he'd realised far too late.

Faunus brought his sight to Magnar, the antler-horned, fox-skulled Duskwalker standing beside Orpheus. *He,* on the other hand, had been a little more welcoming when he found Faunus in his territory.

Perhaps that was out of pity, since he'd been running for his life and had obtained the crack in his skull not long before.

"I know this Mavka," Magnar said, while turning his head to Orpheus. "It is the one I told you of, with the ram horns."

"Our brides are here," Orpheus growled. He took a step back to place himself closer to the house.

Faunus paused and cocked his head, twisting it deeply to the side as his orbs brightened in their yellow colour. *Brides? They have both bonded with a human?*

He'd never known Orpheus had obtained a soul to keep and cherish.

His curiosity faded, leaving a dark and weighty cage around his heart in its wake. They'd both obtained something he would never be able to, and that caused his orbs to flash a bright green in unbridled envy.

He snuffed it, as he did with most of his emotions, so it wasn't prevalent enough to keep his orbs that colour. Instead, it lingered in the back of his mind like a terrible ache.

Magnar stepped closer towards Faunus with his orbs turning a bright yellow in curiosity.

Orpheus took another step back towards the house protectively, going closer to where Faunus figured their brides were. "Are you sure he can be trusted?"

"Yes. I trust him as much as I trust you." Which, in reality, could mean very little. Magnar tilted his head, not seeming to care about Orpheus' hesitation. "Kitty, what are you doing here? You said you never intended to return to the Veil."

With a snorting huff, a little irritated because of his lingering feelings and his restlessness at having to be here in this forsaken forest, he began to change his form. As the transformation shifted his body into one more appropriate for standing, Faunus lifted onto his bare feet.

"I... have some questions," Faunus answered, making sure to keep his sight on the closest threat – Orpheus.

He shook his body free of any leaf litter that collected on him once he was no longer in his monstrous form, especially since he was shirtless and wore nothing but his cloak and pants.

Faunus had never really been overly thrilled about wearing clothing, but the Demons he'd once lived near had preferred it. The only piece of clothing he valued was his cloak, and that was because it hid his skull.

"Also," he started, watching Orpheus more carefully when he approached as well, "my name is no longer Kitty. It's Faunus now."

Faunus lowered his hood so as not to be rude.

He hated it, absolutely despised it, when both Orpheus' and Magnar's orbs flashed white in his direction. The last thing he wanted was sympathy for the situation he found himself in.

There was nothing that could be done to change or fix it, and he'd rather ignore it altogether than dwell on his lingering doom.

Faunus knew he was avoiding how he was feeling, perhaps in an unhealthy way, but he'd immediately accepted it. There had never been a guarantee that death would befall him, only that there was a high chance of it.

He could enjoy what remained of his life, and if it involved a certain tiny human, he would be overjoyed.

Noticing Orpheus looked rather tense, Faunus eased his muscles. He forced a light-hearted chuckle.

"Don't appear so concerned," Faunus said to him, his humour present in his tone. "I apologise for the day I was skulking around your home while you were gone. I was just so curious when I saw a house covered in the scent of my own kind."

"I would apologise for attacking you, but you deserved it for being in my territory." Orpheus folded his arms and turned his head to the side. "But I accept your apology as long as you stay away from Reia."

Faunus tsked. "You're still as sour as ever. I'm guessing this Reia is your female?"

A soft growl came from the Duskwalker, and Faunus gave another chuckle. *Appears he is as territorial about his female as he is about his home.*

His orbs brightened in yellow with humour. He turned his sight to Magnar, who now had his head tilted to the point it was almost upside down. Just by the action alone, Faunus knew Magnar still had a while to go before he was at the same developmental level as himself, and perhaps Orpheus.

"How are Delora and Fyodor?" Faunus asked.

Neither Duskwalker came closer than a few feet, showing that although they welcomed his presence, he wasn't truly trusted.

Magnar's head snapped back into its straight position. "Delora is well. Currently, she is inside with Orpheus' bride, learning to make her own dress. I have no idea how Fyodor is, but I hope they are faring well."

Faunus' head reared back suddenly.

"How can you not know how your own youngling is doing?" He found himself looking around the two males to search the yard for the little baby Mavka with a rabbit skull. "Should they not be here with you?"

Slowly, he watched as Magnar's orbs turned a deep blue before he let out a noticeable sigh. "They are gone."

A cold burst struck his chest as he feared the worst.

Don't tell me... Had what happened to Faunus happened to their youngling?

"Gone?" he asked with a tightness clogging his throat. He was thankful he could speak from his mind rather than from his throat, as he was unsure if he would have even been able to utter a single word.

"They suddenly grew," Orpheus stated with a shake of his

head, seeing that Magnar lacked the thought to expand on this. "They ate a deer and obtained not only their horns but also their sight. They could not stay since they had become an adult and wished to wander."

"I see," Faunus responded while cupping the underneath of his feline jaw. Then he tapped the side of it with a fore claw. "Well, that is disappointing. I was hoping to meet them again."

From the moment Faunus had met little Fyodor, he'd been rather fond of them and overly curious. Born genderless, without sight or a fully formed body, how could Faunus not be curious? It was how he developed, and he was interested in knowing everything about a time he couldn't remember.

Faunus also wanted to spend time with the youngling because he knew he'd never have his own. It was something he deeply desired, but another unobtainable goal for him. *I want to give more than just death. I also want to give life.*

"You mentioned you had questions," Magnar said, his orbs shifting to a colour of yellow that indicated he was joyful about this. "Why me, though?"

"I didn't know you had a bride as well," Faunus commented, turning his snout in Orpheus' direction to indicate he was speaking to him. "I knew you were trying to find one in the many humans you brought to your home over hundreds of years. Perhaps you can both answer my questions, especially since you may know a little more than Magnar."

Orpheus' arms slowly unfolded as understanding took hold. "You have found your own female – one you wish to bond with."

The cage around his heart grew smaller, more suffocating and damaging with each beat within its tight walls.

"Yes," he answered, although a part lie.

Faunus wished to bond with Mayumi, but that would never happen. Even if he wished for it, begged for it, *demanded* it, Faunus would never hold her soul. He couldn't even obtain her love, as it would be meaningless.

He would just be thankful for what he could have, which was her desire and companionship.

"Mayumi has decided not to kill you?" Magnar asked, already knowing about her from when he was last here.

"No, to my surprise." Faunus let out a bright chuckle. He scratched at his chest from the abrupt heat that flared in the cold cage that had been squeezing his heart. "She seems to be rather fond of me."

Spirit of the void help him; he hoped she was fond of him! Especially since he was unequivocally enamoured by everything the bossy, demanding, tiny human did.

He'd cart a thousand trees to her home, cut a million logs. He'd do whatever she wanted. He'd pretended it was an annoyance because it humoured him, and he was hoping to see her flustered by it, but he'd been thrilled that she'd wanted his help at all.

That she needed him for something. That his presence was accepted rather than despised.

Hearing her name coming from Magnar made him tilt his head slightly.

It had been an accident that Faunus had revealed her name to Magnar and his bride, Delora. Apparently it'd been the last thing he'd uttered before he collapsed after nearly two days of fleeing. Mayumi had been on his mind as he experienced all different kinds of regret.

He thought he was going to die and regretted that he hadn't seen more of her, hadn't vowed to protect her when he should have. That he hadn't seen her just one more time, hadn't heard her voice even if it wasn't spoken to him, hadn't taken in her scent – even if it was from a distance.

His hand twitched at the ghost of touching her flesh, like a permanent mark he could still feel.

Her sweet scent had faded from his body over the past several days, but it was there in his mind, would forever be there. He'd taken in her essence and then forcibly woven it into his entire being, every fibre, every cell. Faunus had knotted her to his internal essence so she could ruin and taint him completely for herself.

Orpheus' orbs returned to their natural blue as Magnar's turned green, while Faunus' faded to yellow. They were on neutral ground now, and it appeared as though Orpheus was calmed by knowing Faunus had his own female he longed for.

"I will give you as much knowledge as I can," Orpheus offered, turning his head over his shoulder to look at the cabin behind them. "I understand how difficult gaining a human is and have learnt that I must share what I know. I don't wish for anyone else to suffer as I have."

Faunus cocked his head at that.

Even if he had known Orpheus had a bride, he still would have come to Magnar, as he had been more welcoming to begin with. Magnar had also helped save his life.

Knowing Orpheus was willing to help at all was shocking. He didn't seem like the kind of Duskwalker that would care for the struggles of another, but perhaps he had changed over time. He had humanity, plenty of it, but his interactions with humans had been less than pleasant, which caused his emotional intelligence to become skewed and warped.

Just coming here, in its own way, was degrading for Faunus. The fact that Faunus couldn't navigate this on his own was humiliating, as he'd learnt everything by himself. He'd never needed to lean on another before.

Especially since he'd learned the hard way that no one wanted to help him. That no one cared about him. That he was completely, utterly, and painfully alone in this world – just as all his kind were.

But if I try to learn this on my own, I could hurt Mayumi in the process.

Running his palm up his snout and over the uninjured side of his skull, Faunus opened his fangs to let out a deep sigh.

"Mayumi is... small," he admitted. His hand came down to rub at the back of his neck, revealing how awkward he felt about this. Even his sight turned a reddish pink in both shame and embarrassment. "Magnar, you had a youngling with your bride. And even now, I can smell the lingering scent of sex on both of you."

They both gave a flash of red, perhaps angered that it would mean he could smell their female's arousal on them. Their show of annoyance left as quickly as it came, most likely knowing it also meant they and their females were marked by each other's bodies.

It was obvious, but perhaps blatantly commenting on it was rude. He was beyond caring for formalities.

"How?" Faunus asked, eyeing them both up and down. "Humans are small, and Delora is not much taller than Mayumi."

She may be much plumper, but Delora was small, even to Faunus. A fragile, breakable human.

"How else?" Magnar asked with a shrug of his shoulders. "I don't think it is much different between humans from what I've been told."

"I won't fit," Faunus stated with a shake of his head. "I have already touched, and I know she will not be able to take me within her at all. I will break her if I do. She is small everywhere."

From height to breast to arse to her shallow and tight channel, the only thing that was big about Mayumi was her brilliant personality. But that did nothing to aid him in rutting her the way he wanted to.

And dear spirit of the void, did he want to rut her, so unbelievably *hard*. He wanted to upturn that tiny female until she was at his mercy, and break her mind rather than her body. He wanted to see her squirm and cry and beg and just become nothing but a numb, twitching thing he mindlessly thrust into.

Then he wanted to fill that small, tight, quivering little channel and womb with copious amounts of his seed so that she was overflowing. So overfilled that it covered her, marked her in his sexual scent, while his own body excitedly pumped it into her. He wanted her swollen with it.

Faunus had to quell the violent quake that quivered throughout his body.

He had questions. So many questions that they were moments from pouring from him without thought.

He didn't care if he barely knew these two Duskwalkers in front of him, or that the questions he asked and the answers he received might be disconcerting or uncomfortable for them all.

Mayumi was his priority, and if he missed anything, he would just come back here and ask them then – although he'd rather not.

There was also something else he needed to know, something so unbelievably important that it was perhaps the supreme question of all.

I need to ask how I obtain Mayumi's soul.
He needed to know... so he never, *ever,* took it.

SEVENTEEN

aunus had been hoping for a peaceful walk on all fours back through the mist-clouded Veil.

He'd remained within Magnar's protective ward overnight, recuperating for his long return journey. He refused to rest within the Veil itself, thankful his kind could survive days without rest if they chose it.

It still tired them out, making them less effective and alert, but it was better to keep moving. He'd be vulnerable asleep and more likely to be found if he lingered.

He'd obtained all the answers he sought and even had the opportunity to greet Delora again. She was kind, and he liked that she was so welcoming towards him, but she was also a little timid.

Reia, on the other hand, was like a bundle of chaos from the moment he'd met her. She'd had no qualms about approaching, despite Orpheus' aversion to her doing so, just to speak with him.

At the time, he'd chuckled to himself when she'd placed her hands on her hips and stared right up at Faunus like he wasn't some beast who could swipe her in half within the blink of an eye. She was bold, and he admittedly became smitten with the blonde-haired female who had a sword strapped across her back.

More in a friendly, platonic way than how he was smitten with Mayumi, but he liked that she was strong minded. It was obvious to Faunus that Orpheus needed a woman like her, someone who would put his ill-tempered, deer-tailed arse in his place.

She is the reason he has grown relaxed with others.

Otherwise, Faunus could see the sorrowful and reclusive Duskwalker hiding her away in that log cabin he had near Magnar's.

Faunus mostly understood why Orpheus had become the way he was. He didn't know any other Mavka who had tried so hard to find a companion, only to lose them repeatedly. He'd seen death, had been the cause of it, and if he'd grown to care for any of them in the way Faunus cared for Mayumi, he could only imagine how protective and destructive he would have become.

Pain was a horrible shaper to one's growing personality, and for a Mavka who was still learning, still developing humanity over the years, it would have festered as a dark part of him.

Faunus was thankful that neither he nor Magnar had to go through something so dispiriting.

A small part of him was disappointed he needed to leave. He'd enjoyed being with Magnar, Orpheus, and both their brides. He truly wished to know them more, learn who they had become, and observe the brides who had helped to make their conversations possible, but he didn't wish to be apart from Mayumi for any longer than necessary.

That's if he made it back.

He worried that at any moment, the person he wished to avoid would suddenly appear. Faunus would flee, although he would have preferred to stay and fight.

Before the crack in his skull, that's what he would have done. Now it could cost him everything.

Yet, a peaceful stroll wasn't on the horizon for Faunus. He knew that by the quadruple footsteps he could hear and the scents on the wind brushing his way.

Fuck. He quickened his pace when he'd intended to skulk his way out of the Veil. It didn't matter. Those footsteps were obviously chasing his scent. *Shit. Shit. FUCK!*

Faunus steadied himself and turned to the two creatures coming upon him at a dangerously fast speed. It didn't save him from being barrelled into, one on top of the other, before he was flung between the trees into an area that opened enough to accommodate all three of their massive sizes.

The entire time, Faunus wrapped his arm around his skull to

protect it.

With a deep, rumbling snarl, he turned to them with his orbs red. He also fixed the hood of his cloak to hide his face from anyone who may be looking through magic from seeing him.

"Leave me be!" Faunus bit, wanting to roar, but instead he kept his voice quiet.

For a moment, the two creatures struggled with each other as though Faunus being the centre point of their interest had faded while they playfully fought.

Faunus knew they'd come for him the moment he tried to walk away.

"I knew it was the ram horn," one chuckled, his laughter like a snigger while pinning the other down.

"The one with the cat skull," the other said with a huff, snapping his jaws upwards to get free.

Once they were both on their feet, they turned to him, revealing two Duskwalkers in their monstrous forms. Faunus doubted they owned a single bit of clothing between them, even underneath their forms.

They were overly social Duskwalkers, but that also made them entirely off-putting to all. They were also exceptionally dangerous.

One had bright pink orbs. His skull was that of a bat, with goat horns that curled up and then back over his head. His body, however, was mixed between having long fur and large feathered wings on his back. Those feathers also went down his spine before they turned into a tail of them.

The other had purple orbs with a skull that had once belonged to a raven and the beak to match. He also had goat horns, although small and pointed upwards from his head. He had a mixture of short fur and lizard scales. Lizard-like spikes, twice as many but smaller than Faunus' own, travelled over his arms, legs, back, and down his long lizard tail.

It was obvious they'd shared everything they'd ever eaten, and Faunus imagined they'd fought over most of it. He could picture the two playing tug-of-war with their food.

From what Faunus had gathered over the *multiple* times he'd met them, they were always together. They were likely twins.

These two had no home, from what he knew. They were always in the Veil, safe as they had each other to fight off Demons. A single unit that shared the exact same needs and wants.

Faunus took a wary step back when they both, at the same time, took a step closer. The raven skull stepped his left hand forward, while the bat skull one pushed his right forward. Their pinkies overlapped in the middle of them.

"I don't wish to play," Faunus snapped, especially when they mirrored each other by going in opposite directions to circle him.

"Why will he not play with us?" the purple-orbed, raven-skulled one asked as he tilted his head at the other.

"He used to play with us," the pink-orbed, bat-skulled one responded. *"Perhaps it is a new game?"*

"Kitty always shows us new games," the raven-skulled one stated, drawing Faunus' attention.

Faunus lost sight of the other one when he went behind him. *"My name is no longer Kitty,"* he stated.

"Like hide and tap!" the bat-skulled one chuckled before he shoved Faunus' backend.

With a snarl, Faunus turned and shoved him back to put space between them. Not expecting the push, the bat-skulled one was shoved to his side, but Faunus found himself being tackled to the ground by the other.

A yelp sounded from Faunus when his head smacked against the ground, causing both of them to jump back in surprise. He was sure his behaviour was strange to them.

Faunus had spent many hours playing with these two and inventing new games for them to play with each other. These two Duskwalkers lacked much humanity. They were rather underdeveloped, but he'd found enjoyment in being with his own kind when he could.

They were the two he knew the most, and he trusted them. It was a rarity for him to have such pleasant memories with others – but it had always been brief, as these two easily lost interest, and their small attention spans would turn back to wandering the Veil and its border.

It's probably why they'd hunted him down when they caught

wind of his scent. They wanted to spend time with him, as it was not uncommon for them to do so, for Faunus to steal their attention for the moment.

Faunus let out a small whine when he was trying to find his feet, fighting a small amount of dizziness.

"He cried," the raven-skulled one said, as he lowered himself.

The bat-skulled one hunkered down as well. *"He has never done that before."*

Ignoring them for the moment, Faunus stood on three limbs and steadied himself as he checked his skull. By running his fingertips over the crack, and the additional throb he had, he knew the crack had extended – although only minutely.

White grew in his orbs before he turned to them.

"I said I didn't wish to play today!" he roared, his heart thumping chaotically in his chest.

Fuck! They'd ensured he was closer to the end!

As though they shared the same damn-useless brain, their orbs grew bright red in unison as they snarled. Like all Mavka, they were quick to anger.

Faunus knew he must have pushed back his hood slightly when both came to the same realisation, and their orbs turned white.

"His skull is cracked," the bat-skulled one said as he stepped back with what could only be uncertainty.

The raven-skulled one came closer to his twin. He seemed to need comforting, physical contact between them, since he leaned his shoulder against him. *"This is not good."*

Fixing his hood to make sure it covered his face, Faunus couldn't help thinking they'd stated the obvious.

"Yes," Faunus sighed, before taking a step to the side so he could be just that bit closer to the border of the Veil. To freedom, to safety. *"I have cracked my skull, which is why I cannot play, and now you have injured me further."*

Their orbs turned a deep blue.

"We are sorry."

"We did not know."

"We would never wish to harm you on purpose."

"You are friend."

He didn't know who spoke, since when they were standing beside each other, their voices were near identical.

We are more than friends, Faunus thought sadly. But he knew these two wouldn't understand the concept of family, of brothers, and what that meant.

"It's fine," Faunus answered. Although he was seething with rage, there was no point in taking it out on them. He needed to get out of the Veil before it was too late, and now his time with Mayumi had grown shorter. *"I must leave the Veil. It's no longer safe for me here. Let me pass freely."*

He started to leave, finding his feet moving of their own accord at just the thought of his fiery little hunter.

He'd been close to the border, had almost escaped all this. He couldn't help his own orbs turning a deep, pitiful colour of blue, so dark it drowned out any sort of light. Even the dreary world of the Veil seemed colder, and it caused a shiver to tremble through him.

Faunus looked over his shoulder when he knew they were following him by their pawsteps. Their heads tilted in opposite directions, away from each other, when they noticed his sight on them.

"Why are you following me?" he asked before turning forward. *"I want to escape undetected."*

If he hadn't been detected already because of them, that is.

All was silent, and he couldn't smell any Demons nearby, but their collective, crunching footsteps may be heard. The sound of dead, dry leaves echoed, as did the snapping of twigs and branches under their heavy bodies.

There was no snow, as there rarely was in the Veil, but the wind was strong and cold. Would their combined scents draw Demons closer or cause them to scatter?

"We are trailing you in order to protect you."

"You are safer with us."

A small sense of ease brushed through him. They were right. He was safer with them nearby, even though he'd been trying to do this by himself and had succeeded over the course of many days.

Shame took the place of his fading anxiety. He was a

Duskwalker, a Mavka, something most considered a nightmare. The humans called him a grotesque monster. He shouldn't need their help; he shouldn't *need* protecting.

Everything else should need protection from him.

"Why not... stay?" one of them asked.

"Stay with us. We will protect you."

"No," he answered softly. *"There is somewhere I wish to be."*

One gave a whimper, while the other said, *"But if you die, you will never play with us again."*

For just a moment, white flashed in his orbs. Faunus looked up at the canopy above, wishing to see the sky rather than this foreboding, horrible, gods-forsaken forest.

"I know," he answered quietly, hating the way an iciness spread around his big heart.

EIGHTEEN

Fogging breaths left Mayumi's dry lips, accompanied by grunts, as she swung her axe to cut into the tree branch in front of her. Her foot was resting against the tree trunk, doing nothing but steadying her as she swung again.

Thuk. Thuk. Thuk.

Once she'd gotten the base detached from the trunk, she got to work on cutting the branch into neater, more manageable logs for her fireplace. She also collected the small branches as kindling.

Perspiration dotted her forehead, and she lifted her forearm so she could wipe it away with the sleeve of her jacket. Needing to catch her breath for a moment, she stared up at the mostly clear sky.

Shit. Faunus was able to do this with the bigger axe in a quarter of the time.

Considering the bastard had been gone for a week and a half, and Mayumi only needed to start cutting her own firewood three days ago, she was thankful he'd prepared so much for her.

But at least I don't need to go wandering through the forest to get more.

Her eyes bowed in sympathy for herself when she inspected what remained.

This had been the last branch. After this, she would have to go through the gruelling task of cutting the trunk of both trees and then splitting their large sections into suitable pieces.

Mayumi creaked her neck to one side, then the other, before

rolling her shoulders back. *At least this is keeping me fit.*

She'd spent much of the last week and a half training – whether that was running back and forth across her porch, using the doorway as a place to do chin-ups, or doing sit-ups or push-ups. Mostly because after the twelve-hour blizzard, she'd been kept inside for four days during the snowstorm that followed. It would weaken in intensity only to grow in strength a few hours later.

The snow was up to her thighs and chilling them despite her wearing her thickest leather pants.

Mayumi looked deeper within the forest. *I should go hunting again.* Fresh meat would be good for her, but she also needed it to create her Demon baits.

She figured Faunus wasn't going to come back.

It'd been nearly a fortnight, after all.

At first, she'd been irritated. After the fourth day, she'd been pissed. On that night, she'd finally pulled out her Marianna's Sleeper booze, drowned her sorrows, and then woke up groggy.

Mayumi had gotten over it.

Years of emotional discipline told her not to let her emotions linger or fester, and she just didn't see the point of it. She was alone, didn't care that she was, and she would just continue to live her life like she had done before.

A life of boring solitude.

At least I got to fulfil part of my deepest fantasies, she thought, as she collected her timber logs to take them inside. *Can't ask for more than that.*

She also now had plenty of masturbating material, not that she'd used much of it in the past week. Whenever she tried, it left a burning sensation in her chest.

After placing the logs next to the dying fireplace, Mayumi collected her two travel satchels and strapped them over her torso. Then she strapped on her empty backpack.

She'd already been to town a week ago after the storm, but the thick, fresh, loose snow ensured she couldn't obtain as much food as she wanted. It would have been impossible to carry everything while wading through the dense powder.

Now she was going back, most likely having to grab just as

little supplies. The dead of winter was unforgiving and harsh, especially to those that lived outside of towns.

Most wouldn't have taken the risk she did today by cutting their firewood first. They would have gone to town to ensure they returned by nightfall and cut in the dark if need be.

Mayumi had no such fears, or any at all, really. Being a Demonslayer meant she often found herself travelling in the night where nightmares lurked.

She'd always survived it.

After checking on her charms, she entered the clearing and then the forest. She made it about five minutes before her ears twitched at an alarming sound. Alert and prepared, she unslung her bow from her shoulders and slid an arrow from the quiver at her back.

She turned around and aimed the iron arrowhead in the direction she just came. It only took a minute for the creature to reveal itself.

"You're joking," she rasped under her breath before snorting out a spiteful laugh. "He came back."

Because there Faunus came, walking on all fours in his monstrous form, heading in her very direction through the trees. His pace was fast, but he wasn't running, as if he knew she hadn't been far.

Her deep tracks would have made that obvious, if her fresh scent didn't.

Mayumi cared about no one. That's why she didn't understand the maelstrom of emotions that struck her in that moment.

She'd be *damned* if relief was the one she'd settle on. She refused to be relieved to see that stupid feline skull, or his curling ram horns, or be undone by those swirling, ethereal, unholy glowing yellow orbs of his.

No, it was the other ones, the more negative emotions that she focused on.

Okay, so maybe she wasn't over the fact that he'd just up and left, with no word as to why he was leaving or if he would be back. And then he had the gall to just return a week and a half later?

She pulled back her hooked fingers latched onto her bowstring to tighten it. The spiteful, angry, scorned woman side of her wanted to unleash it straight into his damn chest. The logical side informed her it would mean she'd have to fight to the death with him – and, most likely, lose.

Damnit! She loosened the tension she had on her bow and immediately turned to continue going into town. Her walk was faster than before. It was also less alert and uneven. Okay... so maybe she was stomping!

She hoped he didn't expect rainbows and sunshine to come out of her arse because that was going to be the exact opposite of what he'd be receiving.

Her blood boiled with nearly a fortnight's worth of anger, frustration, and disappointment that she hadn't had a target but her own body to unleash on. She'd trained hard to disperse it from within.

Now, it caused her heart rate to spike, making her cheeks feel warm with it. The burning acid in her stomach almost felt like she'd spit venom the moment she opened her mouth.

The cap of the bottle her emotions were usually shoved inside of was loosened just enough that she could feel it slowly overflowing. Not a good thing.

"Mayumi?" she heard right behind her, his multiple paw and hand steps crunching in the snow loudly. *"Where are you going?"*

"I didn't think you were going to come back," she said quickly, trying not to sound spiteful despite hearing the venom in her tone.

She was trying to put her emotions away, stuff them back into their rightful place where they belonged. To snuff them if she could, since they never did her any good.

"Why would I not come back?" His voice was laden with confusion. *"I said I would protect you."*

"Ha!" Mayumi shook her head and then tried to control her struggling breaths. "Can't protect me if you're not here, can you?"

"Are you... angry with me?" Once more, she heard nothing more than confusion.

"No. I'm not angry with you."

She was livid! But if he didn't understand what he'd done

wrong, then there was no point in taking it out on him. She just put it in the too-hard basket, like she did with most people.

"Where are you going? The town? If so, I will walk with you."

Her gaze narrowed on the trees and the blanket of white before her as far as the eye could see. *Even if I said no, he'd just follow me anyway.*

Her breaths were growing more rapid, the speed at which she was stomping more tiring than the calmer pace from before. She was exhausting herself needlessly to put space between them. That seemed impossible with the way he not only easily kept up with her, but came forward to walk beside her.

"I'm going to Colt's Outpost. I need more supplies."

She considered slinging her bow back over her shoulder, but she kind of wanted to keep holding it so she could smack him with it if he tried to touch her. She grinned maliciously. That'd hurt.

"Would you like me to carry you on my back?" In her peripheral, his feline skull faced her, most likely so he could assess her from the front. *"It will be quicker and easier for you."*

Yes, she would absolutely love that. She'd been hoping to ride him like a mighty stallion to and from the town before he left. She'd even rubbed her hands together while cackling evilly, imagining grabbing so many supplies because he would have been able to carry them for her.

"No, I'm fine. I don't need your help." Mayumi was growing more agitated by the second at his constant desire to assist her. She was feeling bitchy, rightfully so, and his kindness was getting on her nerves already. "Just... go away, Faunus. I'm not in a good mood."

He took a few steps faster and was now slightly in front of her, making it easier for her to see him when she didn't want to right now. She didn't want to see that big, beautiful, bony head of his.

He tilted it at her.

"Did something happen while I was gone?"

Mayumi waited for some kind of apology that would usually accompany such words. Some pathetic explanation as to why he left.

Nothing followed, even after a span of a few heartbeats.

"Screw this," she muttered to herself before loudly stating, "you know what? Fine, I'm angry with you."

The yellow glow of his orbs darkened, perhaps to convey curiosity. *"Why?"*

"Because you just suddenly left, Faunus! Without telling me why or how long you'd be gone for."

His steps lagged for a moment, but he shuffled them to catch back up. *"But I am here now. Why should that matter?"*

It's like talking to a tree!

She knew he was a Duskwalker, but he said he'd been watching humans for a long time. Perhaps she was giving him too much credit, but she thought he'd be a little more understanding than this.

"Leaving right after what we did together is what most people would call a nail and bail. Or a one-night stand, if you will." Her cheeks puffed in annoyance at having to explain this. "Most of the time, the person doesn't come back. It's also a really crummy feeling for the person who was left behind, and it often makes them feel used."

Mayumi was aware she was calling the kettle black here, that she was being a hypocrite, but she couldn't believe a fucking Duskwalker had done that to her! Human men, she could understand. It happened all the time. But him?

When he'd told her it was his first time doing any of this, and the fact he'd jerked off to her riding his skulled face, she'd kind of hoped to have him in her hands after that. To have a curious, needy, horny Duskwalker to play with.

Not for her to wake up alone wondering where the hell he went.

Faunus flinched slightly, and his orbs turned a deep blue.

"I didn't mean to make you feel that way." He came closer and had the audacity to nudge her shoulder almost cutely with his own, like he wanted to be affectionate. *"I needed to go to the Veil to see another of my kind."*

Mayumi ripped her arm away from him and considered smacking him with the flexible end of her bow. She decided against it.

"That's great and all, but you could have told me you were leaving."

Her angry march made sure she remained just that, angry. The snow was heavy and difficult to kick around, frustrating her further. She was sure if they'd started having this conversation back at the house, she would have begun calming by now. But she was moving, and it was making her more stubborn than usual.

He hasn't even said sorry yet. It should have been the first thing he said. It only upset her further.

"So, if that's how it's going to be," she continued, her brows narrowed as she lifted her jutting chin. The flames of spite swelled in her chest and then burst out of her mouth like she was a fire-spitting dragon. "If you're just going to leave randomly and not return for a long time, then I'll go find someone else to fuck since you don't seem to want to."

Mayumi was still pretty pissy about that. She'd offered herself to him, legs open and pussy bared, and he'd chosen to come against the ground. That rejection had left a stinging sensation in her chest ever since... like she wasn't good enough.

The words that were coming from her now weren't the truth, and she knew it. But her hold on her anger was like a sieve. Useless but to let everything fall through.

It'd always been this way for her, which is why she generally tried to keep a good, steady, strong rein on her emotions.

Faunus was suddenly in front of her, facing her on all fours and blocking her path. *"Pardon?"*

His orbs flickered green before they returned to their normal yellow. Mayumi ducked around him and the trees next to him while lifting her chin higher. At this point, her nose was almost pointing towards the sky like some snooty princess – she often made fun of women for doing this.

"I don't wait for anyone," she spouted, which was the absolute truth. "If you're going to just come and go, then I'll just go walk the few hours it takes me to get to town and find someone else to keep me company. There are plenty of people in Colt's Outpost who would be honoured to have sex with me. Actually, I'm going there right now to do just that."

Some of that was a lie. Men either found her forward attitude sexy in a 'full of confidence' kind of way or a deterrent in an 'I'm a whore' sort of way. Most considered it the latter, and her slender but muscular physique didn't scream that she was sensual to play with.

Which was their loss because Mayumi was very sensual when she wanted to be. She could make men come so hard their eyes crossed, and their mouths rambled pathetically.

Women who liked women were a little harder to find, and many were like Mayumi: women who liked both genders. It was difficult to determine if she could steal the woman sitting on a man's lap or not.

The other lie was that she was going to Colt's Outpost for that reason. She wasn't and never had intended to.

A small part of her had been hoping Faunus would return. So, she wasn't quite sure why she was spouting bullshit that would be detrimental to her case of having him stick around.

Perhaps it was her need to punish people, so they didn't make the same mistakes twice. Mistakes in the guild often caused people to lose their lives, and as a high-ranking Demonslayer, it was often her job to give out those punishments.

Mayumi stopped walking the moment Faunus was in action.

He was in front of her again, blocking her path, but this time, he stood. Although he was still in his more beastly state, which curled him forward slightly anyway, he leaned towards her to appear more menacing. Especially when he placed his hands on the trees beside him and growled with his orbs a dangerous colour of bright green.

"No," he snarled, the rumbling from his chest loud and booming.

She hated that her damn nipples tightened in reaction to it!

"No?" she laughed with her eyes bowing in humour. "Did you just tell me what to do?"

"You will not allow another male to touch you."

Her eyebrows nearly shot up to her hairline. Mayumi stepped to the side to go around him, but he instantly followed her.

"You don't get to tell me what to do, Faunus." She just blatantly ducked underneath one of his arms since he was so freaking tall. It was easy, since the gap between his body and the tree to his left was wide. "That's not how this works. I will continue to do what I want, as I have all my life."

Mayumi received no warning before she was face down in the snow, her bow lost in her surprise. He'd grabbed her ankle and tripped her! Then she was flipped before her entire forearm was grabbed this time. She squealed when she was tossed over his shoulder with flailing legs.

He walked away from Colt's Outpost in the direction of her house. Pants had formed on his lower body, meaning he'd reverted into his more humanoid shape to assist in carrying her.

"Put me down!" she demanded with a yell.

Her immediate response was to reach up for her dagger, but Faunus had wisely, whether by accident or not, covered her weapons belt with his arm.

Mayumi beat against his back with the bottom of her fists while kicking her knees into his chest. Nothing stopped the big Duskwalker.

"If that is your intention today in that pathetic human town, then you will not be permitted to go to it," he growled, his voice still beastly due to his rage despite his change in form.

The fact his voice was still a reverberating bass sent a shiver down her spine – one that had her insides clenching with warmth. She even felt it against her stomach pressed over his shoulder as it radiated through her.

Faunus was *mad*. Big mad.

NINETEEN

Mayumi continued to punch him in the back *hard* as she was
carted back to her home. It was like he didn't feel the strength of
her hits at all... like they were nothing to him.

She could feel his sharp claws digging into her side from
where he held her around her hips, as well as the side of her thigh
where he held her legs down. There was a constant growl
emitting from him.

"I said put me down!" she screamed, thrashing against him.

Faunus' heavy footsteps thudded up the stairs of her porch,
and he jumped back a step when he must have hit the barrier of
her charms. She thought that would stop him, but it didn't.

Instead, his growl deepened as he barrelled through it, taking
whatever pain it gave him to get to the other side.

Mayumi never locked her home – there was no point. If
someone wanted in while she was gone, they'd find their way in
somehow.

That meant all Faunus needed to do was open the door.

He flipped her onto her feet and pushed her into her home
right through the doorway, then proceeded to block her exit.

His orbs were an even brighter green than usual, but
everything else about him was threatening. His fur and even his
lizard spikes were standing on their ends. He was puffed, which
made him look like a large, menacing fluff ball. He was also
visibly quaking.

"You will stay," he demanded.

Just as Mayumi folded her arms and opened her mouth to

refute, Faunus grabbed the door handle and *slammed* the door shut on her.

She winced at the cracking sound from her door, or perhaps the frame.

"You can't keep me in here," she flung at him through the door.

Mayumi jumped in surprise when he gave a singular bash to the door with his large fist.

"You WILL stay, Mayumi!" he roared. ***"You will not take another male while I am here!"***

Her arms began to loosen. *Is he jealous?*

Just the mere idea of that had another shiver running down her spine, this time accompanied by her biting at her bottom lip. If he was, she kind of liked him being possessive. She didn't mind the whole caveman 'woman mine, only mine' feral thing.

Actually, it had her insides fluttering in welcome and made the tingling ache of her nipples more prominent.

Then he shouldn't have left me here for a week and a half after not giving me what I wanted.

She also *hated* being told what to do.

So Mayumi did the only thing she could. She walked to the storage room of her house, pulled down the trapdoor to her attic, and climbed the ladder. Then she pushed open the roof door and crawled on top of her cottage.

She knew she'd been heard when she slid down the side of her roof by her hips on purpose. She caught the railing when she went over the edge and saw Faunus had leaned away from the door to look exactly where she hung.

He appeared hulking and beastly on her porch. He was too big for it, a daunting mass of darkness, muscle, and body.

Mayumi gave him a glare as she let go and fell freely into the soft snow below her. It cushioned her fall. She scrambled to her feet when she heard an actual roar this time.

Fuck. Why does that turn me on so much?!

She tried to run, but the thick, loose powder made it difficult. She only made it three steps before she was tackled to her front.

There was no opportunity for her to move when he laid down on top of her and curled his arms around her. He caged her in with his own body, locked her arms to her sides, and only gave her legs just the minutest freedom to kick. She noted he was hot, almost like his body was filled with lava. His quaking seemed to worsen to the point it shook her.

"Never run from me," he warned slowly and punctuated.

A gasp burst out of her when he yanked her and stood. He braved the barrier once more, intending to put her back inside. Just as he opened the door, Mayumi placed her feet on the doorframe to keep herself out of the house.

It didn't work. She had to move her legs, or he'd snap her damn knees with his pushing.

"I need to go into town!"

She needed food and supplies! Screw what she said before. She actually had things to do there today.

The sounds that were beginning to come from him were completely and utterly inhuman. Were they snarls, growls, barks? Or perhaps a mixture of every predator she'd ever heard of?

Regardless, Faunus shoved both of them through the doorway. Before she knew it, he'd crossed through the house and shoved her front against the dining table.

He pinned her down with his entire body. One hand slapped against the table's surface right next to her head, claws *thunking* into it when they stabbed, while the other curled underneath her body and wrapped underneath her jaw.

"Quiet," he snapped, and she realised he'd clamped her mouth shut by force to silence her.

For a long while, he just held her tightly.

The heat coming off him was intense, but now that there was a pause, she could feel how hard, heavy, and fast his heart was beating as it thumped against her left shoulder blade. She still tried to wriggle to get free, but eventually settled when she knew there was no point.

She was trapped beneath him, and since she was forced to breathe only through her nose, she kept taking in his heady, mouth-watering aroma. Her lungs swelled in delight, only to quiver out her breaths.

*"I am **very** angry right now."* She tried her hardest to look up with his hand forcing her head a certain way. His skull was facing

her, his forehead only millimetres from brushing against the table, and she took in the crimson red of his glowing orbs. *"I don't wish to hurt you, but running from me entices me to hunt my prey. And Mayumi, **everything** is prey to me."*

Leaning on his elbow, his free hand came up so he could undo the button of his cloak. She heard the material shift as it slipped to the ground.

"Never run from me again, especially when I am enraged. I am not always in control of my hunger. If you had gone much further, you might not be alive right now."

When she attempted to turn her head side to side so she could free her jaw and speak, he clamped her even tighter. It felt like her teeth would grind together into dust if he pushed any harder. His hand spanned her entire neck and jaw to the point his fingertips reached behind her ears.

Her eyes narrowed into a glare.

The more he spoke, the calmer he seemed to be, but she knew that was just on the surface. He chuckled darkly at her expression, but his voice had finally reverted back to normal.

"You are insane, little hunter." Unable to gasp, the noise that came out of her sounded like a stifled mewl when his claws ran over the side of her hip, down the side of her arse cheek, and then down her thigh. "You have no idea what I have had to deal with over the past few days."

He didn't need to move his body at all to reach down to her boots and slip them off, even when she tried to evade him. One thud followed another. Then he slipped all her bags from her body – showing her he wouldn't be reasoned with in his decision to keep her here.

Then his hand slipped underneath her. He clawed off each button of her jacket, then he yanked it off her and tossed it to the ground. He undid her belt, since it was easy to do just by pulling the tongue to the side, and her multiple weapons clattered against the floor.

"However," he growled. "Now that I have tasted you, made you come upon my tongue, have heard your sweet little moans..." Her pussy clenched not only at the memory but also at him reciting it. "If you ever have the essence of another male on you,

I will leave, and I *won't* come back."

His orbs morphed into a bright green again, and she now knew with absolute certainty that they signalled either his jealousy or envy.

Mayumi stilled completely, her eyes widening. All her anger deflated out of her, and she tried to shake her head. She was given no room to do so.

Faunus forcibly tilted her head to the side so he could bury the end of his snout into her hair. He gave a large exhale as he parted his jaws around her ear, making the strands of her hairline stand on end in reaction to the wrapping of heat. He was smelling her as though he'd waited an eternity to do so again.

"I will take that male's scent into my memory, and instead of protecting you, I will hunt for him... I will hunt for him, I will find him, and I will destroy him." The chuckle he let out this time was even darker than before, filled with menace. "Do you think the walls of towns can keep my kind at bay? We choose *not* to attack because we know we will massacre everyone inside them."

Faunus loosened his hand just enough so that she would be able to speak.

"Do you understand?"

"Yes."

Before she could add anything more, he clamped her jaw shut again.

"If you no longer want my touch," he continued, as he slipped the sharp points of his claws underneath her shirt just above her arse. Her eyelids fluttered against her will when she felt them and his callused palms and fingertips gliding over the small of her back. "Then I will no longer touch you, but I will remain here and protect you, as I have promised."

Mayumi couldn't help bowing her torso into the table, a heavy exhale leaving through her nose when he cut those sharp claws back down her spine.

Then they dug into the waistline of her leather trousers, the backs of his smooth claws cool against her flesh.

"Don't think for a moment that I can't smell your growing arousal, Mayumi. I was hoping to come back here and have the freedom to touch you," he stated as he slipped his tongue over his fangs. "So, choose your answer wisely because I will not ask again. May I?"

The tension around her jaw loosened again.

This domineering side of Faunus was turning her gut inside out, making it flutter and quiver. Her nipples were already hard and aching as they pressed firmly against the dining table she lay upon.

Her eyes flickered between both his glowing green orbs. His face was upside down as he leaned his forehead against the table's surface.

She already knew her answer, but she was stunned that she was in this position, being caged by his entire massive body while being asked this. Never in her life had she ever expected to be overpowered or at another's mercy in this kind of way.

She freaking *adored* it.

"Yes," she whispered.

Her eyes clenched at the burning sensation across her skin as he tore her trousers from her in one swift motion. He'd been holding the waistline in preparation of her answer, and by the cool breeze on her backside, her underwear too.

Then his claws slid up her back, right against her flesh, before he turned his hand over and cut the back of her shirt. It fluttered apart to leave her back bare.

The cold air battled with the heat swirling off him, and she didn't know which one caused her to shiver.

Mayumi was rewarded by him gliding his callused palm across her hips. He slid it down the side of her arse, over her thigh, almost to her knee. She let out a breathy gasp at the rough, tickling sensation.

At the sound she let out, he glided the tips of his claws over the sensitive flesh on the backs of her thighs. This time she let out a quiet mewl, and her back arched as she was given freedom to do so when he lifted his hips off her.

Faunus lowered himself so he could freely lick at the side of her neck from behind, causing a tremor and more soft noises to leave her. A wave of goosebumps rose across one side of her body. His tongue was rough like any normal tongue, but large, long, flat, and wet.

He was still grasping her jaw, but loosely now. It was a possessive hold rather than a controlling one.

"You should have told me you were leaving," she said when his other hand left her, giving her a few moments to collect her thoughts.

"How was I supposed to know that?" he rumbled, his hand coming up to glide over her arse. Against the table, her hands curled into fists when his thumb slid against the outside of her folds, going back and forth but never dipping inside the lips. "I do not plan to leave again. I have learned all I need to know from another of my kind, and I plan to remain here with you as I have promised."

His hand slipped away so he could squeeze it underneath her. The way his palm ran down her abdomen, making a direct path, had her insides spasming.

"What did you need to learn?"

After she asked her question, Mayumi licked at her lips when his fingers slipped through the hair covering her pubic mound and straight into her folds. She spread her thighs apart when he pressed against her clit. He played with it in a similar way to how he'd touched her with his tongue.

"You are very wet," he commented, his tone rumbling with satisfaction. The circular motion he made had her hips going in the opposite direction, hoping to aid him. He went the other way, and so did her hips. Then he moved away, going lower to dab at her entrance. "But you're dripping here."

"Faunus," she quietly moaned when he pressed inside her.

She didn't know how many fingers he pushed in, but it felt like at least the thickness of two of her own. She tried to press onto it, wanting him deeper despite feeling he was as deep as he could go. He swirled to make room, stirring her.

Her breath hitched when another finger speared her, stretching her pussy. "You are *very* tight, Mayumi."

Then he split his fingers, and a sucking sound came from her because of how slick she was. He relaxed his fingers and slowly thrust them, grazing an amazing spot inside that had warmth spreading throughout her entire body.

Any tension within her died at that moment. She started

bucking into his hand. He split his fingers again, only so he could make room to press an additional one in.

Mayumi winced, especially when it seemed he had trouble pushing it in. Her inner walls were stretching far wider than she'd ever had them before, and it burned.

"Not so many," she groaned, trying to get her body to forcibly relax rather than tighten. It was like he was trying to shove his whole hand inside her pussy!

"My cock will not fit inside you. You can barely take three of my fingers."

Only three?! She tried to look down, but with her body pressed against the table, she wasn't able to see.

Faunus pressed the tip of his snout against her ear, and she heard his deep huffs, felt them. It made the side of her whole face tingle. Then she gasped when he shoved that third all the way in.

"Wait!" she squeaked.

She was thankful he stopped thrusting them and sat them inside her. It stung. She felt too full.

Shit. I can only take three? And she knew if he moved, it would only start hurting more. Already her pussy was giving an uncomfortable throb.

The last time he'd fingered her, she'd been soft and relaxed from an orgasm. She wasn't ready to take this much yet.

"You asked for my cock last time, but how are you supposed to take me like this? *I* am not the problem here. You are the one who is small – even for a human."

"I just need to adjust," she pleaded, more to herself than him. "Maybe if we take our time, do this a few times..."

Her eyelids crinkled when realisation settled in. She could adjust all she wanted, but she'd seen his hand grip his cock and knew now that if she couldn't take this, she wouldn't be able to take it. He'd been huge, even in his own grasp.

But I really want it inside me.

She wanted Faunus' weird, tentacle-based cock. She wanted to feel him thrusting over her, taking her as she moulded to his body.

"It still wouldn't matter." Carefully, like he knew he needed to be slow, he removed his fingers from her. He unsheathed his claws when he glided them back up her pubic mound and over her abdomen. "The reason I left, Mayumi, is because I want to do this with you. I *ache* to be inside your tight, little cunt. I long for it more than you know, and I went to speak with my kind to know if there is a way."

His hand settled between her hips, his claws digging in but not cutting. Then his body moved, dipping forward. Her eyes widened when something hard, impossibly thick, and slimy pressed against the tingling entrance of her pussy. Just by the feel of it, she knew it wasn't going to go in, but she still felt him pushing, regardless.

She bit her lip, knowing it was his cock. She tried to spread her thighs further, greeting it, but her body was pushed forward rather than him breaching her.

Why would he be doing this if it wasn't possible?

"And?" she asked. Did he get his answer? "Is there a way?"

His cock slipped upwards. His hips pressed against her and helped to slide the underside through her folds and all the way through her slit to her backside. She lifted her hips to grind against it, feeling there was a deep groove in it.

"Yes, but I need your permission to do it to you. I don't know if it is reversible, but I can... change you to take me. With my magic, I can force your body to fit mine."

Magic? She didn't know he could do magic. *Whatever.* That was the last thing on her mind and something she could ask about later.

"Yes. Okay, do it." He gave her a pleased little growl, one that had her biting the inside of her bottom lip in reaction. He pulled away and pressed the tip against her entrance again, and she tried to back onto it. She even undulated against it, trying to get it in herself. It was hot and hard, and even the strange wetness on it had her insides begging for it. "Give it to me."

He pushed his cock forward just as his breaths halted. Her own were cut short at the stab of his claws slicing through the skin between her hips. He'd stabbed her!

Mayumi's cheeks winced at the pain before cool magic swirled where his hand was. His cock began to slide inside.

Then her body began doing things that were *wrong,* yet it felt so good her tongue fell forward as her lips parted.

Her hips went wider, changing to accommodate him rather than shattering. Her inner walls not only pulled taut but stretched – yet not in an uncomfortable way. It was utterly painless, but she could feel herself growing so unbelievably full she knew she'd never experienced anything like it.

The thick head popped inside, and the rest of his glide seemed easier. But what greeted her sensitive entrance were his little spikes that tickled as each one went in, giving her this wonderous texture.

"Oh my fucking *God*," she moaned, her body shivering and shuddering in bliss – even more so the deeper he went. She felt everything pushing away to let him go further, and further, and further.

"Good girl," he rumbled with a *purr,* an actual purr that vibrated against her back. He licked at the back of her neck all the way to her ear before swirling his long tongue against it. "You're taking my cock so well for me."

She could feel her abdomen pressing deeper against the table by being pushed down from the *inside.* His cock was gouging its way in. It rubbed her most tender place, each one of his spikes grazing it and nearly making her go cross-eyed.

"I'm going to come," she rasped, her eyes rolling back little by little as she blinked wildly. "I'm going to–"

Faunus pulled back before he was even seated all the way so he could thrust forward quickly and go just that little bit deeper. It aided her, this strange way of being stretched, pushing Mayumi suddenly and violently into bliss.

She clamped him, squeezed him – screaming as she came around his cock. So he did it again. He pulled back so he could dig deeper. And then again and again, heightening her orgasm until she was squirming beneath him, trying to undulate and buck.

Then he was seated as far as *he* could go, his hips flush against her backside. She ground her hips frantically against him, even when his tentacles had wrapped around her arse and between her thighs to hold her tightly.

"Nhnn," she groaned, her cheek sliding against the table's surface.

"You came just from me filling you." He *chuckled* deeply, teasing her for it.

She was too languid to bite at him once she started to settle, barely believing that was all she'd needed. She was also relaxed when he suddenly yanked her from the table. Her torn shirt slipped from her and down her arms, discarded.

Something thin and long wrapped around her knee. A brief peek down told her it was his tail. One of his hands wrapped around the thigh of her other leg. They kept her supported with her legs spread apart as he lifted her while his other hand remained around her throat, his forearm keeping her torso to his.

He'd picked her up to turn them, then he walked only a few steps until he knelt down against the ground with his knees parted.

"Is this what you wanted, Mayumi?" he asked, and she watched his tongue come out to lick across his snout through her wall-mounted, full-length mirror in front of them. "A Duskwalker's cock deep inside your snug, hungry little cunt?"

Mayumi's breath hitched when she realised she could see... everything. His tentacles were spread wide, but they didn't hide anything from her. The lips of her folds were parted to accommodate him, pink and swollen and hugging around the base of his purple shaft. She was stuffed to the brim with him.

Her thighs were split wide, with the backs of her feet resting against his furry thighs, revealing that he was just as naked as she was. Between the small valley of her breasts was his fur-covered arm that had little lizard-like spikes running down it.

And Mayumi saw she was... tiny against him. The top of her head sat just below his collarbones, with the way her body was bowed to greet his. He was massive around her. His muscled shoulders and biceps flared him out way past her own, and his thighs were just as dense.

He lowered his skulled, feline face next to hers so he could lick across her cheek from behind. Although his glowing, ethereal orbs had been a bright green before, they were now purple, showing his desire.

Because she hadn't answered him, he slowly withdrew. It was purposeful. It had to be with how far he came back, showing her every inch he'd given her until the flared rim of his cockhead came out of her. The wider thickness of it spread her lips even further.

Her already pink face, heated with arousal, deepened in colour. *Watching* him do that had her growing slicker, despite his cock's natural wetness making her overlubricated. She expected him to come back in just as slowly.

Instead, he shoved in fast and hard, while using all three of his limbs to yank her down mercilessly. "Well?"

"Yes!" she screamed, not only to answer him but to spur him on. "I wanted your cock inside me so badly."

His purr started back up, and Mayumi gave herself over to this, to him, watching as he stayed deep, while rocking his hips with subtle thrusts.

"More. Fuck me. Give it to me. Please, just use my pussy. I don't care how."

"Hold my horn," he commanded.

Mayumi raised both of her hands, but he smacked the left one away with the end of his snout, so she didn't grab the injured side of his face. Her right secured the curve of his curling ram horn, and she grabbed at the long fur on his shoulder and chest with her left.

She leaned her head against him when he started thrusting fast, coming in and out of her so quickly she almost lost sight of him. His hand came away from supporting her throat, but her grasping hands kept her to him as he caressed both her breasts with his rough palm.

His thumb would play with one stiffened nipple, flicking it up and down before going to the other. Then he would pet both breasts with every part of his palm, his claws gliding over her to give a sharp but pleasurable sensation.

"Moan the name you gave me, Mayumi. Tell me who is inside you."

Her head lolled as her eyes grew unfocused... until they caught the side of something odd. She could see where he'd cut her, the small drips of blood, but her wounds were gone like he'd instantly healed her. That wasn't what grabbed her attention.

No, it was the moving *bulge* she could see in her abdomen. From the inside, his cock was nudging her flesh forward, and she knew exactly where the head was as it slid back and forth – as well as a few inches down his girth. She was *watching* him move past her navel while at the same time feeling him bumping there.

She was too small for him even though he'd changed her, and her body was doing the best it could to accommodate his impossible size.

"Faun," she moaned, feeling herself spiralling as she took it all in through the mirror. *"Faun."*

"That isn't my name." He supported her head by cupping under her jaw again when he must have realised it was falling weakly forward. "Or is that a new name for me?" He chuckled deeply. "One you'll give me when I'm inside you, fucking you?"

He pounded harder, faster, his hand on her thigh moving her up and down along with his thrusts. He wasn't being gentle. It was hard, and the heat all around her and inside her had her losing her mind.

His lemongrass and lime scent caused her eyelids to flutter. It completely dissolved her of strength, making her mind go blank.

Her head fell to the side in his palm. She didn't know when she started coming around his cock, but her body went completely lax while her pussy tensed and spasmed, her thighs dancing in twitches alongside it. Her cry was so strong it was silent, her lungs seizing with the overwhelming power of her orgasm.

She was getting what she needed, what she'd *always* wanted. To have something inhuman and strong and feral slamming into her. She'd never been so turned on, and it burned even hotter when she watched her milky come dripping down his embedded sacs.

A few drops fell to the ground.

"That's it, keep watching me fuck you. That's a good little human," he groaned as he turned his head up to the ceiling. "Come around me, for me." He gave a heavy shudder, one that had her jiggling in his embrace. "Fuck, that feels so damn good, smells so damn good." His jaws parted as he panted with his tongue poking past his fangs on each exhale. "I can almost taste it."

The woman staring back at her from the mirror appeared so

lost that she barely registered it as herself. She was a needy person, one with a dazed, misty-eyed expression.

Mayumi couldn't stop watching her... and him. It was so damn erotic, and she knew she'd never forget this moment. It would forever be lewdly ingrained in her brain.

"Faun," she hopelessly moaned, wishing she could say his name fully. She was no longer able to utter anything but a single syllable.

His grip on her thighs tightened when he lowered his head. He moved his hand from her jaw, slowly letting her chin fall, as he cupped her pussy and his cock as it moved in and out of her.

"I'm going to come inside you." His words started as a growl, but they ended on a groan. His cock swelled inside her, making her feel even fuller. "I'm going to fill this pussy with my seed, claim it with my scent." Her brows furrowed, showing her only resistance to this. Seeming to sense this, he added, "Don't worry, I can't get you pregnant. But you will have my essence linger inside you, Mayumi. I want your body to swallow as much of it as it can and hold it for me."

With her worries eased, Mayumi's lips curled just slightly. Panting at his reflection, she whispered, "Yes. Do it."

She wanted to feel it, needed to.

His cock thickened again, and his thrusts became more chaotic. Mayumi was bouncing on his shaft, his whole body in motion to ensure he selfishly chased his own euphoria. She could feel his impending release by how much he pulsated inside her, almost like a squirming flutter.

There was excitement in his motions, made even more prominent by his loud, unhidden groans. His arm came up to hold her across the torso and clamp her shoulder.

"I've waited so long for this," he snarled against the side of her face.

Me too, she thought.

"To fuck you, fill you. To just... be inside you." Then he stilled, his body tensing around her as his claws dug in. He curled forward slightly just as she watched his cock thicken and his embedded sacs lift inside and permanently stay that way against the very base of him. He was shaking, holding onto her for dear life, as he rasped, "*Fuck,* Mayumi."

Mayumi gasped just as he let out a whiny groan.

"W-what is happening?" she cried when she felt something... sharp and stinging inside. She tried to lift her hips, but he held her down.

"Don't move!" he shouted on a choke right before he let out a bellowing roar while lifting his snout towards the ceiling. His tentacles tightened around her hips to the point she thought they might bruise her.

Heat, so much heat, began to splash inside her channel that she clenched from it. His release was fast, quick spurts that filled her so swiftly she barely had time to register it.

Her lips fell open further when she watched his seed begin to burst from her, squirting down the base of him and against the ground.

It was so intense that she spasmed around him. Her cry mixed in with his. Fuck, she'd never felt anything like it. It was *trying* to throw her over the edge. There was so much of it, so wet and hot. And somehow that sharp sting from multiple areas was making her even more sensitive to it.

She was so close, right on rapture's perilous edge. She tried to bounce, regardless of what he said. She kept squeezing him, which only seemed to make him quake even further. His claws dug deeper, just as her toes curled.

She didn't come, but it was still phenomenal.

When he was done, his snout fell forward to plop on top of her head with his fangs parted. They were both panting at their reflections. Her whole body shook as her chest heaved, and she saw her stomach sink around that bulge when she exhaled, making it more noticeable until she breathed in again to catch her breaths.

He pushed just slightly deeper to dislodge whatever he'd done inside her.

"What was that, Faun?" she asked through quick huffs.

"It always happens when I come," he answered with a groan, an aftershock twitching him as he petted the top of her head with his jaw. "I don't know what they are called. Spikes? Barbs? But they harden and sharpen. I didn't want you to move because they've hurt my hands before. I knew I'd tear you."

Mayumi's head shook side to side slightly in disbelief. *Barbs? What the hell?* She couldn't believe the spikes on his cock became barbs!

He'd been locked inside her when he came.

She wasn't upset about it. Not at all. Actually, she kind of liked that he had this strange function, it just... added to the oddity of him.

Her thoughts were silenced when he lifted her while pulling back. She mewled in reaction, a little sore and tender from his thrusting.

His cock bent forward when he fell from her, no longer a hard, upward-jutting rod, as his tentacles became floppy. White semen gushed from her straight onto it before it joined the puddle that had collected between his knees against the floor.

Faunus dipped his head beside hers and twisted it while reaching down. He used his claws and the tips of his fingers to pull the lips of her pussy to one side so he could see what he'd done inside her, see how he'd changed her. He had a little peek inside to see it was stretched and filled with his seed. Her entrance was no longer tight.

His orbs gave a flash of yellow in joy before he raised his head to stare at her through the reflection. His orbs shifted to a dark green, and she would have questioned what they meant if it weren't for his next words.

"Mine," he possessively growled at her.

He was telling her he'd claimed it, that it was his.

She would have denied it if it wasn't true. No human was going to fit there again, so she hoped he planned to stick around because she was going to need him.

His cock jerked in reaction, like it was going to re-harden, when she clenched and a little more seed slipped from her. He grabbed her face, turning it and her body towards his face.

"Tell me it's mine, Mayumi," he snarled.

Being forced to look closely at his feline skull, Mayumi was swallowed up by the dark green of his pretty glowing orbs.

"Yours," she stated, right before she leaned forward and gave the tip of his snout a kiss. His cock jerked again and began lifting into an erection.

Mayumi knew she could live without him if she really wanted to. She'd never really been fond of having sex with humans, and she was sure she could find *something* to compare to his girth and length.

She'd even craft it if she needed to.

But she kind of liked the idea of having this big Duskwalker around for now. She didn't need his protection, but it was nice to have it. She didn't need his help with her chores, but the help would be appreciated.

She didn't need sex from him, but if it was as good as this had been, she didn't know if she'd tire of it.

Before Mayumi could say anything more, a surprised gasp left her when she was pushed onto her knees with her chest against the ground. It was snuffed out by a sharp moan when his semi-hard cock was shoved deep inside her again.

Faunus leaned around her on his forearms and pushed his knees farther back so he could thrust down and into her. Already he was moving fast, drowning her mind so swiftly that it caused it to go numb while the rest of her senses were heightened.

She'd been primed for an orgasm, and already she was reaching for it with soft moans.

"Did you know you cry when you come?" He threaded his fingers into the back of her hair, fisted it, and sharply tugged until she was forced to look at her own face in the mirror. "If you didn't, I am going to make sure you see it for yourself."

I do? She'd never cried before during sex, maybe because it'd never been that good before. Yet, looking at her own dishevelled face, she could see drying tracks down her cheeks.

"It's actually quite beautiful," he panted.

The sound of his hips slapping against hers grew louder as he moved inside her. Mayumi let out a broken cry the moment she finally reached her impending orgasm. It tore through her quickly at the speed he was able to achieve like this. Her own features became murky through bubbling tears.

Despite her unclear vision, there was one thing she could still see, and she gave a heated smile at the mirror.

Behind her, on all fours thrusting into her like a beast, was a

Duskwalker. It was hard to mistake his purple orbs against his white skull in the dim light. Occasionally, they flickered a dark green before switching back.

"I'm going to make you watch me take you over and over again until you're nothing but a numb, broken thing." He slammed in, hitting her harder than he had before. Mayumi cried out, her nails digging into the ground in desperation to hold on as her body uncontrollably bounced from his thrusts. "Because I'm still *angry*. I'm going to make you understand that no human from that pathetic town nearby will satisfy you anymore."

He leaned back while gripping both her calves and lifted them into the air and pulled, spreading her thighs around his waist. Mayumi slid against her front as her back arched deeply. The position forced his cock to the front of her channel as he drove into her, and she reached down to press her hand near her navel so she could feel that bulge moving.

Mayumi couldn't count how many times she came like that, completely powerless as she drooled against the ground. She moaned wildly the entire time, her insides singing with pleasure as her pussy was used by a monster like she was nothing but a ripe whore for the taking.

Just that twisted, unhinged thought had her screaming for him. *Oh God, yes! More. Don't stop, you big, angry, horny Duskwalker. Fuck my pussy until it's raw.*

She wanted to be taken, to be used and abused until she could no longer walk, until her legs ached from being spread all night, until her cunt was dripping and overflooded. Until she was a complete and utter mess of a woman.

Break me. Ruin me. Please, don't stop.

She wanted to feel claws rather than nails, fur rather than skin. She wanted his growls rather than weak human groans.

When he filled her again, Faunus pulled her legs back behind him as he snarled, *nearly* meshing their hips together as his tentacles snapped tight against her skin.

His seed overflowed and dripped down her stomach and her chest until it pooled around her throat like a pearly collar.

Her eyelids shuddered as her face slipped across her own puddle of drool on the ground when she arched into it, into the feeling of his thick, feral seed filling her again.

She could feel every thump of his cock before it shot liquid heat, combined with the little flutters of his heavy heartbeat deep inside.

It feels so good. I feel like I'm going to explode.

TWENTY

The heady smell of lemongrass infiltrated Mayumi's senses. It was hard to wake, her body so lax and yet so unbelievably sore that the idea of moving away from the sublime heat surrounding her was unbearable.

Mayumi was sheltered by a hard, dense body.

Faunus cuddled her with his arms wrapped loosely around her. One arm acted as her pillow, while the other was crossed over her to curl underneath her side. Laying on their sides, they weren't quite facing each other since he was so big.

Her face was buried against his chest, and she nuzzled the soft fur there before sighing in contentment.

I could get used to this.

She knew they'd started having sex in the middle of the day, but they'd only had a few short breaks so she could eat something, drink some water, or nap before Faunus was ruthlessly rutting inside her again. As he'd promised, he'd taken her repeatedly, even late into the night.

This is how women get UTIs, she thought with a frown, yet there was no uncomfortable feeling. Perhaps his lubricant was helpful in preventing it. Or maybe she was just lucky.

Still, Mayumi was tender... *everywhere.*

Not only was her pussy swollen and sore, but her thighs *ached* from being around his much larger waist and being put into different positions. Her chest was partially chafed from rubbing against the ground and his body when he finally turned her over.

She didn't even want to start thinking about her poor knees

and elbows.

Gingerly sitting up, Mayumi rubbed the side of her face while looking for the window, disorientated from waking up upside down to how she usually did in the house. She preferred to sleep with her feet facing away from the door.

Once she saw it was early morning, she turned her gaze down to Faunus, still asleep. His orbs were black, signalling they were 'closed' – or whatever he saw when they weren't glowing.

She rubbed her eyes at the light pounding behind them. *I have a headache.* Who knew that being fucked repeatedly into oblivion would be bad for one's health?

She scoffed at herself. *Worth it.*

What she did know was that she needed water.

The moment she lifted his arm to get up, his orbs morphed to their usual yellow. She squeaked when he tightened around her and pulled her back down until she was lying with her face buried in the fur of his chest once more.

"Sleep more," he demanded with an adorably deep, groggy voice, rubbing the underside of his snout against the top of her head. Then he ground his closed seam against her closed thighs. "Unless you want more."

"You're a menace!" she tried to shout. Her voice came out cracked and so hoarse it was almost painful. She'd lost it halfway through the night from crying out.

"You are the one who started this," he rebuffed. "You cannot blame me when I only intended to come here to protect you. You are the one who *begged*."

Every word from him grew softer, as though he was moments from falling back asleep. He parted his jaws to let out a large yawn before smacking his tongue inside his maw.

"I didn't beg," she grumbled.

Did she beg? She couldn't quite remember. Perhaps asked nicely would be a better way to describe it.

She considered going back to sleep – his embrace was peaceful – but now that she'd opened her eyes and had thought about getting up, sleep would elude her.

Faunus nuzzled his snout into her hair until he'd truly covered his face in the nest of knots.

"I like the way you smell." He gave deep huffs, like he was breathing her in, as his large torso expanded and then decompressed. "Like pumpkin and sleep."

Her lips pursed. "What does sleep even smell like?"

"It smells warm and comforting and makes me drowsy."

That still didn't make sense, but she smiled regardless. She'd never had anyone describe her like that, and the tender, swirling emotion in her chest only deepened when she noticed him purring like a satisfied kitten.

The sound of it always turned her stomach into knots.

"It's time to get up. I need to go to the toilet, and I'm hungry and thirsty." She also noticed something else. His fur wasn't soft along his groin and lower torso, and Mayumi's skin felt cracked and... uncomfortable between her thighs, stomach, and even her chest. "*We* also need a bath."

There was dried seed everywhere. She didn't know Duskwalkers came like a damn waterfall. She tried to ignore the way her thighs easily slipped together with the warm, still moist slick there.

His head dipped as he lifted her higher. Mayumi squirmed slightly when his tongue slipped over the edge of her jaw to the corner before running up just in front of her ear.

"I can give you a bath, my dirty tiny human," he said with an undertone of humour.

He licked at her neck with determined swipes, leaving saliva in his wake.

"I'm covered in your cum," Mayumi answered in a flat tone. "I didn't think you'd be interested in cleaning me of it."

He paused mid-lick against her jugular.

"I don't mind cleaning your pussy since I'd taste you and I mingled together." He removed his tongue from her. "But no, I do not wish to lick my seed by itself from your body."

Now that he'd pulled her higher, she was facing his skull while using his strong biceps as a pillow. They'd never grabbed her bedding, so the ground was hard against her hip.

Thankfully she'd managed to get the fireplace going at some point between their bouts of sex. It was currently dull and dying, but it was still producing a small amount of heat.

Faunus was warmer anyway, and part of the reason she didn't truly want to get up was that he was comfortable. She couldn't remember if she'd ever woken in someone's arms before – she usually always escaped through the front door or the window before any lazy morning cuddles could happen.

I'm glad he came back after all these years.

Staring at his yellow orbs that were already gazing at her, Mayumi reached up and tapped the pad of her index finger against the bone around his nose hole, giving his snout a small boop. His tongue came out to swipe where she'd booped him.

Her eyelids became heavy and half-cast when he caressed the tips of his claws up and down the middle of her spine. It was when his other hand came up to start brushing through her hair, his touch overly affectionate, that Mayumi's heart squeezed sharply. Although she never felt fear, she wasn't impervious to anxiety.

She quickly sat up to break contact between them.

I just want to have sex with him. Nothing more.

It wasn't a good idea to get attached to him and vice versa. Many people had thrown around the idea that Mayumi had commitment issues, but it was just so damn hard to like anyone when they could disappear the next day – forever.

Sure, Faunus had 'promised' he had no intention of leaving again, but she was human. She could die, or they could get tired of each other. Nothing was ever certain.

He'd already left once.

Despite her jarring movements, he only wrapped his arm around her waist and curled around her to continue their cuddle while she was seated upright. He was holding her as though she was a teddy bear.

"Sleep more," he demanded. "As soon as you get up, I know you are going to force me to work. What terrible things do you want me to do today? Remove the roof of your home so you may lay down a new one? Pull up a tree and rebury it on the other side of your yard?"

The fact his desire to hold her seemed more like a prevention of chores rather than to be romantically intimate eased her. Mayumi gave a snort of laughter.

"Just how long have you been studying humans, Faunus?" she asked, raising a brow at him.

His head lifted suddenly. "What do you mean?"

"Well, considering you seem rather versatile in dirty talk and playful sarcasm, it seems you've picked up on a lot."

An irritated, rolling huff came from him as he laid his head back down. "You humans are so annoyingly loud. Sometimes I can hear you long before I see you, and you often play and tease each other. Humans are vocal in everything they do. In eating, in sex, in life, and even in death."

That still didn't answer my question.

With a sigh, Mayumi let it go.

She managed to wrangle her way out of his embrace and crawled on her hands and knees over to the fireplace. She stabbed it with the poker a few times, feeling the cold prickle of goosebumps assaulting her entire body. Her nipples pulled taut in a stingy way, and she quickly threw a fresh log into the embers so it could warm the house.

When she turned back around, Faunus was lying on his side with one knee bent. He'd also bent the arm under him and had placed the side of his head in his palm. His tail swished behind him, but it was his purple orbs that caused her to halt.

They swiftly turned back to yellow, but his position made him look terribly arrogant.

It didn't take her much to realise he'd been staring at her bare arse and pussy from behind!

Mayumi wasted no time. Despite being dirty, she found warm clothing she didn't mind washing again later. There was a noticeable limp in the way she walked – everything from her abdomen down was aching and tight.

I've never been fucked to the point I couldn't walk properly. Currently, she was hobbling around.

A grin spread her lips wide, and she wore it proudly even as she gave little facial twitches of pain.

Faunus remained where he was, watching her the entire time with his tail tapping against the ground. She thought he'd stay there, but he quickly followed her the moment she headed outside.

"Where are you going?" he asked as he ducked through the doorway.

"To the stream."

She battled her way through the snow to the back of the house, holding two logs in her hands and some fire-starting kindling.

Underneath a large stone basin was a heating stove. She opened its metal door and threw everything she had in her arms into it before rearranging it. Then she used multiple matches to get it to light.

Once that was done, she went to the shed and grabbed a pickaxe and a square-mouthed shovel.

Since she was shovelling snow away from a certain spot, Faunus willingly began to help. He used his large hand to dig and scoop it away. With them working together, it quickly revealed a sheet covering.

Mayumi removed it to reveal the top of a stone basin that had been built there. It was watertight since it was sealed with a special clay, but it was mostly made up of the natural large rock wall it had on one side and multiple boulders everywhere else.

She pushed in a little bit of snow, knowing the heating stove beneath it would begin to melt and warm it. Then Mayumi led them to the small stream nearby.

It took her a little while to find the end of the terra cotta pipe her family had buried here long ago. Once she did, she cleared all the snow and dirt around it to dig it out. Mayumi undid the latches that covered the end that kept things like dirt, sticks, leaves, or snow from getting inside and clogging it. It also prevented animals from using it as a burrow.

Since the surface of the stream was frozen, she needed to use her pickaxe to get to the cold but moving water beneath. She dug at the earth so that it would drain into the terra cotta pipe and down the hill. Once she removed the covering at the bottom on the other end, it would drain into the stone basin.

It was a lot of work just to have a bath, which was why Mayumi rarely did this, but a basic wipe down with melted snow water and a cloth just wasn't going to cut it today. Not with Faunus' great big furry ass.

He was walking around without a shred of clothing on him,

and even now she could see the way he was grossly covered in dried seed. It even made his fur clump together, and she was not touching him again until it was no longer doing that.

Mayumi made a *blergh* face when she cringed before marching down the hill. The moment she undid the bottom latch, fresh water slowly poured into the basin.

"While that's filling up and heating," she started while turning to Faunus, "I'm going to have breakfast and some tea."

She noticed his orbs were a darker hue of yellow than usual. He cocked his head at the spring bath before cocking it back to her.

"If you wanted to fill this, you could have just told me. I'm able to use magic to fill things such as baths. It would have been warm to begin with."

Mayumi turned her head to watch the water pouring in. "I guess it's too late now. Maybe next time, since I've already completed the whole process."

It was disappointing she didn't know that earlier, but there was nothing she could do about it now.

Although compelled to follow Mayumi wherever she went, Faunus stayed where he was as she went inside. He stared at the water flowing in, almost hypnotised by it, until it reached a certain height.

After a long while, she came back out to close this end of the strange pipe device.

Even with the distance between him and it, he could see that it was large and deep. He stepped back from it with his tail curling in apprehension.

He began to walk the yard, scouting to make sure he couldn't sense any Demons or coming humans nearby. If she intended to be outside for a long period of time, he wanted to make sure it was safe.

He didn't know how long he was gone, refusing to crowd her or be near the water, but she eventually called out to him.

She was at the back of the house, holding two pieces of long cloth in her hands. He tilted his head at her as he approached.

"Okay, it's ready."

Faunus lifted his head to the small pool of steaming warm water and then brought his gaze back to her. He didn't know why she felt the need to inform him.

He'd seen humans prefer to bathe in private.

He just planned not to tell her he would watch happily from afar.

"Enjoy your bath. I have already scouted the area and know it is safe for you to do so."

Her cute little brows drew together as her lips pursed. His sight grew fixed on them. He'd briefly tasted them a few times yesterday, but he'd been so distracted by the rest of her body that he hadn't quite fulfilled his desire to lap at them.

Because she was so small compared to him, it was hard to reach her face when he was inside her. He'd need to arch his body, which made it difficult to move his hips. He'd taken to licking her when their bodies were separated.

But what he really wanted was to... kiss her.

He'd seen humans do this. They messily locked their mouths together and made these soft little noises that caused his ear holes to tingle.

He could never do this with her, and he wondered if she would grow to dislike him when she realised they couldn't be intimate in this way. Actually, there was much about him that was different and many things they could never do together.

"*We* are going to bathe," Mayumi said with a head shake. "I called you over here to get in with me."

White flashed in his orbs as he took a wary step back, covering his chest with his hand. "Me? No. Just you."

Her eyes squinted into a narrow glare.

"Get in the bath, Faunus." Mayumi pointed at it. "You're dirtier than I am."

His sight turned to the steaming, somewhat deep water before it permanently morphed to white. He shook his head with his heart accelerating, forcing blood to his muscles to make them swell.

"I am fine. I will not fit."

He would fit. He knew he would fit, perhaps even with plenty of room. He just didn't want to.

"You're joking." Mayumi gave a laugh, deep and mocking. "Are you afraid of water?!"

"No," he answered casually, turning his head away dismissively. "I'm not afraid of water."

Was he? No. Maybe a little, but not because of the water itself. He mistrusted it because he knew what it could do, how *suffocating* it could be.

"You are!" The fact her laughter was growing caused his orbs to redden in anger. "I didn't think because you had a feline skull that you would be scared of water like cats are!"

The flare of embarrassment and disbelief in her words caused his body to ruffle. His fur puffed in agitation.

He couldn't believe she'd said something so offensive to him. He refused to be compared to that of a mindless animal. He could communicate and understand – rather than just meowing uselessly or hissing like a fool.

He'd eaten many of them. There was a reason much of him was similar to that of a cat, both domestic and mountain cougars.

"I am not like a cat!" he roared, parting his fangs in warning. Mayumi flinched at the loudness of his roar and the fact he was doing it at her. He immediately winced at her shocked expression, probably because he'd done it so suddenly. "Fine! If it is so important, I will get in the bath just to show you I am unafraid."

He stomped towards the small pool and climbed up the opposite side of it where he could see a human would usually enter. There was a wall here where her heating stove was.

His anger instantly deflated when he placed his hands on the edge to jump up and in. Facing the water, he paused. The flare in his chest was snuffed into an anxiety-filled rhythm of disquiet. He didn't want to get in. He didn't want to put his body in the water.

It rippled when a leaf gently fell into it, much like it would when bubbles broke against the surface from below.

Once more, his tail tip curled in apprehension.

"Faunus?"

Her quiet voice broke him out of the trance that had begun to pull him under, and he turned his head to her. She was no longer laughing, but rather had a thoughtful frown on her expression.

Get in the water, he told himself. *Don't let her know you are... She won't think you can protect her if you cannot do something as simple as sit in this.*

Faunus didn't want Mayumi to think he was weak in any sense. *It's not even that deep,* he reassured himself.

Or was it lying? Was it actually endless?

He jumped up and placed his left leg in. He had to calm his body through the repulsive shudder it gave before he threw the other in. He slipped inside and instantly a horrible shiver coursed down his spine, which caused his fur to stand on end.

The only solace was that the water was warm, which helped to ease some of the tension in his muscles.

There were multiple places in which one could sit on a rock, and he chose the one he thought would be best for himself, as it wouldn't submerge him. He held on tightly to the edges to ensure he didn't somehow slip in any deeper than the bottom of his sternum.

His body was dense, wanting to sink rather than float.

He didn't even know Mayumi had stripped until she was gliding herself inside the water. It came up to well past her breasts to sit around the top of her chest.

Seeing her take a seat in front of him gave him something other than the water to focus on, but it was hard to ignore it wrapped around him. It felt crushing, like it was squeezing his torso rather than just gently lapping at his flesh.

He wished his orbs would stop being white. No matter how much he tried to control his emotions, nothing aided him. He wanted out. He couldn't believe he'd gotten in to begin with. His claws gouged at the rock on the outside of the bath.

The only reason he knew he was shaking was because Mayumi came over and settled him by cupping his snout.

"There we go. Now we can get all nice and clean," she cooed.

He didn't know if she was aware of his unease, but she made no comment about it. She helped to centre him when she turned and sat on one of his thighs while still holding his snout, directing his face to keep his gaze on hers.

He thought he may have sensed a hint of concern in her features with the way her brows twitched. After a small while, his distress lessened.

She is sitting on me. He placed his arms around her so he could hold her.

He didn't like it when she began cupping water in her hands and pouring it down the front of his body, but he chose to ignore it. Faunus didn't take his sight off her, and he tried to feel nothing else but her body on his.

There was no weight since the water kept her buoyant, so he let the side of his torso and his arms take in the touch of her instead.

Her kindness and comfort were what he needed, and his heart flapped lightly in his chest. *She is trying to calm me.* He hated that he needed it, that he'd been so obvious, but he was still thankful for it.

Faunus lifted his hand, which dripped heavily with water, and cupped the side of her face.

"Why are you doing this with me?" he asked, feeling a strange coil of emotion within.

Even though she'd been unobtainable until now, Faunus had... undeniably cared for Mayumi. That was deepening, whether he wanted it to or not.

"Having a bath?" Her brows drew together. "Isn't it obvious? Or do you mean why am I sitting on your lap? If you do, I am just because I can."

Faunus shook his head. "Why are you allowing me to touch you, Mayumi? I am a Duskwalker. I never expected you to feel any kind of desire or affection towards me."

"Oh." Her features fell before she looked away from him to stare out into the forest that backed the house. Then she gave a sharp, short giggle. "Others would think it's weird, but sometimes some people just want to fuck the monsters under the bed."

Faunus gave a quizzical head tilt with his orbs growing a dark yellow, finally fading away from white. "But... I do not fit under your bed."

"Pfft! I didn't mean literally! It's a saying, Faunus. It means that some people are just, uh, kind of attracted to things that aren't normal or human. I hate Demons, but I've found some attractive. Sometimes spooky things turn me on, like monsters and the idea of the boogeyman." She gave him a large grin, one that was so prominent it made the underside of her eyes puffy. "And you're the biggest, baddest, and scariest of them all. From the moment I saw you in the clearing that night, I wanted to jump your bones."

The way his heart turned cold suddenly made him lose the hot sensation of the bathwater around him. He darkened his orbs to black when he knew they were going to turn blue, hiding from her any sadness or hurt he felt from her words.

When he took a steady breath, he opened his sight and was relieved they were their usual yellow.

Then he forced a chuckle from himself and glided his claws up the side of her body.

"Scariest? I have not scented a single thread of fear from you." She squealed when he tickled her. "But it pleases me to know you find me attractive, despite me being a *monster,* as you so called me."

"Is that a sour tone I hear?" she asked with her cheeks puffing.

"I do believe I intended it to be playful."

He knew what he was and what humans regularly called anything outside of humankind. To them, and obviously to her, he was a monster. A nightmare. Something wrong that didn't belong in this world.

Mayumi reached up and cupped the sides of his bony jaw in her small wet palms.

"I find you and that Duskwalker face of yours rather sexy. I called you Faunus because it means forest God, and you can be my bone-daddy forest God any day."

The way her lips curled was heated, her dark eyes glinting with wickedness. The light shone in them, making them appear like pools of rich brown.

"So, when you screamed 'oh my God' yesterday, you were actually just calling out to me." It wasn't a question, but a statement.

It gave him what he wanted, another musical, non-feminine laugh.

"Sure. Whatever you want to tell yourself." Then she stroked his face in a soothing yet appreciative way, being careful not to touch the crack in it. "But I know for certain I wouldn't have entertained touching anyone else but you."

He tilted his head in her hands. "What do you mean?"

From what he'd gathered, she would have done this with another. The fact that a Demon might have been on her menu was a little alarming, but he'd thought that if another of his kind had stumbled upon her, she may have accepted them into her ripe and plush body.

"You saved my life, Faunus. I wouldn't be alive if it wasn't for you. I may not have remembered you well, but I have never forgotten you and what you did for me."

She gave a little sigh and then moved away from him, even though he was desperate to keep her near to save him from his anxieties. He didn't know why she wanted to break contact with him then, especially when she was saying something that made him feel... wanted.

"From the moment you said you were here because you wanted to protect me... I trusted you. That's why I feel comfortable enough to have sex with you."

She sat on the opposite side of the bath again, this time facing her head away into the forest.

She trusts me. I am special to her.

Joy sparked inside him. That was enough. The fact she trusted him and desired him, he would take those things from her and hold them dearly.

"I am thankful for this outcome rather than you trying to kill me," he tried to tease, since she appeared thoughtful. "I will keep your secret safe from the rest of your Demonslayers the next time I go to that big, fortified mountain castle of theirs."

He thought the idea of him waltzing his way into a Demonslayer stronghold would make her laugh. Instead, he watched her right hand curl into a tight fist as her lips drew inwards.

TWENTY-ONE

Why did I turn the conversation around? Mayumi thought with a disgruntled pout.

She'd started sharing her more... private feelings, and she wasn't used to doing that. Her jesting words about 'the monster under the bed' had just been because she wanted to be humorous and distract him from his obvious aversion to the water.

Talking about the fact she trusted him, remembered him, had brought a whirlwind of emotions with it. Emotions she didn't want.

She already knew she liked Faunus. His exterior was a massive part of that. There was an undeniable, divinely dark beauty about him that others wouldn't see – because they were blind fools – but she could also see he was... jovial. She hadn't expected him to be so free-spirited. He could even be teasing.

Then he'd brought up Hawthorne Keep, things about her being a Demonslayer. She wished he wouldn't.

She frowned and brought her gaze to him.

"How did you know it was the mountain castle I went to?" Mayumi asked, drifting her eyes down his body and taking in its oddity before going back up with suspicion. "Although my home is closer to Hawthorne's Keep, there was a chance I could have gone to the Blackfyre Keep instead."

Hawthorne was east of here, whereas Blackfyre was southwest.

Faunus turned his snout upwards as though he was looking at the cloudless sky. His tail swished under the water, grabbing her attention before he sighed loudly.

He turned his head back down to face her.

"You are a fierce human."

Mayumi had noticed that whenever Faunus spoke about her strength, it was always as a human, never as a woman. It was as though he categorised men and women as the same, rather than making a comparison based on gender first and humankind after.

"You are very strong, and I imagine that is because of all the training your Demonslayer father put you through – even when you were a child."

His words made her lips part in realisation.

"How long have you been watching me, Faunus?"

He couldn't have known her father was a Demonslayer since she'd never told him. He also couldn't have known her father had been training her from a young age unless... he'd seen it.

"Currently? The moment you saw me kill that Demon in front of your home was when I returned."

She narrowed her eyes into a glare. "You know that isn't what I meant."

His fangs parted as he chuckled deeply, making it sound more echoed and mischievous. Darker, even.

"Mayumi, I have been coming to this cottage since the night I saved you. I have seen you become a child who slept in tall herbs. Then an even bigger child who tripped and fell while her parent whacked her with a strange wooden sword whenever she made a mistake. Or there were the days where I witnessed you being guided while you hit, kicked, and smacked mounted timber against the stake in the middle of the clearing." The more he spoke in his nonchalant voice, the more her jaw fell. "I have watched you forge your own weapons and argue with your parents. I have seen much of your life. I have also seen things no one else has, things you would not want anyone else to see."

She didn't know if she was outraged, wary, or shocked by this development. It also brought to light that Faunus had probably lived a long time, which only begged the question... how old was he?

"Like what?" she bit, grinding her molars.

"I was following you, making sure you travelled safely by

yourself the day your mother died. I watched you and your father bury her nearby."

Her face paled. *He watched me cry.*

No one had ever seen Mayumi cry except for her mother. She'd hidden any tears from her father from a young age because he wanted to believe she was strong in will. He thought weakness was the sign of a Demonslayer that would die shortly.

"Why are you telling me this? Faunus, this is called stalking! Do you understand how... creepy that is?"

He had the audacity to scoff at her!

"Perhaps it may be *creepy* for a human, but I merely wanted to know if the child I saved was still alive. I have watched many humans and have returned to many homes. I have seen children become adults and then have seen that they never return. You are one of the few who remain in this world."

All throughout their conversation, Faunus' body was as rigid as stone, unwilling to move in the water as though it would eat him alive.

"You cannot call me a monster and then place human morality onto me, Mayumi," he stated, leaning his head to the side as though to punctuate his words. "Is stalking any worse than the dozens of humans I have eaten and killed? You know what I am. You have also made it apparent you understand what being a Duskwalker entails and you know what I have done. I did not get to this level of humanity by sitting still and waiting for my food to crawl into my mouth."

Her lips tightened. *Shit. He's right.*

She couldn't hold human ideologies and morality to something like him, and she'd already liked that about him anyway. He was outside the realm of normal, which is why she was attracted to him in the first place.

She uncurled her fist and let the tension ease out of her body.

"There was no point in hiding it from you," he added. "I would have eventually made it known that I have been watching you by speaking so forwardly. I would prefer to come out and tell you now rather than by accident. It also allows you to know that I understand much about you already, how skilled you are, and that I'm aware you followed in your father's footsteps."

"My ancestors' footsteps," she corrected with her lips pouting and a grumble. "Specifically, the men."

She let out a deep expire and leaned her head back against the wall of the spring bath. Her lids lowered as she watched him, his body still full of tension and unease. Her lips quirked at how stubbornly brave he was being.

"I'm the first daughter born in five generations on my father's side in these lands. He expected a son, someone to sire the next of kin and become a Demonslayer like his forefather and his forefather before that. Instead, my mother gave birth to a daughter and was unable to reach full-term with those that followed me. It's what made her weak when she used to be strong."

She leaned her arms over the rocky wall face to mimic his position. However, she folded one leg on top of the other, since she was naked.

"I think my grandfather would have been disapproving of a *woman* in the family joining the guild, but my father had already been trying to shake off generations of brainwashing. In the past, long ago, women were considered weak and unhelpful. Much had to change with the Demon scourge, but my family decided to hold on to those misogynistic mindsets." Then her gaze fell to the side at a painful throb in her heart. "But my father was protective of me because I was a girl. He wasn't pleased that I wanted to join the guild, and I think he was especially hard on me because of it. He wanted me to live, and I'm still alive because of all his teachings – no matter how hard and cruel they may have been."

"I was angered at first when I saw you receive punishment," Faunus growled, and she swore she heard the crunch of rock chipping away under his claws. "I needed to leave because of the scent of your blood and my rage. I'm glad I didn't intervene."

"Me too," she humourlessly laughed. "He was an Elder. He would have fought you to the death, as I would have, and then neither of us would be here."

His head tilted as he leaned it forward. "You are an Elder too? Could you explain what this means?"

Her jaw clenched before she turned her gaze skyward. "I

never made it to being an Elder. That takes years of experience. I became a Master – a position just below that."

"So you are still a strong Demonslayer."

The praise in his voice nettled at her. She bristled, her ire prickly.

"I'm not a Demonslayer anymore, Faunus. That's why I'm here and not at Hawthorne Keep."

"You aren't? But isn't that what you wanted?" His tone gave her the impression he thought she'd left willingly.

"It was," she growled. "But I broke a rule and was kicked out."

"What did you do?"

Mayumi glared at an oncoming cloud, hoping it didn't plan to start storming again. She was tired of the snow, and it was only mid-winter.

"Do you know what a woman has to do to become an official member and rise from a navy rank Novice to a green Apprentice?"

"Of course not."

She lowered her head and then gave him a spiteful smirk.

"Women bleed, usually once a month. The price for a woman to go up in rank is to have a complete hysterectomy. They cut us open and remove all our reproductive organs. Our uterus, our ovaries, everything. It's to ensure we won't be a liability to our teams when we are out in the field. Otherwise, we'd be nothing but Demon bait, getting our teammates killed."

"I... was not aware that was something you had done."

Blue flickered in his orbs, but whatever the emotion was, he snuffed it quickly.

"I didn't. That's the point." Her head thudded against the rock as she leaned it back once more. "My father was able to pull some strings and have it fabricated to seem like I went through with the procedure. One of the reasons he was unhappy with me joining the guild was that I couldn't continue the family line if I did the surgery. He was the one who told me I should lie, but I had to keep it a secret. For eleven years, I kept that secret. Then, one day, my stupid period came a week early, and I got half my team slaughtered while we were hunting a particularly strong Demon who lingered in the mines. I watched men die because I brought three Demons upon us. I'd been caught trying to hide that I was bleeding, unprepared for it, and that person reported me in outrage because they'd had their hand bitten off and lost their friend."

He said nothing for a short while, eventually bringing his hand forward to hold the side of his snout in thought while looking out into the forest.

She was sure this was a lot to take in.

It had been a lot for her to process.

"No one knows the truth," she continued, weirdly uncomfortable with the silence. "It was announced that I was honourably discharged, and I was given a large sum of money to keep my mouth shut. I can't wear my uniform except around my home, and I report anything I see that might be of use to them – although that is more of a choice than a requirement. They offered to let me go through with the surgery if I wanted to stay, but I declined it."

"Why?"

She'd been asked that very question when she'd told them no.

Mayumi stood and walked to the side of the spring water bath. On the edge was a glass vial of liquid soap made from goat's milk and lavender. Holding the cylindrical vial upside down, she poured a few drops into her palm and washed her arms.

They were having a bath, so she might as well start properly washing her body while they were talking. It appeared he was too uncomfortable to care that she was completely naked before him. Then again, he'd probably gotten used to her body in the last twenty-four hours of delightfully humping it.

"It's my body," she started, watching the soap lather over her flesh. "I didn't want to change it just because the Demons came. Why should I have to suffer that? Most Demonslayers don't even make it past thirty, and many women grow ill and weak in their later years because changing their bodies like that has terrible side effects. I should be allowed to make the choice if I want children and not have that choice taken away from me because of some human-eating vermin."

She was surprised when his orbs turned bright yellow. "Does that mean you wish for younglings? Children..."

Mayumi lifted her shoulders in a shrug before lathering her

chest. "I don't know. I'm not particularly fond of bringing a life into this dying world."

"The world is not dying," he said. "There is much life."

He gestured to the trees and their surroundings.

Mayumi guessed this conversation was eye-opening for them both in different ways. It was nice to learn he'd always been by her side, hiding in the shadows, and it also felt... relieving to vent and share her frustrations.

"Humankind *is* dying," she sighed. "The world is broken, Faunus. We are the last choking embers waiting to die out, desperately burning the last of the light before we're gone. Time is eating us alive, just waiting to cradle us into the grave."

Then she gestured to their surroundings like he had. She stood on top of where she'd been sitting, bringing more of her body out of the water and into the cold air so she could wash the bottom half of her – the place that had truly been dirty.

"Sure, the trees will still be here, but you haven't seen the inside of our villages. It's not just the Demons we need to worry about, but the famine and sicknesses there. Every year, more and more people are suffering. And every year, I wait to see if Colt's Outpost or Reddington town is destroyed, either from within or by a group of Demons. It's worse here in the north than anywhere else because of the large number of mountains we have. There are more Demons, and that makes it harder to trade between villages and towns. Despite what's happening outside the walls, greed is still pulling humankind apart because everything is scarce."

Slipping back into the water to rinse, Mayumi held his gaze as she said, "We are now just generations born to witness the end of the world. The idea of bringing a child into this life, knowing it could end not long after it's born because it grew sick or was eaten, is not something I'm sure I want to witness. Nor do I want to die knowing it could be one of the last humans born."

He was quiet as he thought on her words.

Then his tone was hesitant as he asked, "What... if it weren't human?"

Her brows drew together sharply, not expecting such a ridiculous question. "What do you mean?"

He opened his jaws, only to clip his fangs together. "Nothing. It doesn't matter."

She chose to disregard it since he'd evaded the question. Mayumi wasn't one to pry, especially since she often hated it when others did it to her.

Holding the vial again, she poured a few generous drops into her other hand and lifted them both in his direction.

"Okay, Mr *Forest God.* It's your turn to get clean." Hoping to pull away from the conversation, she wiggled her eyebrows at him as she stepped closer. "I'll make that fur of yours even softer than before."

He didn't move, both his arms spread wide to grip the edge easily with his hands. People could sit on the rim there, but it fit in his large palms.

His head followed her approaching movements, dipping when she was closer. She placed the vial next to his right hand, which gave her freedom to cup some water and pour it down his furry chest.

His firm pectoral muscles clenched when she smeared the liquid soap against him. Then they softened, only to dance with twitches under both her hands as they went up and down. She made sure to get to the root of his fur, going over and between the rib bones that sat outside his body.

Her hands tingled with pleasure at being able to touch and explore him so openly like this.

Faunus gave a grunting, lowing snort as she rubbed the sides of his neck. His head dipped back, allowing her more room before she slid her palms over his arms. They weren't wet, so she had to cup water and moisten them, but he let her do whatever she wanted.

When she started cleaning his chest again just so she could selfishly touch it, something in her peripheral caught her attention.

His cock has come out. At least partially.

She slyly examined it. She'd never seen his tentacles swirl around his cock to shield it. They were a dark purple and smooth on the outside, but she knew they had that spikey texture and were a lighter purple on the inside.

The only reason she knew she'd stopped cleaning him to stare was that he lowered his head and nudged the end of his short snout against her. Since he was sitting on a recess, he was lower. It brought them almost to the same head height.

He may not like the bath, but he was still enjoying her touch. His orbs were purple, giving him away even if his cock hadn't.

"There has been something I've been meaning to ask you," he said, his voice a little huskier than it had been before. "You say 'these lands.' What do you mean by that?"

Mayumi pointed to his groin. "Are you going to want me to do something about that?"

"Not in the water," he bit. Then he placed his hand against the swirling, tentacle-covered tip and *shoved* it back inside. "Because of the heat, I didn't notice it had extruded."

Damn. She'd been hoping to have a little fun.

"Fine. But I'll need you to stand so I can wash the rest of you."

He was standing within a heartbeat, snatching the opportunity to no longer be submerged. His daunting height and the pool's differences made it so she was facing the bottom half of his rib cage, bringing his body all the way to his upper thighs out of the water.

Then he held his hand out, his claws upwards, sharp and caging. "I can do it."

With her lips pressed together and curling upwards, she poured more soap into her own hand and lathered his abdomen. He gave a huff, but she had a funny feeling his irritation was only for show.

Or maybe it was because he didn't want her to see the seam at his groin twitching and clenching because of her touches. The fur dipped inwards at that line. If she'd seen him without pants on to begin with, she may have already realised he had genitalia before he'd revealed it.

"You asked what I meant by these lands," she started, finally getting around to answering him. "My family came to Austrális over three hundred years ago by the sea. They were samurai for one of the daimyo, a land-owning, highly influential, feudal-lord family, which were approved to trade outside their country. The Sakuko policy prohibited most foreign contact, except for a very rare few who had adequate reasons."

Mayumi washed around his hips, making sure she scrubbed hardest here. A human would have been stumbling, but Faunus was completely still, unaffected by her strength. She looked up to find his head was bent down and to the side to watch her.

"Since my forefathers were samurai, military nobles, they were given rights to travel with the daimyo as protection under the will of the emperor." She lowered herself so she could wash his chunky, thick, muscular thighs. "They stepped foot on these lands and then became stuck here when the Demons came. Ships were overrun, and the chaos caused many of them to sink under people's fear and desperation to escape. Some were also spiteful if they weren't granted access, so they went out of their way to sink any ship they could. There are Demons in the sea, so communication to other lands is almost non-existent, but from what we have heard, they are facing them as well."

Then Mayumi let out a long expire as she stood. She eyed his soapy body, seeing that his fur was twirled and disturbed.

"I have bad news for you," she grumbled. "You're going to have to lower your body all the way to your neck to rinse off."

She almost laughed when his entire body went rigid. Instead, she reached her hands up to lay them on his shoulders, trying to pull him down.

"I'll give you a kiss if you're a good boy."

A light growl emitted from his chest. "That is not enough of a reward."

Her lips parted open in disbelief. "Then what would be?"

"Nothing," he bit, his orbs flashing red as he lowered himself. They turned white when the water was up to his chest.

So white shows either his worry or fear.

His fangs parted as he gave distressed huffs when the water was up to his jaw. He lifted his head to make sure none of the bone of his skull got wet.

Mayumi joined him and rubbed his body down to help him rinse. When she stood, so did he.

Then he turned so he could flee the water.

"Wait!" she cried, grabbing his long tail and pulling it. "I need to wash your back."

"No, I am done. I have been cleaned of my seed as you have asked of me."

She fell forward through the water when he jumped out, his soaked tail slippery under her grasp. The wet slap of his feet against the ground was loud when he landed.

Mayumi leaned over the rocky bath wall with a pout. "I was hoping you'd wash mine, though."

Crouching down and stretching with one of his legs back and the opposing hand forward, Faunus shook his body. Water sprayed everywhere, hitting her face, the ground, and even the awning that created a covered area next to the bath.

"Wash your own damn body," Faunus growled.

Despite shaking much of the water off, his body still appeared like a dunked cat. His fur was sagging and dripping. He walked away with his long tail swishing, obviously sulking, while continuing to shake his body to rid himself of more.

Mayumi eyed the two towels she'd brought out for them sitting next to the bath. She gave them a glower.

He drenched them!

TWENTY-TWO

Mayumi swayed side to side as she slightly bounced, her mighty steed between her thighs trudging through the dense forest. The smell of cedar and fir trees was fresh, heightened by the cold dampness that came from winter.

The world was mostly quiet except for the odd bird call, the rustling of leaves, and her steed's large, heavy footsteps creaking and crunching in the snow. There were also their accompanying breaths, hers much softer and calmer.

Faunus' heat between her thighs, and against her arse and hands, helped to keep the worst of the chill away from her body. He was ferrying much on his back since she'd gotten him to take her to the village, and they were already on their way home.

Coming out of Colt's Outpost, Mayumi had struggled to carry everything into the forest to give to Faunus – who had been hiding. She didn't want to go back for as long as she could, weeks even. Though that was doubtful, as her quicker perishables would wither.

This is so much easier with him.

She was riding his back because it was quicker and also because she was lazy. It was even better since he could carry all her supplies.

However, his lizard spikes had taken some wriggling to find a good spot, otherwise it felt like one of them was going to break apart her poor pelvis. They mostly appeared slimline and pointed down his back – unless his body or emotions were ruffled, and then they'd begin to stick upwards. Once or twice, the one she was nestled on top of had tried to lift her.

Letting go of one fistful of fur, she petted him. He was so unbelievably soft – they'd shared a second bath this morning because they'd made more mess again last night.

He was going to have to get used to bath time since it appeared to be a daily reoccurring requirement between them. Faunus had filled the bath with his magic this time by using drops of his own blood.

Mayumi had still gotten the heating stove going in order to keep it warm while they were in it.

Getting him in the second time had been even harder than the first, and it was only the threat of never being able to touch her again that finally got him in. She didn't know how long that was going to work.

He'd gone to sulk afterwards like he'd done the previous day, disappearing for a long while until his fur was dry – which was late into the afternoon. Mayumi just let him be, thankful he was doing something he was obviously uncomfortable with just to please her.

One thing she liked about Faunus was that his annoyance didn't linger. Once he was inside, watching her cook or clean as he laid on his side while resting his head in his hand, he seemed rather content and relaxed.

He was still alert, made obvious by the fact that he'd leave to go check on any noise or scents he picked up, but then he'd return to resume being in her company quietly.

He doesn't like fire.

There was always a noticeable gap between him and the fireplace unless she sought to be near it – which was less often since she just curled into him for heat instead. Then again, she imagined all that fur would make him hot.

He was also very sensitive about his skull being touched any higher than his snout and the corner of his jaw. The crack in it might be painful, so she resisted going any higher than his fangs and nose hole if she cupped it.

And he seems to have nightmares. He often twitched rapidly across his body in his sleep.

Something had happened to him, but she didn't want to pry.

It was obvious he was trying to hide all this, but she'd always been able to pick up on people's odd behaviours.

"Are you still mad at me?" Mayumi asked while leaning back on one hand against his hind.

She was at the centre of his spine, a gap that allowed his big shoulder blades to move while also giving his hips and feline-shaped legs room.

"I was never angry with you," he said calmly, turning his skull to the side to look at her.

His orbs were a dark green. *Yeah, still mad.*

Klaus had put his arm around her shoulders, annoyingly dragging her into a forced hug when she'd been in the town. There were more apologies from all three men, some teasing, and a small update about what was going on in the town – which was uneventful, as always.

Faunus had smelt that she was covered in the strong scent of a single male and the more fleeting scents of many other people. He disliked it to the point he'd surrounded her completely with his arms and legs in a crouch and rubbed his body against hers. Only to then rub himself against a tree just to be rid of it.

There was no mention of what or why he was doing this, but it wasn't hard to figure it out. He was like a creature marking his territory.

"Faunus... where do Duskwalkers come from?" Mayumi asked, wanting to fill the silence.

She was also just so unbelievably curious about him and his kind. The question had been gnawing at her since the moment they'd first spoken.

"The Veil."

She leaned forward and smacked his shoulder blade. "You know that's not what I meant!"

He lifted his head, parted his fangs, and let out a chuckle. His torso dipped slightly, forcing her to lean back so she didn't fall forward when he climbed over a fallen tree.

She held onto the straps of the four bags that had been threaded and knotted together so they could rest over his back. They dangled down on both sides of him, acting like reigns for her to occasionally hold on to.

"We are born, just like you," he said.

He darted his head to the right and paused, as though he heard something she couldn't, before resuming his walk.

"But where? Did you come from the same place as the Demons? We know they aren't from Earth."

"No," he said quickly, with a biting tone. *"We were born here. Our mother was once a human, but she mated with the spirit of the void, our father, by giving over her life in exchange for magical power."*

One of her brows quirked. "Once human?"

"She is now a Phantom." Mayumi shrugged, having no idea what that was, but he wasn't looking her way to see. *"She mated with him just after the Demons arrived here. I believe he came from that world – although he is not a Demon himself."*

"What is he then? I've never heard of some 'spirit of the void.'"

"His name is Weldir, and he is a God. Or at least a part God, or a descendant of one." Faunus shrugged beneath her thighs. *"I'm not quite sure. I have only seen him once in full form, and I have no memory of him before then. But he is everywhere within the Veil. He is the cause of the black mist, and it is his entire essence spreading out among the trees."*

With her lips pursed together tightly, Mayumi thought on what she'd seen of the Veil. She'd been near it many times over her life, often on scouting missions. There were two kinds of mists that frolicked through the Veil.

A white one that appeared to be natural condensation, and then a black one. She never would have guessed the latter belonged to a being.

"So when I called you a forest God, I was kind of right?" Mayumi tried to laugh.

"No, I am no God." He turned his head to show his orbs had brightened in their yellow hue. *"But I appreciate the sentiment."*

"What is he a God of then?"

"The afterlife of all the souls who are consumed by Demons, himself, or Duskwalkers. That is his task, to give them a home since they are not permitted into any afterlife you humans normally have. We call him the spirit of the void because that's

the only place he can linger in his physical form unless he uses a large amount of mana to do so in this realm. He is made up of spirit and mist here." Then Faunus looked to the side and into the forest, his head having a thoughtful tilt to it. "*I have no idea why I was born, what my function or purpose is. Not knowing has been a cause of great distress for my kind.*"

"You don't have to have a required purpose to be allowed to live, Faunus," Mayumi softly said as she patted his back. "Humans have no purpose and yet we are here, uselessly living."

"*Yes, but he* wanted *us created, Mayumi.*" Faunus shook his head with a lowing snort before facing forward. "*But we don't know why. At least, I don't.*"

Mayumi leaned back once again on one arm and kicked her legs back and forth down the sides of his torso.

"Well, how many of you are there?" Then she cocked her head with her brows knitting together. "Wait... you only spoke of your mother and Weldir, or whatever you called him. Does that mean... Wait! Are you all related? Like siblings?"

"*You caught on quick.*" He chuckled appreciatively. "*There are nine of us that I know of for certain, but there could be more. One, however, is not my sibling.*"

Mayumi reached her leg forward and kicked the back of his ram horn.

"You seem pretty smart, I guess," she teased. "Are you the oldest?"

He shook his head. "*No, not by far. I believe I was the third born.*"

She kicked the back of his horn again, and this time he turned his head sharply and gave her a light growl. Then he opened his fangs and chomped at the air, silently telling her he'd bite her foot.

"How old are you then?"

Not believing his silent threat at all, when he looked forward again, she tapped the underside of her boot against the back of his horn.

His only reaction was to huff.

"*I remember many autumns, but I couldn't tell you the exact length of my life, as I remember very little about the beginning. I believe the amount would be at least in the early two hundreds."*

"I see," she said, raising her hand to cup her chin. *Old as fuck then.* "What about the others?"

"There are two younglings currently who still cling to our mother. I am unsure of how far apart they were born, but I believe she is keeping them young on purpose."

"Why and how can she keep them young? Babies grow up."

"There are two I call the twins," he said instead of answering. *"I believe they shared the same womb, and I have never seen them apart. They are very playful, but also rough. Then there is the antler-horned Duskwalker."*

She realised he was stating them by the youngest first.

"The one with the fox skull? I've seen sketches of him," Mayumi quickly butted in. "He is known by the Demonslayers. As is the wolf-skulled one with the twisty horns – the one who takes a bride every ten years."

"That is Orpheus. He is older than me, although not as developed."

"Developed?"

Faunus paused in the middle of taking a step.

"You don't know?" She lifted both her hands to shrug with them when he looked at her. *"I see. Duskwalkers gain more humanity by the number of humans we have eaten. Although I was born after him, I have consumed more humans. He stopped hunting for them when he decided he wanted a bride. He is quite sorrowful. He is also very territorial about his home. Magnar, the antler-horned one, is welcoming, but I believe that is due to ignorance, a lack of humanity, and not having been faced with much adversity."*

Mayumi wanted to continue to learn about him and all these siblings he had, but there was a question that was nagging at the back of her mind.

"The wolf skull one, Oferus, or whatever you said his name was."

"Orpheus," he corrected.

"Yeah, yeah, whatever. Did he kill that last human he took? The western sector laid down a plan to capture him the last time he went to obtain a sacrifice. Is she dead, that woman? I heard he slaughtered all the Demonslayers who went after him. A few watched it happen from afar."

"Reia? Yes, she is alive."

Mayumi hadn't known her name before this.

"No way!" Mayumi squealed while jumping forward, patting him on the back with light, excited taps. "It's been almost eleven months since then! Are the others still alive?"

"No. They are dead. She is the only one who has survived, and she will for a long while. He will never seek a new bride, so once his protection circle fades, the human villages will have to protect themselves."

"I see..."

Not really... She didn't quite understand everything, but she couldn't contain her relief to know the woman was still alive.

There was also something about the way he spoke. She didn't know why, but she had an inkling Faunus wasn't revealing the whole truth. It was as though he was hiding something.

"Okay. So... two babies, the twins, fox boy, you, then wolf boy." She counted them all on her fingers. "You said there were eight of you that are siblings? Who is the last one?"

She'd ask about the ninth one and where it came from later, since they seemed to be close to her home.

"Merikh," Faunus growled, causing her eyes to widen in surprise. *"He is the bull-horned, bear-skulled Duskwalker."*

"I thought he was dead," Mayumi gasped. "The guild killed him over a hundred years ago!"

Faunus tsked. *"No. Not dead. He lives and has far more humanity even than I. It is what makes him so dangerous."*

"You don't like him?"

*"He is **mean**, Mayumi. And if you see him, you will not live long."* The vibration she could feel in his torso was the reverberation of his growl. *"He has no interest in other Duskwalkers and is rather hateful towards humans. He would rather be with the intelligent Demons."*

"Where is he now then?"

She would say it was to avoid him, but she was always up for a challenge.

"I'm not sure. He left the Veil many years ago in search of

something and has not since returned. His cave is empty, but his magic circle still remains. Perhaps he replaces it and leaves again."

The trees began to open up, showing the clearing and her home backing it. The sun was setting, but they had returned much sooner than she would have on her own.

Faunus didn't approach, instead pausing at the rim of the clearing.

"Actually, this reminds me." He lifted one hand while turning his head to face her, balancing on three limbs in order to assist her off his back. *"I wish to lay my protective circle down around your home. I am hoping it remains for the ten years it is supposed to."*

Mayumi kicked her leg over the arch of his spine and slid herself down without his help, much like how she would dismount from a horse.

"Will it stop the Demons from being able to approach?"

"Yes, that is the point."

She folded her arms across her chest and threw one hip to the side. "Then no. At some point, even while you're here, I'm going to start baiting them again. I'm a Demonslayer in spirit, even if I'm no longer one in name."

"Mayumi," he warned, but she just threw her hand up and walked to her porch.

"Don't fight me on this, Faunus. I said you could protect me, and you're welcome to do so, but there are certain things I still want to be able to do."

Actually, she was hoping with him around, she could kill a whole fucking load of them! The idea of that made her grin so wide her cheeks hurt.

"Fine."

TWENTY-THREE

A little disgruntled, Faunus followed Mayumi to her porch. At the bottom step, he reached his arm backwards and clawed at the multiple bags slung across his back to pull them from his body.

He changed his form into his more humanoid one so he could assist in bringing them inside. He was without his clothing, as Mayumi claimed she'd 'misplaced' them.

Since she'd removed her painful barrier when he'd returned, he was given free access inside.

She makes little sense, he thought with a grumble as he went inside after her. *Wouldn't most humans seek permanent protection for their homes?*

He thought she would have made her home secure and found other, safer ways to hunt Demons. Luring them to the very place she resided seemed unsound of mind.

He didn't like it, but Faunus knew if he tried to intervene, his relationship with Mayumi — whatever this was — could change just as abruptly as it had started.

"Here, I'll take the bags and put everything away," she offered after removing her jacket and holding her hands out for them.

I don't wish for her to discard me. He refused to give her the bags and just handed her random items to assist her in any way he could. *I have seen humans discard each other.*

Faunus held multiple fruits and vegetables in his large palm, caging them in with his fingers and claws. When she took them so she could place them on her food rack, he dug into a bag and grabbed another assortment of food.

He watched her, his gaze never leaving this strong, capable, yet undoubtedly beautiful female as she went about putting everything away.

He didn't wish to disillusion himself with the reality of what was between them. She desired him, that he knew for certain, but they never seemed to be much more than that.

It was the same for other human couples he'd seen.

Out of curiosity, Faunus had lingered to watch a particular female who enjoyed having... different partners in her home. The men always left, sometimes more than one, but she never seemed inclined to have them linger.

They usually just completed rather raunchy acts together before she'd wave at them from the door with this satisfied smile on her face. There had never been promises of more, had never been confessions of tender emotions.

Is Mayumi the same?

Would she eventually seek a new partner? He knew he was fulfilling some strange desire she had, but would she eventually grow tired of him?

I'm not human. I cannot give her some things she may want or seek.

He could never enter a human village with her. He couldn't give her younglings or even kiss her, since he had no lips. In comparison to her own kind, Faunus knew he was lacking.

It was selfish, but he didn't want Mayumi to discard him for a human. He knew what marriage was, what a husband and wife were to each other. He could never be this, even if he wanted to.

I will never be able to bond with her. Even if Mayumi wanted to give him her soul, which he doubted, he still couldn't obtain it.

This was as far as they could go.

Mayumi turned with a bright smile when she noted they'd completed their task together. Her warm expression towards him, when he'd seen her be cold, ate at his heart. *But... I want her to... love me.*

For just a moment, bright flamingo pink flashed in his orbs.

No! He quickly covered one eye socket as he pushed down

the emotion, the feelings that were trying to grow, refusing to allow himself to feel even a flicker of that warm emotion towards her. *I cannot. I won't.*

She'd already turned away from him before she could see, beginning to cut up some carrots, potatoes, and various other vegetables he couldn't name. She'd obtained a small amount of meat but threw it into the pot to boil and then removed its wrapping. He'd told her to be careful about any fresh meat around him, and she was taking that into consideration.

Despite his need to kill his growing affection for her, conflicting emotions pounded into his thoughts.

He approached Mayumi from behind to cage her between his slightly bent forward form and the kitchen counter she was using. Placing one hand around her biceps, her strong hidden muscles flexed in his palm as he glided the claws of his other hand under her thick, long-sleeved shirt.

I cannot love her. She should not love me... but I want her to. He wanted that from her. It was greedy, but he possessively wanted to own her heart and steal it from any other she may come across.

Her breath hitched when he slipped his palm against the side of her abdominal muscles, and she leaned into him. *If I cannot have her soul, then I want everything else.*

Faunus wanted to consume her. To consume her thoughts, her heart, her body. He wanted them to be his, to nibble at every part of her essence until every cell in her body remembered him owning it.

Even after he was gone.

"Faunus," she warned, yet there was no fight in her voice nor her lithe body as she pressed even deeper into him. She was accepting his embrace, even turning her head up to him while he towered over her to look down. His orbs were yellow, but he was sure any moment they would turn purple. "I haven't eaten in a while. I need to make dinner before you can play with me."

"Why can we not do both?" he asked, gliding his hand up to brush his palm over her left breast.

He couldn't really hold them. They were far too small, even using just his fingers, but she was very sensitive there. Caressing them lightly was enough to have her scent turning into something wonderous and mouth-watering.

He used the thumb of his other hand to cut off the button of her trousers and dip his hand inside.

Faunus bumped the end of his snout against the side of her head as he rumbled, "You can prepare your food while I touch what I would like to feast on."

She shivered, and her thighs parted just enough so he could dip his hand lower to cup her pretty little pussy, one he'd claimed so no other could.

He'd been concerned about that, and what it might mean for her future, but he was just so fucking ecstatic about her being able to take all of him that it had his cock stirring every time he was close to her.

Considering he did want her to be able to prepare her meal, he kept his touch light, only teasing her nipple and the hard nub of her clit. Before she'd even managed to finish preparing, she *begged* him to go lower, to spear her with his thick fingers.

He refused until she was done cutting up her ingredients and then gave her what she wanted while they were waiting for her food to cook.

Having her on the tips of her toes, gripping both his forearms, while she leaned her pert arse against him and screamed, elicited a loud vibration from his chest in appreciation. Mayumi was *his* human to tease.

"That's a good little Demonslayer," he purred when she'd drenched his fingers, her inner walls clamping and quivering around them.

"Not... a Demonslayer anymore," she huffed. "Remember?"

"Not in name, but in spirit. Isn't that what you said?" He chuckled, then leaving his right hand between her thighs, he cupped her jaw with the other and tilted her head back and to the side so she was facing him. "Open your mouth, Mayumi."

"Why?" she asked, her dazed expression giving a frowning twitch.

She wasn't fond of him licking at her lips, so she'd never parted them for him.

"I cannot kiss you properly, but that doesn't mean I cannot

taste you." He wanted to show her they could at least do this, and that he would claim every part of her body in his own way. "I bet your saliva is just as sweet as you are here."

He moved his fingers back and forth just once to show her where he meant. The fog in her gaze grew thicker, and Mayumi parted her lips for him. She even stuck her tongue forward a little.

She's usually so bossy, he thought as he slowly lowered his head, his heart giving quick thumps at the fact she was being docile and compliant for him. *But she always goes so soft for me when I touch her.*

He liked that he brought out this side of her. It was like a reward once he moulded her in his grasp and upended her.

The first foray of his tongue grazing against the top of hers had them both groaning. Faunus parted his fangs around her face so he could go deeper, and his cock nearly extruded at the pleasure he felt, at the heady taste and texture.

It took her a few swishes of his tongue slipping back and forth, but she eventually lapped back at him. Her lips closed around his tongue to hold it, to keep him inside, and heat flared within.

His joy never reached his purple orbs, but he knew without question that she would allow him to do this again in the future.

Her mouth was another piece of her he'd obtained.

Mine.

The sound of a whine startled Mayumi awake, her eyes snapping open before they immediately drooped.

He's whimpering again.

This wasn't the first time she'd accidentally been woken by Faunus having a bad dream. Although his cries were light and quiet, the sound of them woke her when he squeezed her a little too tight at the same time.

Currently, her forehead was pressed against the cushion of his pectoral muscles squeezing together. He was on his side with his arms around her.

His lemongrass and lime scent made it so hard to keep her

eyes open. It always lulled her, always pulled her under.

Her mind was usually sharp, even when having sex. For him to have this power over her was alarming, but she'd come to just accept it. It's not like he could help how she reacted to his scent, or his heat, or that damn gravelly voice that always had her insides flipping.

Yowling quivered out of him, and his claws clutched in before releasing her.

I never knew Duskwalkers could have nightmares, she thought as she slowly lifted to sit, hoping not to wake him. *Or that they could even dream.*

She stared down at Faunus, whose body gave violent twitches. It was no surprise she'd woken, especially since this time seemed to be a lot worse than others.

Her groggy, dozy gaze flittered to the dying fire.

She eventually turned back to Faunus and tilted her head while leaning over him, balancing her weight on one arm.

What's bothering you, Faunus?

He'd given her absolutely no insight as to why he was wary of a few things. He didn't like short knives, nor fire, nor the bath. He was particular about sniffing her food to make sure it wasn't poisonous, and he didn't like her being buried beneath anything – other than his own body.

Mayumi brushed the backs of her fingers over the side of his jawbone, hoping it might ease him. The arms around her tightened like he felt her touch, almost tugging her closer before they settled.

Should I wake him?

She decided against it. He deserved his rest, especially since he was always so attentive towards her and her body at night.

I really like him. This Duskwalker was worming his way into her stone heart even though it had been impossible for any man before him.

Faunus didn't crowd her, but he was always present. He was so damn lazy that if she didn't give him a task, he'd just lie around her home while watching her. He seemed content to just... do this.

And he was funny, in a weird way. He was playful and teasing, but he was also solemn in other moments. He was serious when he needed or chose to be. Passionate, possessive, and domineering, but would also allow her to take control if she really wanted.

He was a bunch of conflicting aspects, like he wanted to be everything all at once. Gentle and rough, caring and nonchalant, lazy but hardworking.

I never know how he's going to react, she thought with a silent, singular laugh. *It makes him fun.*

She was so used to people being predictable and having ulterior motives. It'd never been hard to guess theirs, but she still hadn't unravelled his true reasons for being here.

She just... she was hoping he didn't plan to disappear. *I want you to stay.*

She took in the ethereal, unholy, yet bewitching features of his bony face. Despite his glowing orbs, his large but empty eye sockets were dark, like they were filled with constant shadows. The arch of his feline brow bone, the dents of his cheeks. His fangs always took her attention, so sharp and menacing, and she often desired kissing the side of the longer ones.

I want to learn more about you. Sometimes he was willing to share everything, and then other times, he was vague.

His stories felt like there were parts that were redacted, information hidden.

What are you hiding?

Mayumi lifted her hand higher, brushing up his snout and then over the side of the crack in his face – being extremely gentle so as not to hurt him at all. It was always sensitive, but she knew that sometimes, if you tickled near a wound, it could feel nice rather than painful.

Red orbs sparked to life.

The moment she brushed the sharp edges of the crevice on his face, Mayumi was shoved to her back. A large hand gripped her throat tightly and *squeezed,* cutting off her ability to speak and breathe. The pressure rendered her gasp into a curt choke.

Her face grew flushed due to the lack of blood and oxygen in her head. Her eyes bowed in confusion in his direction.

Faunus was above her with his fangs parted in a ferocious

snarl, threatening and warning, with his orbs a crimson colour of menace. Mayumi's legs kicked, finding no purchase beneath his three limbs supporting him as he pinned her down.

She slapped at his hands before trying to pry at least *one* thick and long finger from her. It was useless. He was too strong. *Shit!*

The burning ache in her chest intensified the longer she couldn't take in a single breath, saliva collecting and pooling in the back of her mouth. Her throat made a clicking sound as she tried to take in oxygen.

He's going to fucking kill me! Mayumi tried everything, but nothing helped. She couldn't speak as her trachea and larynx were crushed.

She tried to look for a weapon, but there was nothing within reach.

Then Mayumi started to relax, her vision growing dim as black dots swirled. Her head was on fire, like it was going to combust. *Sh...it.* Her mind swam.

A rush of oxygen came into her lungs the moment his hand flung away, and he fell back. His orbs were white. She'd at least seen that before she rolled to her side and coughed wildly.

He tried to choke me!

Faunus rushed forwards, practically straddling his massive body over her much smaller one. She fit easily between his thighs as he placed his hand on the side of her face with more care than usual.

A whimper came from him. "I am so sorry, Mayumi."

"Get the fuck away from me!" she yelled as she smacked his hand away. It came out as a hoarse whisper, since her windpipe and vocal cords were injured.

She knew it was going to bruise. He'd literally been squeezing the life out of her.

"What the fuck, Faunus?!" she yelled, only to go into a coughing fit. Her lungs stung with each intake of breath.

She fell onto her backside a small distance away from him. Her features were twisted into an expression of disgust and disbelief.

"I'm sorry. I didn't mean to hurt you," he responded, like his damn apology was enough! "You startled me when you touched my face."

"That still doesn't give you the right." She rubbed at her throat to feel it swelling already. "Either explain yourself or get out."

Faunus was shaking all over her. His trembling hands reached towards her before pulling back. His orbs were whiter than she'd ever seen them.

She didn't care. Nothing permitted anyone to choke another person. He was a Duskwalker. She wasn't blind to the dangers she faced – and that was part of what turned her on.

He'd warned her of blood, so if he attacked her for that reason, she could forgive him. Especially since he'd openly explained it would mean he wouldn't be in control. His hunger took over his mind, clouding it so completely that he'd eat anything and everything in sight.

But this? There had been no blood. She'd done nothing more than tenderly stroke his face.

She hadn't deserved it.

"I... thought you were someone else," he said weakly. His snout pointed to the ground when he looked down, his position on his knees utterly defeated. "I was confused. You know I would never intentionally hurt you."

"Not good enough."

Something had obviously happened to him in the past, but she wasn't going to be some choking pole for his trauma. She had her own baggage, and she refused to take it out on him, or anyone, for that matter.

She wouldn't allow a human to do this to her. Actually, she was more likely to chop a man's nutsack off or punch a woman's pubic bone if one dared to lay a hand on her – he would be given no wiggle room on this without a good explanation.

He was silent, his fangs opening and closing. Then he turned his face towards her... and she knew. He didn't need to wear skin for her to know.

He's not going to tell me.

"Get out," she said, gesturing with her nose at the door. "Get out and don't come back. If you can't even respect me enough to give me an explanation, then I don't want you here. Don't protect me anymore, don't watch me anymore. Go somewhere else."

Her own words made her heart clench. She didn't want him to leave. Just a few minutes ago, she was thinking about how much she wanted him to stay, but she wouldn't budge on this – even if it was heart-wrenching for herself.

"Mayumi..." he pleaded.

"No."

His orbs turned a swallowing colour of blue, and he clawed at the left side of his chest between his rib bones. He sliced deep enough that purple blood welled between his fingers.

"It is hard for me to explain." His following whine revealed he meant emotionally. "And I don't want you to think of me as weak."

With her chest heaving, she shook her head.

"I won't, I promise." She wasn't going to go comfort him through it, though. Not after what he'd done. She may have before, may have cooed while snuggling into him to make it easier, but she wasn't going to give him that. "But if you don't tell me, I want you gone."

More blood welled as he dug deeper. She knew his hand was right over his heart, that he was having a physical reaction deep within. It seemed he was feeling what she was, but perhaps much worse.

"You touched my face. I told you not to do that." Her bottom lip fell when it sounded as though he was blaming her! "I felt you touch the crack."

"So that gives you the right?"

He shook his head.

"The person who did this to me," he said as he reached up to touch it, "also hurt me in other ways. I was reliving those memories when you woke me. I thought you were him, that is all."

Was this all she was going to get? Some stupid, vague answer, like always?

"What did he do?" she pressed, narrowing her gaze into a glare.

He shuffled back slightly, like he would rather leave than tell her. Yet, he let out a deep expire, his quaking worsening.

"There is a reason I don't like your fireplace or your bath."

She remained silent. She was hoping he wasn't trying to tell her what she thought he was.

"He was trying to figure out how to kill Duskwalkers. And, because I was foolish enough to stay within the centre of the Veil, he decided to target me in particular. I had no home. Demons had come and claimed my cave when I left it for too long. I had nowhere else to go but try to live among them, even though they were distrustful of me. I was by myself the first time he caught me since I never thought he'd come for me. When I continued to live among them, the Demons assisted him the second time. I was only able to escape with the help of Magnar."

"What did he do to you, Faunus?" she repeated.

"The better question would be what *didn't* he do," he chuckled darkly. "Drowned me to see how many times I would breathe again under the water. Buried me to see if I would claw my way out of the dirt. Dissected me. Poisoned me. Envenomed me. Cut off my head. Burned me alive until I withered away into dust and all that remained of me was my skull."

Mayumi didn't think her face had ever drained of colour this intensely before.

Pity pooled in her gut for him. She brought her gaze to the fireplace, unable to imagine being burned *alive* and then surviving to remember how that felt.

"I could not even save myself," he continued, the backs of his hands falling to the ground. A reddish pink lifted into his orbs, and she thought that may signal his shame. "My mother had to help me. She is so small, just like you, but she has strong magic. She was able to fight him off and steal my skull, carrying it under her arm so she could flee with me." His snout pointed the other way. "I was... not myself for quite some time. She helped ease me."

"Faunus," she whispered, going to her hands and knees so she could crawl closer.

It all made sense. This she could forgive. This was a big enough reason to be disorientated when waking up.

"Don't!" he yelped, leaping away from her before she could even place her hand on his forearm. "You promised, and I don't want your pity."

"Hey, hey. It's okay. I don't think you're weak," she cooed while gingerly slipping her hands into his. "I'm actually pretty proud of you. A human would have lost their mind after experiencing something like that. Yet, other than being a little wary of a few things, you still laugh. That's not weakness, Faunus. That's strength."

"But I couldn't save myself," he stated, allowing her to pick up his hand so she could wrap it around her waist. "And the memories linger. They caused me to hurt you, Mayumi. How can I protect you if I cannot do so from myself?"

She lifted his other hand and placed it over her shoulder, curling into him as she slipped her arms around his torso. Mayumi hugged him.

"I can protect myself. Now that I know this, I'll be more careful in the future."

It took him a few seconds, but he eventually picked her up and placed her on his thighs to hold her tightly. He even pressed the underneath of his jaw across the back of her neck and head from behind.

"But you should've told me. This could have been avoided if I'd known what that crack on your skull meant for you. I wouldn't have touched it while you were having a nightmare."

A gasp escaped from her when the burning sensation around her throat dissipated within the span of a breath. She touched her neck.

"I'm sorry." The blue had faded to a different colour, one she hadn't seen before. His orbs were a bright orange. "I have taken your wound so that you don't have to suffer it, but I should not have needed to." He squeezed her tighter. "Perhaps... I should sleep outside from now on."

"No," she snapped while pointing her index finger at his face. "I like waking up to you surrounding me."

He tenderly caressed her cheekbone with the fore knuckle of his index finger. "Are you sure?"

With how quickly he'd changed his mind, she figured he'd never really wanted to sleep outside by himself.

"Yes. Only if you tell me who did this to you."

His hand stilled. She thought he was going to avoid answering, but then he sighed and brushed his claws into her hair.

His voice was sorrowful as he said, "His name is Jabez, and he is the Demon King."

TWENTY-FOUR

Faunus moved his snout to scan the clearing in front of Mayumi's home as his sight moved over the surrounding forest, the blanket of snow, and the brightening sky above. He was sitting on her porch, one leg crossed under him while the other lay down the steps, the backs of his hands limp in his lap.

It was midmorning, which was relatively early for them.

Mayumi tended to stay up past the middle of the night and into the early morning, even before they'd begun to become entangled during it. For Faunus, who didn't sleep many hours, this was a benefit.

He'd only needed to adjust his own sleeping habits minutely to match hers.

When he'd asked her why she did this, she explained the way of life for a Demonslayer was to be active when their prey was moving and out in the open.

Usually, Faunus woke when she did, allowing her movements to jolt him awake, but on this day, he'd risen by himself with his orbs a deep blue. He hadn't slept. The heavy weight in his chest was even more crushing than usual, and laying by her side had not eased him.

I told her what happened to me.

He'd never wanted to.

Regardless of what she said and how she'd attempted to reassure and comfort him, he'd felt no better about it.

He was thankful that the newer memories he'd acquired were of her. Her little cries of pleasure and her brutish laugh. Her enrapturing, crinkling brows and her humour-filled grin. The raking of her nails down his back and her soft touch against his large hands.

Her laughter was as enchanting as the magic he could produce, seeming almost impossible and yet real. Her scent was a dozy aroma, one that had his mind lulling but also had his body stirring – he was truly enthralled by it.

None of this erased what had happened to him.

He still remembered his lungs filling with water, burning him from the inside out in a cold wetness before his mind faded from this world. Only to expel that water suddenly and wake the following day still immersed below the suffocating liquid, breathing it in again, watching his own bubbling breaths hit some untouchable surface from below and make it ripple.

The way dirt had filled his mouth and nose hole was a different kind of agony. To be *blocked* from the places he needed freedom the most was haunting. To eat dirt, just so he could uselessly take another breath and fail – only to wake up again, healed, and instantly choke.

Her touch couldn't remove the echoing linger of the blade that stabbed through his flesh while he was awake or his dense and difficult bones being broken, just for Jabez to show him his own beating heart.

But the worst of all... the one memory that was just as searing as he remembered it was the flames. To feel his fur singe his own flesh before the fire truly took hold. To feel his muscles and blood boiling before he began to burn and melt.

They were the freshest, and they were the most damaging to his mind. He couldn't forget the agony of it, no matter how he tried.

Those memories of fire were the ones he dreamed of the most. They were the ones that caused him to hurt her.

His apology did *nothing* to erase the shame, guilt, and disappointment at realising his own clawed hand had been clasping her small and delicate throat. He'd been squeezing her, her face blistering red – and although not pleading, it had been filled with a glare.

A new nightmare to have.

He'd explained things further since she'd asked him to, but he'd never intended to share these things with her.

Not just because he was ashamed he hadn't been able to save himself, but because he just hadn't wanted her to know he was tormented. His time with her could be short. He didn't want it to be filled with anything painful.

After she'd fallen asleep, Faunus had tried to ease his own aching mind and heart by petting her cheek, neck, and hair, but his whirring thoughts refused to stop turning.

He'd chosen to come outside and watch the world brighten, knowing the number of times he'd see it was lessening by the day.

Faunus wasn't used to being so solemn or sorrowful. He once believed his orbs were yellow because he'd been easy to make laugh or curious. It was only after the Demon King trapped and tortured him inside that inescapable room that Faunus had changed. It could only be opened from the outside.

Things only worsened when he realised his own doom was lingering above his head like a cloud after the day Jabez had cracked his skull with his thumb claw.

He grazed his fingertips over the bone of his eye socket. *The crack hasn't extended since I returned.*

It was sturdy, still strong, but for how much longer?

He worried he'd fall apart at any moment.

Faunus turned his hands over in his lap to stare down at his claws with hunched shoulders.

She told me to leave. She'd given him an ultimatum. Of course he'd chosen the path that would allow him to remain by her side, but the fact she'd uttered it... he felt as though he meant little to her.

He understood enough to know *why* she had. He wasn't so disillusioned and underdeveloped in his humanity to be blinded by the truth. But it seemed her feelings were so lacking towards him that she had come to the decision easily.

All he'd seen was anger and not even a shred of remorse that he may be gone because of her words.

Her body heated and yearned for his. Her heart, however, seemed as cold as the steel he'd seen her wield.

She is like a rose.

Like its petals, she could be soft and malleable. Like its scent, she could be intoxicating and rich. She was just as beautiful, if not more so.

But she could also be as sharp and cruel as thorns.

He had to be careful. Otherwise, he could hurt himself. Her affections could also wither just as fast as the flowering bud above its dangerous stem.

Vicious but delicate, that's what Mayumi was to him.

With every step he took towards her, the more he felt like she firmly held a sword that he would willingly drive into his own chest.

Thinking about this, about his past, about her, his heart hurt in ways he'd never imagined possible. *I don't want to leave her.*

He turned his gaze up to follow a bird that circled above. It flew away just as he noted quick, thudding footsteps.

"Faunus?!" He heard Mayumi's panicked shout before she'd even reached the door of her home. It flew open with a loud *bang* against the wall.

With his skull already looking over his shoulder in her direction, whatever tension she had in her body eased at seeing him there.

She was naked other than the blanket she'd thrown around her shoulders. She often used it to cover the parts of her he was unable to shelter in his warmth at night.

"What is wrong?" he asked, only tilting his head because her complexion was paler than normal.

Her light, fawny colour returned swiftly to glow in the morning light.

"I thought you left," she answered with a croaked voice, revealing she'd woken up with a start and immediately bolted to the door.

She was alert but wobbly, as though she'd only just been lying down. There were even impression lines across one of her cheeks from it lying against the back of her own hand.

"I told you I would remain here."

That hadn't changed because of what he'd told her. The only way he'd leave was if she was to take another male and have his sexual scent all over her. He would never stop Mayumi from doing what she wanted, but he *knew* he would be unable to contain his outrage and jealousy in her presence.

Currently, in spirit, she was his female. He'd marked his territory, and he would feel the need to defend it. Especially since he had no other to fight for.

She was all he had left in the world.

"Yeah, but I thought–" Mayumi rubbed at the side of her neck while giving a pout and looking off to the side. "It doesn't matter. Why are you outside?"

Dropping the blanket from her shoulders, she walked past him.

"Why? Did you miss me?" he asked, forcing himself to chuckle despite his despondency.

She turned her nose up at him. "I was cold."

Then she flung herself out into the snow.

She squeaked when her entire body sunk into it, and he immediately watched her flesh turn pink and prickle. Her cute, perky arse was showing for him. With a swipe of his tongue across his snout, he thought about how he'd like to rewarm it for her. It was firm, and he liked holding it, touching it, nibbling at it.

Faunus often had to force down the urge to bite at her. And not just a delicate little nibble either, but he wanted to sink his fangs into her – show her supple body that he was the master of it. That he could give it both pleasure and playful pain if he wanted to.

He couldn't, as it would be disastrous if he were to taste even a drop of her blood. He often held his breath if he even smelt a small fraction of it – except when he'd changed her body to take his.

He'd been distracted by more pressing desires rather than hunger at the time.

Although she preferred to drink her tea, he'd watched Mayumi do this morning routine many times. Usually, she rose from the bitter cold within seconds. This time, face down, she groaned into it.

"*Ughhh.* I'm so tired."

His heated thoughts died when he realised he'd been the cause of a troubled sleep for her.

When Mayumi returned inside, she debated whether to bathe in the outside spring bathtub or to wipe them down with a bucket of water and a cloth. She decided just to wipe them down.

I wouldn't want to face something I'm wary of after revealing why. After she calmed down from initially thinking Faunus had left, she still found it alarming that he'd been outside by himself.

Usually, Faunus would stay asleep until she woke, or at least continue to hold her until she did. He seemed fond of holding her, and she often woke to him caressing her skin from her forehead all the way to her thigh some mornings.

She didn't know how Duskwalkers processed trauma. If it was anything like a human, she imagined it would be a difficult undertaking – especially considering the severity of it.

Now that she understood why he always placed himself as far from the fire as possible or looked into it seemingly mesmerised, it made her heart radiate with a tender ache. He'd been exposing himself to things he hated or was fearful of, just for... her.

He must care about me a lot, she thought as she wiped down his torso and thighs after already cleaning her own body.

He'd offered to do it himself like he did every time she came at him with liquid soap in her hands while in the tub, but she wanted to do this. She liked touching him. It was as though she was worshipping him in more ways than just sexually.

She considered it aftercare to show she cared too. *A lot.*

Okay, maybe more than a lot, but Mayumi wasn't used to feeling anything for another. People were just in the world to die at some point, and there were so many complications when it came to having a relationship with a human.

He's a Duskwalker, though. To entertain the idea of an actual relationship with him was absurd.

And yet, here she was, contemplating it as she wiped him with long and passionate strokes. It would be just as complicated to form something more solid with him, but perhaps not in the ways she'd noticed within humankind.

Pulling her gaze away from his strong, bulky, muscular chest, Mayumi lifted it to his face. His orbs were yellow and already watching her. Usually, they would have started turning purple by now since she was rubbing his seam. They were both naked, as they often were together, but he just twisted his head at her when she paused.

Is it wrong of me to have feelings for him? Something had shattered inside when he told her about what happened to him.

She'd needed him to be vulnerable. She'd needed to know he'd faced hardships, to understand what it meant to feel pain and sadness.

Faunus had finally revealed something about *himself.*

He already knew so much about her, but up until last night, she only knew of him as a Duskwalker. He'd never revealed where he lived, what area of the Veil he'd come from, what he'd been doing.

She'd known nothing because he often hid things from her.

In knowing more about Faunus, she felt closer to him. Mayumi could share her body with anyone, but her inner thoughts and feelings were often kept deep within.

Staring up at him, she couldn't help the way her heart blossomed with such beautiful warmth that she found herself reaching up to cup his jaw. She paused when she was almost there.

He's told me he doesn't like his face touched. Yet, she'd done it whenever she wanted, not understanding why he was against it until now.

Just when she was about to pull away, Faunus leaned closer. He placed the front of his skull against her hands, letting her brush over everything, including the crack in it.

"I want your touch," he admitted, placing both his hands over hers to keep them pressed down on the hard bone. "I have always wanted it."

"You said it hurts," she grumbled, pushing upwards so she could pet it.

"It does, but only if you aren't gentle."

Faunus pulled his hands away and let her pet him however

she wanted, and she made sure to only use the softer underside of her hands. His orbs eventually turned black, and a bubbling purr began to emit from his chest.

The sound made her skin rush with goosebumps. She placed her forehead against the cushion of his chest and the hardness of the bones encasing it.

When he purrs, it does funny things to my insides.

"Mayumi?" his tone was filled with confusion and concern, probably because she'd been palming his face for so long.

She cleared her throat and leaned back.

"Can I brush you?" She let out an awkward laugh as she looked sideways to avoid his gaze, wondering why she found that more embarrassing than all the times they'd touched intimately. "Your fur is really soft, but I imagine it would be even fluffier if I worked all the knots out of it."

Faunus' large hand cupped the side of her face and under her jaw, steering her back to look at him. "You may touch me however you like."

And just like that, the iron-clad barrier around her heart tried to melt under the power of his words – his trust.

Her smile was the only reflection of the internal, girlish squeal of delight she wanted to release. She quickly fumbled to find her hairbrush, and before long, she was brushing it through his fur across his back.

As a reward, she pressed her lips against the very back of his skull. Her smile only deepened when he brushed his claws over that spot before turning his head one hundred and eighty degrees to look at her with them a brighter yellow than usual.

Mayumi grabbed his head and turned it forward because it was a little freaky that he was able to rotate it to the point there seemed to be no twist in his neck. It was similar to how she'd seen birds rotate their necks, and she wasn't fond of them doing it either.

Speaking of birds... she eyed the empty birdcage she had in her home.

The reason she'd released her messenger pigeon last night wasn't because Faunus had a tendency to stare at it – warning her she might find it eaten at some point. She'd released it because she'd tied a very long, detailed letter to its foot and sent it to Hawthorne Keep.

She informed them of what Faunus had told her last night about the Veil, the Demon King, the Demon Village, and everything else she could think of that might be of use. She never wrote who gave her the information or how she'd come to obtain it, but she thought it was important that they know it.

She'd considered detailing everything she'd learned about Duskwalkers, although she still didn't know how to kill one, but she left that out. It wasn't just because of him. The rest of his kind were his family, and it felt... wrong to share that information with those that would be considered their enemies.

She only shared what she learnt of the Demons and the Veil.

Brushing Faunus' fur all over made him super soft, glossy, and fluffy, and Mayumi eventually found herself nuzzling into it once she was done. It was like a cloud of heaven that tickled her in the most blissful way.

I could do this every day... No, she *was* going to do this every day. She was going to brush him and then snuggle all that fur until her heart was bleeding with contentment.

Mayumi pulled back once she was done hugging him.

"Do you want to help me clear the snow from the yard?" Mayumi asked, rather than demanding it of him.

It was a big task, but she was hoping it would be a good distraction.

When he agreed to help, Mayumi gave him the bigger, square-mouthed shovel, and they both worked on clearing the immediate area around the house. It was at least three feet thick, but Faunus was fast.

When they were done around the shed and bath, they worked their way down the sides towards the front clearing. It was there, however, that Mayumi got a bright idea.

While his back was facing her, she scrunched up a ball of snow in her hand and pegged it at his arse. She pretended to look busy by shovelling when he looked over his shoulder at her. She made sure her back was to him so he wouldn't see that she was stifling a laugh.

The second time she did it, she had two balls. One to peg him in the back with, and the other to hit him in the chest when he turned around.

She expected him to collect his own snowball.

Instead, his orbs turned blue as he asked, "Why are you throwing things at me? Have I upset you?"

He turned his face this way and that, most likely examining all the hard work he'd done so far – which was far more than her. Bending over, she collected more snow and formed a ball.

"It's called a snowball fight," she said while taking a wider stance.

"I don't want to fight with you, Mayumi."

She couldn't help rolling her eyes.

"It's a game where people throw snow at each other while dodging. The person who hits the other the most wins!" She threw it at him, and he watched it fly across the clearing and explode against his dense chest. "Are you competitive, Faunus? Because I am, and I believe I'm four hits ahead of you."

"You... wish to play a game with me?" His orbs flashed a bright colour of yellow.

They'd played many games over the course of the last week. They'd been limited to board games, but she thought this might be more energising.

However, she'd made a mistake. A *very* big mistake. Faunus collected snow to make a ball... and it was the size of her fucking head. It was a snow-boulder.

Oh shit! She ducked when he threw it, practically diving to the side and falling flat on her face.

"You've gotta make them smaller, Faunus!" she squealed when he collected another ball and chased her with it.

She hid behind a tree just before he launched it, hearing her far too late. The tree shook, and white power fell from the branches above to land over her shoulders and head.

Mayumi didn't mind if she got a little hurt in the process. Not when Faunus let out a deep chuckle when she emerged covered in snow while irately wiping it off.

"That counts as a hit," he stated, while laughing and pointing a claw in her direction. "I still made snow fall on you."

Puffing her cheeks, Mayumi quickly reached down and made

the biggest snowball she'd ever made. It was still one-quarter the size of his. Then she swiftly parted her legs with a stomp and raised her arm.

He did the same, preparing himself. The moment she stepped forward to throw it, Faunus bolted to escape. It missed him.

As he was running, he easily swiped up snow and made a ball.

At least it was smaller because she wasn't prepared for it when he suddenly turned and threw it at her. It was a gentle toss, and for that she was thankful as it immediately put her on her arse.

"That's two," he pointed out.

Her eyes bowed as she winced and sat up, digging her hands into the snow. "Ah. Ow! I think I broke something."

His orbs immediately turned white. He bolted for her.

"Did I hurt you? I should have been more careful." He slowly crouched around her and gingerly reached his hands out. "I'm sor–"

Before he could finish, Mayumi tossed a small ball of snow she'd formed in her hand while it was hidden. Her laughter echoed in the clearing as she got to her feet and ran.

"You little liar!"

Mayumi was only chased a few steps before she was tackled. Faunus twisted them as they fell, and they both landed on their sides, so she wasn't crushed beneath his gigantic, heavy frame.

The giggle that came from Mayumi was so light and carefree that she couldn't remember the last time she'd released something like it.

"That was cheating, Mayumi," Faunus lightly growled, which only made her giggle more.

"We didn't state any rules. It was a free-for-all." In retaliation, he scooped up a large handful of snow and dumped it on her head, partially burying her for a split second. "I still won!"

Faunus dug his arms around her and squeezed her into his body. "That was fun," he said. "I have not played in a long time."

"You've played games like this with others?" she asked once she'd pulled her head free.

"Yes. I played with the twins any chance we came across each other. I think they would enjoy playing this *snowball fight* with me."

A flicker of blue lifted into his orbs. She knew she saw it, even if it was gone in the blink of an eye.

Something is making him sad. Which she thought would have been impossible after the way they'd just laughed.

She crawled to lie on top of him with her legs straight and over his. She leaned her elbow on his chest and placed her chin in her hand. "Well, why don't you show it to them?"

"I am here with you, Mayumi," he quickly answered, raising his hands so he could brush his claws through her ponytail. "I cannot show them without leaving."

That caused her to pout. "I guess that's true."

Then he reached down, and from the backs of her thighs, his warm hands glided up her body, over her sides, shoulder blades, and then back down. He let out a sigh when he must have noticed the colour of the sky.

"It is growing dark. If you wish to finish clearing the yard before then, we must resume."

Mayumi shrugged. "We can do that tomorrow. It's not like it matters when it gets done."

After contemplating her words, he let out a single snort of laughter. "You like lying on me."

He was bigger than most single beds she'd laid on! And he was warm and comfortable. Of course she liked lying on him.

Mayumi reached up and petted his skull like she'd always wanted to, from the middle of his forehead all the way down to his snout. Although she avoided the crack, she danced her fingertips over the rest of the cool bone. His orbs went black as he leaned into her touch.

He's magnificent.

There were so many aspects of him she adored. His face, his body, those big sexy claws and fangs, but she also found his personality incredible. Who else in the world could say they'd had a snowball fight with a Duskwalker?

He was thoughtful and yet could be so dangerously playful that it was hard not to... fall for that aspect. He was naughty, and his experience from watching humans made him almost devilish at times, but he was also so considerate.

Sure, there were times he appeared baffled by what she said or did, but he was so quick to adjust that half the time, she barely registered it.

He lets me be myself.

Mayumi had never been comfortable just being herself with another. A grown adult conducting herself in snowball fights and bossy tantrums and whorish body thrusts received judgement from many others. With Faunus, she never had to worry about any of that.

He accepted Mayumi as she was. Hot and cold, messy and clean.

There was just one thing she was uncertain of.

"Faunus, would you let me hunt Demons?" She wasn't looking for permission. She wanted to know what he'd say, especially after the last time they'd spoken about this.

His gliding claws paused in the middle of her spine.

"It matters little what I say on the subject," Faunus stated, already knowing her better than most. "But I would prefer if you allowed me to do so with you. I would not interfere unless you asked me to since I know this is something that matters to you, but I would like to make sure you don't come to harm."

Mayumi buried her forehead against his chest while gripping the soft fur covering it.

That's all she could ever ask for.

There had been a lingering worry that he would try to get in the way since he was here to 'protect her.' She'd been wondering if he would try to stop her from doing something so dangerous, but hearing he would not interfere had her melting on the inside.

"I like you," she muttered against his pectoral muscle. It was more than just a childish crush, but she'd never been good at expressing her deeper feelings.

She knew she was deeply infatuated with him.

"Yes, I know this," Faunus chuckled as he grazed his claws over her scalp, down the edge of her jaw, and lifted her chin. "You like it when I ride you."

"That's not what I mean." She sighed as she lifted herself to straddle his chest. "I mean I like you, and I want you to stay here with me."

He tilted his head in obvious puzzlement, which was something he didn't do often. "I am already staying here with you."

Ugh! Why was this so damn hard?

"I mean like... fuck, I don't know." She gripped the side of her head. "It'd be weird calling you a boyfriend since you're a Duskwalker, but basically the equivalent of that?"

A fuckbuddy was one thing. That was just sex without emotion, but she wanted more from Faunus.

"I will be whatever you want me to be, Mayumi. I have heard that term before. I know it means something more than what we are doing now." He scratched the tip of his claw at the side of his snout. "But wouldn't you want something like this from another human?"

Despite his show of awkwardness, she thought it might be half-false, considering his orbs turned a brighter yellow rather than a glow of reddish pink to highlight a Duskwalker 'blush.'

"People are complicated," she groaned while letting her head fall back, feeling the strain up the column of her throat. "I have dated both men and women, and they annoy the absolute shit out of me. Someone cheats while I'm gone, another just wants my money or protection, and then there are the few who have all these emotions. As much as I've tried, I've just never been able to be myself. I'm supposed to be solemn and think about the cruelty in the world. Don't get me wrong, I do that a lot, but sometimes I just want to have fun for the hell of it. But you're the kind of person I don't have to hide any of who or what I want from. Do you know how freeing that is?"

"I am not a person, Mayumi." His tone was almost bitter.

Mayumi dropped her head forward. "You are to me. You have an identity. It's just unique."

Faunus pinched her cheek and pulled on it. "I find your strangeness cute," he admitted. "No other human would ever be like this with me. It's odd that you are."

He was right, and she knew it too.

She let herself fall until her hands were buried in the snow above his backward curling ram horns, her hair flicking down one side of her face.

"So how about it?" she asked with a grin.

His arms fell into the snow as he rolled his skull and let it fall to the side. He sounded exasperated as he said, "If we must."

The bastard is making it out as if he doesn't want to!

She would have smacked him in the chest, but she knew he was just poking fun at her. He was lucky she was really fond of him.

Jerk.

TWENTY-FIVE

After waking up and begrudgingly crawling to her feet, Mayumi made it about halfway to her front door before a strong arm wrapped around her waist and tugged. She let out a surprised squawk as she fell backwards – into a set of large arms and a warm lap.

She'd thought she'd managed to get up without waking Faunus, but she guessed not.

One of his hands clasped the outside of her bare thigh to hold her to him while the other cradled the side of her neck and jaw.

"Why do you do this?" he asked as he nuzzled his jaw against her cheek. His voice was even more gravelly than normal, considering it was groggy and sleep filled.

"Do what?" she asked back while lifting her chin, allowing him to pet her however he wanted.

"Why do you throw yourself into the snow?"

Since their conversation yesterday, Faunus seemed to be even more affectionate with her. He purred and rubbed against her a little more often.

She did it back, allowing herself to be pampered.

"I struggle to wake up fully, especially in winter." Her eyelids lowered in laziness as she took in his warmth. She still wasn't fully awake, and he was threatening to pull her back under, even now. "I've been doing it since the guild. If I didn't have tea, I'd throw myself into the snow to become alert. Otherwise, I walk around with half a brain for the first hour of my day."

"Don't you have tea?"

"No. I used the last of it two days ago. I forgot to buy more the last time I went to Colt's Outpost."

He purred, not only from his throat but also from his chest. "You could always wake up on my cock."

He was growing more nefarious by the day. She was cheering him headlong into it, hoping he would become more fiendish in this sensual way.

A burst of laughter erupted from her. "You could always wake me with it. I wouldn't mind waking up mid-orgasm."

His vibrating rhythm died as he reared his head back to look down at her. "I cannot do that, Mayumi. You wouldn't be awake. That... that doesn't seem right."

Mayumi carefully lifted both hands to touch the side of his snout, a smile curling her lips.

"It is if I give you prior permission, which I'm giving you now." That smile turned into a grin. "Plus, you've kind of already done it."

A flash of reddish pink lifted into his orbs before they settled back to normal. "That was an accident."

She knew it was, but that didn't mean she wouldn't tease him about it.

Although Faunus often had small, fleeting nightmares, he also had lusty dreams too. Mayumi had woken a few times to his cock thrusting against her, and once inside her, both of them completely asleep before she was eventually woken. Of course, she'd taken full advantage of the situation.

It was nice to know she was sexually haunting his dreams.

"Let's call it a happy accident." Mayumi playfully hummed as she moved to crawl over his lap to face him. Her knees were on his folded ones, forcing Faunus to support all her weight. "You enjoyed yourself afterwards." Mayumi then leaned closer with her hands on his wide shoulders, ducking her head down the side of his to whisper where she thought he might hear from. "It was all nice and slow, and you purred the whole time."

The thick, long fur around his neck stood on end and his fangs parted as he let out an expire through them.

She liked that it was so easy to give him this kind of reaction, even with only a few words spoken in a breathy, light voice.

Faunus slipped the sharp points of his claws from under her arse and teased up to the middle of her spine. She arched into it when he said, "If you want to get up today, I warn that you should watch what you say to me."

This time, Mayumi gave a thoughtful hum that had an undertone of coyness. Slipping her hands from his shoulders to run them down his chest, over the fur and bones there, she leaned even closer.

"You've already told me I can wake myself up by playing with you." With her front teeth, she nipped at his neck just behind the corner of his jaw. She didn't mind the fur, not when the action caused him to stiffen in what she hoped was delight. "And I'm not still fully awake yet, Faunus."

Did they already have sex last night? Yes. Was Mayumi filled with seed already? Also yes, although she'd begun to wipe them down when they were done in order to lessen the need for a full bath in the morning. Did Mayumi mind that she was a little tender and tired? Not one bit.

One of the reasons Mayumi struggled with most partners was that they could rarely keep up with her libido. She often used exercise to curb her sexual needs, but she didn't have to do that with Faunus.

He seemed to be more insatiable than her.

The moment Faunus began releasing what she *cutely* nicknamed a *purrowl*, a growl and a purr at the same time, she knew her little hook had been bitten, and she had a big fish on the line to tame.

When his hands gripped the back of her thighs with the intention of lifting her, most likely to place her on the ground, Mayumi raised her hand. She tapped the side of her index finger against the very tip of his snout.

"However, I want to do it my way." She tangled her fingers together behind his thick neck. "I want you to lay back."

Faunus huffed his displeasure, which only made her lips quirk. "Why do I have to lean back? I thought you liked it when I rode you."

For some reason, Mayumi always found herself against the ground. Whether it was on her knees or stomach or on her back, it was always Mayumi the one being ridden. Faunus liked being in control.

It was her turn.

Faunus clicked his tongue within his mouth. "Are you planning to ride my tongue again? We haven't done that since the very first time." He glided his hand under her thighs to caress them, eliciting a shiver down her legs. "I did like it when you came in my mouth like that."

"That might be on the agenda," she said, even though it wasn't. "But I want to do something else first."

Mayumi had different plans, and she wasn't ready to spill what they were.

"This should be exciting," Faunus purred as he released her thighs and laid back, uncrossing his legs to lay them straight. He folded his arms behind his head so he could watch her.

She couldn't help thinking he looked rather self-important right now, which was how he always looked when lying down.

I want to scramble his damn brain.

She sat back on her ankles, still completely kneeling on his thighs, and licked at the seam of her lips. His tail curled before resting against the ground, and it only added to the vision of him.

Just looking at the feast of a Duskwalker before her, her groggy mind was already a little more alert. Excitement was beginning to throb in all the delicate places on her body.

Yet, the first thing Mayumi did was plant her face against his chest and start rubbing it against him.

"Why is your fur so damn soft?" she asked, taking in its utter softness and his intoxicating smell up close. "It just makes me want to constantly be buried against you."

Leaning on her elbows, she eventually nuzzled herself to the side until her lips brushed against his flat nipple. It was dark grey in colour, much like the rest of his skin that she could see – like his stomach and hands. It was darker, though, and she grazed her tongue over the one she'd been caressing with her lips to see if he liked it.

She eyed him as she did, and his orbs instantly switched to purple. The colour deepened when she bit at it before sucking.

"That feels... strange." His tail wrapped around her thigh to tug her back so she would release it.

When she did, he removed one hand from behind his head and flicked his own nipple in curiosity before putting it back. It had been a new sensation for him, and she figured he wasn't quite sure how he felt.

She'd try again later.

Unbothered by his fur, she bit the top of his pectoral muscle where it was longer before biting the lower part where it was shorter. Then she just kissed her way down until she was slipping between his thighs, and he had to part for her.

"What are you doing, Mayumi?" he asked when her knees were firmly against the ground.

Thankful she'd stolen his pants days ago and hidden them, the tips of her fingers glided over where his seam was. She thought it was adorable when it gave a restraining clench inward under her touch.

"What do you think?"

In all this time of Faunus being here, she'd never gotten the chance to just play with him. She'd seen it, stroked his cock, and held it with her hands, but Faunus was always trying to get something inside of her – whether it be his fingers, tongue, or cock.

She'd tasted his yummy lubricant on her fingers before, but now she wanted to nibble at it from the source.

Leaning forward, she ran her tongue from the bottom of his seam all the way to the top. "Open up, Faunus."

She blinked when the tip of a tentacle wriggled to get free, before curling around her finger when she brought it closer. Then his seam parted, his cock slipping forward, unsheltered by the four limbs that usually encompassed it protectively.

Faunus was by no means a grower.

What came out of him was the same length it always was, and its thickness only swelled slightly. The only difference was that it was still partially soft when usually it was hard as it came out.

It was a strong lavender colour, not a very dark purple, but not light either. Mayumi held it by its thick base and ran her thumb up the side, feeling his spongy spikes move under the pad of it.

Watching her silently, Faunus allowed her to take her time. She knew he was enjoying himself from how quickly it hardened, though, going from being floppy against his abdomen to jutting.

His wriggling tentacles were a much darker purple on the smooth outside, threatening to be a few shades from black, but the spikey insides were the same colour as his shaft. These spikes often became rigid around her hips, but they never grew sharp enough to cut her.

She gave two of the limbs her left hand to tangle with as she glided her right up his big, magnificent cock. His lubricant spread, glistening and wet. It was fat, and when she brought her other hand up to cup the other side, both couldn't contain its girth.

Mayumi bent forward so she could run her tongue over it.

Her eyelids flickered under the delicious onslaught of his lemongrass and lime scent straight on her tongue. It was diluted, but it ensured she started salivating. Faunus' fangs parted slightly on an exhale, his cock swelling in reaction.

Coming down the other side, Mayumi lathered kisses over every single spike on his cock. They weren't uniform, dotting him here and there.

It's amazing that this fits inside me, she thought as she brought her hands up from the base to halfway. She swirled her tongue at the broad head, the spikes around the rim bigger here.

Although it looked proportional to his body, not too long or thick against him, against her own size, it looked... ginormous. The fact she could take it all the way to the hilt was impossible. Which, of course, it was without his gut-rearranging magic.

She hummed in satisfaction at that reminder.

As she moved her tongue, she noticed his abdomen muscles clenched and dipped. By the end of this, she wanted to see them dancing.

Mayumi mainly focused on the head while her hands slipped up and down the root of him, her thumbs gliding in the deep groove underneath. She occasionally came down to rub where she thought his semen might come from, two protruding ovals that clung to the base just past his seam.

The first time she did, he finally uncrossed his arms.

One stayed behind his head to support it with his fist bunched, while the other dug its claws into the ground. He had no idea what to do with his hands, and she would let him figure that out on his own.

"I wish I could fit you in my mouth," she said with a moan when her tongue finally got its first taste of dewy flavoured seed. She was thankful it wasn't that salty liquid she was used to. "You taste so good, I just wanna swallow you whole."

Mayumi pushed down hard, barely gaining even a fraction more of his cock inside her mouth. She wanted it deeper. So deep, in fact, that it was past the back of her mouth and down her throat.

Her teeth must be digging into the plump head, yet he didn't complain. Instead, he rasped, "Mayumi."

His free hand came up to pat over the top of her hair before he removed it like he thought it wasn't a good idea. The fact he could cover the back of her entire head with his hand was awesome, but she knew he could crush it with one wrong tense of his hand.

He wouldn't, even if he was uncertain, but that was something she adored about Faunus. He was unpredictable, dangerous, and strong, and yet he was so conscious about it she rarely hurt. Even if she was, like the numerous times he'd clawed her skin too deep, he would always heal her before she even noticed.

Her hands worked in unison with her mouth, going up and down, as did her head. Her tongue swirled before she dipped to the side to nibble at the rim.

Her tongue was constantly lapping up lubricant that continued to seep from him until it dripped over her hands. She was quick to collect any bubble of precum before it could drip. Her mind was fixated on the hot, hard, jutting, phallic piece of meat she was playing with.

She noticed his thighs twitched around her, his stomach waved and clenched, and his breaths were more panted. But she wanted more.

Exchanging positions, her hands moved higher while her mouth moved lower. Then she swiped her tongue over one of his embedded ovals as she squeezed the slightly pointed head.

"Fuck," he snarled, his voice so much more gravelly and distorted than normal.

He deeply clawed at his stomach as his hips lifted. Mayumi followed, twisting her head the other way to tease the left nut instead. She sucked on it, and his back bowed as his cock swelled in girth.

"Fuck. Stop, Mayumi." The needy tone was decadent to her senses.

"Why?" she asked directly against it, hoping he felt the movement of her lips and her breath.

"You're going to make me come."

His chest was heaving, and he finally placed his hand over her head, trying to push her away with the heel of it as she fought to keep herself there. When he started to win, she turned her head and bit at the fleshy part of his palm – hard. He retracted it.

"That's kind of the point, isn't it?"

Mayumi lapped at the right one again, feeling it clench under her tongue. She brought her hands down the length of his cock.

"I can't give you a proper blowjob unless you have more magic that can help me. I have to use what I've got." She sucked it for a moment, causing his entire body to flinch. "Just enjoy the ride."

Faunus became twitchy, especially when she worked between teasing the overly sensitive base and cock head with her mouth at different intervals. Her hands moved in the middle, always stroking him.

Then Mayumi squeaked when his tail came up to rub all along the slit of her pussy. She was sopping, which aided its glide, and the fur was so short there that it just felt soft.

"You're telling me to enjoy the ride," he lightly growled, causing her eyelids to flicker as she swirled her tongue around the head. "Yet I can smell how turned on you are. Are you doing this for me or for yourself?"

The answer was both, but she just looked up to meet his purple orbs with a smirk on her face.

Her nipples were hard and aching, as was her clit, but she wasn't touching herself on purpose. She was building her own anticipation.

Well... that had been her plan.

It was derailed when she found herself moaning against the

tip of his cock when he slipped his tail inside her pussy. It was thinner than his cock, and it felt more like a tease, but it was enough stimulation.

Mayumi spread her thighs and allowed it to move freely as she lathered his cock in kisses, nibbles, and licks. Her vision was dazed as her body just took control without thought.

Her hands moved fast, her mouth darting everywhere. Perhaps he thought it would be enough to slow her, perhaps even control her, but it just made her greedier, hungrier even.

Mayumi's movements became bolder as she moaned while bucking her hips into his tail.

Faunus' tentacles squirmed like they wanted to grip something, curling constantly. It became a battle when she knew he was growing close.

He removed the arm from behind his head and let his skull fall back, lowering his hand to let those limbs grasp his fingers to settle whatever aching need they had. His other hand was gripping her head in a cage of claws, subtly scraping against her scalp as she moved.

All his muscles spasmed, his hips beginning to dip and thrust. His tail continued to move inside her, but it lost its rhythm and motion.

His spikes hardened and sharpened, his cock swelling completely. She instantly pulled her hands away before she hurt them. Instead, she lowered them and cupped both sacs embedded into the underside of his cock. They were flatter than before, like they'd sunken in, and they throbbed heavily in her palms, hot to the touch.

Every panted breath from him was followed by a tiny whine.

If he wanted to speak, he seemed unable to as she rubbed his pulsating base and suckled the head. He gave an unhidden, bubbling groan.

Mayumi didn't pull away when the first burst of dewy-tasting seed spurted into her mouth. It was powerful as there was so much force behind it, yet she swallowed what she could and the two that followed. Then she gave up and just circled her tongue around the tip while spreading her lips back and forth over it.

"No. Too much," he half-snarled, half-groaned.

Is it because he's not used to movement while he comes?

That only made her go faster, cutting through the ropes of his seed with her tongue as they released.

Faunus fisted her hair and wrenched her head back. She dug her nails into his thighs to balance herself and take away the worst of the exquisite pain over her scalp.

His release splattered against her cheek, chin, and partially between her parted lips. She closed one eye when a rope of thick liquid came far too close to it.

Since she'd stopped swallowing and because he'd yanked her back, there was cum everywhere. It dripped from her face and covered his cock and seam completely. He released his tentacles, and they flicked white liquid all over himself and the floor.

He shuddered as he came, and she watched in delight at him becoming undone by her. She clenched around his tail as its thrusts matched each spurt, both the sight before her and it turning her on further. Her cheeks and chest flushed with deep arousal.

We made a huge mess now.

Well, there was going to be one anyway, but at least it had been controlled to dripping down all sides of his cock before.

"You're not allowed to do that again," Faunus rasped as he loosened the tension he had on her hair. His tail slipped from her, never giving her an orgasm but making sure she was primed for one.

She lowered her head and began giving appreciative kisses to his floppy dick, making his body spasm. She also held him with both hands, ensuring she got semen all over them as if she was playing with it – she *might* have been.

"Why not?" she hummed as she attempted to lick him clean with her frolicking tongue.

"Because it was so damn nice until I felt like you were trying to make me explode."

"You kind of did," she mocked.

His tentacles began swirling around his cock when it started to retreat. Panic struck her. Mayumi quickly climbed on top of him with her knees over his protruding hip bones and sat on his cock. She made sure it was nestled between the lips of her pussy and ground her clit against it.

"Hey, don't you dare," she threatened. "If you think we're done, you're mistaken. We've only just gotten started. I didn't even get to orgasm."

"I'm not what you humans call a *buffet*, Mayumi," Faunus rebuked with a chuckle. "I'm not endless."

"I didn't think you'd reach your limit so quickly with a measly half-blowjob."

She stabbed her elbows into his chest so she could lean her chin on her hands and grind into him.

"I came so hard my cock hurt."

"I did kiss it better," she retorted playfully.

"Barely." He turned his skull down to face her, his orbs a bright purple and reflecting that his irritation was nothing more than a façade. "You're a horrible, wretched human. How has any of your kind ever dealt with you?"

A smirk curled her lips. "They haven't, which is why they are no longer around. You're the first to have ever satisfied me completely."

His head twisted at that.

"Really?" His voice was filled with astonished pride before he gave a singular, dark laugh. Then he glided his claws over her arse just because he knew it always made her shiver. "Why am I not surprised? Fine then. Play with me until your little cunt can't take any more."

It wasn't like she was going to go give him much of a choice either way.

"Thank you." She crawled up his body and leaned down to kiss the tip of his snout. "That's very sweet of you. You're such a good boy."

When she pulled back, she licked at the seam of her lips to collect the rest of his seed there, knowing she'd left a kiss mark of it behind. Then she ducked her hand between them to lift his cock and mount the tip, having to wiggle her way back down to his hips since it was so long she couldn't have raised above it.

She winced a little at how her body always had to stretch despite him changing her. It seemed she was still just slightly too small for him, but Mayumi liked the sting, knowing that something unbelievably fat and long was opening her. It also forced her to feel every one of his spongy spikes slipping past her entrance.

Faunus hissed in a breath when his soft dick kinked in the middle before popping further in. "I'm not even erect yet, Mayumi."

Once she was seated all the way, she could feel her answering smile all the way in her eyes. "I want to feel you get hard inside me."

The chin of his bony snout was resting firmly against his chest. He was looking down to where they were connected, and already he was beginning to balloon in hardness within her. He was as excited about this as she was, which was made evident by how he licked at his snout with orbs deepening in their purple colour.

Incidentally, he removed the white kiss mark.

He was also releasing his strange *purrowl* again, and his big, rough, warm hands came to cup under her arse. He tried to thrust upwards, but with her on top of him, it did nothing but lift both his hips and her into the air.

Her smile grew more devilish. He wouldn't be able to control anything with his thrusts unless he lifted her with his hands.

TWENTY-SIX

The moment she started moving, Faunus' gaze trailed upward from where the lips of her folds were widely spread around his shaft. It trailed over the tentacles that gently rested just over the arches of her small hip bones, creating a vee just below her navel.

His gaze climbed higher as he watched a bulge moving, her body unable to completely contain his within hers. Then higher still to her small, pointy, and perky breasts jiggling every time she pushed forwards and backwards to stroke him inside.

He could see her muscles bunching and twitching. He felt her clenching as much as he saw it.

Finally, his sight fell on her lovely face. Her lips were parted so she could quietly moan – her cries progressively increasing until he knew she would eventually become a crescendo of them.

He'd always thought of a human's moans as uncontrolled and loud. He'd enjoyed them because they'd been erotic in their own way, but the song of Mayumi's lungs was somehow both lewd and so damn fucking cute – especially when her face would grow terribly flustered.

Even now, she already had a pink tinge over the bridge of her nose, and her bowing eyes grew more dazed the more she moved. She was staring at him; she unfailingly did.

If she wasn't facing him, he noticed she'd always find his reflection somewhere within her home.

He wished the vibration of both his growl and purr emitting at the same time didn't worsen when he connected his sight with hers. It was scratchy and almost painful, his chest and vocal cords doing two different actions simultaneously with the same parts of him.

It always made his breaths raspier, showing how needy he would become or how much he ached for her.

It didn't matter how many times they did this or how many times he witnessed this body in motion and bared to him. Faunus was enamoured by her. Every flex of muscle tantalised him just as much as the first time he'd seen it twitch.

Faunus tried to stifle his groan, but it echoed past his parted fangs as he panted at her.

Usually he pounded into her, desperate to fill her, desperate to make her mind frazzled with pleasure. To satisfy and please her as much as he could with every part of him he had available.

Anything in hopes she would always want more.

She wants me to stay. Her words and request to him yesterday had birthed a deeper feeling within his chest. He hadn't stopped thinking about it. *She likes me.* Not just his cock, but *him.* Just knowing that made his mind shudder with bliss as much as his body beneath hers.

He caressed his hands over her until one was palming her chest, rubbing her hard nipples to abrade them. The other held her hip so he could use the pad of his thumb to pet her clit, sheathing his thumb claw so he didn't cut her somewhere so delicate.

Her movements were minor, but with the way she gripped the fur on the sides of his body with her nails digging into his flesh, he knew it was enough for her. Her inner walls spasmed the moment he touched her, and she seemed to be angling her hips in a certain way that had her breath hitching.

His own breaths quivered out of his lungs under each draw of their mingled scents. The smell of his lubricant, his seed-covered cock, and her arousal mixed to create something feral that always caused his mind to fog.

"Is this what you needed, Mayumi?" Faunus groaned at her. "Did you want to ride me like you did my tongue?"

Fuck, he *liked* asking her all kinds of wicked questions. She would answer them every time without fail, giving him what he wanted to hear no matter how raw it was, knowing he would react violently.

"Mhm," she answered with a nod, biting at her bottom lip.

He pulsated and swelled within her, the first bubble of his precum leaking from his enthusiastic dick.

His hands never stopped petting her nipples and swollen clit. Faunus wanted to help her to go over the edge as fast as she could, just so they could build her up again.

"Are you enjoying fucking me instead?"

He hoped so because he was thoroughly enjoying her on top of him. It was different, more controlled, but watching her bouncing on him was hypnotising. He didn't want her to stop, and the fact that this was more like a tease ensured he was going to take a while.

"Yes," she answered on a moan, her eyes shutting briefly.

"Are you making me hit all the nice spots?"

"Fuck, Faun. Do you ever shut up?" She palmed her own stomach, her fingertips dancing down where he was moving inside her until she was gripping the back of his hand. "Of course I am."

Her body bowed, and her head fell forward as she let out the most delectable moan. She'd called him by the nickname she only used when they were doing this, her brattish question nothing but a ruse to make his hackles rise.

"It feels so warm and tight inside you," he rasped, moving his hand up to palm her stomach. He came back down when she tugged on it so he would continue playing with her folds. "It's so nice, like a hug to the core of me. Do I feel as good inside your cunt as you do around my cock?"

His chest was on fire, his own playful humour burning to make him chuckle. Yet the pleasurable ache in the root of his shaft, spreading deeply throughout his groin, only made him quake instead.

He was thankful he'd witnessed many humans doing this so he could say all the right things. They pushed him just that little bit closer to his own release, but they also heated her as well.

"Faun..." She tilted her head up just enough to briefly look at him as she whispered, *"Yes."*

"I fucking bet it does," he growled. "Because right now, there is nowhere else I'd rather be."

There was no place in the world other than being with Mayumi. He knew she'd think just inside her, but he meant totally. Where she was, no matter what they were doing, that was where Faunus was determined to stay.

"Show me how much you like it. Make yourself come for me."

Faunus didn't need to wait long until her core squeezed him in a snug vice grip. He couldn't stop his back from arching, and he held her tiny waist as he steadied himself through it.

Every time Mayumi came, it was like she was strangling his cock in the most exquisite way. It choked his lungs and almost halted his blood flow until it threatened to make him dizzy.

Her scream was ear piercing, rattling inside his brain. Nails dug as she pulled on his fur, clinging to his body in every facet possible.

Only because her movements became erratic and uncontrolled as she orgasmed, Faunus lifted her up and down on him. He forced her to come for longer, to drench his cock until he could feel her liquid pool in the space around the base where his tentacles were connected.

He also continued to move her when her body lost complete tension, and she slumped. He wasn't going to allow her a moment of relief. She wanted to be on top, then she could suffer through his necessity of motion, his need and desire aching for its own liberation.

It was only when she leaned back on her own and started going up and down that his hands released her.

"Fucking hell," she moaned, her shoulder giving a twitch in aftershock. "That felt so damn amazing." Her head fell back before it rolled to the side, and then she smiled for him. "You're not allowed to leave again. I don't think I could live without this now that I've felt you."

Faunus purposefully purred in answer, but he also did it so the vibration within his chest would erase anything dark her words could inspire. He didn't want to feel a hint of regret or pain, not when he had this beautiful woman claiming him in her own way.

I want to possess every part of her, Faunus thought as he

glided his hand from her breasts so he could palm her throat and jaw. He dipped his index finger, claw and all, into her mouth to play with her tongue.

His cock couldn't fit inside here, but she'd given him a taste of it earlier, teasing him with lips and tongue and teeth. Her face was still covered in the pearly white liquid of his release, and she'd drank that down.

He gripped her arse with his other hand, kneading one cheek with rough grabs. *I want to take everything and make it mine.*

Faunus wanted every strand of hair, every bit of flesh, every drop of blood, every cell, every fibre that belonged to Mayumi to be his. He wanted to greedily consume it and have her consume him in return.

She didn't suck on his finger as he'd hoped, but she did curl her tongue around the tip as she parted her lips in welcome.

Faunus wondered how far he could go.

He had good control of his tentacles until he was spending, which is why she was able to ride him without them hindering her. He slipped two opposing ones sideways.

One sat between the lips of her dripping pussy to tease her sensitive clit, while the other tentacle nestled between the cheeks of her arse. It wasn't the first time one had been there, since they often moved around, and she didn't seem to mind.

They were both wet, seeping lubricant.

Faunus tilted his head to the side so he could look down their bodies from a different angle as he concentrated. Mayumi gasped when he curled the one between her arse cheeks and the tapered end found the little hole there. The tip slipped inside.

Mayumi paused, and he twisted his neck so his snout was pointing in her direction, so she knew he was meeting her gaze. Faunus licked at his snout, silently asking her if it was okay.

He wanted to learn if she would take all of what he had to give, but also know everything he could about her desires.

"I have seen humans play here, both men and women," he stated.

Before Faunus could continue speaking, Mayumi rested back on it. Not far, but enough to show her acceptance.

"Just be slow and gentle, okay? I haven't done anything like this in a while. I wasn't going to put your cock there, but I don't know how well it'll go with both inside me."

"You've done this before?"

"Had a tentacle in my arse? No," she laughed, her eyes alight with humour. "But you don't fuck like I have and not try everything. I didn't mind doing it in the past, and I'm kind of curious to know how this will feel."

Her skin broke out in goosebumps when he went deeper. She even shivered. However, Mayumi's head fell back as her chest rose, her lips parting to moan.

Faunus couldn't feel much sensation with his writhing limbs, but that didn't mean he wasn't doing this for himself. She accepted him wherever he wanted to go, and he was satisfied when she lowered herself to the base of his cock and took his tentacle wholly inside her too.

It was tapered, slowly stretching the tight ring. The base was thick, and she gave it a little wiggle. The woman was still trying to tease him! And he experienced that side-to-side motion with his cock, causing him to gnash his fangs.

"I didn't know you could control your tentacles like this."

It'd taken a long time, and he'd needed to consume a lot of humanity in order to wield this part of him. A lot of practice too – which he gave himself plenty of with his own hands.

When she raised herself, though, Faunus grunted. He had to focus when she almost lost it. *This isn't going to work.* But she seemed to like it.

"You know what feels good about this?" Mayumi moaned as she spoke around his finger. "It's the fact that it feels almost *wrong.* That's what makes it so damn hot. Things going where they're not supposed to, fucking something I shouldn't."

She eyed him with fierce, hungry intensity as she moved, her hips picking up rhythm even more than before. Her face was such a cute colour of pink all over, and he could see sweat dripping down her temple. He followed a drop, his tongue tingling to taste every bit of her.

Trembling all over, Mayumi's inner walls throbbed and thumped faster, her quickening heartbeat fluttering around his cock. She almost lost his tentacle again when she rose up.

This definitely wasn't working. However, Faunus knew what would, and she'd already let him tease her pussy with it earlier.

"More, Faun. *Please.*" Her eyes widened when Faunus laid back properly, held her waist with both hands, and removed his tentacle. "Hey! Wait, no. I said more, not stop."

"You're an impatient, needy thing, aren't you?" he teased as he dipped the tip of his tail into the pooling lubricant around the base of his cock and tentacles.

"What's that supposed to–" Faunus pressed the tip of his tail against that tight hole instead. "Oh!"

There was a difference between the base of his tentacle and the thickness of his tail. It took her a moment to accept it, and she squirmed the entire time. A gasp was wrenched from her when it slowly penetrated.

Her body seized to the point her hands fisted, and even her toes curled against his thighs. With her back in a deep arch, her body barely moving and instead just shuddering, he was unable to see her face properly.

It was an exceptionally tight fit, with his cock already inside her. Faunus lifted a hand to tangle it in her hair and cup the back of her head.

"Are you okay, Mayumi?" he asked with concern.

He wanted to take it out since she had stopped properly bucking, but now he feared removing it. She was even shaking with tremors.

"Please... move... me," she begged with a broken voice. *"Please."*

Unsure of what was happening, Faunus gingerly lifted her up and down. He also started removing his tail, but Mayumi quickly reached back to stop him from doing so.

"Oh, fuck," she panted. "Oh, fuck. *Faun.*"

Faunus ground his fangs when he realised Mayumi was only using singular syllables. He moved her faster when he knew what was about to happen.

She let out a bellowing cry as she came, her cunt rippling around him in intense waves, as did her arse around his tail. Faunus let her waist go the moment she bucked herself over him, her hips going backwards and forwards as she tried to go up and down. There was no pattern to her actions as she gave herself over to her orgasm.

He snarled as he moved his tail back and forth, her release seeming endless.

Then he placed one of his hands against the ground and lifted his torso. He curled his spine in a deep, unnatural arch so his hips could remain flat against the floor. With his other hand, he gripped her hair and pushed her head forward so he could drag his tongue over her face.

He lapped up his own seed, but he'd tasted worse things in his life. All he cared about right then was filling Mayumi's mouth with his tongue. He stifled her sounds, muffling them as he licked across her tongue while panting heavily.

She wrapped her arms around his neck, using his shoulders to balance herself. Leaning into his mouth, she accepted his fangs, this *kiss* of dancing tongues as he filled every available hole she had at the same time.

"Consume me, Mayumi," he demanded, feeling her riding his cock in her pussy, his tail in her arse, while his tongue was pushing back and forth inside her mouth. "I want you to dissolve me until you have taken every bit from me."

His tongue only dipped away from her mouth long enough that he could swipe across one of the salty tracks of liquid dripping from her dazed eyes.

"These are the only tears I want you to ever cry for me." He dipped inside her mouth before licking across her other cheek. "I like how messy you get, how sweet every part of you tastes."

The sounds that came from him no longer sounded human but rather animalistic and strange. In one breath, he was growling, the next purring, the next snarling, until one was a whine as his semen sacs clenched tightly.

So much was happening. There was so much for him to focus on, but Mayumi writhing and lost above him had him swiftly approaching his own release.

Yet he wanted nothing more than to continue until the world crumbled. If he could have chosen a moment to live in forever, it would have been this one.

He no longer knew if she was still coming or if she was just doing so repeatedly. His own release was climbing, causing his mind to blank as a terrible yet beautiful ache clutched at him. Both were in motion, in a state of complete and utter disarray as they reached for their bliss.

His deep sounds overlapped her feminine ones while squelching played in his ears. Their mingling scents were strong to his sensitive nose, but aided in making his collapsing lungs heavier than they needed to be. Faunus quaked while she trembled, and they clung to each other while their torsos were parted.

It was too intense. His body felt far too hot. His blood was boiling in his veins under the waves of her heat and passion. It wasn't supposed to be for something like him, and yet he was the only creature who could survive being eaten alive like this by her.

Faunus wrapped his arm around her midsection. He squeezed, rending a choke from her when he knew it was too late to tell her to stop.

His spikes hardened, the barbs released, and Faunus wrenched his tongue from her. He had just enough time to lift his head back and release his distorted roar to the ceiling as his seed broke free.

He so desperately wanted to thrust. He wanted to rut her. He wanted to roll them over and pound his seed into her body until he forced it to take root in her belly.

Instead, he was compelled to be stuck in this horrible limbo state where he couldn't move, or he'd tear her insides with his very own cock.

He'd released hard before, but not like this. Not to the point he thought his heart was going to stop. Mayumi had lifted her hands to cover her ears under the loudness of his roar, but his orbs faded to black – uncontrollably losing his sight.

His quaking intensified until the last bubble of semen gave way.

Disorientated and head swimming, his arm buckled underneath him. He shoved her down when he fell back to unlatch his spikes so as to not hurt her, and she fell onto her stomach on top of him afterwards.

He gently removed his tail from her as he covered his slightly throbbing face. The crack was pulsating, but that quickly eased as he huffed to catch his breath while she did the same.

The way she nuzzled into the fur on his chest made his heart take flight, and he couldn't have stopped his orbs from turning bright pink even if he fucking wanted to. He just lifted his head back to make sure she couldn't see to question him about it.

She always compared him to a damn cat because of his feline skull, and yet she was the one who rubbed against him constantly. His ribs tickled with the urge to laugh.

She must be the strangest damn human in this entire world. He wrapped his arms around her shoulders to hold her. *I'm glad I saved her rather than eating her and that I came back here. Who would have ever thought she would have accepted me like this?*

Faunus couldn't stop himself from running his fingers through her hair to untangle the knots she had.

Too soon she rolled her hips while leaning forward to slip his cock from her. Everything he'd just released within her gushed onto his torso – not that he really minded.

However, he did mind when she slapped both her hands against his chest and happily stated, "Well, I'm awake now."

With a growl, Faunus used the arm still around her waist to keep her to his chest as he rolled them over. She gave a girlish squeal that sounded *odd* coming from her.

And then there she was below him, completely and utterly trapped beneath him, which was exactly where he liked her to be. Caged in by his body, imprisoned by his massive size and strength, cornered by this vicious predator.

She was also undoubtfully free. Faunus' cage was only as strong as sand against her.

Her hair was a thick, messy pool underneath her head, cushioning it against the hard timber flooring. He leaned forward on his hands and forearms so that he could lightly bury his head into the crook of her neck and shoulder, letting what few strands hadn't fallen back cover his face as much as her warm skin.

Her sleepy scent directly against his snout caused his mind to go quiet as he slipped his arms underneath her. He tried to be careful of his claws, but her breath gave content twitches whenever they glided across her bare body.

He lowered himself further at the same time as he lifted her by her arse with one hand and her ribcage on the opposing side. Her chest grazed his, and his fur parted until she was directly against his firm flesh, pulling her to the very base of them.

"Are you trying to have sex with me again?" He heard the groggy satisfied tone in her voice.

"No," he answered, hearing that wasn't what she wanted – nor was it what he was doing.

Faunus' orbs went dark when her hands slowly caressed over his sides, dived into the fur across his back, and then gripped two fistfuls. Her abdomen even bowed so it was pressed more firmly against his torso.

"Is this your way of giving me aftercare?" she asked softly, which made the moment feel even more intimate than it already had been.

He didn't know what aftercare meant at first, but it didn't take him much to put it together.

"Yes," he answered just as quietly as he drew her tighter against him until he was squeezing her.

But that wasn't the whole truth, although it was something he would consider doing better in the future. He didn't really understand what emotion it was that had caused him to hold her like this.

It was heavy and sparked a pleasant tenderness and a painful throb across his chest at the same time.

Although the raunchy acts they'd just done together might have meant little to her, for Faunus it meant she had accepted anything he'd wanted to do anywhere upon her body. It just showed how deeply she trusted him, and he valued that trust more than anything.

After a few moments, he pulled back just enough so that he could dab his tongue against the corner of her jaw. Then he paused, remembering she wasn't always fond of him licking at her.

"It's okay." She reached up and pressed against the side of his snout to push the tip against her neck. "It actually feels really nice, and... I think I need this from you right now."

Was she feeling as unguarded as he was?

A purr broke loose from his chest as he slipped his tongue more forcibly across the entire column of her throat. He avoided her ear completely, knowing she hated when he tried to play with it, and instead focused on her neck, jaw, and cheek.

Mayumi was the one who turned her face towards his and licked at one of the long top fangs, causing him to flinch in surprise.

Pulling his head back, he stared at her. Her eyes were dark in the dim morning light that was washing inside her home, but they were like two pools of glinting crystal obsidian. They held warmth in them, warmth that was directed at him.

It was her lips quirking into the smallest smile that had him bending so he could lick at them. She instantly greeted his tongue with her own, not allowing him inside but allowing them to brush against each other.

"You are the most beautiful being in this world," he rasped, only moving away from her mouth because she tilted her head back so he could lick other areas.

She parted her lips to say something, perhaps one of the general retorts she always spilled whenever he'd tried to compliment her, but then they shut. When he realised this, Faunus took the opportunity he could while it was available.

"So pretty. From your eyes." He licked across her cheek just below her left one. "To your face." He slipped his tongue down the edge of her jaw and down her throat. "To your soft skin."

"It's not fair that you can speak, purr, and lick me at the same time." Her voice was so small and dozy that she sounded unbelievably weak. Hearing it and seeing how docile she was right now had the spikes going down his limbs and back quivering. "It makes it so hard to deny you."

Going over her collarbones, Faunus went lower. He dabbed at the centre of her chest, feeling her hard sternum pressing against his long, flat, malleable tongue.

"Even your little nipples are cute." He nipped at one, and she let out a gasp.

"I'm really sensitive all over right now," she croaked, pushing at his nose.

He moved away, going back to her sternum to not overstimulate her. He was enjoying petting her like this, appreciating her body in a completely different way.

I like every part of her. From her bold personality to the soft, satisfied side of her.

He moved his hands behind her, one going up so he could caress her lovely shoulder while the other ran down her hip, hoping to feel her strong legs. He would even appreciate her cute, dainty feet if she let him.

Suddenly, her scent became hot in a way he'd never smelt before, and something pinched the very tip of his tongue as he brushed it over the centre of her chest.

A bright light flashed.

TWENTY-SEVEN

Faunus reared his head back when the pinching at the tip of his tongue didn't fade. Then something weighty caused it to flop downwards while it was still sticking out.

There was also a strange light still emitting between them.

Digging his arms out from below her, he raised his hand so he could cup underneath it. Something small and warm slid into the centre of his large palm as he lifted it. His tongue followed until it was released, just as a little flame became visible when he raised it past his snout.

Everything within Faunus paused – his heart, his lungs, his very mind – when he realised it wasn't just a simple flame but a woman made of it.

Is this... her soul?

It was currently resting on its hip, with its two little, shapely legs curled to the side while resting on a single arm. Its hair was long, lifting up from its shoulders before falling and then rising again, almost like it was being billowed by waves.

But he knew it was her soul when it turned its gaze up to him, with two little sharp dark pools for eyes, and had the audacity to fucking grin at him in the same way she did. It reached up to him with both arms, almost like it wanted him to embrace it. It was like it wanted to go with him.

The world around him faded as he grew rapt with Mayumi's soul.

It was mesmerising, perhaps even one of the most stunning things he'd ever seen. The only thing that could compare to it was Mayumi herself.

And it looked exactly like her, from her stout height and muscular legs to her dainty hands and feet.

Faunus lifted his other hand so he could brush the back of his black, curling foreclaw under the same rounded jaw he enjoyed licking. Her soul tilted its head back in welcome while gripping the sides of his finger.

The sound that came out of him was more like a childish giggle than anything else as his sight changed to a bright, radiating, flamingo pink. His heart felt as light as the very soul in his palm. That heavy feeling as it dangled from his tongue must have been from pulling it out of her body, yet it truly weighed nothing.

Her soul came to me. That same childish sound of adoring delight escaped him. He couldn't believe he was staring at it, holding it. That he was petting it.

His mouth watered, knowing exactly what he was supposed to do with it. He considered it, his palm lifting closer.

A small, fleshy hand wrapped around the side of his own and the world opened up again. Mayumi, the physical one, had dipped his hand to the side while leaning up so she could see.

"What is it?" she asked as she repositioned herself onto her knees.

His reality set in, and the warmth and tenderness were overshadowed by an intense, cold-like grief.

"It is your soul," he answered, his voice twisted with awe and agony.

Mayumi's eyes drew away from what lay in his palm to him. She held his gaze, waiting for an explanation. When he didn't give it, hoping she'd let it go, her brows drew together.

He knew her question even before she said it.

"Why did it come out of me?" Then she looked down to pat her chest. "I don't feel any different. I've never heard of something like this happening. I didn't even know my soul could come out of my body."

I don't want to tell her. He would have to share the truth.

However, he knew Mayumi would pester him about this. She would ask and ask and dig. This was something far too strange and significant for her not to. It was her soul, after all. She would want to know about something that had to do with herself.

With a heavy sigh, one that even caused his fangs to part just enough to let it through, he moved his sight away from Mayumi to her soul. He petted it again with the back of his claw.

"From what I know, my father is a soul eater. He collects them and then keeps them in the void. He can eat as many as he wishes, though he can only keep one for himself – my mother. Duskwalkers can only consume one soul, and that soul will become our... bride."

His sight flittered to Mayumi's face just long enough to take note it appeared somewhat confused.

"You asked me about Orpheus, the Duskwalker who would venture to a human village every decade for an offering. You asked me if the last one he took, Reia, was still alive." He gestured to the soul in his hand by bouncing it in her direction. "This is why she is. She gave Orpheus her soul, he consumed it, and she is now eternally tied to him. She is his bride."

He thought Mayumi would be angered to find out that she was at risk of this happening to her, considering he was holding hers, but she just leaned closer with a thoughtful expression crinkling her features.

"She is also a Phantom," he continued.

Mayumi shrugged. "I've seen Ghosts, but I've never heard of a Phantom before."

"Ghosts and Phantoms differ in what their anchor is and how they died. Phantoms have living anchors, and that is what we Duskwalkers become when we consume a human soul. The Phantom's life is dictated by the length of ours."

"Is that why you took it?"

"I don't think this can be taken." His tone was serious, but it didn't reflect the way his heart suddenly quickened in his chest. It swelled with tenderness, suddenly feeling overfull. "The better question would be... why did this come out of you, Mayumi?"

Her gaze finally met his with her eyes widened ever so slightly.

"It must be given," he stated.

Could she perhaps... feel something for me? More than just desire and general fondness in his presence?

"I don't know why it came out of me," she answered with a shrug.

Then she turned her head away from him, her shoulders turning inward. He thought he may have seen her bite her lips together before her face disappeared from his sight.

Orpheus told me Reia gave him her soul because she loved him.

With his free hand, Faunus reached towards Mayumi and cupped the side of her face. When he tried to steer it towards him, she struggled while trembling. But from the glimpse he'd managed to catch, her face was blistering red. She'd never blushed with embarrassment with him before, and even the ear poking out from her hair was flushed.

Letting her keep her face hidden, he released her as everything within him suddenly went into motion. His heart sprinted, causing his breaths to struggle. His body grew warm just as his flesh ruffled, causing everything sticking from him to puff and lift.

Realisation was dawning.

He didn't know the true depth of her feelings, but he had won some part of her heart. His orbs, which were already pink, brightened in colour.

"Well..." she grumbled from under her hair. "Are you going to take it?"

Even after what I'd just told her, she wants me to take it?

Like someone had unleashed an arrow straight into his big heart, he was pierced with a sharp coldness. Deep, swallowing blue infiltrated his sight.

Gingerly, he slipped his free hand under one of hers and lifted it. Then he placed the back of his other hand into hers.

"No." He carefully shuffled her soul into her palm and then released her. "I will not take your soul."

"What?" she gasped, turning to stare at him and then her soul floating above her hand. It didn't seem so small now that she was the one holding it. "Why not?"

That invisible arrow managed to somehow twist within him. "Because I cannot."

Her brows drew together just as her lips pursed. He thought he noted a hint of anger.

"Obviously it wanted you, so take it." Mayumi shoved it at him, and Faunus shuffled backwards on his knees. When he shook his head, her features turned into an obvious glare. "I won't offer it again, Faunus." Her voice croaked, and he *hoped* he mistook the hurt in it.

"Then don't," he stated coldly, trying to hide the pain in his voice. "I don't want you to."

Her mouth opened and closed as her expression fell before she drew her soul closer to look down at it.

"Why don't you want me?" Her cheeks flared again before she added, "I mean... *it*."

And just like that, the shaft of the arrow broke off, leaving the sharp head lodged within him. He never thought he'd ever see Mayumi look crestfallen like this, but he also never thought she'd want to give him her soul.

"I want to take it," he answered truthfully, unable to bear that she could think she was the problem.

He didn't want her to feel rejected or unwanted, not when he desired what she was holding in her palm more than anything in the world.

"Then why won't you?"

"I can't tell you that."

Her pretty eyes lifted to his blue orbs, then they turned spiteful.

"Yes, you can." Mayumi crawled on one hand and both knees to her shirt that had been discarded on the floor from the night before. "This obviously has something to do with me."

Faunus stood when she placed her grey tunic on, and it fell to just below her arse when she rose to her feet. He hated that he was crouched forward because he didn't fit in her house, the spikes between his shoulder blades scraping against the ceiling.

She was still holding her flaming ethereal self in her palm, and she spun to him with her other hand on her hip.

"I know you're hiding something from me. You've been doing it from the very beginning." The darkest part of him wanted to chuckle when her soul stood as well and placed its hands on its hips. "Tell me the truth, Faunus. Now."

"Are you going to tell me to leave again if I don't?" he asked, taking a step towards the door.

He thought it might be better than telling her the truth.

Mayumi side-stepped to get in the way. "No. I won't let you leave until you tell me why."

A soft growl left him. "I don't want to."

"Too bad! You will give me a reason why my damn soul isn't good enough for you!"

Faunus lowered himself so his skull was only an inch away from her face. "Why are you so determined to give it to me?" he bit, wondering if she would say it out loud.

Spirit of the void help him... he *wanted* her to say it out loud.

"Why else?" she snapped back, having no fear as she craned her neck so she could stare up at his towering form.

His growl deepened. "Why should I have to tell you the truth when you cannot even do the same?"

He made his way to the door, needing out of this house before the truth burst from him. He would return later, when her anger had hopefully subsided, and she wouldn't pester him about this.

Even when Mayumi got in his way again, he grabbed her shoulder and pushed her to the side – making sure his strength didn't knock her over.

She gripped his arm and tried to tug him back with one hand. "Faunus, stop! Please tell me!"

"You are such a stubborn human, but you cannot win against me. Especially when you won't even tell me the truth yourself." He placed his hand on the doorknob, trying not to crush it in frustration. "You can pretend you can control me, Mayumi, but I don't have to–"

"I've never told anyone I've loved them in my entire life!" she half-screamed. "How am I supposed to do that with a creature who told me they don't want me?!"

Faunus paused, his head whipping to the side to stare at her. It was indirect, but did she just admit it to him? Admit that she loved him?

She was even still holding her soul, like she didn't want to put it back inside her body in hopes he'd suddenly take it. Pain and sympathy bubbled in his chest on her behalf, especially at her crinkled, wounded expression.

"That's not what I said."

His words landed on unlistening ears. Mayumi wasn't done screaming at him with her eyes closed and her face scrunched up – like she was against speaking the words that fell from her pretty lips.

"Do you know how hard this is for me? I don't even know what I really feel or why. People all my life have called me cold or cruel because I've never been able to give them any piece of me, because I always preferred to be by myself since it was easier. Yet, here I am, trying to give you my soul – right after you just told me this could tie me to you forever. I didn't ask you to come here. You're the one who decided to come to *my* home, to protect *me*." Still holding his wrist, her head fell forward so her hair would hide her face. "So why are you the one rejecting this?"

Guilt flashed in his orbs as the colour orange, right before they became white.

His emotions, his feelings, everything started boiling over under the power of just this tiny human's words. He was confused about her, about her feelings towards him, about why she even wanted him in the first place. Shouldn't she be overjoyed that he wasn't demanding to take her soul? Why did she want to give it to him at all?

I don't know what I'm doing with her.

All this precious time with her felt like some fantastical dream, and he worried that at any point he'd wake up drowning in Jabez's castle again.

"You can't even give me the decency of telling me fucking why. It doesn't matter if you understand humans or not. It's not an excuse."

With his fingers splayed and filled with tension, he turned to her with his claws at the ready, wishing there was some foe he could destroy to stop the terrible way he felt in that moment.

He never wanted to be the source of her pain, yet he couldn't seem to stop hurting her. First, with leaving to get the answers he sought, then with his damn hand around her throat. And now this? How was he supposed to carry all these burdens, along with the many others he already wore?

It was too much for something like him. He didn't know how to handle it, how to cope with it, and the way her face appeared right now was more painful than anything else.

"Being left in the dark about something like this... It's not fair to me, Faunus. And you trying to leave is worse."

Those words were the last thing to lodge the invisible arrowhead deeper into his frantic heart until he thought he'd start vomiting up his own purple blood.

"Because I'm dying, Mayumi!" he roared.

Her face paled before it shot up to his. "What?"

He came closer and cupped the base of her skull in both his hands, his fingers and claws tangling into her beautiful hair. He kept his gaze on her wonderful eyes, wishing they'd never look at anyone but him.

"*That* is why I cannot take your soul." He drew his thumbs over her pale, stricken cheeks. "I won't take your life along with mine."

She tried to tug one of his hands free, but he wouldn't let her.

"What do you mean you're dying?" Her eyes flittered down to search for some kind of wound on the body she'd been staring at for weeks.

"The only way to kill a Duskwalker is to destroy our skull."

"Your skull?"

Her eyes shot up and then widened at the crack running down the left side of his face. He removed one hand so he could brush the backs of his foreknuckles across her cheek instead.

"I wish I had come here sooner."

With every fragment of his being, he wished this.

She'd told him she'd been here for six months... and within those six months, he could have been here with her rather than alone with the memories of his torture.

He could have been learning all these different facets of her, about sex and what curious things his tail and tongue could do, along with his tentacles and cock. He'd already known she was wonderous, but he hadn't realised she'd be this stunning, this warm and tender towards him.

"If I had been here sooner, even just a month ago, I could have accepted your soul." The chuckle that fell from him was humourless and dark. "I came here because I wanted to spend what remained of my life protecting you. I wanted to give away my life for you."

"But you're fine now," she said, covering his snout with her hand and letting her fingertips brush right next to the crack. "As long it doesn't break further, you'll be okay."

"I can feel the end, Mayumi." He leaned into her touch. "It may not be today, or tomorrow, or even a year from now, but something could happen that will break it further. I am weakened, and I cannot bear knowing that if I bonded with you, I could destroy you along with me. I came here to protect your life, even if it is at the cost of my own. I won't take even a single second that is meant to be given to you."

"That's not your choice to make."

"It is," he stated as he drew away from her.

"What if you live for another hundred years?"

Faunus let out a terrible expire. "And what if I don't? That's not a risk I am willing to take with your life."

Then he grabbed her hand and turned it so that it was flat against her chest, forcing her soul to go back where it belonged – within the shelter of her body.

She was too distracted to notice what he'd done, that she was no longer holding it. "Why didn't you tell me sooner?"

"I'm sure you will come to hate me for it, but I didn't want you to change. I know it is selfish, but I wanted you to accept me. I wanted a taste of what I could have had if I'd come here before the Demon King cracked my skull."

He braved trailing the tip of his claw under her jaw, being careful to not cut her buttery-soft skin.

"I have wanted you for a very long time. When you were small, I just wanted to protect the one creature that had been... kind to me. I wanted to see you flourish in this world filled with teeth and blood. I wanted to know I wasn't just capable of death, but also something... good. As you got older, I realised you didn't need me at all, and I was in awe of you for that." Then Faunus drew his claw down the centre of her body, brushing it over her tunic. "I did not know what desire was until a little after you had already left to become a Demonslayer, but suddenly I wanted more than just to watch you, protect you. I thought you would never return my desire... or my feelings. I am no better than a Demon to your little warriors."

"I became a Demonslayer eleven years ago," she mumbled. "I'm twenty-nine now."

"And it has felt like eons for me," he rasped. "You cannot imagine the longing and yearning I have felt in that time. I spent my time with the Demons at the centre of the Veil because I hated being alone when I couldn't be with you. Some of them eventually accepted me, but I was never trusted. If they wouldn't truly befriend me, creatures who are just as much of a monster as I am, what hope did I have that you would? I expected you would try to kill me if I came here and you discovered me."

"You couldn't have been more wrong..."

"I know that now, but that does nothing to change my future. It doesn't change what has happened."

Not even the Witch Owl had been able to heal him of his wounded face, and if she couldn't, nothing could.

He watched as the softness in Mayumi's features hardened. She squinted her eyes at him. "There must be a way we can save you. I *will* change your mind, Faunus."

She's so damn stubborn.

She said that now, but when she realised it was futile, he was sure she would come to resent him. He'd changed her body for himself, played with her, when he knew there would never truly be a future between them.

"You can try."

Despite everything, he refused to pull away from her until she started to. He would take everything he could, even until his last breath.

TWENTY-EIGHT

Mayumi lifted the clumpy spoonful of porridge she'd prepared, watching as the honey she'd drizzled over the top stretched from the bowl before she tipped everything from her spoon sideways. The quiet *splat* did little to distract her as she thought deeply.

After their eventful morning, going from a sexual high to an emotional low, Mayumi had requested some time alone.

Faunus left, probably to circle the house or sit in some tree – or whatever Duskwalkers did.

Do I love him? She picked up another spoonful and just let it... splatter back into the bowl. *I kind of just went with the whole moment, but I don't really know how I feel.* She stirred her steaming porridge, just playing with it rather than eating it. *Then again, I'm pretty shit when it comes to understanding my own feelings.*

Still leaning against the kitchen counter, she took her eyes away from her food and looked out the window at the white wasteland before her.

A month is a little early to really develop feelings for someone... right?

It was hard to deny it when her literal soul had called to him. It was like her body was speaking on her behalf – it always did that.

Her gaze changed its focus, and she stared at her own reflection. *But it hasn't really been a month, has it? I've kind of always felt a shadow in my mind ever since I was little.*

The dark entity of her desires, the shadowy creature her mind had been fantasising about, had always been *him*.

"Is that why I've never been able to get attached to anyone?" she quietly asked her own reflection.

Mayumi laughed darkly at herself as she turned her spoon upside down and slipped it into her mouth, only gaining what had been coating it.

"Be pretty stupid of me to wait around for someone who may never have come back... or may never have existed in the first place."

She could almost hear her own reflection tell her she was that stupid.

"He's dying, huh?" She gave a sour scoff. "Hard to imagine a Duskwalker dying when the guild has done everything possible to kill them."

The story of the great bear-skulled Duskwalker was that it'd had its throat cut and then fell into a river. They'd thought it drowned, and because it had never been seen again, they thought they'd killed it.

She'd never fought against a Duskwalker herself – she imagined she'd be dead if she had.

They couldn't even hold them back properly with enchanted weapons. She'd heard they would just rip their own limb off to escape. Then it would be seen again, full bodied, like it had never had an arm or leg torn off.

But she knew his facial crack wasn't healing simply because it hadn't since she'd first seen him in the clearing, nor had it in the two weeks since he'd come back after leaving her to go to the Veil.

Why is this happening? she thought, as she finally shovelled some porridge into her mouth. She was hungry. She hadn't eaten today and starving herself wasn't going to solve her problems.

Regardless of anything that may or may not happen, Mayumi was glad he'd come here. She was thankful for everything she'd experienced with him. She just refused to accept that this was it. That there was no solution.

All her life, Mayumi had never looked at things as unfixable problems. Everything had a solution. Sometimes it just required an out-of-the-box thought pattern.

He said it hurts.

So gluing his skull back together with certain adhesives would be painful. She tried to think of anything she could bear placing over one of her own wounds, and anything she knew would burn was immediately taken off her list.

She also couldn't nail it back together. That left her with very little, and what remained tended to be short-term fixes.

Sitting on her counter was a teacup.

Her father had shown it to her when she'd been young, and he'd explained the significance of it.

What had once been a broken cup was now worth more than most things in her modest home. Her grandfather had bonded it back together with the use of gold dust mixed with tree resin.

If only I could just take his face off and do the same thing. The resin would sting, and she'd need to get into the crack from both sides for it to be effective.

Anything that required a similar bonding, where both sides needed to be worked, was also taken off her list.

"Screw it," she bit out as she picked up her bowl and finished what remained. "Standing here thinking about it isn't going to help."

Mayumi washed up her bowl, spoon, and the pot she'd used to make her food and then stomped to the coat rack where she had her weapons belt. Then she slung her bow and its matching quiver over her shoulder and went outside to shove her boots on.

Placing her thumb and middle finger to her mouth, she let out a loud, ear-piercing whistle in the clearing. She flinched in surprise when Faunus fell from the sky right in front of her.

He'd obviously been sitting in the trees.

"I'm not a dog." The irony of him saying that when he was in his more monstrous form didn't miss her. *"Don't call for me like one."*

Mayumi rolled her eyes. "Whistling is a form of communication we use in the guild for long-distance calls. I didn't know how far you'd be."

He snorted a huff, which she took as him accepting her reason. He did seem a little grouchier than normal, but she figured that was because of earlier.

He'd just revealed he was dying, and she'd asked to be alone to deal with the way being rejected and the truth of everything hurt. Probably not her most sympathetic or wisest choice, but she didn't know how to deal with shit like this. Whenever Mayumi had grieved in the past, she preferred to be alone.

In her own way, she knew she needed to accept this possibility and prepare her mind just in case things didn't work out. That didn't mean she wasn't going to try everything in her might to prove him wrong.

"Can you take me to town?" His orbs immediately turned green, and she didn't miss the little growl he tried to hide. So, for good measure, she added, "Please?"

"I just took you there a few days ago. You said you wouldn't have to go back for a few weeks."

He really doesn't like me going there.

Mayumi stomped closer, grabbed him by the underside of his snout, and pulled his head closer as she leaned forward. She pressed her lips against his fangs.

Terrible with words, she'd rather her actions speak for themselves.

"Just take me there?" she said while she was so close to him that her lips brushed over him as she spoke. "I forgot to get tea, and I want to ask a few people about something."

"Hmm." He cocked his head like he was thinking, yet his orbs had morphed from green to yellow from her kiss. *"Only if you give me another."*

Her lips quirked with humour. "I can walk there myself."

"Not if I don't let you."

"Are you going to put me in front of the mirror again if I try to?"

"I believe I do that already."

He did. He was rather fond of forcing Mayumi to watch him take her, making sure she understood he was the one inside her.

Considering his size, tentacles, claws, and growling snarls, it was impossible to think of anyone else.

Even though she could go on forever with their playful banter, Mayumi wrapped her arms around his neck to lean in closer and placed her lips against his fangs again. The tension she'd been able to see the moment he'd landed in the clearing eased. She gave him another just to make him happy.

"Hop on then."

He stepped backwards and lowered himself while turning so she could climb onto his back.

"We need to be quick," she told him when he shifted to all fours and started walking. "I decided to go there pretty late, and night will fall soon."

"I can protect you on the way back, even if it is dark."

"That's not the point. The shops will close within an hour of nightfall."

Once the shade was too long, humankind tried to hide within their homes if they could – even in the soldier-protected, wall-surrounded cities and towns.

"How fast do you want me to go?"

"As fast as you can." She knew that was a loaded statement considering his kind were really freaking fast.

"I don't think that is wise," he refuted.

Mayumi kicked her heels in like she would with a horse while placing her torso flush against his body. She used her mostly empty satchel as a barrier between herself and his spikes, hoping they remained streamlined.

She gripped his fur tightly as she said, "Oh, just giddy up, you fucking scaredy cat."

"I'm not a cat!" he bellowed, a flash of red illuminating in front of his face.

"It's just a say-ING!" she screamed when Faunus suddenly burst into action.

If it wasn't for the fact she could feel his strong body in motion beneath her, she would have thought they were flying with how fast they were going.

Every tree they passed was a whistling blur, and she was never given the opportunity to see a single one as they shot past. The air was unbearably cold, immediately cutting through her thick winter clothing to make her shiver.

Eventually, she just laid her face down to hide it from the freezing wind assaulting her poor skin and tried to hold on. She could feel it when he stepped wider to avoid and duck around tree trunks or when he jumped over fallen ones.

After a few minutes of just feeling his glorious body moving while listening to his huffing, deep, reverberating breaths, she turned her head to the side to peek at the forest.

Everything was a disorientating smear of colours.

Despite her arms and legs being tired already, Mayumi's face shifted into a massive grin. *This is awesome.*

Then, after what could have only been twenty minutes, if not less, he eventually slowed.

She sat up while looking around to figure out where they were. There was usually a route she took to and from the town, and she wasn't particularly familiar with the trees currently surrounding them.

"Why'd you stop? I told you I'd be fine."

"We're here."

"You know what..." she said as she climbed off him. "I should have figured as much. You know that's usually a three- to four-hour walk for me, right?"

"That's because you humans are impossibly slow." He lifted one of his arms to steady her when it was obvious her legs were wobbly with exhaustion from holding onto him. *"I've always thought it was impossible that humans haven't been hunted into extinction yet."*

She lifted her chin up at him. "We may not be fast, but we're exceptionally clever."

"Just hurry up and go into your human village. I will wait here." Despite this, he grabbed her forearm when she nodded and turned to walk away. She faced him and found his orbs were a dark green. *"Remember my warning, Mayumi. That hasn't changed."*

"I don't think I'm particularly fond of the colour of jealousy on you," she answered with her eyelids lowered in annoyance.

She was coming here to find a way to help him, not to go bouncing with human men.

Plus, it would be the equivalent of throwing a sausage down a hallway at this point after taking Faunus' brilliant cock. How many men would she need to take now just to feel somewhat full, three or four at the same time? It sounded like too much work, and she doubted they'd reach anywhere near the same depth.

His clawed hand slipped up her arm and cradled the back of her head. He yanked her forward, bringing her closer before he drew his tongue up her neck and over the corner of her jaw.

Then, right when his skull was next to her ear, he growled, *"The colour does not signify jealousy, my foolish Demonslayer. It signifies my possessiveness of you."* She couldn't contain the little naughty tremor that tickled down her spine at the depth of his gravelly voice and dark words. *"Currently, you are **mine**, and I will destroy anything that touches what is mine."*

She opened her mouth to refute him out of usual habit when someone said that to her but closed it when she realised she was rather content with that notion. She opened it again to mention that he wouldn't take her soul, which meant she wasn't actually his, then closed it again when she understood *why* he wouldn't – not that she agreed with it.

I could only live another year or two.

She baited Demons to her home; she could be killed by one. She could easily die from a sickness, a broken bone, drowning in the tub, choking on a piece of bread. A human's life was feeble and weak.

But she was terrible, and she enjoyed messing with him.

"I take it back," she whispered, perhaps a little raspier than she intended. "I like this colour on you, then."

A chomping sound came from him, which he mainly did when he opened and snapped shut his fangs when he was stunned speechless for a moment or sometimes annoyed.

He leaned back while still cradling the back of her head. He twisted his own. *"You... like me being possessive of you?"*

"Only because I think you would actually go out and kill anyone for touching me. It gives far more meaning than anyone who's ever tried to say it to me before." She leaned in closer and whispered against his fangs. "It's like playing with danger, except I'm in control of other people's lives without them knowing."

"Why are you like this?" he groaned, wrapping his arm around her to pull her closer.

"I have to go into the town, Faunus!" she squealed, noticing his orbs flash purple.

"No, you don't. You don't have to get anyone else's scent on you. Only mine is worthy enough to be on you."

He brushed the fur covering his neck against her, but she was sure she already smelt like him. *Well... he did come inside me this morning.*

Oh my God! I just realised I'll be walking through the town with Duskwalker come inside me. She didn't know if she was concerned by that fact... or turned on by it. *No one would ever suspect what I've been doing with him.*

She almost wanted to laugh when she realised she was more perverted than she ever thought.

She smiled when the tension she'd been able to feel since their conversation this morning was burned away by this one. It was what she'd been hoping for.

No matter what happened, Mayumi hadn't wanted things to change. She didn't want Faunus to withdraw from her, and she didn't want to do the same.

I'll find a solution, and until I do... I'll just pretend nothing bad will happen.

It was odd that the most cynical person she'd ever met – herself – was willing to believe in blind hope like this.

TWENTY-NINE

"What the hell do you mean you can't think of anything else?" Mayumi shouted in an attempt to show her outrage, while also trying to speak over the unusually loud chatter of the tavern she was in.

Cornering Klaus and Yoshida at the same time while they were both off duty was a miracle. However, they were being as utterly useless as they usually were.

"Sorry, Yumi," Yoshida answered with a shrug, bringing his mead-filled mug to his lips. He accidentally spilled a small amount down the front of his shirt and wiped it off. "I just can't think of anything other than casein, or the animal glue you suggested, that would be available in the city."

"What about beeswax?" Klaus interjected. "People use that for glue sometimes."

Mayumi groaned while sliding her arms forward onto the table and face planting it.

"That's not strong enough. I need something that wouldn't fade over time, that won't melt under heat or crack when frozen. I need something that is malleable, yet firm enough to hold under pressure."

"You're asking for the impossible," Klaus said with a frown crinkling his stupid forehead between his stupid red eyebrows. "You haven't even told us what this is for."

Music was playing, albeit just loud enough to add to the noise but not overpower it. Someone knocked into the back of her chair before stumbling into their table and then walking off like nothing happened.

The tavern smelt horrible, like alcohol and sweat, and she *knew* that was all going to cling to her. If she'd be able to smell it on herself, she worried how Faunus was going to feel.

"So animal glue and casein, that's all we can think of?" she asked instead of answering.

How was she supposed to say she was trying to glue a Duskwalker's skull back together? If they didn't call her insane and throw her in the prison cells, they would round up an army and surround her home to take Faunus on.

"Yeah, but both of those can become brittle over time, and it also depends on if what you're trying to glue back together is porous or not," Yoshida reminded her. "If you're trying to glue something together that is smooth, there's a chance neither of those things will work since there isn't anything to bind to. Plus, you'll need to clamp the pieces tightly together. Otherwise, it's pointless. So if it's round, good luck."

"Thank you *so much* for explaining the obvious to me," Mayumi grumbled as sarcastically as possible.

I'm being mansplained to! She'd worked with plenty of glue in her life. She didn't need someone to explain it to her like she was five years old.

"I'm just trying to help," Yoshida grumbled with his mug to his lips. "You're the most ungrateful person I know."

"I'm paying the tab for your help, so shut up."

"It would be good if we had Henry here," Klaus chimed in, waving for his mug to be filled at the reminder that she was paying.

"Where's the smart one when you need him?" Mayumi cried pathetically against the table, her shoulders giving a false heave as though she was truly weeping.

"Never thought I'd hear you say anyone is better than you at anything," Yoshida scoffed. "And he isn't *that* smart. He tripped over his own boot yesterday."

"He's more of a smart*ass*." Klaus chuckled, staring at the huge tits of the barmaid serving him.

It wasn't his fault. She was smiling while obviously trying to shove those soft, round, yummy things in his face.

"Yeah, and you both are like two halves of a whole idiot."

"There's three of us here, so that makes us all one-third each of a whole idiot."

Mayumi lifted her head and pointed her index finger at Yoshida's face with a glare. "I came up with the animal glue idea."

She'd already checked if she had some at home in her shed. Her reserves were low, and she was a little worried about how old it was.

"Yeah, and at least I came up with casein." Yoshida then pointed his thumb at Klaus. "This one here hasn't brought anything good to the table since he roped you into hanging out with us when we were kids, and I *still* don't think that was his greatest idea."

Her nose crinkled in annoyance.

He was joking, she knew he was, but she still wanted to be childish and twist his nipple so he'd squeal like a little bitch – just like when they were children.

"Awww, don't be like that," Klaus pouted while wrapping his arm around Mayumi's shoulders, making her cringe at the physical touch. "She was useful. She was the smallest and helped us get into some really tiny places. Remember when she–"

"I didn't come here to reminisce!" Mayumi shouted as she shoved her hands against the table to stand. "The markets are closing soon. I'll pay the tab, so anything you drink from here on out comes from your own pockets."

"You didn't even have a drink with us!" Klaus exclaimed as she walked to the bar to pay. "I have to show you up from last time."

Mayumi didn't bother to answer. She'd bet them many times in the past that she could drink them both under the table – sometimes winning that bet, sometimes having to be carted out over someone's shoulder because she couldn't walk anymore.

But Faunus was waiting for her, and she really needed to get what she came here for.

Okay. Get my tea, figure out who sells the glues I need, then get out. That should be easy enough.

It wasn't. About five minutes after finishing her tasks, as she was about to leave this wretched city, she heard the voice of one of the many people she would rather avoid.

"Mayumi!" a woman shrieked, sending a crawl of dread up her spine.

Her immediate reaction was to find somewhere to hide. A barrel, behind a counter, she'd even use a small child as a shield at this stage.

Oh God. Oh shit. She searched and found nowhere. *Fuck!*

"Clara!" Mayumi shouted with false joy as she spun around, trying her hardest to smile warmly.

The blonde-haired, buxom, and curvy woman had lifted her frilly skirt up to walk at a fast pace in Mayumi's direction, probably to make sure she couldn't run without it being obvious.

Mayumi's hands lifted partially in greeting. They were also a half-hearted shrug, the awkwardness of this causing heat to prickle on the back of her neck.

She couldn't have just pretended not to see me, could she?

"Look, I'm sure I have some explaining to do," Mayumi said with warmth in her eyes, understanding why Clara might be rather upset with her. She had every right to be, after all. "I'm sorry I–"

The resounding *slap* that struck her had her head twisting to the side from the sudden unexpectedness of it.

"I told you last time I wasn't interested in a one-night stand," Clara bit, shaking her hand as the back of her knuckles turned pink. "And yet, you disappear in the middle of the night... again? Right after you promised me you wouldn't? Then you even left coin on my nightstand, like I'm nothing but a filthy whore. You're lucky I'm not brave enough to walk through the forest to that very home of yours!"

From the heat Mayumi could feel in her cheek, she knew that slap was going to stain her face for some time, possibly even swell.

All the warmth and niceness in Mayumi's expression died as she turned her piercing, narrowed gaze in Clara's direction. The woman, who had been filled with fire just seconds ago, tensed her lips together and shied away a little.

Mayumi had always been all sweet talk, playfulness, and patience because it always got her what she wanted – a half-decent lay. She was used to being yelled at by those from her sexual past and having awkward conversations.

But she'd *never* been struck by one.

Placing her hand on the hilt of her dagger, Mayumi rolled her shoulders back while lifting her head.

A small crowd of people had stopped to witness the spectacle, needing the dramatic entertainment. The people's nosiness was disgusting.

"You shouldn't have done that, Clara," she said through gritted teeth before taking in a calming breath. "Was that really the wisest choice, the only action you could have taken?"

"You deserved it." Clara eventually crossed her arms and turned her nose up at her, deciding to ride the wave of her stupidity. "You can't do anything to me, not if you don't want to be arrested."

One thing Mayumi hated was violence towards another. She wouldn't permit anyone to lay a hand on her or on another person. Death and pain could be for Demons and bandits.

She pulled her dagger out and inspected it, just because she *could.*

"Sure, I can't hurt you." She pointed the tip at her, although they were at least a metre apart now. "But there's no law in place that says I can't cut that pretty dress off you and make you parade around naked for all to see."

Mayumi wasn't sure if that was a lie or not, but no one was going to follow her into the forest to arrest her for something like that. Plus, Clara was from the peasant sector. A rich person might be able to hold some power and sway, but she was a nobody in Colt's Outpost. Just a very pretty face.

"You wouldn't!" Clara squealed, clutching at the skirt of her dress with both hands as she stepped back.

"You people seem to think that just because I mind my own business and try to be nice that I'm not dangerous. I'm sorry for hurting you, but that still doesn't give you the right to hit me. Go home, Clara." Mayumi nodded her head in the direction of the woman's home. "Now, before I change my mind."

"Bitch," Clara muttered under her breath, before running off.

Mayumi watched her, only because she was trying to reign in

her anger. *She has the hide to call me a bitch?* She placed the back of her cool hand against her radiating cheek.

She was still being stared at.

"What the fuck are you all gawking at?!" she yelled, turning to the witnesses. "Want me to cut off your clothing instead?"

The crowd scattered, not wanting to piss her off. Mayumi was known for getting into fights and winning them – even if there was more than one opponent, even men. She'd also bite and scratch if she was held back, like a feral, untameable beast.

The guards nearby who overheard the commotion did nothing to intervene. They didn't overly care what happened in this town so long as it wasn't truly criminal, like murder or severe assault. Other petty crimes, like causing a disturbance, were seen as nothing – even if someone actually needed help.

All they cared about was that people didn't steal from the rich and that there were no riots. Riots meant bloodshed, and bloodshed meant an army of Demons.

It was one of the reasons the poor didn't revolt against those within the inner rings.

A bell rung in the distance, informing the town's residents that the gates would soon be permanently closed for the day. They didn't want a Demon scuttling its way in at night.

I want out of this hellhole.

Mayumi stormed her way out of Colt's Outpost.

When the gates shut behind her, she pressed the back of her hand to her mouth, this time to make sure it wasn't bleeding. It wasn't, but her face just hurt a whole bunch.

I only left her money because I stole a bottle of her booze while she was asleep. She'd just been making sure she paid for it, not for her time with Clara. Mayumi was many things, but she wasn't a thief.

She scanned the meadow in front of her, trying to remember where Faunus was in the trees beyond it.

This is what I mean, Mayumi thought as she crossed the meadow. *I just try to do something nice, and people take it the wrong way. Yeah, sure, I should have been upfront with my intentions with her, but for fuck's sake. I'm sure plenty of men have done the same thing to her.*

It'd happened to Mayumi many times in the past, men skulking away before she could.

She'd always just shrugged it off, made sure he hadn't come inside her, then moved on with her life. Sex for her had been nothing but a transaction of release, wanting to feel something good.

I've spent my whole life training.

She'd tired her body out with exercise and worked to make herself strong. Demonslayers also went to towns that had been destroyed by Demons to help them rebuild and protect them while they did.

They were also hired to fight against human bandits.

Mayumi had been shot with arrows, marred by claws, and bitten. She'd almost lost her life a handful of times.

Is it so bad to just ask for a good time occasionally? Nobody was perfect. So what if she made a few mistakes?

When she entered the forest, she found Faunus waiting for her. The trees weren't the same as earlier, so she figured he must have followed her approach.

She paused when she saw his yellow orbs.

That's why I like you. Because you're not like them. There is no expectation with you, Faunus. Everything is decided by me.

He took her brattish behaviour and her superiority complex and pushed back with his own brand of playfulness. She didn't have to hide, didn't have to pretend.

In just the little time he'd been here, he'd made Mayumi content in his presence. He'd moulded himself around her, not the other way around.

She continued to walk to greet him. When she got closer, his snout bounced up and down as if he was sniffing.

His orbs turned green, and an echoing growl bounced off the trees and snow as he approached. The little hairs on her body stood on end with a thrill, the sound like music to her damn depraved senses.

"You smell terrible," he snarled when he was right in front of her. *"There are too many scents on you."*

He swiped at his snout in disgust.

Mayumi's mood was still rather sour, but he made her snort

out a laugh even when she thought nothing else could.

"I thought I might."

He lifted his head back and up, in a way similar to how she would when she was about to be purposefully mean. *"I don't even want to put you on my back."*

Her eyelids lowered. "Well, that's rude. Here, have some."

She rubbed her hands over his snout.

He gave a sneeze and backed up from her. Then his orbs turned a dark yellow as he leaned forward to sniff at her face.

The growl that came from him this time was menacing. He crouched, his spine curling forward as he leant on one hand and then reached up to touch her cheek.

Mayumi winced. She tried to step back, but his hand darted forward to cradle the back of her head to hold her in place.

"Your face is swelling, Mayumi. It's red and bruising." His orbs morphed into a terrible red, glowing only inches from her face. *"Why?"*

She hid it with the back of her hand, letting the coolness in her fingers aid with the swelling. "It's nothing, Faunus. Don't worry about it."

"It looks like someone struck you." He ripped her hand down and used it to yank her closer when it was obvious she was trying to get away. *"Who did this to you?"*

With a sigh, her eyes found the forest, wishing he'd just let it go.

His tongue swiped across her cheek. Just as a sting started, it quickly faded as a yellow glow of magic brightened between them. It was cool – his magic always had a chill to it – but it caused the ache to dissipate.

"Nothing is allowed to harm you." She let her gaze remain averted, but he just took the opportunity to come closer to be right next to her ear. His voice was low as he growled, *"I said you were mine, and I will protect what's mine, destroy what hurts mine, and make sure it knows fear as it takes its last breath."* The dark chuckle that fell from him, almost overshadowed by his growl, was... evil. *"And there is only one scent on your face. It'll be easy for me to follow."*

Mayumi reached up and covered the top of his face with one

hand and grabbed his ram horn with her other. She pushed him back so she could face him.

"It was just a silly girl, and I kind of deserved it."

"I. Don't. Care."

"Faunus," Mayumi said in a stern tone. "I'm saying *no*."

She slipped her hands up so she could place her arms around his neck. She couldn't believe she was here, trying to calm down a Duskwalker from killing someone.

"Thank you for healing me. She has a meaner slap than I thought she would, but I'm fine now. Plus, do you really want to leave me here in the forest by myself while you go and cause havoc in the city?"

If his skull is more fragile than normal, what if one wrong hit causes it to break?

She could feel how heavy his breaths were, how full of rage he was as he quaked. He wanted to mete out retribution over something so small and insignificant.

His long and strong arms wrapped around her, his embrace swallowing her up before she felt the light stab of his claws on both sides of her navel.

"You could take care of yourself until I return. It wouldn't take me long."

It's like talking to a menacing wall.

"I just... really want to go home. I've had a terrible day." She didn't think she'd had a day this bad in a long time. "It'd be nice to spend time with you. I can finally teach you how to play shogi since you've picked up chess so well."

After a long while of Mayumi hugging him, even patting the back of his puffed fur, Faunus eased.

"You stink," he eventually grumbled. *"I don't like it."*

A laugh burst from her. "I don't think I'm going to be able to get rid of it anytime soon."

A rolled huff shook his torso against her. *"If it will remove the mixture of others' scents on you... then we will have a bath when we return to your home."*

"Really? It's that bad that you would suggest having a bath?"

She couldn't believe it! His tail almost always curled between his legs the moment she suggested it.

"You rubbed it all over me, so I need to have one with you. Otherwise, it will not matter."

"You know night is falling, right?"

"I will be there with you."

Mayumi looked up at the pinks and purples of the sky on dusk, just glimpsing it through his fur and the trees. *I've never had a bath outside at night.*

The smile that curled her lips was weak and solemn. *I guess it would be fun.*

THIRTY

Faunus hated the way the bathwater appeared calm and inviting. He hated the way the cloudless night sky made it appear black, as if it was endless, boundless, and immeasurable.

He hated the way it swallowed up Mayumi in its abysmal depths. She was so small, so delicate, as she carefully chose which natural rock step she would take to get deeper.

The naked beauty of her slowly slipping in, even as she stepped *into* the stars, wasn't enough to distract him from how easily he could lose her.

Her hair became a black floating wisp against the dark pool when her neck reached the surface. His muscles swelled in fearful anticipation of having to dive into the water and save her from drowning, as he had many times.

I should not have suggested this.

At least throughout the day, he could see the bottom of her spring bathtub.

He knew it wasn't that deep. He knew the water only surpassed the bottom of his ribcage if he stood in the middle. It did nothing to ease him.

"Mayumi," he begged.

This wouldn't be enough to completely rid her of the scent of *many* others, but he would accept it. He would accept what tainted his fur if she would just come out of the water and onto the safety of land.

Her smile was small, yet so gentle, as she turned to him and offered her hand.

"Come on, Faunus," she sweetly cooed. "Since you used that water spell, it kind of feels like you."

Her words caused his head to tilt slightly. "Feels like me?"

He couldn't possibly be compared to such a remorseless, unforgiving element. At least he held *some* regret for taking life – some.

"Well," she said as she looked down at it. "It feels the same temperature as you, and I *swear* it even smells a little like you. And it reminds me of the colour of your fur... it even tickles a little."

This wasn't the first time he'd used his blood to fill this bathtub, even though it cost him a lot of it to do so. Currently, there were drops of purple liquid dripping off a few of his fingers and staining the snow beneath him.

But it was the first time she'd made such a remark about it.

Her hand bounced lightly, beckoning him to come closer and take it. His orbs shifted to a reddish pink in shame when he realised she was only saying it because he was obviously more hesitant than usual.

Faunus reached down to take her hand so he could pull her out.

However, the second before their palms made contact, her face turned upwards to the sky. "This is really beautiful. I'm not stupid enough to take a bath outside at night, but I've always wanted to."

Such heartfelt words of longing made the power of her pulling strength much stronger than his own, his heart lost to her awe.

All the fur and spikes covering him puffed out in repulsion when his pawed foot slipped inside the pool of darkness. The rest of him followed Mayumi's lead as she brought him in deeper.

Faunus despised this next part, especially since she softly pushed him into the lowest recess, and the water gobbled him up all the way to his chest. He preferred to sit on the other, shallower side.

His claws scraped and dug into the rock to steady himself as the heels of his feet slipped out from under him so he could be seated. His legs were wide to account for their long length in the relatively small but deep bath.

As he always did, despite feeling the bottom, he held on for dear life.

She laid herself on his lap, which she didn't always do, and made herself comfortable on top of him.

Then she grabbed the bottle nearby, poured herself a glass of liquid that caused his nose to sting, and took a sip. She'd already informed him that she wanted to drink that alcoholic concoction. They both just hoped the water would help to ease the scent of it on her.

What was one more? He'd prefer it over her smelling like a hundred humans – which was how she currently smelled.

Faunus braced his feet against the bottom and finally curled his arms around her so he could feel she was safe.

Despite his unease, he carefully listened out around them. The forest was quiet; not even a mouse scuttled, or an owl hooted.

The water lapped at his fur, warm and relaxing even against his own aversion to this. She was right, it did feel like his own warm temperature, and he was sure the furnace beneath them would fight against the frost surrounding them to keep it comfortable.

He eventually braved moving in it so he could brush the back of his claw against her soft cheekbone. Red flashed in his orbs. They'd been consistently white since the moment the water started rising.

Mayumi pressed a finger to the end of his snout with a cute little glare.

"Don't," she warned. "I'll be really mad at you if you ruin this. You already healed my face."

His long inhale was followed by a huff of annoyance.

He didn't understand why she would allow someone to hit her and let them live. He hadn't understood it when she'd been fighting those human men either.

The only reason he hadn't hunted them down and slaughtered them was that she'd been stained with blood. She would have been hunted by Demons had he left her alone then.

He knew he could've snuck his way in over the wall of that puny little human village and found the woman who had harmed his female, covering his snout so he wasn't able to smell her blood before he clawed her throat open. Then he would've exited the village all before the sun had even finished setting.

Would he have been seen? Probably. But Faunus was *very* swift and agile. He was sure he could have figured out a way in and out without going into a rage.

Honestly... he wouldn't have cared. He wanted to destroy every scent that had been clinging to her. Any scent that could possibly touch her again in the future – even if it was as innocent as a rub to her shoulder.

He lifted his head to look up at the stars when he knew his sight had gone a dark green, hiding it from her.

She swallowed deeply before she reached for the bottle again, and he ignored it as he looked skyward. He stared for a long while when a collection of sparkling dots grabbed his attention.

"I have always wondered what is beyond," he said quietly.

"Why?" she asked once she was comfortable again. "I've always found it pointless to wonder about things I can't see or touch. All I know is that the sky is a vast amount of nothingness."

A small billow of wind fluttered the dry fur around his neck and cooled his face, highlighting the silence that fell upon them.

"Sorry," she mumbled. "I probably should have just shut up and let you talk."

He was a little relieved she'd stopped him. "It's fine."

"No, it's not," she lightly bit as she grabbed his ram horn and forced him to look down at her. He was thankful his sight was back to its usual yellow. "Talk, Faunus. I want to know why you want to know what's beyond the stars."

He shook his head with a chuckle. "It doesn't matter. I don't think humans would consider my thoughts peaceful."

From what he'd gathered so far, she wanted to enjoy the bath for its rarity. He was sure his words would have been dispiriting.

"There is another side of the tub I can go sit on," she threatened.

A spike of anxiety struck him, and his claws dug into her a little. He thought if she were to leave his lap, he might bolt out of the water – and that would ruin this for her.

"Speak."

With a sigh parting his fangs, he turned his snout upwards to stare at the stars again.

"I don't know if other Duskwalkers feel the same way, but I don't... feel like I belong here. I don't feel like I belong anywhere. I cannot stay on the surface without eventually being hunted by Demonslayers, and I cannot remain in the Veil or I will be hunted there, too. If I cannot go to these places and live peacefully, where else am I to go?" He twisted his head at a cloudy, glittering spiral he could see way out in the expanding distance. "I know of how I came to be, but not why. Yet I wonder if there are more of my kind somewhere out there."

He could feel by how she was sitting that she was holding her glass with both hands.

"Well, you said that your father was some keeper of the void. Are you able to go there?"

"I don't know if I can come back from that place. It is an afterlife, so I have never been tempted." His sight fell onto the moon. It was bright and near full, so he examined its shadowy craters. "The reason why I have not gone in search of a new world is because I'm worried it will be the same. We Duskwalkers *need* violence. We must feed in order to develop. What if I find another place that hates us just as much? Or one where my kind are undeveloped, and I am still left on my own, unable to speak with them since they do not know how?"

"Are you... lonely, Faunus?"

As much as he tried to stop it, he knew it was her question that caused his orbs to shift to blue.

"Very," he grated. After a short silence between them, Faunus forced out a chuckle. "See? My thoughts are not very pleasant. Perhaps we should talk of something else."

"Don't do that," she quietly grumbled. "Don't invalidate your own thoughts and feelings just because they're unpleasant. They aren't unwanted, Faunus."

He turned his head down to her, and two black pools filled with twinkling lights, just like the water around her, glittered at him. The moon had found her eyes, making them even more alluring and spellbinding than normal.

"I have thoughts like this too," she continued, her eyes flicking over his skull. "Sure, I don't experience loneliness in the way you have. I can go almost anywhere humans live and be accepted, but..." Mayumi let out a humourless laugh as she rubbed the back of her neck. "I haven't always felt like I belong. I don't think like everyone else, and I'm quick to be violent or cold towards others. I've tried. Fuck, have I tried to fit in. But too many people make me feel claustrophobic, and once I've spent too long with them, I start to get annoyed by the person next to me just breathing. It's like there's a wall around me when I'm on a busy street, and the longer I'm there, the more I feel it getting smaller until I feel like I'm choking. The only time I really felt comfortable being around others was when I was out in the field with the guild hunting Demons. It was the only time I felt like I fit in."

Mayumi rested her glass against her chest and stroked the fur over his chest with her free hand. She stared at her hand moving, almost like she was avoiding his gaze.

"People start to feel sticky when I spend too much time with them. After a few days, their skin feels wrong next to mine and my own starts to crawl."

His heart constricted painfully as he asked, "Do I make you feel that way?"

Her lips curled upwards as she turned her face up to him. "Not at all. Maybe it's because you're covered in fur."

She stroked her cheek against his chest, which only made it feel lighter under her touch. He even began to radiate a contented rumble.

Mayumi gestured back towards her house. "I know it's not much, or very big, but you at least fit in here... just like me."

"But I don't fit in here. I can't even stand properly inside your home."

"I feel so bad, but we can't just lift the roof and make it bigger. You're wanted here, is what I meant."

His orbs brightened in their colour of yellow. "I know."

She gave a pout when she realised he'd been teasing her.

Faunus knew Mayumi wanted him, and he was delighted to know that she would have hated anyone else remaining here as long as he had.

"Have you ever had alcohol?" she asked, lifting her glass

slightly.

"Never." Why would he have? This was a human drink, as far as he knew.

He tried to remember if Demons had ever imbibed, but couldn't think if he'd ever been to a place within the Demon Village that offered it. There could be, but maybe he'd just never been there.

He wasn't particularly welcome there. All Duskwalkers weren't. Even more so now, since he'd learned from Orpheus and Magnar that their kind were banished from the Demon Village by Jabez.

"Try it," she demanded. "You won't know if you don't like it unless you try it."

By the smell alone, he was uncertain. However, she was right. He couldn't say he disliked it until he tried.

"Perhaps we should try this when you have a second glass?" he asked as he examined it.

He didn't have lips or a mouth that could drink from such an item.

"Just poke your tongue in it, Faunus! I've had it in my mouth enough times not to care."

Damnit. He'd been hoping to use that as his excuse.

He leaned forward, his tongue smacking at the inside of his mouth in wary agitation before he dipped it into her glass. The moment his tongue touched the hard bottom of it, every part of him stood on end. His fur, his spikes. It was like his bones wanted to jump out of his flesh and run away.

"Blergh!" he retched, bringing his tongue away.

He coughed when he accidentally swallowed a drop, trying to get the offending liquid out of his maw. He didn't have lips, so he couldn't spit, and the only thing that saved him was the drool that began filling his mouth.

Mayumi giggled as she tried to help, scooping up a handful of water so he could drink it without having to shove his head down into it.

"Disgusting!" He gave a full-body, repulsed shudder. "How can you drink that?!"

"Because it makes me feel all warm and fuzzy inside. It

relaxes me." Her giggles were stemmed when she took a sip of it. "It's not about how it tastes, but how drunk it can get me."

Faunus couldn't think about anything else but how it made his throat burn and his stomach gargle with disgust. He thought his tongue was trying to shrivel in his mouth!

"It is offensive and vile, and you are lucky I don't toss it into the forest." He gave another shudder. "I am never trusting anything you try to make me eat or drink again."

"Awww, don't be like that."

Her cute pout was not enough of an apology.

"Here, let me make it up to you," she said as she placed her glass down on the rocky edge and picked up a vial.

The liquid soap she dribbled onto her hands was pretty smelling, and she dipped them into the water before she lathered his left shoulder with it. An irritated huff left him, but he couldn't stop his head from lifting in welcome when she scrubbed at his neck.

Everywhere she touched him relaxed his fur. She'd soothed him fully by the time she was going down his other arm after rubbing and massaging the first.

With his sight black and his snout pointed skyward, a groan fell from him when Mayumi straddled his lap and rubbed his back with soap. It took him a little longer than it should have for him to realise why he'd groaned when she was only cleaning him, even though her scratching nails felt sublime.

It was because something soft had rubbed the underside of his shaft.

Why does this keep happening to me?

Something about having Mayumi's hands on him while the water surrounded his body made his shaft slip from his seam without him knowing. It was nestled in heat and wetness, and the throbbing in it was a common occurrence around her.

He opened his sight to find it was purple.

She dug her nails into the fur of his chest and torso after applying more soap to her hands. It rinsed away quickly under the water.

"I hope you don't mind... but I'm not really in the mood tonight."

"Mood?" he asked, not knowing what that implied, as he turned his head down.

Her lips weren't pouted, nor were they pursed, but somewhere in the middle as she looked down.

There was his cock, fully hard, resting between them. His tentacles were surprisingly still and languid, not seeking and searching like they usually were – as if they were soothed by the heat.

It was odd to hear her say she *didn't* want it when she usually took any chance she got to make it come out of him.

Faunus cupped the back of her head and caged her pretty face with his claws to make sure she didn't look away from him.

"You never have to do anything with me if you don't want to. I cannot help the way my body reacts to you, but that doesn't mean I require anything."

He pressed the palm of his other hand against the tip and pushed down so he could at least put some of it away – he knew he was too hard to push it fully within his seam.

"I am just enjoying you touching me. I didn't even know I was becoming aroused until you slipped against it."

Mayumi reached down and grabbed his wrist with both hands to stop him. "You don't have to do that. I don't mind that it's out, and I'm sure it's more comfortable than trying to shove it in."

"Are you sure?" He really didn't mind.

He was a little embarrassed that this kept happening.

"Yes. I'm just tired and worn out." The smile she gave him was completely and utterly false. "It's been a long time since I've had an eventful day."

"Mayumi... if this is about this morning–"

"I don't want to talk about it right now." Her smile fell, her features becoming stern as she reached for more soap.

Faunus' body tensed in reaction. Was this the beginning of Mayumi changing? *But she was playful with me before she went into the town.* She'd been her usual self. She'd nettled him, bossed him around... she'd even kissed his snout more than she usually would.

He was unsure of what to make of her actions, especially since she was here cleaning him herself.

He pulled his hand away and let his cock freely float in the water when she lathered the fur covering his chest. She also cleaned the bones of his ribs, which felt wonderful.

As she went lower, Faunus grabbed her and cradled her in his large arms. "The rest of me is clean enough. Just relax."

Honestly, he just didn't want to stand in the cold because he knew he'd want to leave the water the moment he did. Her head being so low had also worried him. She could die from a simple drowning, not that he would allow it.

Then a thought crossed his mind, one that had him licking at the outside of his snout with deep interest.

Before she could finish opening her big mouth to speak, he asked, "Could I wash you?"

He was feeling a little more comfortable in the water than normal, perhaps because of constant exposure. Even though she didn't want to be sexual, he still wanted to touch her – maybe even make her feel good.

Being washed by her was pleasurable. He wanted to soothe her in the same way.

Mayumi grabbed her glass and drank the rest of it. Then she grabbed the soap vial and handed it to him, which he took as her way of saying yes.

She tried to give him one arm, but Faunus took both her hands in his after sheathing all his claws. Her mouth pouted to the side as he rubbed his long and large fingers into her dainty, small palms while his thumbs rubbed over the backs of them.

Despite her strength, he knew one wrong move could have him snapping her feeble human bones. He was gentle as he moved up her forearms and tried to massage them in the same way she did for him.

Sometimes Mayumi would scratch at his fur as though she wanted to get to the root of it. Other times, she dug her thumbs and fingers into his muscles deeply. He followed her movements from memory and lightened his press whenever her dark brows twitched.

Since he didn't trust himself, he closed his thighs and made her sit on his knees, turning her so her back was facing him. He wanted to see what he was doing as he washed her back.

Faunus' touch was light when he wrapped his hands around her hips and pressed the pad of his thumbs into the muscles hugging her spine. He did little circles, just like she'd done to him a few times.

He paused when she gave a little mewl, until she leaned into his hands for more.

"It actually feels really tight there," she commented when he was just below her shoulder blades.

Tight? She just felt soft everywhere.

He realised he wasn't the right person to know what felt right and wrong in a human's body.

She wriggled back on his legs, hers parted, and braced her hands on his closed knees. She looked over the treetops to peer at the sky.

He brushed her thick, silky hair over one shoulder when he started going higher. She let out another soft noise, one she only ever made when she felt good. He couldn't stop his cock from jerking every time she did.

It was beginning to strain now, since he'd been hard for so long, untouched. Thankfully, the water kept him moist. Otherwise, he didn't think it would be possible for him to be here doing this with her right now.

Just when he was about to reach her shoulders and neck, he caressed his fingertips down her back and started from the bottom again. He was thrilled when she didn't stop him.

He was supposed to be washing her, after all.

"Have you ever been to the sea, Faunus?" she asked with a breathy voice.

"Why do you ask?" He wasn't sure why she wanted to know this.

"Because you make it really hard to get to know you. You said you've wandered all over the world. I wanted to know if you'd seen the sea."

"Yes, I've seen it. I have walked almost all the way around the land."

"But I'm guessing not the south beaches?"

His head tilted. He was surprised she'd know that.

"No. It is very difficult for a Duskwalker to go there."

"Demons can't really go there either," she said, and he swore he could hear her lips quirk in humour. "We, in the north, have the most fortified Demonslayer guild, but the south has more humans. They battle the land and the sea from Demons, so I imagine getting there would be difficult for your kind too."

"There aren't many trees for Demons to hide from the sun, and it is far from the Veil," he responded.

"I asked to be stationed there for a while. I think I'm one of the rare humans that has been almost everywhere. Where did you live? Um... your cave, I mean. Before it was stolen by Demons."

"West, I think. There was a village that burned down not far from my cave. It was many years ago... but I watched it from the forest as a large number of Demons took advantage of its burning walls."

Mayumi stiffened and looked over her shoulder. "Are you talking about Leeside Town?"

Faunus shrugged in answer. "How would I know what a human town is called?"

"Did it have a big bell in the middle?"

"Yes. It was annoying to me. I could hear it all the way from the Veil, which is why I went there when it wouldn't stop ringing."

She covered her lips with the fore knuckle of her index finger. "Leeside burned down around a hundred years ago."

"I... obtained much humanity that night."

Eventually, the smell of blood and burning meat had sent his mind into a thoughtless craze. He'd spent days fighting with Demons while trying to get to any human who had unfortunately found themselves trapped under house rubble.

"Why did you want to go to the sea?" Faunus asked, becoming uncomfortable with sharing those memories – especially since they were hazy, as most bloodlust episodes or rages were.

He could only imagine what he would have looked like to another. A mindless, roaring beast in the middle of a destroyed, burning town that was being overrun by Demons, surrounded by the sounds of screams and that damn bell ringing until a Demon took it down.

Then a sudden quietness, which only left the sounds of

crackling, dying fires and bloodthirsty creatures sniffing and searching.

"I wanted to know more about you, not the other way around."

Mayumi gave a little moan when he finally worked his thumbs into the tops of her shoulders and the sides of her neck. He used the soap to help make his strokes more slippery, just as much as he used it to wash her.

"I don't have much to share, Mayumi. I have spent most of my life wandering what I can of this world."

"What were you searching for?"

"Everything," he admitted. "And nothing. I just didn't know what else to do. I felt lost."

I have always been searching... So why did I stop when I found her? It was when he'd found Mayumi that night that he stopped wandering and began visiting homes in curiosity, learning. He'd even started trying to befriend the Demons.

The moment that little child had reached for him and asked him not to leave her again... Faunus finally stopped seeking something.

"Fine," she sighed. "My father's family has always lived in this house, so I wanted to see where my mother was born."

"She was not from here?"

He expected her mother to be from one of the closely residing towns.

"I think she was insane. She had to be to have chased my father all the way to Hawthorne Keep." When Faunus' hands halted, and he tilted his head, Mayumi turned around and sat sideways over his lap to face him. "If my father was stubborn, I think my mother was more so. They both said I was more like her than him, not just in the way I looked, but also her personality."

Faunus didn't say anything as he curled his hand around her hip to hold her to him. She eventually looked down her body, then back up to his face as she cocked a brow.

"Well?" she asked, her smile turning a little more mischievous than usual. "There's still plenty of me to wash."

"Will you tell me more if I keep going?"

He'd only stopped because he was waiting for more.

Her smile fell as her brows furrowed deeply. "Why?"

"Because I want to know everything about you," Faunus grumbled.

He wanted to know how she came to be, so he could learn how he came to find her in his bleak existence. Perhaps that would be the answer to why he found her so astonishing.

"There isn't much to the story. My father was still climbing through the ranks of the guild when he was forced to go south. There was a big issue with Demons attacking the border wall and breaking through, so many sectors sent Demonslayers south to help them while they rebuilt."

As she spoke, Faunus reached to grab the soap vial, but she grabbed his hand to stop him. For some reason, she didn't want him to wash her while she spoke of this.

"The south is different from anywhere else. They cut down most of the trees and built a big wall that crosses through the entire land to block out most of the Demons. They still have walled towns, just in case, but it's like a first blockade. They already had to deal with Demons coming from the sea, so they were trying to prevent constant harassment from both sides. A lot of them farmed and fished."

She looked down at both her hands gripping one of his. She drew patterns in the rough palm of it, causing his fingers to twitch.

"You'd think at first glance that she was a meek woman, especially in her later years... but she was actually a soldier. I think that's why my father was drawn to her at first. If he was a poised man, my mother was a bear. He was a lot more brutal when no one was looking, so I think he liked being able to throw her around." She snorted a laugh as she said, "He hated it when she put him on his arse a few times when they sparred as I was growing up."

"He bonded with her because of this?"

"No. Like I said, she chased him to Hawthorne Keep. My father spent a lot of time with my mother when he was in the south, but he eventually left her there when the wall was rebuilt, and he was called back. I don't even think he really considered staying because his home was here – he's always refused to abandon it. And I know everyone in my family history has had to chase people away who have tried to take it for themselves when it was unoccupied." Her pretty eyes finally drew up to his orbs, and the humour in her expression was a little dark, perhaps twisted. "After he left, my mother travelled north all by herself and bashed on the guild gates until they opened them. She wasn't afraid. She'd always been a determined person once she set her mind to something. When they finally let her see my father, she demanded that he take responsibility for getting her pregnant. My father, being an uptight and fundamental man, agreed to marry her and let her guard this house for him. In return, he made sure she and I always had money, and he visited to take care of us both when he could. She trained me just as much as he did."

"She was not upset that she had to leave her home?"

He'd been forced to leave his own, so he didn't understand why someone would choose to.

Mayumi shrugged.

"I told you my mother was an orphan. Her parents died when she was really young, and the people who fostered all the orphans were forced to move around a lot. Not many villages, towns, or cities wanted to house so many collective, unwanted children because they are often afraid of everything – the Demons, the dark, their futures. They were pushed out of a lot of places. She felt no tie to the lands she'd come from and had never put down roots. She'd been renting a room with her wage. She saw no point in staying there, and she wasn't going to raise me by herself when there was a father available – even if he was far away. She didn't know she was pregnant until he left, but that wasn't going to stop her. She told me that if she'd died along the way, then it just wasn't meant to be, but she knew she wouldn't have been able to travel that distance once I was born. I would have cried and brought the Demons upon us."

Faunus lifted his head to look at the sky, thinking deeply. Once he'd made his decision, he turned it back down and leaned forward so he could stroke his tongue across her cheek.

"They were right. You must be more like your mother then."

"Excuse me?!" she squealed. "You didn't meet either of my parents, so how would you know?"

"She was foolish to wander the world by herself with you

inside her womb. Just as you are often foolish."

Mayumi gripped the horn on his good side with both hands and shook his head wildly, causing the rare occurrence of bones to rattle from him.

"That's really mean, Faunus!"

"Is it not true?" he chuckled. "Currently, you are shouting when we are outside in the middle of the night. I can barely hear if a Demon is approaching with how noisy you are being."

Her lips parted in disbelief. Then she made this weird *harrumph* sound as she crossed her arms over her lovely breasts and turned her head away from him with a pout.

"I have upset you," he said while trying his hardest to hide his humour. He snuck his fingertips under the crossed section of her arms so he could palm her chest. "I can continue bathing you to make you feel better."

"I think I'd rather get out after that." Her tone gave a hint of a lie.

"You are not getting out of this water until I know for certain you don't smell of others," he warned, green immediately lifting in his yellow orbs – the heat of his desires had died during their conversation. "I will rid you of their scents, even if I have to force you."

Her eyelids bowed and crinkled with thought before she loosened her arms, and they eventually fell. Her head was still turned away, though.

"Now that's a good little hunter," he purred as he reached for the vial of soap.

He started with her throat and hair after he dunked her back just far enough to wet it. He knew Mayumi had become content again when he played with her hair and massaged the soap into her scalp.

She was always easy to coax sounds out of, and his sensitive hearing picked them up, no matter how quiet she was.

He cradled her entire body with one arm, holding her in the water, as the other danced over her supple flesh.

"Thank you for sharing all this with me," he eventually said as he washed her breasts, lingering there because he liked the way she twitched. Her nipples were hard, and he knew she enjoyed it when he petted them. "There is only so much I could learn from afar, and I have always wanted to know more about you."

"You could always ask me," she said quietly, her eyes closing in what could only be contentment.

"I don't always know what I need to ask," he said truthfully. "To be honest, I don't know what I'm doing with you or why."

Her eyes peeked open slightly. "What do you mean?"

"I have been to many places and seen many humans, but it has only ever been you that has brought peace within my mind." He brushed his soap-covered hand down her stomach, palming her all the way down as it dipped and concaved under his rough callouses. "All I know is that whenever something... unpleasant has happened to me, you have been the only thing I can think of, the only thing that could ease me."

Faunus pushed past her pubic mound to go to her legs, knowing if he was to touch there, he may want to return to it when he'd already promised this would be as far as they'd go tonight.

His thoughts weren't aided by the fact his sight was purple again, and he could feel the underside of his re-hardened cock brushing against the side of her arse. Even one of his tentacles had curled into that cute little crease she had where her arse cheek met the back of her thigh.

Even when Jabez had me in that room, she was the only creature that kept me... sane.

And every time his mind had finally drifted off, it was her beautiful face that he'd see right before he succumbed to his pain, or lack of air, or when his heart would temporarily stop beating.

She'd unknowingly been his salvation.

He gripped her muscular thigh tightly, never wanting to let it go, as he said, "I am inexplicably drawn to you, Mayumi."

THIRTY-ONE

While crouched, Mayumi carefully selected her footing to make sure she didn't stand on any leaf or stick debris. She even tested the snow she was walking on top of to make sure it wasn't deeper than usual and wouldn't create noise.

Her breathing was shallow and quiet, her pulse calm and steady.

On the other side of the deer, deep within the trees, she could occasionally see two yellow orbs. Faunus was ensuring he didn't spook the creature in the wrong direction. For a beast that was so massive and heavy, his steps were almost silent when he wanted them to be.

He was being just as cautious as she was; however, for a completely different reason.

There was a chance he could be sent into bloodlust, a hunting rage, if the deer ran. She'd originally been hoping he could chase the deer down and kill it for her, but he'd informed her that would be too dangerous.

He could turn on her once he finished eating.

His face was covered by a cloth that was saturated with perfume to hide the scent of blood from him. His jaws were also tied shut, just in case, by an enchanted rope she still had from being a Demonslayer.

She had a small arsenal of enchanted weapons.

They had been blessed by Priests and Priestess in one of their temples. They refused to live with the guild or in most towns, choosing to seclude themselves unless they had their own temple within the town. With limited space, having a temple just for a small few was unachievable.

Mayumi had always been apprehensive of those face-covered, mysterious people. The fact that they were the only humans who could use magic and hid their identities and even their bodies in long cloth and cloaks... she couldn't help finding them anything but suspicious.

She was aware she was calling the kettle black, considering Demonslayers also covered their faces, but that was more to stay hidden within the dark than anything else.

Still, she had always been thankful for their magic.

It had been a massive help as a Demonslayer, but currently it was protecting her from her big, bad, sharp-toothed monster.

This was their agreement.

Nothing could cut the rope other than a small knife made of blessed obsidian, which she had on her weapons belt, and it would keep her safe... ish. His claws could still go for the kill, but she also had an enchanted whip looped at her hip.

Most enchantments were only for binding and protection. Nothing seemed to kill or cause additional damage.

Honestly, she could have done this herself, but the idea of carrying such a large creature sounded tiresome. She was game enough to take the risk if it meant she could be lazy.

She had someone who could carry the load for her, so why not utilise him?

Mayumi crawled her way closer to the doe she hunted. She searched for any sign of Faunus but couldn't find him. He was watching, waiting.

I need to come up with something else, she thought as she locked her sight on her target. *The animal glue didn't work.*

Lining up her shot with her bow and arrow, she took a breath and held it. The world quietened in her ears as she narrowed her eyes.

The glue melted right off his face.

She released the string.

The arrow met its mark, and the deer made a lowing, distressed bleat and reared back. While it was upright on its hind legs, Faunus launched through the trees.

It was given no chance to run as he grabbed it by its head and twisted. Minimal bloodshed, minimal chance for the creature to be in lasting pain, minimal chances of it squirming. A clean kill, in her opinion.

But now she had to wait, ducking down just enough to make sure she couldn't be seen. His orbs were red, and he was standing above it on all fours.

The full-body shudder he gave was easily visible before he sat back on his haunches and gripped at his skull. He shook it side to side in his hands like he was trying to shake his very own thoughts from his mind.

He eventually sagged and lowered his hands to look around.

"It is safe now," he said, not raising his voice since he knew she would be nearby.

"Are you sure?" she asked... just to make damn sure.

He changed his form so he could stand on two legs, his furry butt naked to all. She still refused to give him his pants, enjoying seeing him in all his glory.

His tail curled in what she *knew* was annoyance as he bent down to scoop the deer into his arms.

"I would not have called you over if I didn't think it was safe," he stated, before turning in the direction of her voice. "Please let us hurry. I am uncomfortable with my jaws clamped shut like this. I also cannot smell properly, so I can only hear if danger is approaching."

Mayumi bounced to her feet and dusted the snow from her knees. "I told you it would be fine."

A huff snorted through his nose. "It was still risky. I don't know why you wanted me to help you so much when you could have done this on your own while I stayed back and scouted the area for other dangers."

Her shoulders bounced as she shrugged.

"I haven't hunted with another person since the guild, and I wanted to see how compatible we were in the field. I also thought it would be fun."

His snout lifted like he was thinking on her words. "Are we *compatible*, then?"

"Absolutely. They often require multiple shots. I was able to hit in the spot that would make it rear back, and that meant you were able to finish it off." She reached up and patted his biceps. "It would have taken me a few hours to weaken it and then I would have needed to bring it home alive. This way, I was able to hunt it right before dusk fell, and it's big enough to still attract Demons without bleeding it like I did the boar."

"Sounds complicated," he huffed.

"It is. Baiting Demons is an art we needed to perfect." She crossed her arms behind her head as they walked. "I live too close to two villages, which means I have to either have a fresh kill or a large one."

"Although I have already stated that I will not stop you, I still don't understand why you are doing this."

"It means there is one less Demon in the area to go poking its ugly head near those villages. That's all I care about, doing my duty even if I was discharged. I still have two legs, two arms, and a heartbeat, and I will use all of it to kill them until the day I die."

Faunus let out a growl at her final word, but she refused to hide the fact that death could come for her at any time, just to stop him from being upset about it. The more he came to accept that she would die one day, whether he wanted her to or not, whether he was here or not, would only further build her case to him.

Having Phantom abilities would be so useful.

He'd further explained it to her, and Mayumi was absolutely one hundred percent on board with the idea of turning intangible.

Imagine all the Demons I could sneak up on and kill.

Faunus would turn her into the ultimate Demonslayer.

Her eyes fell to the side to look at him, knowing he was slowing his pace for her. *Spending whatever time I have with him sounds... pretty good, too.*

So what if he was destined to die sooner than eternity? With the way she lived, she only had a few good years left anyway.

Her arms fell from being crossed behind her head as her heart gave an uncomfortable throb. Her lips pursed as her brows crinkled into a tight frown.

I thought I could convince him if the glue worked, but his body heat literally melted it off his face.

She'd used animal glue, as she hadn't been able to obtain casein. Everything else she'd found within Colt's Outpost would have stung his constantly open wound. It had been her only shot, and it failed.

I can't strap his horns because he said pushing the crack back together was excruciating.

She didn't mind staring at leather over his face or even the yucky yellow of the glue on him if it helped to keep him alive for longer. She just wanted to make him feel confident enough to take her soul.

I've tried the glue twice in the past week just to make sure. She wasn't about to give up just because of a failed attempt. *What else can I do?*

Being a Phantom was just a bonus, but bonding with this big guy was what her mind had stubbornly grabbed hold of. Like her mother, she was foolishly determined.

Call it love or infatuation, but she *knew* Faunus was the one person in all of existence that she could picture being... happy with.

It wouldn't be easy. Already they had their difficulties, but this was the first time she ever wanted to persevere through those challenges instead of salmon diving out the window to freedom.

Why couldn't that be enough?

"You have that look on your face," he eventually said after some time of them walking.

She snorted half-heartedly. "The one where I'm up to something?"

"I believe your face is permanently like that." He chuckled, making her jaw drop in disbelief. The audacity of this Duskwalker! "No. The other one. The one where something is bothering you."

That made her jaw instantly shut. The corner muscle knot of it ticked when she clenched her back molars.

"You're also quiet," he stated casually. "You're rarely quiet. You're usually bothering me and harassing me. It worries me when you don't."

With a false huff and a very real eye roll, Mayumi picked up her pace. Which meant nothing because he just matched her as she tried to trudge through the thick and dense snow.

"I'm usually a pretty quiet person. It just depends on my mood and who I'm with," she said.

Ahh, misdirection at its... lamest. Her internal cringe had to be snuffed so it didn't twitch her cheek.

"I'm just getting my mind ready for tonight," she added. "You must be in the right frame of mind when hunting creatures who tend to think of you as prey."

The lie was bittersweet, as it was partly true.

She just didn't want to talk to Faunus about her feelings, how deep they were, or how much she wanted to give him her soul.

I'm not a poet. She didn't know how to be soft and gentle with her words, didn't know how to formulate them almost musically.

She had half a mind to pry his jaws apart while he was asleep and shove her soul down his throat so he couldn't stop her. There. A solution. Then they could argue about it together for eternity, or however long they'd have left together.

Currently, she saw any dialogue on the subject not going her way, and she wasn't the type of person to fight a losing battle. She'd rather delay the fight until she came up with a strategy where she knew she would be the victor.

Before Faunus could pry any further, the top of her chimney came into view and she almost sighed in relief.

"Come on, quick," she said, knowing she was the one slowing them down. "The shadows are almost long enough that Demons might start approaching."

After a few minutes of jogging on her part, they made it to the cleared centre of her front yard. She instructed him to tie its hind legs together by a long rope before he just... lifted the thing so she could tie it off at a height she could never reach.

Mayumi checked the rope leading to the ground hook to make sure it was perfectly secured. Then she ran inside and immediately dumped her weapons on her coat rack and up against the wall next to it, with Faunus following in behind her.

Walking halfway across the main room, she was already stripping her clothes off. She dumped them in a messy ball on the single-seater couch she rarely used and walked into the storage room.

"Okay. So first, you'll block your nose and then cut open the deer to attract the Demons. I'll be in my usual spot on the roof, and you'll be in the trees or on the ground, whichever you prefer," she said while jumping back into the main area with one foot inside her Demonslayer pants as she tried to get the other in. She almost tripped onto her face and had to steady herself. "I'll watch your back and make sure you're safe from harm."

"I feel like we're going about this the wrong way," he grumbled with his arms folded across his chest and leaning against the door frame. "Aren't you meant to be the one hunting them, and I protect you?"

His orbs were yellow, but she swore they flashed purple when she stood and placed her hands on her hips. It was probably because she was wearing nothing but her pants right then, her breasts out for him to see.

"Do you know what a hunting dog is?"

She groaned when he licked at his snout and quickly shoved her skin-tight, long-sleeved uniform shirt on. She tucked it into her black leather breeches to make sure it wouldn't ride up and expose her back to the elements.

"I have seen dogs with humans, yes. Are they not just companions?"

Going back into the storage room, she grabbed her special boots from the personal chest she had sitting on top of another. Her personal items were often used, so they caused little dust to flurry into the air.

She always had the urge to sneeze in this room, though.

"They are, but they're also specially trained to hunt down other animals and kill or trap them, depending on the command given." Once more, Mayumi was hopping her way back into the room, a single foot thudding against the ground. "It's a different way to hunt. The human protects the hound as it runs headfirst into danger."

Faunus gave a mean growl. "I am not a dog, Mayumi."

"I never said you were one!" she shouted as she got her second foot in her specialised boots. "But you have claws, fangs, and are super fast. You're also really fucking strong, and I just can't help myself from wanting to use your full potential."

When she realised their talking had caused her to mix up her boots and put them on the wrong feet, she groaned and sat down to take them off. It was an easy mistake... when rushing.

She gave a shrug with one arm.

"Did you know you are literally the apex predator? It goes Duskwalkers, Demons, bears, wolf packs, and then mountain lions. Humans are barely even on the scale, even with all our swords and arrows." She stood once her boots were on the right feet and tucked her ponytail into the back of her leather uniform shirt so she could bring the hood over her head. She turned to him once she'd fastened the mouth covering over her face. "Look, I have a Duskwalker here, and I happen to think you're pretty freaking awesome."

Mayumi smiled under her face covering when his orbs changed into a reddish pink in embarrassment.

"Why can't I use you as an extension of myself in hunting, Faunus? We got the bait together, brought it back, and now we *both* get to lure Demons here and kill them. You, being the better half of our team, will take them down, while I, being the slow, weaker half, will be on the roof with my arrows. I will take any chance I can to kill them myself and make sure you aren't taken from behind."

The colour of his orbs darkened in their reddish-pink hue. He even fidgeted slightly by turning his head away, then looked up before coming back to her.

A frown crinkled her brows. *I've complimented him before. Why is he acting so shy now?*

She wondered if it was too many at once or if it was because she was complimenting his strengths rather than his body.

Regardless, Mayumi internally shrugged and came forward. She lifted her hands up and removed the cloth covering his snout before untying the enchanted rope clamping his jaws shut, thankful she didn't have to cut it.

He spread his fangs apart, moving his bottom jaw side to side while rubbing it before clanking them shut.

Mayumi then reached up and dragged his head lower, cupping the top and bottom of his snout, as she kissed it through her face covering from the side.

"I trust you, and you're the first person I've ever wanted to hunt with like this who isn't from the guild." She leaned her forehead against his bony jaw. "This is a big part of who I am. It brings me a lot of relief to not only be able to do this, but also do it with you. I don't want you to protect me as though I'm incapable, Faunus. I want to protect you as though I'm strong and cunning."

"I trust you, too," he said, as he rubbed his jaw against her. "But if I become enraged, my mind won't be what it normally is. I won't be able to see the difference between you and them, friend or foe. Everything will be prey, and you will smell much more enticing. I'm worried I will turn on you."

"You won't," she stated without a doubt. "And even if you do, I'll just tie you up and wait you out." A chuckle left her right before she said, "Maybe we can have fun with that when the Demons are gone."

He returned her chuckle. "I thought you said you had to get your mind ready."

"Thank you so much for this, Faunus. I'll wave at you from the roof when I'm ready."

Mayumi rushed to her coat rack and took her belt off it, her quiver following it. Once they were on, she grabbed her bow and slung it across her body.

She knew Faunus had gone outside by the cold chill that billowed inside the house. Then she grabbed a brick-hard section of bread she'd cooked the day before.

He was standing by the stake when she climbed through the ceiling hatch and onto the roof with her brown cloak covering her. His skull followed her movements as she crawled until she was in position.

When she waved at him, he dug through the snow until he had a clump of sloshy dirt and proceeded to shove it into his nose hole. Still preparing herself, she pulled an arrow from her quiver and nocked it just as he walked over to the deer carcass, shoved his claws into it, and tore it open from its hips to its chest.

Its entrails spilt against the ground.

A large grin spread across her face at the odd sound in the distance, like a froth-filled, gargling roar. It was familiar... and close. It may have been sniffing around where Mayumi and Faunus had originally attacked the deer.

She'd shot the deer, which had left a small amount of blood behind.

The moment the Demon broke into the clearing, Faunus leapt for it from where he'd stepped back to hide from sight. The Demon didn't even stand a chance. He just tore it to shreds with his claws the moment he got his hands on it.

Thankfully, he didn't start eating it, but she didn't understand why he left it there once it was dead. Or why he pulled it apart even further once it'd ceased breathing. Honestly... it was a little morbid and grotesque.

He turned his skull in the direction of the roof, his orbs already a dangerous colour of red.

"You better prepare yourself." His voice was almost like a growl in itself. "You want to kill Demons?" He pointed to the one on the ground. "That is bait. That will bring more. I will try to go for as long as I can before I eat everything."

The expression that lifted into her features was most likely malicious as well as prideful as she stared at him.

Demons were cannibals. They ate their own kind, and she couldn't believe she'd never thought about pulling one apart to make the scents in the air stronger after she'd hung up her bait and killed one.

Faunus retreated to hide once more, unable to see her grin hidden behind her mask.

Happy hunting.

Not long after, another Demon approached. She pulled back her string and aimed it in the direction she knew it was coming from.

It'd been far away, and she'd needed to wait for a long time. The moment it came out of the tree line, Mayumi released her arrow – uncaring if it truly hit its mark, since Faunus would protect her if it changed directions and targeted her. She'd hit right between the Demon's eyes, and it slid against the ground to halt right between Faunus' hands since he'd been running for it.

It was a clean kill, and she met Faunus' gaze when he turned to her. He was on all fours now, at some point shifting to his more monstrous form to be faster.

His spikes, which were usually streamlined down his body, were currently sticking straight up from his spine, forearms, and calves. He looked threatening, savage, wild, and oh-so-freaking sexy that it had her biting her lip.

I need to fuck him while he's like that.

She *knew* that if things went well tonight, and she was able to mostly watch him be his beastly, predatory self, she was going to be picturing it all night.

Looks like I'll be breaking multiple Demonslayer rules on the field tonight.

She almost laughed as she recounted them while nocking another arrow to her bow string.

Rule one: don't be afraid until your last breath. An easy rule to follow. She couldn't remember if she'd ever been afraid in her life.

Rule two: be prepared to die. Another easy one. She was always prepared for the worst possible outcome.

With Faunus by her side, she doubted death would be coming for her tonight.

Rule three: never be distracted. She'd already broken this rule, instead picturing Faunus' on all fours with her beneath him. Pinning her down, dominating her as she screamed with abandon.

Her heart stammered at just the mere thought.

Rule four: keep your scent minimal.

It was late into the night, the waning moon rising higher, and Mayumi thought she had such a deep puddle between her thighs that it was soaking her underwear.

She wondered if Demons could pick up on her arousal, but she also cared very little if they could.

As the night continued, she recounted more rules.

Rule Nine: never take your eyes off your target.

She nocked another arrow and unleashed it into the back of a Demon that was sneaking up behind Faunus while he faced off with another.

They'd managed to attract multiple Demons, more than she'd ever seen before, because of the number of bleeding bodies they'd collected. Faunus had eventually lost his mind to whatever forces caused him to go unhinged, but he never got the chance to turn on her.

By the time he started eating everything around him, another Demon would come to steal his food – and then die.

Rule twelve: if your companion is injured, do not try to help them. Protect them from a safe distance until the sun rises.

That was a dark, foreboding rule. If someone tried to help a bleeding companion, there was a chance they could be killed themselves trying to bandage their wound – a wound that would continue to attract the Demons.

It was better to protect them from a distance and hope they could both last until the sun rose.

Mayumi had *always* followed that one rule, even when she didn't want to. She'd been hated for it by many as a team leader, and she couldn't count the number of human deaths that were a result of her decision. She'd also saved many more by doing so.

But she'd break that rule if Faunus was in serious danger. She'd leap from this very roof with her sword raised above her head if need be – even if it put her in his enraged sight – so long as his skull didn't crack further.

She'd do it in a heartbeat.

Rule seventeen: if you see a Duskwalker, you may choose to either fight it and die, or run and die – there is no escape.

Here she was, fighting alongside one while also wondering how she could get herself on top of its cock without being mauled to death. Her breaths were laboured, her cheeks warm with arousal.

She even considered fanning herself when he let out a nipple-pearling, pussy-spasming beastly roar to the sky, covered in blood from bony head to pawed toes. She wanted him to roar like that while he was ramming into her and forcing her to drown in the waves of bliss-filled oblivion.

Rule eighteen...

THIRTY-TWO

With her head resting on the pillow of Faunus' shoulder, Mayumi let her eyes slowly peek open.

As dust motes danced all around them in the sunlight that filtered into the room, the first thing that greeted her was his bone-encased, furry chest slowly rising and falling as he lay on his back for her. The leg she was lying on was straight, while her other was bent and thrown over his torso. It was the same for her arms.

Her entire body was pressed against him, although not nearly enough of them were touching since she was wearing a shirt.

There was a slight stab of claws into the backs of her thighs since his hand was cradling her arse, his middle finger dangerously close to being between her legs.

She rubbed her drowsy face against him to wake herself further before letting her gaze fall onto one of the windows next to the fireplace.

It's definitely past midday, she thought, noticing how bright the sky was. A bird flew overhead, giving a tweet she didn't fully take notice of.

Instead, she let her eyes fall back to his chest so she could follow her fingertips diving through his fur. *We were awake even after the sun rose.*

Hell would have frozen over before Mayumi let Faunus in her clean home, saturated from skull to pawed foot in Demon blood. A bath had been ordered, and he'd grumblingly accepted the demand.

A smile quirked her lips.

He didn't complain when I gave him a massage, though.

Actually, he'd managed to get sleepy while still partially in the water with his arms and upper chest lying over the inground bath's edge. She was certain he'd been purring the whole damn time.

In pampering him after fighting Demons throughout the night, it'd been Mayumi who had eventually fallen asleep lying over his back.

She had no recollection of being carried inside. Maybe she'd even walked the distance half-asleep. Regardless, she hadn't managed to do what she wanted to.

Continuing to sift her fingers through his long fur, her cheeks ballooned when she gave a puffed pout. *I wanted to appreciate him for all his hard work.*

Or rather, she wanted to appreciate him for the magnificent show he'd put on throughout the night. Although she'd occasionally helped, it'd turned into more of a spectacle for her.

With the moon barely illuminating his movements, he'd been so fast in the shadows of the trees that if she stopped watching him even for a moment, she'd lost him. Perhaps it was because there had been no strong Demons, but the ruthlessness he showcased in destroying anything that came into the clearing was awe-inspiring.

Sure, he'd gained a few wounds. She even brushed her fingertips near one that marred his chest, but it hadn't slowed him down at all.

Should I wake him? She brushed her hand lower and eventually found the dip where his seam was. A small smile filled her features when it twitched under her light touch.

He did *say I could wake him up with his cock.* She eagerly licked at her lips.

When his seam dipped and clenched as she stroked upwards over it, Mayumi made her decision. She carefully wriggled herself down until the side of her forehead was resting over the bottom sunken rib bone of his chest. His palm stayed stuck to her arse as though, even in sleep, he didn't wish to relinquish it.

She stroked his seam up and down with a feather-light touch, teasing it. After dancing her fingers over it a few times, a slight bulge pushed up from underneath his flesh.

It didn't open, but the tip of a tentacle came out to curl around one of her fingertips as if to say hello before slipping away again.

This was going to be a lot harder than with a human man. Their dicks were always hanging out, making it easy to wake them with either a hand job or a blow job.

"Faunus," she lightly called, noticing his cock wasn't pushing through.

"Mmm?" was the only answer she got.

When more coaxing didn't work, she gently fingered her way in. The tension holding him back wouldn't permit her, and she huffed out a breath.

Fine then. She shuffled her way over him until she had kneed her way between his thick thighs.

"Mayumi?" he asked, in the groggiest, sleepiest, most gravelly voice she'd ever heard in her life as she pressed her lips to the middle of his seam.

She gave a tiny, appreciative moan in contentment at the sound of his voice before she pressed purposefully loud kisses to him.

"You have to open up if you want me to touch you," she stated between kisses, looking up to see Faunus hadn't moved an inch, nor had he seemed to open his sight.

She knew he was awake when he reached down and patted the back of her head, scraping his claws through her hair and over her scalp. Just for the little shiver he gave her, she licked up, and his seam twitched like crazy under her tongue. The bulge grew exponentially bigger.

"Say please," he groaned, his hips lifting slightly before settling. He was trying to keep it from her on purpose, the bastard!

The smile that curled her lips was devious. Mayumi had been gentle so far, trying to coax him out nicely.

She drew the tips of her nails up both his inner thighs, starting from his knees and making his legs clench and shudder as she swirled her tongue in patterns.

There would be no please from her, not when she could feel him parting despite obviously trying to hold back. Mayumi shoved her hand in, slowly but with force this time. She breeched his seam and knew by the texture that greeted her that his tentacles had swirled around his cock, impeding its release – or they had been until she shoved her hand in.

His cock pushed forward to the length of them as his back bowed.

"Why did that feel good?" he groaned, just as his skull pointed downwards, and she watched his orbs light up.

Purple greeted her. Bright purple, in fact.

"You tell me," she murmured with her lips against a tentacle, trying to get them to unwind so she could get to the yummy centre of him. "Now, are you going to give me what I want, or shall I start peeling tentacles off you with my teeth?"

"I'd like to see that," he half-heartedly chuckled.

She carefully bit into the tip of a tentacle and pulled. There was a lot of resistance, but when she finally made it let go, she noticed his spikey cock was throbbing heavily. Even the veins on him were visibly pulsing.

"You're making this hard on purpose."

"You–" he started, right before she dipped her tongue into the gap between his tentacles that she'd opened up and licked his slick-coated cock. "*Nhn*. You win."

They finally released, and his full erection pushed all the way forward. Mayumi immediately grabbed it with both hands and licked the head before he could do anything to stop her.

"You're not usually this... active in the morning," he rasped, fisting her hair.

"Kept thinking about last night." Her answer was muffled by what she could get inside her mouth. "I don't think I've seen anything as hot as you fighting off Demons for me."

A bated breath fell from him when she began moving both her hands up and down the heavy girth of him as she swirled her tongue around the tip. Then she sweetly suckled it for him, giving a content hum against him at the taste.

"Even I know that is an odd thing to be aroused by, Mayumi."

She laughed. "I thought we'd already come to the conclusion that I get turned on by odd things."

Hell, she was here nearly drooling at the mouth each time she collected a heady taste of lemongrass, lime, and Duskwalker cock lubricant. She suckled over one of his spikes on the side of the shaft between her hands, her tongue dabbing before she moved to another.

Then she bit the side of him decently hard. Faunus groaned as he fisted her hair tighter to the point a sting radiated across her scalp.

"Why would me watching you being amazing be any different, my big, sexy, murderous, Dusk–WALKER!" Mayumi squealed when Faunus rolled up to be seated while forcing her mouth away from his cock.

Before she could even orientate herself, her shirt was removed from her while she was lifted. Her back was shoved against something hard, and the ends of her limbs partially dangled over the edge. The cool air brushing over her now naked body caused her already hardened nipples to tighten.

Faunus had laid her down over her coffee table they often played games on.

Then he was all around her, his bigger frame allowing him to lean on his knees and a straight arm against the ground with her elevated by the table.

"Hey," she said quietly with little huffs, breathless from his swift actions. It reminded her of all the times her eyes couldn't keep up with his speed last night. "I wasn't done."

Her head shifted when he used his free hand to claw his way under her head and support the back of it.

"Amazing *and* sexy?" he purred, burying the end of his snout just behind her ear and breathing her in. He nipped at her neck. "I'm starting to get the feeling you liked seeing me in that form, Mayumi."

"Mmm." She lifted her chin up and to the side so he could have better access. Her jugular was given a rough, swiping lick in return. "Maybe a little. I wouldn't mind if you fucked me like that."

"You have a *monster* in your arms, and you want him to be even more monstrous." His voice was rough and husky, hinting with just the right amount of teasing humour that it evoked a shiver from her.

Mayumi's skin grew even more flushed than before, and she gave a little mewl.

Then she reached up so she could run her hands up his torso, over his chest, and into the fur on his neck that connected to the back of his skull. The tips of her fingers brushed his ram horns.

"I like all of you, Faunus."

His fangs gave small nibbles at her skin, almost shyly.

"You smell so good," he groaned, his hand coming out from under her so he could brush it down her body in the opposite way she had. Her chest lifted when his large palm flicked over both her sensitive, aching nipples at the same time. It caused her abdomen to rub against his cock and tentacles, smearing wetness on her. "Usually, your scent is tainted by me and leather, but you don't smell like anything but pumpkin and sleep. You smell clean."

The longer he breathed her in, the groggier his voice sounded – like he wanted to fall back asleep above her.

"We did have a bath before we went to bed." Her body flinched when his rough palm swept from her right breast to her left, his hand slipping over the near flatness of her chest to play with them, to tease them since there was little for him to hold. Her voice was even quieter when she said, "And we didn't have sex yesterday."

Her breath hitched when he slipped his claws down her torso, and her insides spasmed, her abdominal muscles tightening in anticipation under the points of them.

"It makes me want to make a mess inside you."

"Faunus," she moaned, spreading her thighs when his fingers brushed through the hair curling over her pubic mound. She fisted the fur at the back of his neck.

"You smell so wet for me, Mayumi. If I touch you, will you soak my fingers?" The bastard just danced the tips of them above the slit of her pussy.

"You already know the answer. Just touch me."

Her clit was tingling and begging for attention, while her insides were throbbing with a desperate need to wring something. She'd wanted this last night, to be touched and teased. If she hadn't been so tired, she would have made sure he'd fucked her to sleep rather than falling asleep in the tub.

His index and middle fingers slid into her folds to caress the needy bud of her clit from both sides. A sharp moan slipped from her lips, and her hips rose, pushing him all the way through until the tips tickled her entrance.

An appreciative *purrowl* emitted from his chest.

She pressed her chest against him so she could feel that rumbling vibration against her nipples, even if it was only for a moment since he leaned back.

As he stared down at her, he prodded her by dabbing at her pooling entrance. She just panted at his divine, unholy, skulled face, knowing her own was pink with deep-seated arousal. At any moment, she worried her very breath would begin to fog from the heat that was building within her.

"Do you wa–" Cutting off whatever stupid teasing question was about to come out of him, Mayumi messily swiped her tongue across his closed fangs.

"Oh!" she cried when his claws sheathed right before he rammed those thick fingers inside her wet, quivering cunt.

The moment her lips were spread and her tongue poked out a little, Faunus parted his fangs and buried his tongue inside her mouth. Her moan was muffled, and it grew quiet but consistent as he thrust his fingers in and out.

She tried to get her tongue to frolic with his. She even chased it when it left her mouth. The squelching from between her legs was distinct, revealing just how sopping she was, how much liquid he was moving around.

How pathetically turned on she was.

There was a short moment when his fingers left her, and she felt his arm moving. Mayumi tried to wrap her legs around him when she knew he was stroking his cock to coax his lubricant to rewet him, hoping he was preparing to push it inside her.

It almost felt cruel when it was his slime-covered fingers he slipped back inside, but he rendered her quiet when he palmed her clit. His thrusts weren't fast, but he pushed each one upwards against the front of her channel to find the tender spot that would make her break apart for him. He grazed it, pampered it, gave it attention when he found it and then drew his fingers in a circle over it.

Eventually, her arms wrapped around his neck. It was rare she got to hug him like this, since she was so much smaller than him. She usually had to hug his torso. That or he would have to awkwardly arch his back.

And now that she was accustomed to it, she adored having his long, flat tongue in her mouth for her to suck.

He always makes me feel so good. With her feet finding purchase on the edge of the table, she bucked her hips into his hand with her knees wide. *I fucking adore doing this with him.*

The only reason he broke from their strange kiss was that Mayumi had stopped greeting him. She could barely breathe, and she was thankful for the reprieve since she was moments from dissolving into a happy puddle.

Oh, God. His fingers are so long and thick. She didn't feel snug around them, but they were wonderful nonetheless. They could target, could stir her in the most sublime way.

"Inside me," she begged, uncaring of how pathetic her voice sounded. "I need you inside me. I'm about to come. Please."

She wanted that thick girth pounding into her. She needed it, ached for it, fucking craved it. She even looked down, trying to search for it through the gap between their bodies. She wanted to look at what was going to be inside her.

"Not until you come for me like this," he stated – just because he knew she was desperate by how much she was undulating into his hand.

And she relished him for that.

"I like it when you're all needy like this. When you beg me for it with your mouth or with the way your pussy hungrily sucks my fingers."

Mayumi's head tipped back, her back bowed deeply and her toes curled as she let out a powerful, high-pitched scream. She yanked on his fur as she came hard, liquid building inside her channel. His fingers moved in and out of her faster, and she thought she saw stars in her murky, darkening vision.

Faunus buried his bony face against the exposed column of her throat and let out a deep expire, almost like a breath of relief or gratitude.

"There we go. That's a good little human giving me what I wanted," he rumbled when her spasms began to soften.

She relaxed underneath his heat, but her heart was still beating quickly when he finally slipped his fingers from her.

His head was facing her to make sure she saw when he lifted his hand and smeared her orgasm over his nose hole and snout to stain it with her scent. The show felt almost primal, feral even. Then he spread his jaws and used his purple tongue to lick the rest of her cream from his fingers and palm.

His bright-purple orbs darkened to black as he deeply groaned, like the taste of her was delectable against his tastebuds. She even noticed the inhuman parts of him ruffled and shuddered as he sampled her taste.

Her dazed eyes softened at having this remarkable person above her. Just him doing all this had her satisfied body priming for more.

Then his hand shot down to her thigh, almost slapping it, so he could grip it tightly and keep her legs open. His hips surged forward, and her breath hitched when the tip of his cock slipped over her folds. The soft spiked length of him followed, and she tried to close her legs so she could capture him between them. Only one moved until he let the other go.

"I swear your cock was made to do that," she rasped, pushing her hips into it.

He placed his hand next to her head again to support his massive body above hers. "Do what?"

When he pulled back to thrust through her folds again, she couldn't contain the lewd mewl that fell from her.

"My clit fits perfectly in the groove on the underside of you." She bit the inside of her lip on the draw back and grabbed both his biceps to hold on to him, to touch him in any way, as she steadied herself through this. Her body was sensitive now, and the wet slide of his lubricated cock was like beautiful torture. "It feels so damn amazing."

The sensitive bundle of nerves was nestled within that deep groove and being sinfully petted from all sides.

The heat spreading over her sternum was familiar and welcome but so searing that it had her chest quivering to the point that even her breasts jiggled.

She looked down to watch, refusing to look at him, as she whispered, "It's like you were made to do this to me, Faunus."

The idea that they were 'made' for each other was a silly notion. They were nothing more than two creatures whose fates had incidentally intertwined. Deep down inside, she knew they weren't meant to be together. He was a Duskwalker, and she was a human. They were so vastly different, and yet... she couldn't help thinking Faunus was the only perfect man for her.

A bright light glowed between her breasts just as a wisp of fire passed through her flesh.

She noticed his cock swelled in reaction to seeing her soul trying to emerge, causing a heavy drop of precum to well at the very tip as he thrust harder. It even dripped to her stomach to leave a sticky line joining them.

He pushed his palm against the glow.

"I can't take it when you do that," he rasped? Groaned? His body did that weird *purrowl* thing she teased him for – like his insides wanted to sing for her in every way imaginable.

She liked that she could give him such an intense reaction, and her eyes crinkled as they bowed, her lips curling knowingly.

There was nothing he could do or say that would make her contain it.

She could feel tiny little movements, like her soul was bashing wildly against his palm with its hands and feet. It was desperate to come out, desperate for him to steal it.

Faunus lowered himself so his chest was the one containing it and could freely slip both his hands underneath Mayumi's smaller body. Gripping the creases where the bottom of her arse cheeks met her thighs, he lifted her off the short coffee table and sat back with his legs crossed.

Although this position meant she was hovering in the air, she trusted him. Her own legs wrapped around his waist, but he was much too big for her to cross her ankles.

Mayumi only had her arms around his neck for a few seconds before she was forced to let go when he'd positioned her over the head of his cock and shoved her all the way down to the hilt in one fluid, hard, and fast motion.

Her surprised, yet raspy, moan was drowned out by his much louder, deeper one. Both their heads tilted back at the pressure.

The heat within her was so immense that it had her softening around him, and yet, their bodies were so snug she knew she must be strangling his cock. She didn't know if it was his lubricant that made her feel like she was soaking wet, or if it was the orgasm he'd given her, but it allowed her to lean back with ease by gripping his fur and grind him inside her using her calves.

She stirred his cock inside her pussy, as she leaned back further to look down at their pelvises flush against each other, watching avidly.

The movement separated their bodies, and the bright-orange glow crested through her flesh as her soul ducked its head out.

When it did, Faunus released her arse so he could grab her hands. He yanked at the claw-like grip she had on his fur and shoved her hands behind her back with both of them folded.

It arched her back, forcing them together once more. Her chest compressed tightly against his torso every time she breathed.

"We can't move like this," she stated.

At least, not with her thighs around his waist and his legs crossed.

He leaned his head down and brushed the end of his snout against her hair. "So impatient. Always so needy and demanding for my cock to be moving inside you."

Faunus brought his tail forward and wrapped the middle of it around her forearms to lock them together. She curled her hands into fists, each one resting on the back of her waist.

"You will stay," he demanded, grabbing her arse again and giving each firm cheek an enthusiastic knead.

He lifted her slowly up his cock, and the higher she went, the more his lungs and torso seemed to shudder. With the head being just slightly bigger, she felt her entrance parting for it from the inside before he dropped her all the way back down.

His head tilted back as he let out a rumbling groan, moving her up and down his fat cock in such a slow, agonising pace.

"Contain your soul, Mayumi." She didn't know if it was a demand or a plea, but it sounded as though he *ached* for her to do so. "It's so hot I can feel it." Then, his voice faded into a whisper as he said, "It's right there. I can feel it calling to me."

Her breath hitched at the direness she heard, like he was growing frantic at it trying to come out. Mayumi moaned when her inner walls clenched him in reaction, the idea he might be losing his mind over it making her shiver with goosebumps.

"No." She *wanted* him to be tormented.

She wanted him to ache all the way to the very core of his being until she knew she'd shaken him completely.

The growl he gave was the only warning she got before the end of his tail wrapped around her throat. He pulled her head back as he turned his downwards to her, his orbs flaring red for a few fleeting seconds.

There was nothing she could do. She couldn't even kick her legs since they were as wide as she could get them, and she couldn't bring her knees to her chest as that would uncomfortably change the angle of their bodies meeting.

With her arms still behind her back and his tail around her throat, she was completely trapped.

"You have no idea what I want to do to you, Mayumi," he said, his up and down movements increasing in swiftness. "There are things I desire, things I crave, that eat at me."

He made his cock go shallower, only fucking her with half of it, so they were more eye-level. The head now kept repeatedly digging into the swollen spot inside her.

Her lips parted as her moans became sharper.

Just as she parted her lips to tell him to keep hitting her right there, the pressure around her neck squeezed.

"And every time I see your soul, you push me just that little bit closer to taking it from you."

The pressure was constricting enough that it made her head warmer and swim. It was like a warning, a threat, one that made sure she knew she was the one at his mercy, that he was in control of everything. Her life, her breath, and even her blood flow.

The throb that tingled in all of her delicate places, like her cunt, her breasts, even the bundles of nerves in her wrists, pounded harder. Suddenly she wanted him to squeeze harder – it was too soft right now.

She could breathe currently, but she was fine with not being able to for a moment. Blood was flowing, and she was happy for him to strangle her jugular if it would push her even faster to orgasm.

Not once had she ever been dominated like this, taken control of to this degree. She'd been pinned before, but she'd never been absolutely incapable of doing anything.

They were barely having sex. It was more like he was using her hole as a masturbation tool as he lifted her up and down over his massive, inhuman cock.

"Tell... me," she choked out.

"You may not like all of it," he warned.

The purple of his orbs stared straight at her as she was forced to look up at his ethereal, unholy face, making her mind grow numb. Right then, she thought he could tell her anything, lay himself bare to her, and she would accept it, would welcome it, would give it to him so long as he kept moving inside her.

Her eyes watered as her tongue poked forward, like that would help her to breathe through her strangled pants.

"Faun..." It was all she could manage.

She hoped he understood what she was trying to convey.

A growly groan came from his parting fangs before he lowered his head and bumped his snout right above her left temple. He thickened inside her, swelling and making her feel fuller before it went back to its normal girth.

"I want to take that cute little soul of yours and consume it. I want to make it mine, so no one else can take it, so no one else can have you," he rasped, and his hot breath over her ear made the hair behind it stand on end.

"Take–" Before she could finish telling him to take it, he slammed her all the way down on his cock to render her quiet.

Fuck, I'm so close.

He was going just slow enough that she was teetering on the edge. She was right there, about to explode and shatter into a million fragments, like glass.

She wondered if he knew. He must with the way her insides were constantly quivering, with how her thighs twitched and legs kept writhing behind him. Her toes curled, and her feet arched to the point mini cramps assaulted her and she had to wilfully relax them.

She was a tangled mix of pleasure and pain, and she wanted more of both.

"And then once I have taken it," he rumbled, his tentacles clasping her hips as he rammed himself with deep, short strokes. She fit him perfectly now, but she could feel the very tip of him pushing against her cervix over and over again. Not hard, but enough to show his wonderful depth. "I want to take you to the Veil. I want to hide you away, shelter you within the dark where no one can find you, where no one can take you from me, and..."

His voice trailed off like he was hesitant about what he wanted to say next.

Yet, his cock swelled again, and his tentacles gripped so hard she was sure they were bruising her. His claws dug into her skin as his hands gripped her arse tighter. Even the slams of his shaft were faster.

Whatever he wanted to say was sending him into a frothing lather.

His tail pushed her more against him by her arms while it yanked her head back at the same time, just as his own turned upwards towards the ceiling.

The full-body shudder he gave was so intense it even shook her. He looked so excited.

"Fuck, Mayumi... I want to breed that tiny body of yours." She choked out a gasp, and he lessened his grip on her throat minutely as her body tightened at his words, clenching him. His groan was haunted, constantly resonating between frantically panted breaths. "I want to pump my seed inside your womb and watch you grow my youngling. I wish to see your stomach swell and know that you hold a Mavka inside you, that I claimed you like this – in a way no other has."

She didn't know what made her heart speed up into a deafening roar in her ears. Was it from worry that he wanted to do something so life altering to her body? Or was it in yearning for him to do so?

She'd been against having a *human* child in the horrible, twisted, dying world. Something weak and feeble. But a

Duskwalker's child? *That* wasn't something that was going to die of a sickness or become foolishly eaten by a Demon – not if she could help it.

"But we can't."

He'd already told her they weren't able to, which had been a relief to her since having all that warm, overflowing semen gushing out of her once she was filled to the brim was utterly satisfying. Walking around and knowing she was holding a part of him inside her was as much of a turn-on as having the hard source of it stretching her.

The chuckle that came from him was wicked, echoing from both his skull and his chest in a gravelly bass that made it sound even more ungodly than it should have.

His head turned down to her and twisted so he could be right next to her ear. "We *can* if I take that soul you're so willing to give to me."

Suddenly his movements became frantic as he bounced her, her thighs and small breasts jiggling every time he hit the end of her. Even her hair was beginning to slap and tickle down her back and trapped arms.

"W-wait," she pleaded when suddenly it felt like it was too much. She was growing hazier by the second, her breaths knocking out of her until she was beginning to play a game of catch-up.

Mayumi didn't know if it was his balmy breath grazing down her neck, his mouth-watering scent clogging her senses, the way his soft fur tickled her nipples while his hard chest massaged her breasts, or even just the constant, glorious slide of his slime-covered cock annihilating her insides in such a rapid-fire rhythm, but one or all of them had her melting.

She let his tail support her head and back as she let go, let her body take over. Every muscle in her body, from her pectoral muscles, abdomen, and even calves, tensed alongside her pussy.

Mayumi screamed as she came, and his answering snarl right next to her ear rendered her silent. Her lungs collapsed, her orgasm so intense that she became nothing but a writhing, lust-crazed thing he used to stroke himself off.

She desperately wanted to move, but his hold on her barely

allowed her to do little more than tremble.

"I want you to do that around my cock, to milk me of my seed like you want me to drain every drop inside you." He swelled again, a lot longer than before, warning her of his own impending doom. "I've been *trying* this entire time."

Her head lulling to the side as she let him continue taking her. She still gave no resistance.

Her bloodstream was filled with lava, carrying lust and need and submissive obedience she'd never have granted another. There was nothing that would make her stop him right now, not until he was done using her, until he was satisfied.

His tail lifted to her jaw to steady her bobbing head and forced her to look up at him.

"A part of me feels like you kept your womb waiting and ready for me," he admitted with a shudder. She knew by the way his tentacles clasped tighter that Faunus was nearing his own end. She tried to spread her thighs further apart in absolute welcome of it. "And I so badly crave to take your soul and then fill you. I want to be more than just destruction and death. I want to be pleasure and life too. I want to share that with only you."

"Faun," she moaned lowly, her voice broken and croaked. *"Faun."*

She didn't know what she was trying to say. She could barely formulate more than his damn name in her cloudy mind.

"Mayumi," he answered. One of his hands slid over to take her arse completely in its palm while the other reached up to grab her shoulder, shoving her down harder. "Fuck. Give it to me, Mayumi. Take it from me." She gasped when she fleetingly felt multiple sharp tugs deep within as he swelled thicker than ever before. "Take it. Take it. Take it!"

Faunus shoved her down hard, yanking her body deeply on his cock until she felt pressure trying to push her insides. The sacs on the bottom of him had sunken so tightly against his cock that she thought he was threatening to shove them within her as well.

There was pleasure. There was a dull pain. He was pushing too far, beyond what he'd done to magically alter her body.

Then Faunus tensed around her as he squeezed and squeezed,

right before a poor, choking whine came from him. She knew he wanted to thrust by the minor twitching hip thrusts he gave as he held her down, but they ceased immediately when his barbs latched on and forced them together just as much as his tentacles.

His claws dug in, but not enough to puncture, as he let loose a bellowing roar when a heavy gush of cum splashed right against her cervix he was nearly pulverising.

Her tongue poked out, shivering in delight at the heat, the liquid, at him filling her. Any ache she felt was melted in the toe-curling bliss of his release.

She happily accepted all of it – there were no repercussions to him doing so.

Can't have what you want if you don't take my soul. It was obvious he longed to, and that made her smile dazedly at the sunlit ceiling with her heart swelling fierily.

Everything seemed brighter, like her pupils were heavily dilated. It even made the dust particles sparkle more than before, showering them in glitter. At least his lack of thrusting allowed her mind to spiral back to reality at a nice, relaxing pace.

The last of his release squeezed out of her.

She was pretty sure it had leaked all over his hand and legs, but he didn't seem to mind. Especially when he slumped over her, wild aftershocks making him twitch, shudder, and jump against her.

His tail released her, and she buried herself against his frantically heaving torso. Well, only her face did, since her arms were fucking numb and filled with grainy pins and needles from being behind her for so long. They hung languidly against him.

She nuzzled his fur, hoping he thought she was being adorably sweet, when really she was just getting rid of any evidence of drool or tears she unfortunately shed when she was that far gone.

Mmm, lemongrass, her groggy mind murmured.

"A baby, huh?" she said with a quiet, teasing tone. "Never thought I'd hear that from a Duskwalker."

Or that one wanted to mate and breed her specifically.

Fuck knows what I'm doing anymore, but that usually would be a major turn-off for me. Instead, she was pretty sure that was one of the reasons she'd come so hard. *At least we don't have to worry about it for now.*

For now.

When she realised he'd never responded to her, she pulled back so they could face each other. He wouldn't let her, instead hugging her tighter like he didn't want her to look at him. Was he feeling vulnerable? Had he been too caught up in the moment and spilled a secret he suddenly regretted sharing?

She hoped so, wanting to dig up every buried puzzle piece of him.

"I have always wanted to know how you would feel about it," he said quietly. "It was not even something I realised I truly desired until recently."

"Because of me?" she asked just as softly, a tender smile curling her lips. She adored that she could be the one to make him realise things like this about himself.

His response had her pouting.

"No. Magnar, one of the Duskwalkers I have mentioned, managed to have a youngling with his bride. I have witnessed humans with their own younglings, but I never thought it was possible for a Duskwalker, so I never cared. I am not the kind of creature to wish for things I could never have."

Except for me... right?

"And then I came along and showed you how amazing I am?" He better fucking tell her that because her pout was about to turn into her biting the ever-living shit out of him in retaliation. "That it's possible."

"And then you came along," he echoed, which lessened her pout.

He brushed his claws in what was obviously a nest of hair from the light sting as he untangled the knots. Perhaps he was doing it to soothe her of her concerns, since she always relaxed against him when he did.

"When I met their youngling, Fyodor, I was very curious about them. It was odd seeing what I may have looked like when I was small, and even though it wasn't mine, I felt this undeniable burning desire to protect them. When Fyodor held my finger in their tiny hand, I knew then that I wanted my own... even if I no longer could."

Even if I no longer could...

Mayumi sighed, knowing if she offered her soul so he could, he'd still deny her.

"As happy as I was for them," he continued. "I was also very... envious. I had only just obtained the crack in my skull, so it felt like my pain was worsened by learning of their creation. It made me realise there was more that I would never be able to experience."

"Faunus," Mayumi gently called, as she leaned back with her brows knotted together so tightly she knew it screwed up her whole face.

His large, warm palm cupped the side of it, and he brushed his thumb over her cheek.

"I'm glad I came here. I am glad I am here with you. It is more than I ever expected, and I cherish every moment with you." He licked at her other cheek. "You're very naughty. It is all worth it to feel you cuddling my cock with your warm little cunt like you are now."

Faunus was the damn king of misdirection.

It wasn't enough right then to unwrinkle her features as her eyes bounced over his skull and horns. There was much she wanted to say, but like always, it was as though she'd swallowed her tongue.

Her forehead bashed against his chest as she released a defeated sigh. She continued to knock her forehead against him, although rather lightly, as she thought, *Why? It's not fair that this is happening. There has to be a way.*

"I'll warm your cock for you as much as you want," she grumbled against his chest. "It feels really nice for me too."

Although he'd been rather limp, any tension he'd built during their conversation eased out of him as he chuckled.

"It would be terrible for you if you didn't like it because I'd still want you to do this to me."

Devious bastard.

"You know what?!" Mayumi playfully burst out. "You can warm your own—"

Faunus suddenly held her tighter when she went to get off him, and a sharp pain scraped her insides. An acute gasp tore from her.

"What the–?" she asked as she frowned and pursed her lips. "Why are you still latched to me? That kind of hurt."

His barbs usually went down by now, or he made them somehow.

His orbs turned into a reddish pink. "I'm stuck."

The colour drained from her face. "What do you mean, you're stuck?"

"I usually do not come so deeply within you so I can push forward and release my barbs, but I, uh, shoved you onto my cock as hard as I could while I was coming."

"So you're as deep as you can go right now?"

She didn't think his orbs could turn any brighter in embarrassment, but they did.

"I was really turned on, so I wasn't thinking clearly." He rubbed his fangs against her like he was trying to be playful in this distressing time. "I don't think you understand just how badly I want to breed this tiny body of yours. I bet your stomach would grow so big for me."

Her lips parted in shock, and she looked to where they were joined. His tentacles were floppy, the ends caressing her bruising skin as they slowly moved like they were happy and content.

"You'll go down, right? Like you'll soften and then be able to push in and unlatch, yeah?" When he didn't say anything for far too long, her heart raced, and she looked up with panic forming on her face. "RIGHT, FAUNUS?"

"I'm sorry." She could hear the wince in his voice! "This may hurt a little."

Mayumi gripped the fur of his chest like one might do to a person's shirt and tried to pull him closer with every bit of seriousness in her expression.

"Don't you fucking dare!"

"I promise I will not pull back far, and I will heal you right away."

"No. Nonono," she whined as she fell against him. "Let's... let's just stay like this for a bit."

He rubbed her back comfortingly.

"My cock only goes soft, Mayumi. It does not get smaller,

and I'm too deep inside you to go any further forward."

"I know... just... I think I need to build up to this. I'd rather just sit on your cock for a bit longer."

She was thrumming with contentment. She'd rather not ruin that just yet.

"I was hoping this would never happen," he growled. "Why do I even have this function when my tentacles already lock us?"

"I don't know, but I guess that means we're stuck for the moment." Then she forced a laugh as she said, "Let's look on the bright side. At least we'll get to spend some quality time talking for a bit."

She guessed now would be the time to ask him anything she wanted, since he couldn't get away from her.

Then her lips tightened. "But you better pet me the entire time to make it up to me, you jerk."

THIRTY-THREE

Faunus tipped his head to the side as he watched Mayumi use a clamp to pull a metal rod from a blazing fire.

The large area at the back of her cottage between the shed and her spring bath was a smithing station fitted with a furnace, anvil, and metal workbench. There was an awning shelter above to keep everything dry.

She'd already smelted her own ores of iron into liquid and poured them into a mould for her rods.

He was curious about what she was doing, especially when she held the metal rod upright and smacked the end of it into an anvil. She explained that she was upsetting the metal at the orange, hot end of the rod, but he didn't quite understand how metal could feel emotions.

Apparently, that wasn't what she meant when he asked her, and instead it meant that she was compressing the hot end so it would be denser. He just nodded his head as though he understood when he absolutely did not.

She shaped the end so it was flattened into what she called a fin. While this piece of shaped rod was heating back up in her furnace, she grabbed a new one and began doing the same thing.

There were thirty pieces she was working with, all at the same time.

He was thankful she was wearing thick gloves to protect herself, as well as leather from head to toe. The area was hot despite them being outside, and he could see trickles of sweat running down her temples and neck.

The soft glow from the fire and the rod she was working with lit up the features of her face. She appeared serious and stern, and he wondered if that was because of this morning.

Unlatching from her had been painful for them both. Her because of the sharp pain he was sure she'd felt, though he'd immediately healed her so it wasn't prolonged, and him because he hadn't liked hurting her.

Faunus had apologised profusely, and she'd just laughed it off afterwards, but she'd come out here and had been working ever since.

She was unusually quiet.

"Why are you doing this?" Faunus asked as he stepped closer, crowding her before she crudely elbowed him out of the way.

"I used most of my arrows last night while we were hunting Demons. I'm making more." She curled the flat fins when they were hot again, bashing them to manipulate them into a cone until they were ready to be shoved onto a different kind of rod to shape them further. "Smithing is a trade most Demonslayers must excel at before they can rise through the ranks. There is no point in being able to shoot a weapon or cut with it if you're unable to make them yourself."

She wiped her brow with her sleeve and then began the process of using a triangular metal brace to cut the arrowheads she was working with away from the iron rod. She then threw those pieces back into the furnace so they would glow red hot again.

The tinging bangs she produced with her metal mallet rang in his ears. It was disorientating, but he remained with her in order to watch. He'd bear the way it pounded his mind, so long as he could stay close and observe her.

"Don't get me wrong," she continued. "It's tiring, and this isn't the best station to produce the finest work, but when you're just making arrows or doing minor repairs to your weapons, it's more than enough."

She used her clamp to pull the loose arrowheads from the fire once more so she could flatten the closed, rounded ends – the cone side was open to slot onto an arrow shaft – making them almost leaf shaped.

"Does that mean you made your sword?" he asked, seeing that what she was making now looked much more... barbaric in comparison.

"No. Items such as my sword... I can't replicate that quality of work. It's one of the best swords anyone can get their hands on." She looked at him from the side. "It was courtesy of my father that I obtained it. He had it made for me when I reached Silver rank to congratulate me." Mayumi then looked down as she raised her mallet and brought it down, her lips pursing momentarily before relaxing. "He was never big on words – maybe I got that part of his personality – but it was his way of giving me a precious gift. He valued practicality over the heartfelt."

"It is hard to tell whether or not you liked your father," Faunus stated.

A dark chuckle left her lips.

"I cared very deeply for my father. He was tough on me, and maybe those who saw us from the outside would think he was abusive in the way he trained or disciplined me, but it was never done out of malice. He wanted me to reach my full potential, and he wanted me to outlive him. If he had been uncaring, he wouldn't have done everything he did. He wouldn't have travelled to one of the best blacksmiths in the north and had my sword made for me. Even with his leg injury, he'd limped his damn way through one of the most dangerous mountain paths just for me. Hard not to feel fondly for someone who risked their life just to give me a sword worth more than most of what I own collectively."

I wonder what kind of relationship I would have with my own father had I been born with humanity.

His memory of the beginning of his life was foggy, and much of it was of hunting various moving creatures until his mind began to... think.

Leaving them to cool in oil, which she said would help to make sure they didn't rust, she went inside to make herself some food.

Faunus walked around the yard to make sure it was safe.

There had been a great deal of blood due to the number of

Demons that had come during the night. When he first emerged from the house, he'd done the best he could to hide it by covering what he could find with snow and dirt. The area still had a certain reek to it, one he'd managed to mask but not fully remove.

Thankfully, Demon blood was rather off-putting and foul. It didn't particularly stir hunger in his kind, but it was difficult for him to smell through. Mayumi said she couldn't notice anything once he'd covered it all.

When she emerged from the house, she went to the back again and filed the arrowheads into sharp points with a grinder. He watched her foot press up and down on a pedal while it made some kind of rotating, whirring noise.

His orbs darkened in their yellow colour as he examined the machine with profound curiosity. He'd never seen anything like it.

Just as he crouched down and went to touch it, she smacked his hand away.

"Don't shove your fingers into things you don't understand," she bit. "That's how you hurt yourself or lose one."

He looked up to her and noticed the concerned, disapproving frown of her brows.

"I've already told you I will heal within a day, no matter the injury." Except for his skull, of course.

A gruff sigh came from her as she rolled her eyes.

"Just because it'll grow back doesn't mean you should be so careless. It'll hurt a whole bunch, and you might break my tool."

"Hmm." He hadn't thought of that.

He stood and just continued watching her.

His hackles rose when she pulled out the same glue she'd used to put his face back together. He was hoping she wouldn't try to do so again.

Faunus had been... hopeful when she tried. The fact she cared so deeply about him that she was willing to fix his face had been heart-warming.

It hadn't helped. Instead, it had only further dismayed him. She'd asked if she could use her other glue, and he'd rejected her offer. The animal glue she'd worked into the sensitive crack of his skull had stung in the same way that even water getting into it hurt.

The failure had stung far worse.

I've already accepted my fate.

Thinking there might be a cure or a way to fix his injury just reopened the cavernous wound in his heart. He'd much rather ignore it, push it to the deepest, furthest place of his mind, and just live in the present with her.

Relief washed through him when she used the glue, once it was heated and liquefied, to attach the hollow edge of the arrow to shafts she already had prepared.

It appeared this lengthy task was one she did often.

When she started using her mallet and a special blunt tool to dent the arrow and shaft together, he couldn't help but ask, "What is the point of using glue if you are binding them together this way regardless?"

"It makes them sturdier," she answered when she was doing the last one. "I can use these arrows right away, but the glue helps prevent them from coming apart if the metal or shaft distorts for any reason."

Faunus followed her when she picked up all thirty arrows in her arms and walked them to the front of her home. She placed them on the porch as she headed inside to grab her bow before coming back outside to his awaiting form.

All the way from her porch, Mayumi picked up an arrow and nocked it onto her bowstring. Making sure he didn't get in the way, she raised her bow and aimed.

She unleashed the arrow, and it landed straight into the stake in the middle of the clearing. Doing this multiple times, most of her arrows embedded themselves into the thick wooden pole.

Faunus looked up to the sky, noticing the sun was not far from finishing its descent, and already the shadows were long enough to shield the house completely.

Dusk. It was a dangerous time of the day, as Demons who were brave enough to risk getting minor burns began to hunt on the surface.

I've always enjoyed this time of day.

He observed the blast of colour that was painted in the sky. The varying oranges, yellows, purples, and blues. He especially liked that very brief time when even stars would begin to twinkle. Sometimes, he even caught the moon in the bright sky.

It often reminded him of himself. Both night and day blended into one. Just like every Duskwalker he'd met, each dusk was different.

"I'll need to tweak those that didn't hit their mark," she grumbled, referencing the arrows that had missed the target and flew off into the forest. "Do you think you could get them for me while I pull out the ones in the stake?"

"Of course," he answered with his tail curling, an animation of his glee. He enjoyed assisting her in any way he could, even if it was playing fetch. "However," he started with a chuckle as he headed into the forest. "Are you sure you didn't just miss because you cannot aim?"

"Rude!" she laughed back. "I'll have you know, there were only a few in the guild who were as good as I am at archery. I rarely miss my mark, thank *you* very much."

He began his search, following Mayumi's scent that lingered on her arrows as well as the smell of the metal, wood, glue, and even the feathers. For a moment, he wondered if she had sent him off to go find them because she had been intelligent enough to know he'd be able to use his senses.

I believe I counted seven missed?

The lingering smell of blood made it a little tricky to smell through, but he was able to slowly find them.

A thought did cross his mind, especially when he could hear her struggle to pull out the deeply stuck arrows.

"Mayumi," he yelled casually.

"Yeah!" she screamed back while groaning. Then she yelped, and he heard the shuffle of her feet before a dull thud.

She fell on her arse. His sight brightened in its yellow colour as the urge to laugh tickled him.

"I think it would be wise if you remained inside tonight. I'm not sure if we are at risk, but there is a lot of blood in the air."

"Ooh! Are you saying we can lay in wait and hunt for more Demons again?"

She's so bloodthirsty, he thought as he plucked a third arrow from its resting place – inside the very base of a tree. He inspected it, wondering what could possibly be wrong with it when it appeared perfectly made. *I'm forever grateful to whatever being made her the way she is. It would have made it a lot harder to protect her if she had been trying to kill me the entire time.*

His orbs brightened even further in their colour as his tail happily curled again.

Faunus chose not to respond to her, knowing she would make up her own mind on what she wanted to do tonight with the information he'd given her. He doubted he could change her mind either way.

At this rate, they'd have a permanent hunting ground. He bet that'd make her ecstatic. Would their new normality become fucking throughout the day and Demon slaying at night?

I'll admit... it feels good to slaughter them.

If Jabez wanted an army and was willing to kill Duskwalkers to do so, then Faunus now wanted to absolutely get in the fucking way after what he did to him. Revenge felt good. It was so sweet he could almost taste it on his tongue.

You crack my skull, and I'll crack all the ones in your army.

When he was just picking up the last arrow, a whooshing sound caught his attention. It sounded like a bird in the distance, and at first, he ignored it.

That was until he realised it was moving faster than any animal he'd ever heard, and... it was coming right this way. The loud rustles of leaves informed him that the creature was also very large and flying through the forest rather than above it.

It's avoiding the last of the sun. His head turned in the direction of where he could hear Mayumi still in the clearing. White flashed in orbs. *She's in danger.*

Faunus, still holding the arrows just in case he was wrong, *hoping* he was wrong, sprinted through the forest. He wasn't far from her.

It was too late.

Just as he broke the tree line, something black shot through a different section of the forest. It swooped, grabbing Mayumi, who had been standing on a low arrow with her thighs hugging the stake to grab another that was higher.

She gasped in surprise when a large, winged Demon grabbed her shoulder with its prehensile foot.

"Mayumi!" he roared as she was dragged into the sky just as the last of the sun faded over the horizon. He jumped to reach them, but the tip of his claw just scraped the underside of her boot.

She said nothing, made no demands to the Demon as if she knew it wouldn't matter. She didn't even scream.

With Faunus circling below them, he watched Mayumi narrow her eyes upward and begin bashing on its foot. When that didn't work, she tried to peel one of its clawed toes back to release herself.

Her legs kicked in the air as if she was trying to find purchase. She was forced to lift her body by just her shoulder so she wasn't loosely hanging there.

"A Mavka?" the Demon asked as it turned its angular, near bat-like features to Faunus. It was hard to tell that it was male, especially when his voice was rather distorted and high-pitched. "Did I steal your meal?"

The sniggers he made were more like clicks as he hovered in the air.

"Give her to me!" Faunus bellowed, his sight turning a pale red.

Fear and anger warred within him, one cold and the other unbearably hot. His heart felt as though it was moments from freezing over, whereas his extremities were about to burst. His fur and spikes stood on end, and his tail straightened as it puffed.

Faunus looked to the trees, and the Demon used its wings to flap away from them. When he turned to the top of the house, about to leap to it, the Demon fluttered the other way.

The way he bobbed up and down in the sky was like a taunt, coming closer only to suddenly bounce upwards in height.

"I didn't think when I followed the scent of blood that I would come across a Mavka. No wonder the smell here is strong, and yours lingers. Have you been working with this human?"

His hands clenched until his claws were stabbing into the plump flesh of his palms. *I should have realised sooner that it was a Demon.*

How could he mistake that whooshing as its wings flapped?

Even now, it was hard to smell him through the lingering blood of his dead kind. Faunus had been upwind of the Demon, making it even more difficult to sense.

The growl that Faunus produced was beastly, even to his own ears. "If you harm her, I will hunt you to the very ends of Earth and rip you limb from limb."

He would make it his only goal in his disconsolate life to annihilate this winged Demon. Then, and only then, would Faunus march towards Jabez's grand castle within the Veil and use whatever strength he had left, whatever remained of him and his broken skull, to kill that monster. Even if it cost him his last heartbeat.

After everything he'd experienced with Mayumi, every tender touch, every heart-achingly beautiful word they'd shared, he knew he'd see no other point but revenge if she were to be taken from him.

She had been the centre point of his life for too long, his obsession. Without her, knowing she no longer shared her breaths in the same plane of existence as him – even if he could not be with her – Faunus thought he might give in to his mind and let it go.

What was the point of his humanity then, if he couldn't have the one creature he'd sworn to protect? The one creature he'd grown to... love.

Mayumi's and the Demon's voices overlapped at the same time.

"Faunus!" Mayumi shouted while reaching down to the hilt of her dagger. "Catch!"

"Wait..." the Demon said with his red eyes narrowing at him. "I know you."

Shit! He only had a second to get into position before Mayumi stabbed her blade into the calf leg holding her and drew it down. The Demon screeched, hands tightening in pain and tension as his body dipped.

He released her, and Faunus caught her mid-air when he leapt. She was silent as she fell until she landed in the cushion of his arms, where she gave an impact oomph.

"I knew you'd catch me," she said quietly, a glint of tenderness and trust in her eyes.

Her expression hardened when she looked upwards.

"You're the feline-skulled Mavka! The ram horned!" the Demon shrieked.

"Fuck," Faunus gasped out, his orbs turning to such a stark colour of white it blinded him for a second. He tossed Mayumi to her feet, and she stumbled before righting herself. "Stay inside."

He began to change, morphing into his monstrous form. Fear and panic were settling deep with every second it took to change.

"We'll fight him together, Faunus. I'll get my bow and–"

"I must let him know!" The Demon yelled. Before they knew it, he dipped to the side and flew into the forest. "I must let our king know!"

It was exactly what Faunus anticipated.

No!

"Stay here, Mayumi!" Faunus shouted as he turned from her and gave chase on all fours. *"I will return!"*

He would, at least, try to.

Even if she wanted to follow, both Faunus and the Demon would be too fast for her to keep up. Within minutes, they'd covered a large distance, the Demon's wings making him near impossible to catch, even for a Duskwalker. *Near* being the keyword he was hoping would aid him right now.

His paws and hands thudded heavily against the dirt and snow, and his snorting huffs were just as loud. The wind was icy against his bony face with the speed at which he sprinted, but his long fur and adrenaline kept his temperature at a boiling point.

He hoped Mayumi wasn't foolishly following. Night was minutes from being fully upon them. He couldn't stay, even if he knew her home was now a dangerous baiting ground.

I can't let this Demon escape. I can't let him go. Now that he was no longer near her home, he was able to easily track the Demon's scent in the wind and on the leaves he brushed with his expansive wingspan. *I can't let him tell Jabez where I am.*

He didn't want the Demon King to find him. He didn't want him anywhere near his precious tiny human. It didn't matter that she was fierce or strong. It didn't matter that she was brave.

Jabez would kill her just to hurt him. The wretched, vile half-elf would use her against him.

And there was the doubtable guarantee that she would be allowed to live even if Faunus did hand over his life to him. He'd probably kill her just because Faunus had touched her. He might even eat her just because he was evil, hateful, and selfish.

I have to trust her. I have to trust that she can protect herself while I'm gone.

He just hoped he didn't regret his decision to abandon his promise to stop this Demon from getting away.

Because... even if he pretended he was okay, even if he had accepted his eventual demise, even if he lied and hid how much his heart ached every second of every day with her, Faunus *desperately* wanted to live.

Even more so now that he knew the one creature he'd ever wanted to keep wanted him in return.

With an arc that started low to the ground and then swiftly shot upwards through the air, Mayumi's blade sliced open the torso of a Demon she'd already chopped the forearm off of.

She spun and used the momentum to glide her blade across its throat. Blood gushed down the front of its body before it dropped to one knee and fell to the side. It was already a corpse by the time its head smacked against the ground.

Her eyes found the brightening sky as her chest heaved with heavy, sawing breaths.

Three Demons. She thanked the heavens that day was finally breaking free after being awake all night.

Faunus had been right when he'd warned her that the area would now be ripe for baiting Demons.

She turned her gaze away from the purple sky to the three dead carcasses around her. One was hanging from its neck and the low tree branch her whip was attached to. Another had an arrow shaft jutting from its eye socket. Then, of course, the one she'd just killed that lay at her feet.

Usually Mayumi only fought one, maybe two Demons whenever she baited them. Even for her, this was a lot to fight on her own, but thankfully they hadn't come at the same time.

She'd scarcely eaten, and the last two fights had taken time to win. Most of the time, she just remained on the roof and shot her targets from far away, either killing them straight away or weakening them with arrows before she fought them claw to blade.

But there had been no animal to bait them. This made their movements far more erratic and unpredictable.

I can't believe Faunus left me alone to deal with this mess by myself. Then again... he must have had a good reason to.

Her head drifted in the direction she'd seen him go. *I hope he's alright.*

It was already morning, and he still hadn't returned. That didn't indicate anything good. *If he doesn't come back, when I find him in the afterlife, I'll beat the shit out of him for leaving me.*

She would confront any God that existed to permit her to do so, even if she had to cross over planes of afterlives.

A solemn sigh left her shaking lips, her body trembling due to exhaustion. She was terribly fatigued, hungry, and thirsty.

Yet, when the sun finally broke and splashed its light on her home and made it safe, she didn't go inside to rest. Instead, she went to her shed and grabbed one of her shovels.

I don't know how long he's going to be gone. If it were days, then she needed to reduce the scent that was now loitering in the air disgustingly.

She went to the far reaches of her clearing and began digging, keeping to the sun, as she threw snow and eventually dirt to the side.

I think I've dug the same number of graves for Demons as I have for humans. It would help to hide their scents, so she didn't have many coming tonight as well. Otherwise, she may end up in a cycle of slaying Demons nightly without rest.

She needed a break, especially so she didn't become overworked and make a mistake. So far, she hadn't obtained any new injuries, except for the claw marks she now had on her shoulder from the flying one, and she'd rather keep it that way.

The wound was small. She'd barely bled since her thick, furred winter coat had kept her protected.

Currently, she was wearing her Demonslayer uniform since it was more effective for hiding in the darkness. It was soaked in blood, and her stomach was tight, but otherwise, it wasn't that upset by the putrid smell. Exposure to it over the years had deadened her senses.

Sweat covered her flesh, causing her uniform to cling to her in an uncomfortable, clammy way. It only made her shiver, despite the rise in her temperature, as the chilly air turned the perspiration covering her icy.

She was at risk of getting a fever if she remained like this.

Once I've done this, she thought as she dug in one of the many places she usually did when she intended to bury Demons. There were five locations, and she rotated between each one so the earth, worms, and bugs could eat their corpses and get rid of the evidence of them besides their bones. *I need to wash my uniform with the specialised soap I have. Have a bath, then eat, and then fucking sleep. Man, I need to sleep. I'm so freaking tired.*

Hopefully, she would wake to Faunus returning at some point in the day to come curl up beside her.

She listened out for him and potential danger all throughout the morning as she slowly worked at getting all the Demons into the hole. Once done, she covered them with dirt, then snow, and patted the ground to compress it.

He better come home soon. I kind of already miss that big guy purring at me. She'd rather have him be here right now, teasing her about being slow at all her tasks, than out there by himself in danger, not knowing if or when he'd return.

Her brows furrowed deeply.

He better come home to purr at me, she thought, her lips puckering into a tight, almost childish pout.

THIRTY-FOUR

For two nights, Faunus had chased the winged Demon. He never stopped, no matter how tired he became, no matter how much he needed to rest.

I almost had him, he thought with dismay as he walked on all fours back through the forest in the direction of Mayumi's home. *I can't believe I almost had him.*

There had been one moment, just one, where Faunus had managed to catch up to the Demon. Not long after he'd begun chasing him, Faunus had gotten close enough where he could climb a tree and leap from branch to branch.

I had ahold of him.

Faunus had grabbed him by the leg with one hand and was being flown through the forest, tearing at his calf and slipping as he tried to climb. Faunus knew he'd nicked his wing, but the Demon had kicked him in the damn skull.

The knock had caused agony to pulsate throughout his face, and he'd accidentally let go when his whole body seized in reaction. His skull cracked just that little bit more under the impact.

After Faunus smacked into multiple branches and then needed to claw his way down a tree to slow his fall, he'd broken several more branches with his legs and groin before he landed on his paws.

The injuries he'd sustained had been painful enough that the Demon had flown a large distance from him while Faunus tried to right himself. Jagged spikes of branch pieces had broken off into his legs that he'd needed to rip out, or he couldn't bear to move them. He knew blood had been streaming heavily down his right thigh, as well as a steady trail down his skull.

His groin had protested any movement like it was contused, but adrenaline and fear kept him going.

He didn't take long to look over the rest of his body to assess his injuries. He just took note of them and followed the fleeing threat.

After that, the Demon remained above the trees during the night, flying freely, whereas Faunus was slowed by his wounds and had to dodge his environment. At that point, the Demon's scent had been difficult to track.

It was only throughout the day when the Demon needed to slow down to fly through the shade of the forest to avoid the direct sunlight that Faunus had managed to locate it again.

He thought he might be able to catch up the second night, but by then, he knew it was too late.

Even if he kept chasing him, it was likely the Demon would lead him to the Veil. He would have essentially been handing himself over to Jabez, and he refused to do so.

He could go no further.

Faunus paused to cover his skull, groaning in frustration and anger. *I've brought danger to her.*

If he thought it would help, he wouldn't return to Mayumi if it meant Jabez would never find her. But, if the Demon brought him there, Mayumi would be in danger regardless.

He'd rather be there to bargain for her life or kill the Demon King – either would suffice, so long as she was safe.

The cold pit that had dissipated since he'd begun to protect Mayumi returned tenfold when he understood his end might be a lot closer than it had been before all this.

He wouldn't blame Mayumi for baiting Demons and doing what she had been doing all her life. He'd never wanted to stop or change her. That's not why he'd come to her.

All he wanted was to be by her side, even if it was a risk to his life – but never hers.

His gut twisted with worry, more than he'd ever experienced before. He hadn't even been this mangled inside when his skull had originally been cracked.

All he'd needed to care about then was himself. Now... he feared for his pretty, wonderful, tempting little human.

What have I done? He thought as he brought his hands away from his face to stare at his claws. *Why couldn't things have been different?*

He wanted the happiness he felt with her to be untainted by anything else. It was always there, a lingering dark cloud, and he just longed for the constant drizzle to clear away and give him true brightness.

Are Mavka not allowed to experience true happiness?

Yet, Orpheus and Magnar had seemed... happy. He envied them for that. A part of him hated them for it. Why could they have what he'd longed for? Why did he have to be the one suffering through this?

Why did Jabez have to target me?

He'd emotionally tormented Orpheus over hundreds of years, but Faunus was the only one he'd managed to get his hands on and truly brutalise.

I should have just lived alone. I should have just accepted the loneliness rather than try to live among the Demons.

Look at what it'd gotten him. Nothing but pain, and now everything he'd ever truly wanted was at his claw tips, right fucking there within his reaching grasp, and yet so much further away than ever.

Faunus continued to make his way to Mayumi's home, needing to go back more than ever. His sight constantly switched between white and dark blue the entire way, his mind rotating with desolate and terrible thoughts.

They didn't dissipate, not even when he saw her home and could smell that she was awake by the evidence of a cooking meal wafting through the air. He'd long ago been able to smell the sweetness of her fireplace.

Although the area smelt ripe with Demon blood, just as he thought it might, it was somewhat hidden underneath musky, overpowering incense. From what he could see, there were two hollow, round incense canisters that allowed the aroma to slip through their lids.

These two scents made it difficult to smell her sleepy pumpkin aroma beneath it. He desperately wanted to breathe in that sweet scent and know she was safe.

I want to hold her.

He wanted to be comforted in that special way Mayumi did – the one where she didn't use words or an explanation and just soothed him in the silence he needed.

He didn't want to talk, didn't want to share his pain and longing and fears right now. What he needed was her warmth and arms around him, clutching or nuzzling at his fur. He needed her acceptance and understanding that she showed rather than said with pretty words.

His fingertips found the painful barrier of her home. He considered shouting out so she could remove her charms but decided against it. Outside was cold, and he'd long ago begun to feel... sheltered in her home that was far too small for him. It had been safe.

He pushed through it, shuddering at the pain.

Faunus had seen humans greet each other by the male or female running into the arms of the other. It had always touched his heart and made it swell in a profoundly heartfelt way.

He craved for her to gift him with such a greeting. As though she longed for him, missed him, and wanted to reach out to him just as much as her soul did.

He placed his hand on the door handle.

I just hope she isn't mad at me for leaving her here for the past few days.

With nothing but her black breeches on, and her upper torso left bare, Mayumi took in a large gulp of Marianna's Sleeper to moisten her tongue and give her liquid courage. She was going to need it.

She shoved a partially saliva-damp cloth between her teeth and breathed in quick, shallow huffs through her nose. She tried her hardest not to close her eyes, the corners of her eyelids crinkling just as deep as her forehead, as she shoved a needle through her skin.

Her lips twitched under the power of her cringes.

Her left arm shook as she clenched her fist, but it was nothing in comparison to the agonised tremble her right hand gave, especially when it worsened when she did the other side of her wound. She swore she heard the pop of the needlepoint breaking through the layers of her skin after it'd been tenting her flesh.

Her teeth gnashed the cloth in her mouth to stem her scream throughout the whole process. She pulled the thread attached to it so she could close that section of her freshly bleeding injury. She tied the blood-coated string before cutting it.

She removed the cloth from her mouth and panted for a few seconds.

Drinking alcohol was thinning the blood that continued to seep from her, but none of her major arteries or veins had been sliced. In reality, the three-fingered claw mark spanning diagonally down her forearm could be much worse.

It was deeper near the inner part of her elbow than her wrist. However, more damage had been done near her wrist, as it had less muscle to protect it.

I still can't feel my ring and pinkie fingers.

Unsure if that was trauma or because the muscles and tendons controlling them were fully severed, she looked at them. They weren't shaking like the rest of her, and they appeared to be permanently stuck in a semi-curled position.

No tears fell from her eyes, but they welled and pooled before she blinked them away.

This wasn't the first time she'd tended to a wound she'd obtained. She had a pretty gnarly one on her thigh she'd patched up herself, but she thought this might be the worst injury she'd ever received.

Faunus had been gone for four days.

As much as she didn't blame him for abandoning her when he knew it could have been dangerous, it would have been damn helpful had he been here.

Had I known he would leave, I never would have used such a large bait like the deer. And his way of killing things was to absolutely shred them to pieces, spraying blood and body parts everywhere.

Most of her kills had little bleeding, and she was sure had she baited the Demons by herself, she wouldn't have made such a large mess that would have continued to lure more.

Rule fourteen: never get in over your head.

This wound could have been prevented if she had just been paying attention.

Only two Demons came last night. She could have taken them on easily by herself if it wasn't for one minor detail she hadn't considered.

Rule three: never be distracted.

I know this is why they kicked me from the guild, she thought as she took another gulp of booze and shoved the cloth in her mouth. Mayumi held her needle and thread again. *A woman with her period on the field is a lure, is distracted, is a risk.*

She'd started menstruating yesterday. The first day was always the hardest for her. At one point last night, while she was on the roof, she'd gotten a cramp so bad she thought her pelvis was on damn fire.

Once more, Mayumi shoved the cloth in her mouth, so she didn't bite down on her tongue or ruin her teeth by gritting them. She purposefully screamed as she threaded the needle through her flesh again. She tied it, then did another, wanting to get this over with as quickly as possible, all the while trembling terribly.

I never bait when I'm on my period.

She did what every smart woman did when she lived in the forest. She lit incense canisters to help mask the smell while burning whatever evidence she had collected in her pants.

Currently, she was wearing a belt of pouches that had strong herbs inside them.

But when she'd been inside while wearing her guild uniform and heard a Demon scuttling outside, she knew she needed to go fight it. Then she stayed on the roof, fatigued and in pain, so she could protect her home and herself.

It'd cost her, and here she was now, sewing her arm while she boiled food because she hadn't eaten in hours. She had a pot full of hot water on her kitchen counter, ready with herbal antiseptic cloths. She planned to wrap them around her arm before she bandaged it properly.

Once she was done closing her wound, she looked at the numerous wadded up pieces of blood-covered cloth on the table. She used another to wipe her forearm as she inspected it.

It was a pretty decent job, if she did say so herself.

She touched her numb ring and pinkie fingers, her lips pursing tightly. *Fuck. If these don't get better, I'll never be able to hold a bow properly.*

It was also doubtable that she'd be able to hold it up with the lack of strength she'd have in her healing arm. She could be permanently shaking from now on.

I should still be able to wield my sword, though.

She took another large swallow of booze before pressing her forehead against her fingertips as she leaned her elbow on her dining table. Her head turned towards the kitchen window to stare out at the midmorning sun with aching, puffy, tired eyes.

Her arm felt searingly hot and swollen, so much so that she thought lava was beginning to form in her veins. Ugh, and the throbbing was making it hard to think of anything else!

With one foot steady, the other was on its toe tips as she bounced it up and down.

If Faunus comes back... Her foot bounced faster. *If Faunus comes back, he can heal my arm, right?*

She'd bear this wound if she had to. If he never came back, she would just accept it, but she couldn't hold back the possibility that there might be a solution.

There was no way she'd let this get in the way of her life.

Although honourably discharged after something similar had been done to his calf, her father had continued to bait Demons and protect this house just fine. She wouldn't throw in the towel that easily.

She had never been cowardly.

Death will come for me regardless, and I'd rather go out fighting. Screw living a long and semi-peaceful life.

It was just as useless as surviving.

What else would she do? Sit in this house and do nothing? She had no such aspirations. She wanted to make a difference in this world by killing just one more Demon.

And I won't live in the towns just to go mad and rot behind those walls. To her, living there was like nothing more than cattle in the stocks waiting to be slaughtered for meat.

The throbbing in her arm was only because it was so fresh, but she inspected her wound again to make sure it was clean. *I hope I don't get an infection and go septic.*

What a pathetic way to die.

What am I going to do tonight, though? I can't fight like this right now. She stood and removed the pot of porridge from her cooking hearth top.

Then she stepped to the side and pulled strips of antiseptic-soaked cloths from the now cooled pot. She laid them over her arm, wincing at the stinging agony it brought. Her arm, somehow, throbbed even faster as the heat got to her wound.

She worked on bandaging her forearm properly to keep everything secure.

Once that was done, she served herself up some porridge and sat down with her eyes growing heavy. She'd lost a lot of blood, and she hadn't slept much yesterday since she'd been cramping.

And being injured could really take it out of a person.

She played with her food to help it cool down, the entire time thinking she didn't particularly feel like eating. Instead, she looked at the chaos within her home.

Her guild uniform shirt was on the ground where she'd dumped it near the door, ruined. She'd just burn it since she had others. Her pants were covered in liquid, and she wasn't sure if that was her own or Demon blood. She hadn't taken her shoes off – it'd been the last thing she'd thought about, all things considered.

It looks and smells like an infirmary in here. She sighed as she ate. *I need to clean up before I sleep.*

With her head pressed against her palm, Mayumi began to fall asleep under the weight and events of her night.

The sound of heavy footsteps crossing her porch had her suddenly alert. She didn't know how long she'd been asleep – probably a few minutes? Her head had begun to fall towards her bowl on the table, and she almost gave herself whiplash as she reared it back.

"Who's there?" she shouted, hoping to the heavens it *wasn't* a certain Duskwalker.

Those footsteps made it to the door and turned the door handle. Mayumi stood and then looked down at all the mess.

Fuck. Don't be Faunus.

"It's me, Mayumi," he called back just as the door began to open.

"Don't come in here!" she roared, running to the door so she could slam it shut.

She didn't make it there before she was face-to-face with his feline skull and massive body in the doorway.

Blue orbs turned stark white as he searched within the house. She noticed he took in a deep, curious breath right before it shuddered out of him.

"Blood? You're injured?" he asked as he took a step backwards. Both his hands lifted to cover his snout, but before he did, his orbs had swiftly turned to red.

Shit. That's not good.

Mayumi backed up while reaching for the side of her weapons belt. She grabbed at the air, having forgotten her sword was outside.

"You need to leave, Faunus," Mayumi said calmly, keeping her voice especially soft when an echoing, bubbly growl emitted from him.

She tried to grab her dagger, but her injured, trembling fingers fumbled it when he lowered his hands so he could fall forward and land on them. Her skin prickled with goosebumps in dread when he took a step forward into her home on all fours, his bubbling growl turning more ferocious by the second.

He shoved his wide shoulders in, making her doorframe creak.

His orbs are still red. And they were focused on freshly bled prey. Her. *Shit.*

She narrowed her eyes, keeping her heart steady even though her body was shaking with weakness.

"Hey there, my big sexy Duskwalker," Mayumi cooed, backing up from him with a hand forward. She could sense the danger from him like it was something thick and tangible. "I know you don't want to hurt me. You'll be really angry with yourself if you do."

She knew he was gone to whatever forces made the bloodlust silence his thoughts when he skulked low and kept coming. He was no longer listening. He no longer seemed to be her sweet Faunus.

There was no point in talking to him now, and she wouldn't waste her breath on doing so. Instead, she just took a mental stock of where all her available weapons were.

Other than the dagger that now lay on the floor between them, the only available weapons were her father's sword resting on top of the fireplace mantle and her whip looped on her belt.

When Faunus' fangs parted, and he snarled, she braved flicking her eyes to the fireplace.

She had anticipated that he might leap if she took her gaze off him, and when he did, she dived to the side as he charged. He stepped on top of the coffee table, breaking it in half as he came at her.

Her heart accelerated under her stress. This was the last thing she needed after the damn night she just had!

He missed her when she rolled to the side in front of the fireplace and came up in a crouch. She grabbed her father's sword, but it flung out of her hands when his chest shoved her as he tackled her much smaller, huddled form, thankfully too low for his swiping claws.

Shit! He's so damn fast. She flipped onto her back as she hit the ground and pressed against his chest with her feet to keep them separated while he savagely snapped his jaws above her. His fangs created a sharp clipping noise not even centimetres from her nose. *Of all fucking days for him to come back, it just had to be this one?!*

Only a minute had passed since he'd come inside, and already she was on her back! A human could never outmanoeuvre a Duskwalker, and she was weak and slow from blood loss.

Think, Mayumi.

Her father's sword had partially slipped from its scabbard, but it was just out of reach – and those teeth were snapping dangerously closer.

Grabbing the fire poker lying in front of the flames, Mayumi shoved it between his fangs and used both her knees and hands to push him back, screaming in the agony that radiated up her injured arm.

Faunus obviously thought with his fangs in this state because he just used his arms to steady himself above her while trying to get her head in his mouth. Drool splattered against her cheek as she kept him at bay.

Her arms were weakening, though, and her eyes widened when the iron poker began to distort. He was bending it!

Fuck. Fuck! She needed to do something, and quick.

She darted her head to the side to give her arms a break and let him come forward to bash his snout against the ground. At the same time, she reached down and unclipped her whip from her belt.

Just as he reared back, Mayumi kicked the underside of his jaw to shut his fangs and quickly threaded the whip around his deadly maw.

He backed up to scratch it off his face, the poker stuck behind his back fangs. While he was distracted, Mayumi reached into the fireplace and grabbed the non-flaming side of a burning stick that was half inside the flames.

Terrified of fire, Faunus yelped at the splatter of embers that cascaded around his face as she swung the stick, buying herself an extra moment to manoeuvre. The sound squeezed her heart in pity for him. Actually, this whole situation only had her feeling pity for him.

She reached for her father's sword and pulled it from its scabbard, chucking the stick back in the fire just as he roared.

Cut his head off. That's what he told her to do if there was ever a situation where he was attacking her in a blood-hungry rage. *He said he'll come back if I cut his head off. Maybe I can fix his skull while he's unconscious.*

Mayumi brought her shoulders in to make herself smaller when he slammed his hands around her. She held the sword sideways out in front of her, the bladed side towards him, and she steadied the flat edge with her foot. It lodged in his throat as he descended.

Once more, she was just holding him at bay.

At this rate, he's going to kill me.

She felt no fear, but the adrenaline coursing through her veins made it feel as though her stomach and heart had switched places. The back of her throat burned on each inhale and exhale of breath, her lungs shrivelling as they squeezed.

She had one hand holding the hilt of the sword with her opposing foot pressing it in. Her other foot was against his chest to keep him back, but he was stronger than her. She was sure the only reason he wasn't completely bearing down on her now was because of the pain he must be in.

Dark-purple blood oozed onto the silver blade of the sword as it cut deeper and deeper into his throat. Faunus came closer and closer, like he didn't care as long as he got his meal in the end.

Mayumi had always known this was a risk. She'd been mentally prepared for it. She could handle dying. It had been ingrained into her personality to be aloof about her own death.

But the reason her heart raced with worry wasn't for herself, but for him.

He'll never forgive himself if he kills me.

She could only imagine the aftermath of this. How he would handle knowing he'd been the one to take her life.

He'd never said it, but Mayumi knew he loved her. It wasn't hard to see it in the way he held her dearly, like she was the only thing that mattered in the world. She also felt it in the way he stroked his claws over every single part of her body, from her feet all the way to her thick hair, as though he worshipped every part of her.

He treated her like she was the most precious thing, and the words he spoke were deep affirmations of affection.

It was hard not to return those feelings when they were so freely being shared. She preferred them over the uselessness of one single word that was so lacking in expressing one's endearment.

Mayumi narrowed her eyes in stubborn determination. She did the only thing she could think of.

She shoved her fingers all the way into his nose hole since he didn't have eyes for her to poke. The big Duskwalker shuddered from the unexpected intrusion to his nose and reared back. He hacked in repulsion, giving her a chance to bring her foot back.

He swiped a claw and nicked the point of one of them against her cheek, slicing it when she turned her head to evade the worst of it.

The sword was firmly lodged in his throat now, and she aimed the heel of both her boots at it when he came back down. Both feet hit it, but then her left one slipped off.

Mayumi crossed her arms over her face, expecting the worst when that gave him the freedom to finish coming down.

A sharp gasp tore from her throat. Pain radiated in her right knee as it hit something hard and curved. She didn't worry if something in her knee shattered when she thought she was moments away from her arms being bitten into.

Suddenly, Faunus slumped over her, crushing her beneath the weight of his massive form.

It took Mayumi a few seconds of wild panting to realise he'd completely stopped moving.

Did I do it?

She wasn't going to lie here and wait to find out – not if it meant she could be wrong.

Clawing her way out from under him was exceptionally difficult. She had multiple injuries, and he was so damn heavy as a limp being that it was like trying to lift a bear off herself.

However, as she wriggled herself upwards and to the side, trying to crawl out from the junction of his neck and shoulder, she could see his head was still firmly attached to his neck. She'd barely got the sword halfway inside his thick, dense throat.

If it wasn't his neck that put him out, then what–

Mayumi didn't think she'd ever experienced anything like the ghastly chill that crept down her spine at what she saw. Never in her life, even after everything she'd seen, done, and experienced, had anything made her heart nearly shatter in her chest.

Seeping heavily from the wide-open crack of his skull, a puddle of purple blood was forming underneath his head.

"No!" she yelled, leaning forward to ghost her fingers in the air above it.

It was obvious he was still alive by the way his laboured

breaths lifted his chest, but that did nothing to ease her.

"No! Fuck!" She sat back on her arse and brought her knees up. At the same time, she covered her face with her shaking hands. "I broke his skull further."

It must have been his horn she felt bash against her knee.

She broke it, her! She'd been trying to fix him, not be the reason he was even closer to death! He'd never take her soul now, not with the way she could see it was gaping and revealing bits of strange looking muscle.

It was barely holding on, the underside loose while the top part of the crack was all that was left holding him together.

It's all my fault. It's all my damn fault.

Mayumi didn't know how to process this. What she was supposed to do.

She just crossed one foot on top of the other as if she was trying to make herself smaller to the world, unsure of how to handle the growing grief swirling all the way down to the very core of her being.

No tears formed. She hadn't cried when either one of her parents died. Faunus, from what she could tell, was at least still alive, but there was an uncomfortable tingle in her sinuses like she wanted to.

She was in so much pain. Her arm was bleeding through her bandage, and she knew she'd popped multiple stitches in fighting him. Her face hurt from where he'd cut her, and she was certain something was horribly wrong with her knee.

It's all my fault. If I hadn't wanted to bait the Demons, the winged one probably wouldn't have come here.

The Demon had mentioned something about a king. She knew Faunus had run after him because he didn't want the Demon King knowing where he was.

Faunus wouldn't have needed to chase after him. I wouldn't have been left to fight off Demons by myself and gotten injured.

He wouldn't have come back here while she was in the middle of patching herself up and cleaning her home. She wouldn't have been covered in her own blood.

She wouldn't have caused all of this.

Lowering her hands, she stared at him with her eyes bowed

deeply. Bile rose to her throat like acid, her gut churning with emotions that she couldn't bottle down no matter how hard she tried.

Her heart painfully clenched, threatening to snap the tendons holding it in place. It stole the rest of the agony she felt, more prominent than any of her physical wounds.

How am I meant to save him now?

"I'm so sorry, Faunus."

THIRTY-FIVE

Faunus' mind was discombobulated as he woke. It was the kind of groggy one would feel after a deep sleep.

No, that was wrong. It was dizzy, like in the way he remembered being poisoned felt. His hearing was muffled, like someone had shoved cotton into his ear holes. His sight was shifting, vibrating in and out of light and dark, as everything appeared to move slowly. There were trails and a strange split in his vision he'd never witnessed before.

His skull was unbearably heavy, but it also gnawed at him with a pounding that forked all throughout his entire face like strikes of lightning in the sky.

It was the strangest sensation, but it felt as though his being, his essence, his very *soul*, was severing in two.

A mixture of his own blood and intense herbs, like dill, basil, and multiple others, was all he could smell. Something was covering his bony snout and partially filled his nose hole – although not fully. It was uncomfortable, and he didn't like not being able to sense where he was.

What... happened?

Usually, when he slept or passed out or even temporarily died, he would remember. He'd even vaguely remembered the many rages he'd had.

Now there was only blankness.

The last thing he remembered was that he'd given up on chasing the winged Demon. *I remember falling from the tree...* There was nothing else in his memory.

Another attempt at looking around revealed he was in a cottage, a mostly familiar one despite the fog of his vision.

Did I make it to Mayumi?

Faunus tried to move his arms but was unable to. He wriggled when he realised his limbs had been tied together behind his back, and he was rendered immobile against the ground. *Enchanted rope?* That was all he could think that would be binding him this way.

A form and a half came into view, and Faunus only knew it was Mayumi kneeling on the floor next to his skull when she came close enough to slip through the veil of his filtered, idled mind.

"You're awake." Her voice was distant. "It's been a day since you came back."

Faunus focused on her and noticed, eventually, everything began to settle.

The pain in his face remained, worsening even, while the world steadied. But there was a partial dimness that didn't fade on the left side of his sight, and he swore his hearing was off on that same side.

A curt, lung-shuddering whine echoed out of his lungs.

"Why do I hurt so much?" He wriggled again, his tail curling in aversion to being captured this way. "And why am I tied like this?"

With something clamping his jaws shut, he was lying face down with his arms behind his back and his legs together. He could see he was inside, a safe distance from the fire, but was still within range of its warmth.

"You don't remember?"

When he shook his head, Mayumi looked to the ground.

Her hair was shielding the side of her face, and he was surprised to find her in a dress. He'd never seen her in one before, and although it was grey and plain with an underdress beneath it, he thought it suited her.

"I couldn't stand to leave you outside by yourself when you healed, but I'm currently on my period. I covered your snout, hoping it would help hide you from the smell, and I tied you up in case that didn't work."

He was surprised she avoided eye contact with him, since Mayumi didn't often avert her gaze for long periods of time.

She appears tired.

From what he could see of her face, the underneath of her eyes was bruised and heavily creased. She also appeared paler than normal.

"Although a few drops would not send me into a craze, that was still wise of you."

But with Mayumi being a Demonslayer for eleven years, he thought she must know ways to get around this feminine issue.

She became silent, which always made him worry.

"Mayumi?"

When she didn't turn to him nor respond, Faunus turned his head more towards her. He yelped. The need to touch his face and discover why it ached so badly ate at him, and the inability to do so nettled him.

"I'm so sorry, Faunus." The despairing tone in her voice made his fur and spikes puff. "I've put a salve on your face to aid with the pain, and I don't even know if it's helping, but... I've cracked your skull further."

White lifted into his sight. It was then that he understood the dimness he could see in his left orb and why his vision was partially split... The reason he couldn't hear properly was because of his skull.

He wanted to be angry, but he found he could never be so with her. He allowed all the tension that had shot through him to ease.

"How? What happened, Mayumi?"

She covered her left arm and turned her head away to face it completely the other way.

"You attacked me. Well, you nearly killed me, to be precise. I tried to cut off your head like you told me to."

He looked at the arm she was covering with her hand, and panic struck him.

"Are you injured?"

"Did you know your neck is really fucking thick?" she asked instead of answering, which only made his panic worsen. "When I tried booting the sword into your throat, my foot slipped, and you ended up head-butting my knee with your horn. You collapsed after that."

Could Mayumi hear his heart beating against the floor? She must be able to – it was as heavy as a drum. Every word she uttered left a metallic, sour taste in his throat.

"Did I hurt you?" he asked, struggling to get out of his bonds so he could check her. When she didn't say anything, he began to growl. "Answer me, Mayumi!"

She spun her head to him, her teeth gritted and revealing a bruised cut she had across her cheek.

"Worry about yourself, Faunus!" She reached forward, leaning on one knee and a foot, to undo the binds on his legs and then wrists. "I'm not the one fucking dying here, I don't think. My arm looks really bad since I popped most of my stitches, and it's black, but I'm not the one with half my damn face falling off!"

When he was freed, she stood to put space between them. He didn't like it, didn't like she was trying to hide from him, run from him when he wanted to check on her wellbeing.

"I shouldn't have been so careless. I knew about your crack, but I thought we could protect each other. You protect me while I protect you. I thought everything would be fine, but if I hadn't wanted to lure Demons here, none of this would have happened. I'm so freaking selfish and stupid."

"Are... are you limping?" he asked as he made his way to his paws. He was unsteady, like his equilibrium was off, but he adjusted to it swiftly.

Nothing prepared him for the new onslaught of pain that would bombard him once he'd risen as far as he could stand in her small home. He raised his hand to touch his skull, wincing at the sting that movement brought, but he just bore with the pain so he could physically inspect how bad it was.

His tail curled downwards. It was bad, really bad.

"Faunus!" Mayumi shouted as she turned to him. "Why aren't you angry with me?"

He stilled as he stared at her. She stared back with her little brows furrowed, as though she was awaiting something.

His white orbs turned blue at the sight of her. They deepened even further when he took a step towards her, and she stepped back.

He was right, she was limping. Her face looked haggard, tired and hurt, pale and crestfallen. But no matter how far she limped back, even when her arse hit her dining table, Faunus didn't stop chasing her.

He gently slipped his clawed fingers under the soft lines of her jaw until he'd cradled underneath it and the base of her skull with his massive hands.

"Because, Mayumi," he rasped as he lowered his skull, turned it slightly, and pressed the side of his forehead against the middle of hers. He winced when even that little contact caused pain. "You are alive. That is all that matters. You fought against me and won, no matter how. I would rather my skull be broken further than to have come to my senses and realised I'd killed you."

He darkened his sight, relieved to know that she was here when he had almost ended her life. He couldn't remember how, but if she said he'd nearly succeeded, then he knew she must have done everything in her feeble little human power to overcome him.

Despite the sickening pool of terrible emotions swirling within him, he couldn't help the pride he felt.

While holding firmly onto her precious head, cupping the underside of it completely, he resisted when Mayumi bashed against his chest. She beat it, slapped it, tried to push him away, but he refused to let her go – just like he hadn't truly been able to from the moment he first met her.

At the same time, the cool wash of his magic radiated between them as he took her wounds for himself.

"No!" she yelled, her hits becoming more aggressive the more he healed her – it was like he was giving her strength to do so. It only made him realise how badly she was hurt. His knee threatened to buckle, and his arm was in agony. "It's not fair!"

"Quiet, my adorably fierce hunter," he said in a gentle, soothing tone. "Everything will be fine."

He knew it was a lie, but he just needed her to calm down. She'd obviously spent the last twenty-four hours spiralling, and he couldn't bear to see her this way when she was usually so reserved and controlled.

Her slaps softened before she eventually fell against him.

"But it's not fine," she muttered, gripping at the fur of his chest. "I feel like I've killed you."

Leaning back so he could face her, he found her colour had returned significantly. That fact alone made him feel better.

With the back of his curved claw, Faunus tenderly pushed a clump of tangled hair behind her ear.

"I know this would have happened to me eventually since I already injured my skull further chasing the winged Demon. I always knew what my end was." He drew his claw down her fragile jugular so he could feel it pulsing with life. "I always knew my future was limited. This is not your fault, Mayumi. It is no one's fault but my own, and the choices I made that led me to being trapped by the Demon King."

Somehow, her brows furrowed even further, this time her lips pouting along with it. He found her sadness charming because it showed just how deeply she cared for him.

"But–"

"You can choose to dwell on this, but nothing will change it. I have chosen to just... live, so long as it is by your side. No matter how long that may be. That is all I have wanted since this happened to me." Faunus pressed his forehead against hers once again. "I do not wish to taint whatever time I have left with you with misery." He skated his claws down her side with a warm chuckle as he added, "When I would much rather it be filled with pleasure."

"I don't know how to do that," Mayumi muttered, tipping her head forward. "I can't just forget what's happening, Faunus. My mind wants to find a solution. My heart wants to fixate like it always does when I've decided upon something."

"Can you not decide on something else?" he asked, using a fore knuckle to lift her head back up. "I have never seen you in such long, flowing clothing."

He was trying to distract her – especially since she usually let him.

"Let me guess. It suits me? Looks better on me? I should wear it more often?" Her snarky tone gave him hope.

"It looks easier for me to get into," he said, thankful his orbs were beginning to go back to their normal yellow. He was forcing them to as much as he could. "But I do think I much prefer you in pants. You don't appear like yourself dressed this way."

The corner of her mouth twitched, the nag of a smirk teasing her lips before her expression fell.

"Is the salve helping you?" she asked as she reached up to ghost her fingers close to his crack, but thankfully never touching it. "Your left orb looks much smaller than the right."

"I'm unsure of what it is like without it, so I don't know if it is assisting with the pain."

"I can make more, so let's not find out." Her lips tightened momentarily as her eyes danced across all his features – from his orbs to his horns to the rope and cloth covering his snout. "I tried strapping your face together while you were unconscious, but I heard a cracking sound and stopped. I wish there was more I could do for you."

Faunus grabbed her hand and held it down against his sternum, hoping she could feel his heart radiating beneath it.

"Just being with you is enough for me."

Her gaze was mingled with far too many deeply conflicting emotions for him to truly understand all of them.

"But it's not for me," she croaked before burying her forehead against his chest.

The way she clung to him felt wrong.

It was filled with warmth and tenderness, but there was a slight tremble to the way she hugged him. She was fisting his fur tightly, and since he smelt no fear, he knew it was anxiety.

He was causing her distress. He wished he was selfless enough to put distance between them when he knew what the inevitable was. To help make this easier for her.

But he wasn't selfless. He knew it the moment he wrapped his arms around her and squeezed her to him like his life depended on it.

THIRTY-SIX

Days had gone by, but they felt like nothing more than seconds to Mayumi. Time was flowing on a set construct she couldn't change. One where she was watching the grains of sand beginning to sprinkle through a time glass belonging to a being who was meant to be given an unlimited amount.

It was delineated, painting the very boundary of fate's tethering of a person to this world.

To watch those fate strings beginning to unravel, to know those glittering pieces of sand were running out, was arduous and punishing to witness. Especially when there was nothing she could do to help.

She didn't understand how immortality could be so fleeting.

Despite the constant bitterness this gave her, she was thankful for it. At least Faunus wasn't alone.

She was thankful the Demons had mostly stopped coming since she'd been trying to kill them with as little blood spilt as possible. Especially since, over the course of the last few days, both their minds had aligned to do nothing more than spend time together.

And with the sand running out, she showed him all that she could. They'd built snow creatures, hers being a snowman and his being a snow Duskwalker. He'd helped her fix the coffee table he'd broken when he attacked her, so they could play every board game she had available.

But, perhaps the most tender of moments had been Mayumi bringing Faunus into the cluttered, uselessly sentimental room of her ancestors.

Even though she'd vowed to never go rifling through things that were better left forgotten, she explained the history of everything she had knowledge of.

What painting belonged to whom, which great-grandparent wrote some sappy or depressive poem. Why there was a single small left shoe, but not a right.

For most, this could seem like an unimportant task, but Mayumi had wanted to finally share why this room kind of... scared her a little. To know she might be the last one to live in it, to pass this information on to another, was cruel.

The fate of her bloodline rested in her hands, and instead, she'd gone and fallen for a monster – one who may not be here for much longer.

She was someone who was repulsed by affection from humans but revelled in it from him. How was she supposed to settle for some lesser score after all this?

No one and nothing could compare to the greatness that was Faunus.

Of course, he'd given her his complete and undivided attention. Whether or not he was feigning interest was beyond her care. It was better than them both sitting there in deafening silence and dwelling on the bleak future.

Her libido, which was usually ripe and hungry, had been drowning in an ice bath. She wished it had stayed that way rather than roaring to a burning inferno when she watched this big, dark, fluffy fucker hold her own tiny baby shoe in his massive palm.

Especially when the ending of their intimacy had Mayumi feeling as though she'd been slapped in the face by the two droplets of purple blood that splattered against her cheek. It'd shocked her so completely that her entire body clenched around his cock, which only made her wince when she felt his barbs.

With Faunus huffing wildly above her, his body heaving with heavy breaths that ended in acute but quiet whines, she watched blood dripping from his nose hole and down his face.

A third droplet splashed against her lips this time.

"Faunus?" she asked, concern ladened in her voice.

She lifted her hand to wipe it away, hoping to remove it. More light droplets followed in thin rivulets down the white bone of his face.

"I thought I could do this," he panted before he shook his head slightly. His orbs morphed into a deep blue. "But I cannot. My heart is beating too fast."

With his cock fluttering in a frenzy, he pushed forward to unlatch his barbs from deep within her channel.

"I cannot even take satisfaction in scenting you and I mingled. I can barely smell anything." His nose hole was pooling with his own blood, and it sprayed around her when he gave a deep, wet snort. "Perhaps that is for the best."

For the best? She thought as she watched his clawed hand come up above her.

A gasp tore through her, one of pain and surprise, when those claws came down to stab into her stomach. Mayumi's back bowed even deeper when she felt cool magic radiating all throughout her abdomen.

"What are you doing?!" she tried to scream, but it only came out as a whisper.

"If I can shape you to me," he growled lightly. "Then I must be able to undo it."

"No! Don't!"

Her request was ignored.

Her legs trembled and twitched as he withdrew – or maybe she was now pushing him out. It was hard to tell. All she knew was that her body was changing like it once had, but this time going back to the way it was supposed to be.

She hated it.

Seed she could usually hold gushed out of her right before his softening cock fell from her.

Faunus steadied himself above her on all fours once he was done, while her back straightened and laid flat against the ground. His body was shaking around hers, trying his hardest not to collapse.

Mayumi shoved at his chest. "You didn't have to do that!"

"I did," he grated, his whines still apparent. He was in pain, and she wanted to sympathise with him, but she couldn't after what he'd just done. "I cannot taint the rest of your life because of these few blissful weeks we have shared."

He didn't get her permission to do it, her consent. He'd done what he thought was best without even asking her if she wanted it.

"That is not your choice to make!" she yelled, wishing he would stop being so damn selfless and sweet just for one fucking second. It wasn't fair.

It was painful. She'd rather he be a bastard all the way to the end, be possessive and jealous until his last breath. This knight in shining armour bullshit was doing nothing more than twisting her insides tighter than they needed to be. At this rate, she'd be knotted into braids.

She wanted him to growl *mine,* not fix her so she could take another person's cock!

"I have told you many times," he chuckled darkly. "I am the one in control."

"Undo it, Faunus," she demanded as she glared up at him.

"No." He finally collapsed to the side, his body languid as his chest rose and fell. "And I would rather not fight with you. I can still pleasure you, even if I cannot receive pleasure myself."

"I don't want to do that."

She didn't think she could handle being touched without being able to reciprocate. Giving was just as satisfying as receiving for her.

Faunus pulled her against him, forcing them to cuddle on the ground of the dust-covered, cluttered storage room.

"Then show me more of your life and your family's too. I would enjoy nothing more than to learn everything about you, knowing you would trust no other but me to hear of it."

Mayumi bit her lips shut to quell the whimper that wanted to escape from her.

It's not fair when he pulls on my heartstrings like that.

The threat of tears tingled her face, and she turned her glare towards the ceiling to stem them. But they were getting harder and harder to control and hold back the more time they spent together.

She wanted them to be closer than ever, yet Faunus was shoving walls between them.

I... I wish someone would tell me what I need to do.

Faunus slowly untangled Mayumi from his limbs, the tiny female holding his fur tightly with her clutching little human claws. He rose to be seated with his legs crossed, wishing he could lay his forehead in his palm to rest his head, but he couldn't bear the pain that even touching the good side of his skull brought anymore.

I cannot sleep, he thought as he looked at the darkness of her home, the sun soon to rise but not yet shedding its light upon the world.

Currently, his face was bandaged. It was done at his own request to prevent dust and dirt from getting inside his constantly open wound. The salve she placed in his crack did little to ease the throbbing, and he was constantly in agony.

He tried his best to hide the extent of this from her, but even he couldn't stop the sudden whines that burst from him during certain tasks now.

There is no point in me being here any longer.

Other than being a presence in her home, Faunus could no longer assist Mayumi in any strenuous task – no matter how much he tried.

Anything that accelerated his heart rate caused his injury to worsen in its severity of pain. It was only when his heart slowed again that he was eased, but sometimes he'd bleed through his crack and inside his nose hole.

His sense of smell was hindered, as was his hearing on the left side of him.

He couldn't move trees for her, cut kindling for her fireplace, or even cart it inside. He couldn't shovel snow or even walk around her home. He could do nothing without feeling dizzy or weak.

I cannot touch her.

He could hold her, he could speak with her, but nothing more than that.

Faunus felt... useless.

He doubted he would be productive in protecting her. If a fight were to occur, he knew his increased heart rate would be a hindrance in his sense of judgement. The dizziness that overwhelmed him caused his mind to be slow.

He could end up becoming a distraction for her.

She will seek to protect me.

Which, in turn, could end with her coming to harm. She'd already made that obvious by hanging up her protective charms each night while he was sheltered inside her home.

She was trying to keep him inside even if there was danger, knowing he couldn't pass through it with the way his skull was. It didn't further destroy it, but it was too painful for him to pass through now.

Faunus turned just enough so he could touch his fingertips to Mayumi's sternum.

A soft, orange glow lit beneath her flesh as though her skin was the surface of water – it even rippled when he lightly touched her. A wisp of fire fluttered out before a round head followed.

Her soul was limp as though half-asleep since he was the one pulling it from her rather than it aggressively jumping out.

He didn't need to grab it as he pulled it from her. Instead, her soul fluttered through the air below his fingertips until he brought it in front of him. He cupped beneath it with his large, dark-grey palm.

Sitting on its hip with its legs curled underneath itself, her soul looked up at him. He swore his very essence quivered when it appeared as though it smiled at him. Two dark spots lazily blinked.

He carefully brushed it underneath its tiny jaw with his forefinger. His sight morphed to bright pink when it leaned against him in welcome.

Her soul is mine to touch. Unless it was a Duskwalker like himself, no other being would be able to share in this kind of intimate moment with it. *Whether or not I get to keep it, it is mine.*

He knew it was true when he managed to coax it to its feet and began... playing with it. A sad chuckle almost escaped him when he thought he may have tickled it when the back of his claw caressed up and down its side.

Her soul held his finger, and he thought he saw tiny lips puckering into a pout. To remove the expression he had seen far too many times on Mayumi's very own face, he twirled his finger around her soul's body like a tornado.

It spun in a circle, wisps of fire swirling up his finger from its floating hair. It didn't appear dizzy once it settled, and it took its own initiative to hold his claw to balance itself so it could almost... dance with his finger.

Of course, it was doing whatever it wanted, just like Mayumi often did. His heart was swollen, overflowing, and unable to contain the emotions that wanted to burst it.

I wish I could take it.

He eventually lifted his palm so he could nuzzle it with the front of his snout. He felt warmth and pressure, but it didn't hurt him like anything physical might. Perhaps he didn't care. It was nothing in comparison to the longing bruising his chest.

Once more, he brought his palm down so he could caress it. He rubbed it underneath its jaw, down its side, and even brushed his claw up its spine. He sifted two claw tips through the fiery, floating hair.

Faunus flinched in surprise when two hands rubbed over the back of his shoulders, then over the tops of them, before coming down his pectoral muscles. Mayumi leaned her weight against his back as she brought her head beside his own.

"You're thinking about leaving, aren't you?" she whispered. Her voice was croaky and sleep filled, and so decadent to his ears that his fur puffed when goosebumps lifted it.

"No," he lied, looking at her from the corner of his orb – even if she wouldn't be able to tell where his sight had fallen.

Then he gazed back down to her soul, continuing to touch it even though he'd been caught in taking it from her without her knowing.

It'd been an accident that he'd discovered he could just will it from her body without her knowledge. He tried not to do so often, worried that the constant exposure would cause his dying willpower to finally crumble, and he'd eat it.

I want it. I want it more than I can stand.

It was there, right in front of him, glowing for him, fucking reaching for him with its slender arms, and he couldn't take it. He didn't think anyone could understand how miserable that was.

It was haunting him just as much as he had begun to feel like he was haunting Mayumi. He was just a presence now, a Ghost holding on by a thread to this world, and he knew he was going to fade soon.

"Don't lie to me, Faunus," Mayumi whispered as she brushed her lips against the side of his neck – so light and feather-like in touch. "Just stay here with me."

His orbs turned a deep well of blue despite his efforts to not let them.

How did she know I was saying goodbye to it? he thought, as he held her soul in his hand so he could pet the pad of his thumb over its torso.

His intention had been to touch her soul one last time before giving it back and leaving. He couldn't bear to say goodbye to Mayumi herself.

He didn't think he could handle watching her hurt or deal with her convincing him otherwise. He also didn't think he could handle his own reaction to her, his own internal longing and sadness.

Figured she would find a way to meddle, regardless.

Why does she want me to stay? What use was there in him remaining? The last thing he wanted was for her to see his decline or the end.

I had planned to go into the forest and pull my skull apart myself. It would be easy, too. Whether it was his internal or physical hurt, both were as prevalent as the other. Both would push him to do so.

He wanted to be rid of it.

"Your silence is convincing me that I was right," she said as she buried her face against the fur of his neck. "I am used to people dying, Faunus. I am used to watching it. I have seen people die from wounds and from sickness. Some deaths are quicker than others, but I have always found that the person is brought comfort by having someone by their side."

"I am not a human, Mayumi," he quietly bit. "It would bring

me no comfort to have you watch me. There is no pride in it for me, and I don't need you coddling me. I was brought into this world alone, I have lived it alone, and it is best that I leave it alone."

Alone.

"I could try to guilt you into staying," she said, making him growl in reaction. "But I won't. I'm just... asking you to. I want to spend every moment I can with you." She nuzzled her face against him. "I want to take in your scent, feel your warmth, and hear your voice for as long as I can. Is that so much to ask for? A second more is better than a second lost."

"I cannot help you." He turned his head so he could show he was looking around her home.

"How many times do I need to remind you I don't need your help, Faunus? I have never needed it." She slipped over his shoulder so she could lie on his crossed legs. "But I would like your company. You can still hand me vegetables to cook. You can still play board games with me. You can still talk to me until the stars are beginning to fade and we watch the rising sun. I have never needed help, but I have always needed someone to fill the void of my home." Then she gave him a small, forced smile as she said, "And you do take up a lot of space. You make it cosy."

But was that enough? He wanted it to be.

I don't want to leave.

What if Jabez came here? How would Mayumi face the Demon King by herself with him gone? He'd most likely think she were lying if she were to say that Faunus had just left.

He was completely torn between what he wanted.

I don't want to leave her, but what right do I have to stay?

THIRTY-SEVEN

A light sound thudding beyond her front door spooked her into alertness. Mayumi rushed to crouch so suddenly that her feet nearly got caught in her blanket and tripped her.

"Faunus?" she shouted, standing as she took a step towards the outside, uncaring that she was in nothing more than a sleep shirt.

"I'm right here," he answered from the back of her home where her lounging chairs were.

She turned to find him sitting by the window and staring out at the early morning light. He was leaning up against the wall with his shoulder, one leg straight and the other bent, his body so brightened in colour that his fur almost had a blue tinge to it. Even his skull seemed to glisten.

Fuck, she thought as she brushed the tangled knots of her hair from her face. *I thought he left.*

Even though it was only a night ago that he'd been playing with her soul in the dark, Faunus had never promised he would stay here. Since then, Mayumi had been on edge.

"Why are you over there?"

"The sun was shining on my face, and it woke me."

It was a lie, an obvious one. She knew his orbs weren't the same as human's closed eyelids passing light through. It also wasn't that bright yet.

He isn't sleeping. She knew he did a little, but he was no longer the lazy, sleepy Duskwalker she knew him to be.

Mayumi bit her lips to stop herself from responding before

she rounded and went to the kitchen.

She wasn't going to coddle him. He'd asked her not to, and if she tried to, if she treated him like a lost, sick puppy, it would push him to leave. She tried to act as normal as possible. Which is why she transferred some of her drinking water to a pot so she could boil it for tea.

When she grabbed the ceramic container and opened it, she shook the very last few leaves that were inside it. She slyly let her eyes drift to the corners of her lids to inspect her dwindling supplies.

I have two or three days left of food. And it wasn't good food either. Her potatoes and onions could last, but already her carrots, pumpkin, and beets were going soft, and her broccoli and cauliflower were withering.

This was the point at which Mayumi would start considering going to Colt's Outpost. Actually, that was days ago. Her dwindling food was a choice, and she'd been rationing in order to stay here with Faunus.

I don't know how well he'll do making the journey to the town... or if he'll leave once he sees me go inside.

She couldn't ride his back like before. Even though her weight was light for him, she wouldn't want to add any extra pressure to his body that could accelerate his heart rate. *But if I don't ride his back, he'll think he's weak and unhelpful.*

A cooing sound beyond her front door had her ears perking and her head turning that way.

"It's your bird," Faunus told her while keeping his skull pointing upwards and outwards to the cold, wintery outside world. "I didn't want to fetch it for you in case it flew off. I doubt it would trust me."

"I guess I better go get him then before he freezes," Mayumi sighed as she threw the last of her tea leaves into the pot.

Since she only had her own light body sweat to deal with, she quickly wiped herself down with cold water to clean herself. Then she pulled on her brown deer-hide pants, a cream tunic, and her usual white wolf-pelt jacket so she could brave the elements. Of course, she donned her weapons belt, as the sun was just low enough that Demons could still be hiding in their shadows.

Her boots were outside, and she put them on just in case her pigeon decided to be skittish.

"Hey there, boy," Mayumi fondly murmured as she reached her arm out to her pigeon sitting on the railing of her porch. "I've been waiting for you."

When her messenger pigeon was resting upon her forearm, she lifted him so she could check his leg for a message.

There was nothing there.

That's odd. I expected them to respond to me this time.

The guild had never responded to a single message from her. However, with the fact they'd kept her pigeon for a month when usually they'd return him sooner, Mayumi had been expecting correspondence.

"Did you lose it?" Mayumi asked as she scratched her fingertip against the front of his neck before going up the side. "You were gone a long time, so did you not come home straight away?"

It wouldn't be the first time her pigeon had taken its sweet time returning.

Mayumi turned to her front door and then paused at it, the weight of her pigeon seeming heavier than normal.

Maybe I should go back, she thought as she stared at the distressed timber of the outside wall. *I could go through with the procedure and return to my rank. They said I could return at any time if I chose it.*

It would be better than sitting in this cold, empty house by herself once Faunus was gone. Her house was becoming a tomb of painful memories.

Her mother's coy, brash laughter was gone. Her father's stern but protective gaze was gone. And already Faunus' radiating personality was dimming.

What would she do here? Drink herself stupid and lay in the dark thinking of all the fond memories she had of all the people who no longer existed?

Her mind would decay.

Once her mind was made up, she pushed her door open.

I'll go back. I'd rather that.

So lost in thought, Mayumi didn't hear the crunching

footsteps entering her clearing until it was too late.

"You're becoming negligent after being away from the guild so long," a familiar, deep voice stated. "You even let us sneak up on you, Mayumi."

Her sudden spinning around spooked her pigeon, who flew off to the side before going into the air. Her door naturally slammed closed behind her.

Mayumi's gaze scanned over the five men and four women clad in black, each one bearing a golden crest on their Demonslayer uniform.

"Elders?" Mayumi asked with her brows furrowing before her gaze finally landed on one additional person. It narrowed at the medallion glinting against their chest. "And Head Elder, Cordon Hansley?"

Resting neatly over his Demonslayer insignia etched into his uniform, the medallion caught the bright sunlight showering into the clearing. The big chain links reached a round, golden medal that had a sparkling black crystal in the centre. It was polished from chain links to stone, all of it glinting.

"Long time no see," Cordon said as he bowed his head slightly. Not far, just enough to show his respect. "Your father almost took my position, and I worried for a long time that you would do so as well, considering you are so much like him."

His voice was light and filled with humour, but the way his head reared back and stood high showed his obvious superiority. His eyes were hard, unfeeling, and she'd always thought they appeared hostile – like he expected a Demon to burst through the chest of every person he passed.

Mayumi strode a few steps forward until she was standing at the very edge of her porch. She folded her arms across her chest.

"What are you all doing here?" The suspicion in her tone was unmistakable.

These were the last people she wanted to see here. She was currently harbouring a Duskwalker in her home, one who was injured and most likely unable to fight for himself.

Stay inside, Faunus. She knew he would be listening and *willed* him to stay hidden. *I'll get rid of them.*

It was impossible to see their faces under their black hoods and masks to the point Mayumi struggled to make out who was who. There were more Elder members than this for the northern sector. Three times as many, in fact.

"Are we not allowed to visit?" Cordon asked.

"We told you we may return at any point to speak with you," Claudia, one of the female Elders, stated matter-of-factly. Her voice was distinct, as she had the same deep tone Mayumi's did.

"It's a three-day journey in the dead of winter, if not more, from Hawthorne Keep," Mayumi replied blandly, her gaze slipping to Claudia.

There weren't enough hours in the day this time of year, and the snow made it treacherous. Just getting to the base of the mountain could take a day of careful walking on sleet-covered steps, and that was still within the ten-mile radius she had to avoid.

"If I expected to ever be visited, it would be by an Elder and a handful of lower-ranking members. That, or you would call for me via a messenger bird."

"Due to your circumstances, we can't allow lower members to come into contact with you," Jace explained. She only knew it was him by the weathered tone of his voice, as though he was tired and bored of the conversation. "As you know, your discharge was done under secrecy. We couldn't allow you into the keep, and you are not permitted to step foot nearby."

"And I have kept to my oath and told no one as to why," Mayumi snapped back in his direction. "So why are there so many of you here?"

There were nine Demonslayers at her doorstep. Such a large group was uncommon for delivering nothing more than a message or request. This was bigger than the size of a hunting party. It was safer to travel in a small group.

Then again... the distance to here is quite great.

If the message was a matter of priority and urgency, then a large party was to ensure that, hopefully, one person survived to deliver that message.

That didn't explain why Cordon Hansley was here himself. He rarely left the keep unless it was for a council meeting with the three other Head Elders who were in control of the other districts – south, east, and west sectors – of this continent.

Cordon stepped forward to be in front of the others.

Margo followed just behind him. The woman was a mountain of a human who stood even taller and bulkier than the men beside her. She was generally with Cordon, and many considered her his most faithful guard dog.

Mayumi may have barked at her a few times.

"We have a matter that must be dealt with and questions we need answered. I am here to ensure we have obtained what we need, and that everything is completed."

Mayumi allowed her head to slightly tilt in the direction her pigeon went.

"You have been storing my bird until your arrival," she stated before bringing her sight back to Cordon's icy-blue eyes and the pale skin she could see encasing them – the only parts of him she could see. "You baited me into coming outside so you could approach me out in the open. Why?"

"We wish to speak with you," Cordon stated.

"You could have knocked on my door for that."

One of the men in the back shuffled his feet before leaning towards another to whisper something while keeping his eye on her. The one he spoke to lowered their head and squinted their eyes in Mayumi's direction.

She took a step back as a grand smirk curled her lips. Placing her hand on her sword hilt, she turned her body slightly to make herself smaller. She further turned when she noticed one of the women holding a bow tightening their grip on the weapon.

"You were hoping I'd come outside unarmed." She chuckled in realisation. "Inside, I have weapons, hidden ones you wouldn't know of. You wanted me outside where you could trap me. What do you want? It's against the guild's fundamentals to harm a civilian, which is what I am now. I am no bandit or felon, nor have I further broken any rules of the guild."

Cordon sighed heavily as he placed his palm on the pommel of his sword to rest it there.

"We wanted to further discuss your message," he said as he shook his head. "You have gathered strange information that is pertaining to the Veil and Demons. Did you not consider the weight of your words and what they mean?"

A small amount of tension eased out of her.

"Well... yes. I knew it was important and would be invaluable to the guild." She lifted an arm to shrug. "We know so little about the Veil and what's within it. Even though I was discharged, I still stand for our mission and the pursuit of freedom for humankind."

"Which is why I am here. I am the Head Elder, the one who collects and holds all knowledge." He gestured his hands backwards. "These are merely the bondsmen I have chosen to learn of such secrecy in order to ensure my journey was safe."

I guess that makes sense. She released some of the grip she had on her sword.

"I'll be happy to answer any questions you have, but I'm afraid I don't know much more than what I wrote in my message," she conceded as she placed her forearm across her chest and bowed slightly, not that she really wanted to, but formality would probably assist the obvious tension. "I apologise for my rudeness and quick tongue. It is hard to trust anyone."

"Of course," he said, his shoulders visibly easing. Although his hand had been lazy on his pommel, he'd been ready to strike it forward and draw his sword. "We have come to your home unannounced and perhaps in ways that are alarming. The information you gathered is critical, and we were worried you would be resentful towards the guild after your dismissal. People tend to hold grudges. You understand, correct?"

"There are just as many Demons within us as there are among the trees," she stated, a common saying among the guild.

"Excellent. You have informed us of the Demons who have begun mimicking humankind and have created their tree village. Do you know the safest path leading to it?"

"No. Like I said, I don't have much more information as to what I specified. Maybe the swamplands, though?" Then she realised they wouldn't know what that was. "Apparently, if you walk into the Veil from the southwest, not too far in is a swamp and marsh. The creature that guards it is hostile and dangerous, but it is a deterrent to other Demons. There is also a musk in the air that may hide our human scents."

"I see... a swamp with a monster that even the Demons are afraid of." Cordon waved his hand, and one of the other Elders pulled out a leather-bound book to record the information with a quill pen. "How about Jabez's castle? Do you know what direction it is from the village and if he has any defences?"

"That, I'm not sure about," she sighed. "I only know that the Demon King has a vast amount of power and that he is half-El..." Her words faded out as her brows drew together tightly to crease the centre of her forehead. She tilted her head with her eyes turning hard. "I never wrote his name in my message. How do you know it?"

"Is sunlight the only weakness you've come to learn about the Demons? Is there anything more you have learned about their possible weaknesses?"

He evaded my question.

"No," Mayumi stated with a clipped tone.

Cordon's eyes squinted at her before they darted down to Mayumi's tightening hold on her hilt. "Do you know where the portal he has leads to, and if there are people there that will aid us?"

"It will take us to an Elven world, but I already told you of the Elves," Mayumi said before she chuckled, realising he'd pretended not to know who or what the Elvish people were when she'd definitely wrote about them in her message. She ran her fingers through her hair in disbelief. "You knew. You already knew all the information I gave you. Didn't you?"

"We have gathered some information from Demons we have tortured, yes," Cordon confirmed.

Mayumi threw her head back and laughed. "Then why the fuck are you really here? I doubt I have any information that could be of use to you. I told you everything in my letter."

"Watch how you speak in front of our Head Elder," Margo snapped with her high-handed, bitchy attitude. She even pulled on her hilt to reveal part of the blade of her claymore sword.

"Calm yourself, Margo," Cordon said as he threw his hand out. "I only wanted to know if you knew anything more. I doubt you were able to write all of what you learned in a message your bird could carry."

"I have given you all I know of the Demons and the Veil. If that is all you wished to learn, then please leave. Your presence is no longer welcome, and the longer you remain and saturate your scents into my clearing, the greater the likelihood that you'll bring forth an army of Demons upon my home when night falls."

"I do have a final question," Cordon said. Mayumi didn't trust the pause that followed or the way she could see his jaw tick under his tight mask. "How did you come to learn all this?"

"By myself," she said while folding her arms. "You could say I had a bit of a death wish after I was shamefully discharged and thought I would go for a wander through the Veil for a bit. I wrote my message when I returned and was able to fetch my bird from the nearest pigeon station."

"Doubtful," Jace piped up, as he elbowed the woman next to him. "No human has been able to walk into the Veil and return."

"We must know who you obtained this information from, Mayumi," Cordon stated. His tone was flat, which didn't match the beseeching façade he was attempting. "They may have more we can use."

She snorted a laugh, knowing they wouldn't leave and instead would pester her until she gave them a name, any name. She needed to make it believable too.

The best way to do that was to spin a half-truthful lie.

"You want the truth?" Mayumi took in a large breath before she sounded it out. "I obtained this information from a cat-skulled Duskwalker."

"I beg your pardon?" Cordon stuttered.

"He decided to share some information in exchange for me saving his life from Demons." She lifted her hand to convey bashfulness as she scratched at the back of her neck. "Guess he took a liking to me after I patched up his wounds. He knew I should try to finish the job, and he could have killed me in the blink of an eye, but we found an unlikely companionship within that moment. It was a truce, especially since I was out in the dark by myself and there were Demons around. I needed his help as much as he needed mine."

Silence bled between them for several long, tense moments. Cordon turned his head to the other Elders, assessing their reactions by their eyes.

"How do we know you're not telling a lie?" Claudia asked.

"Why would I lie about something like that?" Mayumi responded in disbelief. She even twisted her hands upwards, so her palms were facing the sky, and used them to shrug. "No human would be able to give me this information. Only a monster from the Veil would know the inner workings of it."

"If that's true–" Cordon started.

"It is," Mayumi interrupted as her back stiffened. "It's why I didn't say who gave me the information in the letter. I befriended a Duskwalker when I should have killed him, and I didn't really think the guild would believe me."

"If that's true," Cordon repeated more firmly, "and you have given us everything you know, then we are done here. I have nothing more I need to ask of you."

"I guess we are," she answered, a breath of relief expiring out of her when he waved his hand to make them turn around.

Good. They are leaving.

Faunus was safe.

A whistling sound caught in her ears.

She instantly leaned to the side while dipping her body, the action so swift and sudden that Mayumi fell against the side of her arse with an oomph.

Her head turned upwards to the *thunk* she heard against her front door, and her eyes widened at the arrow shaft quivering from its impact.

It had been aiming right for her chest.

There had been a tenth Demonslayer hiding within the forest in preparation – possibly even more. She turned her gaping face to the people in her clearing, who were now bearing their weapons in their hands. The deadly points of them all were aimed in her direction.

It didn't take a genius to figure what was happening.

They planned to kill me... Her lips parted in shock. *What fucking for?*

THIRTY-EIGHT

Shit. I don't have my bow, Mayumi thought as she spun to her feet to get into a crouched position.

She hid behind the support post that held her roof upright where her stairs were. Pulling her sword from her scabbard and holding it upright, she mentally prepared herself for a battle.

"What is the meaning of this?" Mayumi shouted while eyeing the door, choosing her words carefully.

Stay inside. Please, for all that is good in the world, just stay inside, you big, protective oaf.

Thank goodness it was winter as the thick snow created enough sound for someone with trained, alert hearing to notice footsteps crunching closer.

And closer they were coming.

"It's nothing personal, Mayumi Tanaka," Cordon said in a grand voice. She could almost picture his hands out, facing upwards as though he was giving a stupid apology. "Out of respect for your late father, we let you leave the guild rather than imprisoning you for your crime."

Since her ear was turned to the left so she could listen, she almost missed someone coming towards the right side of the house with their bow armed. Mayumi dived to the other corner post of her stairs to take shelter behind it and the railing.

"Then why the hostility now?" Mayumi looked left and then right to make sure it was safe. "I aided you, gave you information."

She noticed there was a darkness under her door in the middle.

Faunus was listening, and by the fact that darkness moved, she knew he was considering coming out.

"Because you're privy to information you shouldn't be. If all this information got out, if civilians learned there is a Demon King and that Demons are becoming like us, there will be chaos. The people are already afraid, and you know how deadly that fear can be."

There was someone approaching her stairs, and the person from the right side of the house was beginning to emerge to a point where they'd be able to freely shoot down the porch.

Fuck. She bashed the back of her head against the timber post. *Guild secrets. I should have known. Why do I keep trying to do the right thing?*

Baiting and fighting Demons had gotten Faunus injured further, and for what? Humans that were going to become extinct no matter how many she killed? For a guild that had tossed her to the side rather than compromising with her after all the years she gave them?

I'm starting to feel like I'm fighting on the wrong damn side. She eyed the bottom of the door once more. *I'd rather fight on his side.*

"You don't want to do this," Mayumi pleaded, knowing it was useless but trying regardless. "You know I won't tell anyone, and I'm harbouring things you *really* don't want to come out."

She shouted that last part, hoping Faunus understood she meant him.

Within the blink of an eye, a pair of feet made a double thump on the porch right next to her while the person swung their sword downwards.

"Shit!" Mayumi raised her own with one hand to block their attack.

The *ching* of their weapons colliding rung right before the front door opened with a loud *bang.*

Faunus was nothing more than a black blur as he tackled the Demonslayer and launched them through the air. They both hit the ground just beyond her first step, but the Demonslayer was dead since they landed with Faunus on top of them with his claws embedded into their chest.

"It's the cat-skulled Duskwalker!" one of the Demonslayers shouted.

With a growling groan of irritation, Mayumi chose that moment to finally come out of hiding.

The guild members were discussing how she had him in her house, that they were friends and she'd been hiding him all along, and so on, but Mayumi cared very little.

They were stating what she already knew.

Her plan had been to run from the Duskwalker that was about to go nuts. She wasn't going to fight so close to where he could accidentally make her his prey, but he turned to look at her standing at the top of the steps.

Then he walked towards the Demonslayers in the middle of the clearing.

"Faunus?" she asked his back.

"I will protect you for as long as I can."

His mind isn't turning over. That was odd.

Whatever, it didn't matter. He was on her side, and she really fucking needed that right now. Especially when she heard the roar of three more humans entering from the forest with swords raised.

Great! More Demonslayers. She mentally threw her hands up as she dodged another arrow that came from the forest. She ran down the stairs with her sword raised.

She couldn't leave Faunus out there by himself.

"Duck!" she shouted.

Faunus lowered, but he didn't know it was so she could literally step on his back and use him as a bouncing pad. She wasn't going to have him at the front line – not if she could help it. He could protect her from behind.

With her sword raised above her, she came down silently on Cordon. He lifted his sword and redirected her while stepping to the side.

She crouched down to avoid an oncoming sword from the side. Then she squealed in surprise and had to pivot to her toes to avoid an arrow lodging into her arse!

A clash of different swords rang out beyond her peripheral gaze. Mayumi expected that she and Faunus would be surrounded with weapons pointed at them by now, but that never happened.

"What are Colt's Outpost soldiers doing here?" someone yelled.

Just as she went to investigate the newcomers, Faunus grabbed the hood of her jacket and yanked her back. A whip end struck the air right where she'd been standing.

"Thanks," Mayumi mumbled to Faunus.

He snorted a huff in response, which sprayed a small mist of purple blood through the bandage covering his nose hole.

"Mayumi!" a familiar voice yelled.

She turned to Henry, finding Klaus and Yoshida were with him. They had already taken up arms against the Demonslayers, seeing she needed the assistance.

She noted only Klaus and Henry were wearing armour. *Did they abandon their posts to come here?* Why?

Yoshida was in his everyday leather, and his hand held his scabbard, using it as a shield, with his sword in his other hand. He had no weapons belt, and she figured he'd probably been off duty.

Since Faunus stepped in their direction, she got between him and them by placing her back against his big shoulder and chest. He'd morphed into his more monstrous form at some point and was leaning on his hands.

It was easier for her to talk to him since their heads were near a similar height.

"They're my friends," she told him as she assessed the battle field with her head turning one way and then the other. Enemies were approaching, and Mayumi was deciding who to strike against first. "I don't know why, but they're here to help."

Mayumi wondered if they'd been hiding in the forest and watching to see what would happen before running out.

"I figured they were on your side when they started attacking the Demonslayers," he answered plainly.

Faunus wasn't attacking. He hadn't made a single move to confront a Demonslayer after killing the first one. Faunus was choosing to be her shield rather than her weapon, and her heart tightened.

He knows he shouldn't fight.

Mayumi was about to correct him that they were on *their* side, but Yoshida, the brave, stupid bastard, proved Faunus right. With a roaring battle cry, he sprinted at Faunus with his sword raised to attack the most frightening and freakish thing in the clearing.

Mayumi spun and clashed their swords together, glaring when he righted himself with his eyes wide.

"What the fuck, Mayumi!?" Yoshida yelled, his brown eyes flicking to Faunus behind her.

She saw the confused fear in his eyes.

"He's my friend, Yoshida." She shoved her head forward to punctuate her statement. "The Duskwalker is on my side."

There was a hesitancy in his expression. He stared at Faunus again, and she could see he wanted to sprint past her to take on the Duskwalker.

Despite the situation, she was proud that her friend's survival instinct was to fight what frightened him rather than piss his pants and flee from it. He would have made a great Demonslayer had he walked that path alongside her.

His brown eyes found hers again.

"Oh, fuck it," Yoshida bit as he gave her his back and pointed his sword at a human enemy. "If you say he's your friend, then whatever."

When she placed her back against his so they could fight together, she couldn't help the way her heart warmed at the quick trust he just handed to her.

"Thank you," she said quietly.

"You're a freak, you know that?" he murmured right before they both broke contact to deflect a blow each. Their backs returned to be a comforting warm press. "Figures you'd get yourself in shit and befriend a monster. You just could never do things the easy way, could you?"

She noted that Klaus and Henry had taken a similar stance with Faunus between all four of them.

"Shut up and concentrate," she commanded.

Then she kicked her leg back and hooked the front of her boot against his shin. She tripped him so they could avoid both an arrow and the whip headed for them. She rotated above him, grabbed his arm when he raised it, and pulled him to his feet as she spun.

"What are you guys even doing here?" she huffed when they were taking a stance once more.

Her heart raced like a sprinting predator chasing its prey, and her breaths were already sawing in and out of her to the point it burned.

They weren't fighting stupid, careless Demons. They weren't even fighting half-brained bandits.

These were trained warriors, and it was currently eight against five. The odds weren't in their favour, not in number, not in skill, and with their Duskwalker mascot in the state he was in, not in strength either.

"They visited Colt's Outpost before coming here. They asked for directions to your house, and we knew something was wrong." His voice quietened when he said, "We couldn't just leave you to deal with them by yourself."

She wanted her eyes to stray to the sky so she could thank the heavens that these three brave men were her friends. But rule three of the Demonslayer code was never be distracted, so she kept her eyes on her current enemy, the humans fighting for the guild she'd once been a part of.

If we survive this, drinks are on me.

Faunus kept himself steady as best as he could. Occasionally, one of his arms suddenly bent as though he was about to collapse, but he straightened and stepped forward to fight the shake in it.

I'm so dizzy.

Having run out of the house in a jumping, swiping launch had set his fury-filled heart into overdrive, and the adrenaline sweeping through his body ensured the pressure in his vascular system stayed high.

It was causing his vision to turn murky. Blood was pooling in his nose hole and eye socket, soaking through the bandages that covered most of his face.

He hadn't opened his jaws in days because of the intricate web of cloth tied over his face. He clawed the bandages away when he tried to part his fangs and the web pulled on his horn – like it was trying to break his skull further apart.

A fountain of blood that had been held back poured from his nose hole to the crisp, white frozen ground, but the scent of it was blocking the smell of the humans, their fear, their red blood.

It was aiding him. The dizziness was pushing back those invisible, invading hands that were trying to cause him to lose his mind over to the madness of a frenzy. There was prey everywhere, things for him to sink his fangs into and munch away at.

Why? he thought. The desire to cover the sides of his skull was overwhelming, as the constant chime of metal upon metal obliterated his sense of hearing. *Why is everything so loud?*

Ching. Clack. There was a bellow from a man here, and then the warble of metal vibrating from a heavy impact. *Skerrrrp.*

The pain was miserable, but Faunus tried to ignore it when he swept his arm to the side to knock a Demonslayer sprinting at him with their sword pointed at his side.

Mayumi and her friend, the one she just said was named Yoshida, separated. Yoshida was forced to move away in order to fight a foe one on one. He was on the constant back foot, having to defend rather than attack. It was obvious his skill was lacking in comparison to hers.

Mayumi ran into the fray while pulling her dagger from her belt and held it with the blade coming out from the bottom of her left fist. She began using her dagger to attack and her sword as a shield. She blocked a sword coming downwards to slice her from above and forced it back before spinning and swiping her dagger in a quick strike across their body.

The Demonslayer let out a distressed choke and held their wound. Faunus started making his way closer when he saw that wasn't enough to put them down.

I must go to her.

She didn't need him. By the time his wobbly form was almost upon them, the Demonslayer's wound had slowed their movements until Mayumi was able to flip her dagger and stab it into their jugular.

He only knew the name of her other companions, Klaus and Henry, because he overheard them calling to each other. She'd also spoken of them many times.

Together they fought against a small human and a woman who appeared to be taller than the rest – he could only tell it was a woman by her breasts tightly clad in her black leather uniform.

Faunus was thankful it was easy to see who belonged to which side. He only needed to attack those in black, and in his hazy vision, they appeared like nothing more than Demons.

Something wrapped around his back paw and tugged. The strength of the human was minor, but it still caused him to trip forward.

Faunus steadied himself on his forearms to prevent his skull from bashing against the ground. Then he let out a bellowing roar when something long and sharp speared him all the way through his torso.

His orbs had been white from both worry and pain, but they often flickered to red at his fury. They were red when he twisted his head to the Demonslayer, who had just shoved their sword through his torso with both hands.

They tried to yank it out, but the clenching of his muscles kept it locked inside. The Demonslayer pressed the base of their foot against Faunus' side to tug, gaining back their sword inch by inch.

When they realised Faunus had turned his sight to them, they left it inside him and backed up.

It was too late for them. Faunus reached his hand down his body before they could take a single step and stabbed his claws through their shoulder. He felt bones snapping as he brought them closer. Their dying scream was cut short when he clamped his jaws around their head and shattered their skull.

His following yelp was high-pitched and sharp.

The quick shutting of his own fangs shot excruciating agony like a lightning bolt throughout his face. He went to cup his skull, but stopped himself before he made contact.

I cannot even fight with my fangs! Faunus lifted his paws and roared to the sky in frustration. *It hurts. Why does it have to hurt so much?* Could his final moments not be filled with pain? He was riddled with it, both inside and out.

It was debilitating. He hated the shame it brought – even more so when he saw Mayumi was fighting by herself.

She ran through the middle of the clearing and jumped for the stake. She used one foot to bounce off it while turning to the side, spearing her sword through the chest of the second opponent that had come to fight against Yoshida.

She had seen her friend was struggling by himself against two enemies.

Her eyes found Faunus on the other side of the clearing, her hair whipping around her face as the wind blew.

"Behind you!" she yelled before she twirled to block a blade.

Faunus didn't have the chance to assess the two people who cornered her and purposefully separated her from the rest of those fighting.

Instead, he turned just in time to see a Demonslayer utilising a whip and brandishing it against him. It had been aiming for his neck, perhaps to thread around it like a collar. He threw his arm up, and it caught around his wrist.

Their eyes widened between the slit of black material covering their face before they narrowed on him. They pulled, just as he did.

They let go of the handle, and it caused him to stumble a single step in surprise. Faunus unthreaded it from his wrist and carelessly threw it to the side.

"Fuck!" Yoshida spat out.

Faunus, about to launch himself at the Demonslayer in front of him, managed to catch the male throwing up his own arm to take the blow of a sword directly against it. Yoshida had lost his own weapon to the ground and had nothing else but his own body to defend with.

The man's following bellow was one of pain when his arm was sliced down to bone.

Lost in watching, the slash of the whip sliced across the flesh of his neck. He also took a new arrow close to his heart. It buried into his body until he felt the sharp point of it each time he took in a lungful of air.

He was growing more injured by the second and was doing

very little to help in fighting. Yes, he'd killed two Demonslayers, but so had Mayumi.

And she was currently fighting off two by her damn self.

I am growing weaker.

He was losing too much blood, even for a Duskwalker. He hadn't even realised he was littered with arrows until the last one punctured his lung.

He was a distraction for the Demonslayers, helping to spread out their attention, but that was it.

He couldn't believe he needed help. The one with the whip and the bowman he could see were too far away from him to fight. They were keeping their distance from his slicing claws.

He was just standing here, struggling with his limbs that were trying to cave in. His lungs felt as though they were filled with dust, blocked and aching, and it made every breath he took burn in the back of his throat.

It was in that moment, when he was deciding the best course of action he could take to aid those on Mayumi's side, that he watched Yoshida be speared in the torso with a sword. He was the only one of her companions who wasn't wearing plated armour, and it left him vulnerable.

Yoshida gaped at the weapon inside him before raising his head to the Demonslayer with blood bubbling at his lips. It poured down his chin.

He was going to die, that much was obvious. Faunus usually wouldn't have given a damn about a human's life, but he currently did – only because it meant Mayumi had one less person on her side. He cared naught for their friendship.

I will not last much longer. Faunus watched the Demonslayer twist the weapon inside Yoshida's chest. *But he can.*

Using all the strength within him, he sprinted in the direction of the man.

Faunus shoved the Demonslayer away hard enough that he went rolling to the ground. The accidental flick of his wrist sliced claw marks into his leather and, hopefully, his flesh.

Yoshida stared at Faunus instead when he gripped him by the throat with one hand and swiftly yanked the sword from him with the other. Crimson liquid squirted from the gaping hole in his stomach when the blocking pressure was released before pouring down the front of him.

Then a bright yellow light glowed from underneath Yoshida's flesh as magic radiated coolness between them.

Even just using his own magic had Faunus shaking, but he refused to relent, even when an arrow embedded into his back. He flinched but held strong.

The gargling from the dying man grew stronger rather than softer as he was given back his strength, his blood, his breaths, while Faunus' own dwindled far more rapidly.

Yoshida gained the vigour to hold Faunus' wrist to lift himself up, his human legs writhing so that his leather boots brushed and kicked the dirt and snow.

"Why?" he grated out. "Why save me?"

"Protect her," Faunus pleaded, his breaths turning more laboured at the gaping wound forming in his chest. His arm burned with the transfer of magic. *"Protect her with the life I have granted you."*

He was healing him, taking his wounds for himself.

Another horrible yelp escaped Faunus, one far worse than ever before when something wrapped around the horn on the bad side of his skull and pulled.

He went with it, at the same time dropping Mayumi's companion as a crumbling heap to the ground, to prevent it from snapping the last tether holding him together.

The Demonslayer kept pulling, and Faunus' paws almost came out from under him.

Despite the differences in their strength, pain was a cruel weapon – one this puny, feeble human didn't know they were wielding.

He grabbed the line of the whip with his fist. It was difficult to hold as it was so small and thin within the crease of his large palm. He was also holding it with the arm that was now wounded due to the new injury he'd gained in saving her friend from death. But he held it as tight as he could to lessen the tug and went with the Demonslayer, finding himself stumbling away from the battling field.

His sight desperately searched for his tiny, little, precious female in the clearing.

Klaus and Henry had managed to kill one of their two enemies, but they both struggled against the big human woman that rained down heavy striking blows.

Yoshida, the one he had saved, killed the man who had originally sought to take his life. He could have gone to his friends, who were struggling together against a singular opponent, but he instead entered the forest.

There were more arrows around Faunus' and Mayumi's paths, the enemy seeking to take them down first – he was hoping Yoshida had noticed this invisible bowman's intention and wasn't scuttling off to be a coward.

His sight finally took in the glorious vision of her. There she was on the outskirts fighting off two Demonslayers.

By herself, she not only managed to block one opponent with her sword but shove her dagger at the torso of the other, who dodged by jumping back. Then she was swift as she crouched down on one knee while straightening the other so she could lean to the side and be even lower. She evaded a sword slashing through the air just a hair's distance from her head.

Low to the ground, Mayumi threw herself forward with her arms crossed over the top of her head. She crashed into the legs of one man to make him completely lose his footing. His feet went over his head when he crashed against the ground on his own face, and his sword was lost due to his spindling arms cartwheeling through the air.

Just when Faunus thought she would slide across the ground on her front and give the other enemy her vulnerable back, she rotated in the air before she made contact. The flexible, nimble woman, who he had seen bend and twist in ways he'd never known possible, rolled onto her side and dug her dagger into the snowy ground.

She used her weapon to turn around as she found her feet.

Even from a distance, even with his vision so dim, he knew that woman was giving the enemy still on their feet a cruel, menacing glare. A glare of determination and utter stubbornness.

Just look at her. She was wild, a power to be reckoned with.

If he hadn't been here to give her the information that brought these people here, had he not been here to make her want to attract Demons that caused the winged one to come, had Faunus never crossed paths with her, he knew without a shred of doubt, she would have survived.

To see her do what she was obviously born to, battle the world and all the enemies it had to offer, struck awe into him.

This magnificent woman appeared to be the most dangerous thing in the world with her meagre weapons and fragile humanness.

Despite this, he still couldn't stand to see her doing it alone.

One small detail could see her lost to this existence forever, and the one with the medallion was still standing. That glinting round golden medal was shining in the sunlight.

Faunus' didn't know why, but he couldn't help thinking the black crystal within the centre of the golden ore was like a symbol of the humans. Surrounded by something bright while harbouring darkness within.

This very fight showed that they were easily swayed to do wrong. Mayumi and Faunus had done nothing to deserve this, and yet here they were, fighting for their lives – just like the Demons they sought to destroy.

Faunus kept his position as the Demonslayer behind him tried to pull. He stayed strong and stepped forward, only to backtrack by two steps when the whip slipped through his grasp and rendered a yelp from him. His hands were covered in melted snow and blood, slippery and hindering him.

Just when Faunus thought Mayumi would take down the medallion-wearing foe, he retaliated with more vigour than before and put her on the back foot.

He was silent, just as she was, both only occasionally letting out minor grunts from impact.

The other man was still getting to his feet after she'd tripped him, but Mayumi's own sword was lost to the ground at her feet. The Demonslayer had struck downwards with both hands on the hilt of his weapon while she'd been crouching, the obvious overpowering force too much for just one of her arms to take by itself.

She did have the cross-guard of her dagger supporting the

long edge of her blade, but it'd only been enough to stop her own weapon from cutting back into her under the bounce of force.

Mayumi abandoned her sword and instead drew her whip once she was finished rolling to the side to miss the second downward swing.

It was only then that he noticed her clothing had been cut, and her blood was soaking through the sleeve of it. She was hurt.

I must help her. She no longer had a shield, but Faunus was more than prepared to be one.

He turned to the Demonslayer behind him.

They ran to the side to keep the tension, realising long ago that he hadn't managed to fight them off for a reason. On his slow, wobbling legs, he was forced to chase them. When he was almost within claw striking distance, they released the hold they had on their whip.

Since he was such a large target coming towards them, they didn't need to aim. They just pulled two daggers from either side of their weapons belt and blindly threw them with a swiftness that not even his arms could knock away.

One lodged into his shoulder, doing little to stop him from coming. The other lodged straight into the centre of his throat, clogging it and his airways.

Faunus choked and reached up to pull it out, giving the Demonslayer the opportunity to grab the handle of their whip once more. He yanked the dagger free and dropped it. Then Faunus grasped that dreaded line again in his fist before any more damage could be done to his skull.

Faunus was facing the Demonslayer that now had their back to the battling field.

His blood turned to ice in his veins when he saw Mayumi fighting the medallion wearer, while the foe she'd tripped was on their feet and had found their sword.

He was unsure if she knew that she was being snuck up on. He also didn't care. He'd been separated from her for too long, hadn't been by her side to protect her.

If I cannot let go of this tether...

He eyed the Demonslayer whose feet slipped against the ground to get purchase as they walked to the side to draw him away from the battle... from her.

Then I will take it with me!

With a snarl, Faunus twisted his hand around the whip line until it had made a singular loop around his fist. Then he dragged that sorry excuse for a human with him as he stomped in the direction of Mayumi, walking on his paws despite usually being on all fours in his monstrous form.

The medallion wearer allowed his arm to be caught in her whip and then grabbed it with his fist. He yanked it as Mayumi was pulling, and she staggered forward. She wisely let it go so she could stab her dagger forward, then leapt backwards to avoid being hit.

He didn't know when it had happened, but Mayumi's cheek was bruised, and his little female was limping. The medallion wearer had a slice across his cheek and a nasty gash across his chest.

But the second Demonslayer was slinking ever closer, and Faunus knew when she stepped backwards blindly towards him... that she didn't know he was there, coming for her.

Just when he was almost upon them, he was jerked back. Faunus looked behind him to see the whip holder had shoved a discarded sword into the ground as a stake. He turned his skull to Mayumi.

He was almost there, almost to her. They were almost at his claws' tips.

The enemy rose their weapon behind her as the medallion wearer spoke to Mayumi, shouting some grand speech he cared little to listen to.

"Mayumi!" he roared.

She began turning her head towards him but halted when the medallion wearer took a step forward with his sword raised. She couldn't greet Faunus' gaze, which would have let her know of her oncoming demise from behind. She couldn't safely take her eyes off of the enemy in front of her.

But she was distracted already, the medallion wearer lining her up for a surprise attack from another.

There wasn't time. He could see that. If she stepped one way, the two enemies circled each other in opposing ways to match her. If she escaped one, the other was sure to get her.

I came here to protect her. His grip on the whip line tightened. *My life is already fading.* His heart pounded in fear at what he was about to do. *Nothing can change my fate.* His breaths huffed in and out rapidly to take in courage as though it was in the air. *I will not watch her die and do nothing.*

A deep breath stuttered out of his nose hole, spraying blood, just as he let go of the whip line and his final tether to this life.

With a bellowing roar that was cut short when his skull broke apart, he leapt forward.

All his pain faded, as did the sounds around him, and the smell of his own blood. Sensations like warmth, iciness, and the very wind died away to nothingness.

With the last of his sight, Faunus watched his body break away into tiny pieces of glittering black sand that plumed around him. *I must reach her.* As his body faded, he reached, and reached, with all his strength, will, and might.

The last sensation he felt as his form dispersed from his neck before going down his limbs, was the very tips of his claws catching on something.

He didn't know if he managed to kill the Demonslayer as his sight exploded in darkness, but he hoped he had done what he'd come here to do.

To protect her even if it cost him his life.

Mayumi...

She would be the last thing on his mind as he finally faded to the afterworld, and he held not an ounce of regret in the action that caused it.

THIRTY-NINE

Mayumi glared at Cordon with every bit of resolve within her.

She'd intended to kill Cordon herself, the man far too skilled and experienced for any of her friends to take on. At the same time, she'd been fighting Jace. He was strong, but not to the skill both she and their Head Elder wielded.

The only reason Mayumi hadn't reached the Elder rank, despite being recommended multiple times, was because they rarely left the keep. She had chosen not to progress to remain in the field killing Demons, rather than training new Demonslayers within the safety of a fortified mountain castle.

She spared a glance to her left, just the barest peek.

Yoshida had only just emerged from the forest, having taken down the bowman hiding within it, and was assessing the clearing.

Margo, the fucking mountain of a woman, was holding back Klaus and Henry by herself.

Margo and Mayumi were evenly matched in polar opposite ways. Where Mayumi was swift and agile while wielding enough strength to hold her own, Margo was pure brute strength with just enough speed to make her a frightening opponent. Both were cunning, both were intelligent, and both would fight with every part of their bodies, from their hard heads to their strong, sharp nails if need be.

They both could wield any weapon handed to them, Mayumi hitting her target dead-on every time, whereas Margo would give an impact that could shatter the whole target altogether.

No wonder poor Klaus and Henry were struggling.

But I have never seen Cordon fight.

The rumours stated he was deadly. As quick as a snake, as strong as a bear, and as cunning as a fox.

All of which she experienced now.

Her knee had been bashed from the side by one of his kicks, and her cheek was hot and aching from when he'd smacked the pommel of his sword into her face. Then there was the shallow sword slice she had down her arm.

She'd managed to slash him across the cheek and torso, but it wasn't enough. She'd given up her sword, and he'd just taken her whip.

Standing back, she caught her breath when he did. Her lungs were on fire and wheezing dry breaths burned her throat. Her heart was a deafening drum in her ears, and her skin was slick with sweat. She was so hot that not even the frosty chill in the air could cool her.

Cordon's blue eyes still held a piercing, unrelenting gaze that had not once fallen since the fighting started, but his shoulders lifted and fell with each of his heavy breaths. She'd been giving it her all, and he was obviously tiring just as much as she was.

She expected him to sprint at her. Instead, he opened his stupid mouth to prattle at her – and she hated when enemies did that. *I'm big, strong, smart enemy, you small, dumb woman. Me fight you and win. Grrr,* her brain supplied over Cordon's voice as she tried not to roll her eyes.

Ugh, she couldn't think of a more idiotic way to waste breath.

He didn't lower his weapon as he spoke, but even if he had, she wouldn't have dared lowered her own.

"...could have been one of the best of us," Cordon continued on with a shake of his head, his words finally registering. "Had you not been so foolish as to keep that blood sack within you, you could have been one of the greatest Demonslayers in all of history. At the request of your father, I made sure you were trained by the best. He knew you would exceed all of them in skill, and you proved him right. I was almost to the point where I was going to give you the rank of Elder, despite your rejections, and take you on as my underling. I was going to hand over my position to you had you lived long enough to receive it. You could have had power, secrets, and lived a long life within the safety of the keep."

Mayumi's features twisted into a sneer. "Your position sounds cowardly."

"Cowardly?" he chuckled. "How so?"

"You hide yourself behind walls and send out people to die."

"They made that choice, as did I when I enrolled. I didn't get to this position by twiddling my thumbs. I got here by earning my place." He took a step forward and held his sword out flat to point it at her. "You talk of cowardly, but how about your stupidity? How many people died because of what is between your thighs? Was the potential of being able to bring a child into this world so important that you thought so little of your comrades?"

"Why are we talking?" Mayumi asked with a mocking tone. "Have you grown so immobile in your years as a Head Elder, surrounded by parchments and quills, walking around the keep with your hands behind your back and looking down your nose at everyone else, that you require a break?"

The only reason she knew he was smirking was because of the way the corners of his eyelids crinkled. "Not at all."

She heard her name being called by Faunus. She was about to turn her head to him, but Cordon changed his stance in preparation to swing his sword.

She took a step back and to the side to create space, hoping to get closer to her sword lying on the ground so she could dive for it.

The following roar sent a chilling shiver down her spine. The tiny hairs covering her flesh stood on end like her bones were filled with buzzing insects, a physical reaction to the anxiety that flew through her at Faunus' call.

He needs me.

He needed help.

She had one weapon left, and she'd been gripping it for dear life this entire time. She no longer cared as she tossed it straight into Cordon's meaty leg in order to stop his attack and slow him down.

There were weapons littered upon the ground; if she ran to Faunus' aid, she was hoping to take up a new one – maybe even her own.

She turned so she could run, only to come face-to-face with Jace. Her face paled when she realised Cordon had set her up in a trap.

No wonder the bastard had started uselessly speaking.

He wasn't prideful. He didn't care who took the final swing as long as the goal had been achieved.

"Shit," she breathed.

She thought it would be the last thing to come out of her mouth. Shit, what a graceful final word.

Suddenly Faunus emerged like a moving, towering shadow behind him. Or, at least... part of him.

The moment was slowed in time, everything growing eerily quiet as she tried to register what was happening.

What Mayumi saw was a cloud that was partially physical, while the rest of him was a floating mass of black sand that swirled to the ground. He was a plume of glitter.

A small fragment of skull was hurled backwards, while the rest fell forwards. She watched as his red orbs burst into an explosion of small fires in front of his eye sockets before they dispersed.

Faunus was approaching by a long leap, while Jace's sword was inches away from her head. That moment seemed the longest, as though minutes, months, possibly even years passed. Even her quick, sharp gasp was echoed as a long inhale that burned in her chest while her next heartbeat was slow to come.

Then everything sped up.

Jace's body almost crumbled upon itself sideways when he was thrown to Mayumi's left, his entire back torn to shreds past his spine and into his organs.

With Jace gone, Mayumi was showered in the black, glittering sand of Faunus' essence. It was surprisingly warm against the sweat-coated skin of her face, like a final lemongrass-and-lime scented breath. His skull fell through the middle of it as though it had suddenly been dropped, and it landed not far from her feet.

The lightest part of him was face up, and she saw the gaping hole in his beautiful skull. The blood that had been streaking across it in little rivulets glittered into dust as well, leaving behind nothing but pure white bone.

The black sand never truly made it to the ground, fading away into nothingness with sparkles.

She stared down at what remained of his skull in shock, her lips parted in horror. "No," she whispered.

A part of her splintered when she understood that Faunus was gone. That he wasn't going to come back.

No, her mind repeated.

She'd thought she'd be given the chance to at least get to say goodbye. Instead, he'd obliterated into fucking glittering dust! Gone. Poof. Never to be seen again.

Cordon's bellow behind her was a war cry.

There would be no chance to grieve.

She would be given no chance to breathe in this everlasting, painful breath that didn't seem to end, no matter how much she huffed and panted.

She was almost choking on it, and all the things that were left unsaid... she wanted to hurry and utter them now in case his spirit, at least, was still here to hear it. Her dreams, her hopes, her stupid feelings she'd been too freaked out by.

The way Cordon's yell ignited her into an inferno of vengeful fury was so sudden that she screamed when it felt as though lava had replaced her blood.

The usually silent, stoic Mayumi was a screeching banshee as she turned to the Head Elder.

You wanted me to live, Faunus? she mentally asked whatever remained of his spirit, sprinting towards Cordon with all her might. *Then I'll fucking live!*

Caked in dirt and sweat as she darted, the screech she produced was broken in the middle of her tones – wanting to be high with her grief but deep with her determination to have retribution for the loss this had all caused. It scratched at her throat.

Mayumi had no weapons. There wasn't one between her and Cordon, who was moments from slashing his sword across her torso.

Using the slick of the snow, she tipped her body until she was sliding on the side of her left leg while using her palm to steady herself. Going underneath the sword, she dug her fingers into the dirtied snow and turned her body just enough that her legs tangled with Cordon's.

When he realised he was coming down above her, he directed his sword towards her body. She bent her knees to get his under hers and bashed his blade with her arm while throwing every bit of her weight behind it.

She managed to reverse their positions until she was above him.

Then, with her lips pressed tight and curling downwards like a snarling grimace, her front teeth gritted so tight behind them she thought they'd shatter if she pressed any harder, she knelt over his torso. Mayumi shoved her thumbs into the only part of him she could see, his callous, icy-blue eyes.

The man screamed and scratched the ends of his gloves into her jacket to stop her. When that didn't work, he slammed his fist across her face, snapping it to the side.

But Mayumi didn't relent until her nails dug deep enough that blood welled. Then she brought her hands away so she could punch the lower part of her knuckles against his cheek with her right hand while the other held his jaw right where she fucking wanted it.

She was small, but she was strong enough to knock some sense into the man – the sense of realisation that he had messed with the wrong damn person this day. That the tide of a battle could be changed merely by a person's newfound rage at seeing another die at their own hands. When they stopped caring about self-preservation and let their body take control rather than the cunning of their mind. When they would throw themselves foolishly into danger rather than courting it in a graceful dance.

Revenge wasn't better left cold; it felt far better when it was hot and scalding.

Fuck the guild. Her fist came back down on him. *Curse this wretched, dying world.* She drew it back and then brought it down again until she struck against bone. *There is no light in it.*

In people. In anything.

She grunted when Cordon managed to grab the end of her ponytail in his blind flailing. It forced her to roll off him, but not before she tugged on the whip in his weapon belt.

He wheezed, coughing blood and a tooth or two against the ground as he got to his hands and knees.

"Like a wild animal, you went for my eyes!" He was beginning to get to his feet when Mayumi came from behind. "You've become like those barbaric human savages in the mountains. There's no honour in blinding another. If you fight against another human, you should fight fairly until your death. That is part of our code!"

"Fuck your code," Mayumi sneered as she wrapped his own whip around his neck. His back arched as he went upright on his knees and dug at the braided cord around his neck. "Death is death. There's no beauty in it. There is no honour in it. There is no grace in it." Then Mayumi leaned closer to his squirming, struggling form until her mouth was right next to his ear. "And I'm not going to give you the respectful burial you deserve, our great, honourable Head Elder. I'm going to let the Demons eat your corpse while I watch from the safety of my home."

Not one for many words on the battlefield, she decided that was sufficient. She wasn't going to give him any more time to get the better of her.

She loosened the left side of the whip just enough so that when she pulled to the right, it twisted his neck until she heard the most *satisfying* pop.

When Cordon went limp, Mayumi let him fall.

Since his breath had left this world, so did his existence to her.

Her eyes found Yoshida battling the one she knew had torn Faunus' skull apart. Beyond him, Margo was lagging and now on the defence against Klaus and Henry. She was not far from falling as well. Those two enemies were all that remained.

She no longer cared about the fight when she could see it was ending.

She walked away from the clearing to where the bigger section of Faunus' skull lay. She fell to her knees next to it and scooped it into her arms so she could cuddle it to her chest.

I knew this was going to happen... You told me you were going to die, but I just refused to accept it.

She still refused to as she curled her entire body around it. No tears formed, only because she denied this, denied that he was truly gone.

There must be something I can do. This can't be it for you.

She pulled back so she could stare down at the white bone that lay across the top of her folded legs.

But what? What can I do? The glue didn't work, and she doubted strapping his face together now would be enough.

All the fire she'd felt not even moments ago sizzled out of her, leaving her feeling unbearably cold – especially in the centre of her chest, where her soul often tried to emerge. Mayumi shivered, her hands trembling as her teeth clattered.

Come on, Mayumi. Think.

So deep in contemplation, it took her longer than it should have to notice that someone was approaching her from the tree line.

The setting noon sun allowed a large stretch of shadow to come almost all the way to her, but it was also completely out of reach.

When a pair of bare feet, dark in skin with little claws on their toes, stopped and crouched a metre away from her, she turned her head up.

She didn't know why she didn't spook and immediately reach for a weapon. Perhaps it was because she was tired and hurting, and this person wasn't covered in the clothing of her once fellow Demonslayers.

Red eyes set inside the features of an other-worldly face screamed dangerous as they gazed down at her. She blinked at them for a moment, trying to register why there were red eyes on an obviously human face.

Long white hair wisped to the side before a few locks fluttered down the front of a male's shirtless, bulky torso. She thought he was naked until she noticed the dark-blue, loose-fitting pants he wore.

"So..." the man started with a serious, thoughtful expression. "He's dead, is he?"

She was about to ask him who he was, but her eyes finally slipped lower to find black streaking marks over his sides and arms. They bounced from the golden bands and looping chains over his body, to a singular pointed ear poking up through his blueish-white hair before they fell on the two dark horns curling back over the top of his head.

All of this informed her of who he was.

"This is what you wanted," she almost growled – if a human could growl. She nodded her head in the tree line where she saw another Demon standing there – their big wings awfully familiar. "You watched us fight. You saw it. Why the fuck are you asking me for?"

She bet it had been entertaining for him to see humans fighting each other.

When he grinned, he revealed sharp fangs. She cringed in disgust when it looked like what she'd seen inside the mouth of sharks from sketchbooks.

"Testy, testy, for such a tiny human." He even clicked his tongue in his mouth at her. "Was he your dear friend? Or did you let him ride your cunt like the other whores the Mavka have taken? I can smell his scent all over you."

"Come into the sun and say that," she bit in response.

"I could, you know." He raised a brow at her. "I, unlike the rest of my subjects, can withstand the light for a short period of time. It comes with my Elven blood. You wouldn't even be able to run since I can teleport to what I can see."

Is that how he was able to get here so quickly?

She clutched Faunus' skull tighter when Jabez, the Demon King that Faunus had told her of, laid his hand out.

"Give it to me."

"No, I refuse. You can't have it."

"Mayumi!" Henry yelled, and she turned her head to the side to find all three of her friends running towards her.

Jabez threw his hand out to the side, and brown tree-root vines broke from the earth and twisted around their bodies. All three were pulled to their knees before they fell to the ground. They struggled to get out of their bonds.

"Stop!" Mayumi demanded.

Jabez twisted his head until he was facing her once more. "Or what? It's obvious that stupid Mavka told you who I am, which means you know what I can do."

She struggled for an answer, but she doubted anything she said would've prevented him from doing what he wanted. He'd tortured Faunus. Mayumi would bet on her life he didn't care about anything other than his own desires.

Then he chuckled brightly. "You know what? After watching you fight and finally seeing that ram-horned Mavka die, proving my theory, I'm willing to be benevolent. I'm not evil, nor cruel."

Mayumi mentally snorted. *I beg to differ.*

"Keep the skull and your friends. I came here to end him; that's all I truly cared to achieve."

Despite crouching for so long, the position seemed so natural for him that he didn't even sway on his legs. The balls of his feet were deep against the ground while he rested his forearms over his bent knees.

"Why are you doing this?" Mayumi couldn't help asking as she shook her head. "What are you targeting the Duskwalkers for?"

Jabez gave a curt growl against his closed fangs when he bared them at her. "Because they keep killing my kind, and they are in the way."

Mayumi laughed so hard that her eyelids crinkled with the depth of her dark humour.

"That's not enough. Humans are killing just as many, if not more, of your kind, but I don't see you going to all the Demonslayer strongholds with all that apparent vast power you have." She noticed his red eyes, tipped with white eyelashes, narrowed on her as one side of his jaw knotted. "So, what's the real reason?"

"Very intuitive of you." He cocked his head to the left with a sneer. "Why should I tell you?"

"Because I'm just so damn curious. Why else would I be fucking asking?"

She wanted to know why! She wanted to know why it was so important that the person she cared for had to be destroyed. She wanted there to be a legitimate reason other than cruelty and menace, hoping that might help her accept this loss.

He threw his head back and laughed.

"I like you. Why not come with me to the Veil? I watched you fight. You would be a formidable soldier for me. You could help me train my army, so they aren't so useless. They can be fumbling buffoons at times, and they need discipline." He offered his hand out again. "I won't even use you like you let that useless Mavka. I need smart soldiers. I don't care what breed they are."

"I'd rather die," she bit. "If you weren't listening properly with those freakish pointed ears of yours, I should inform you that I am a Demon*slayer*. I'd never help you."

"Tsk. Then you will get no answers from me."

Jabez took a single step back and then stood to remain in the shadows. He didn't step back enough since a streak of sunlight washed over his shoulder, causing burning smoke to form. He hissed and dropped his shoulder forward into the shade.

"I enjoyed the show, and for that, you can keep his broken skull as a glorious trophy for defying the odds against you."

It would never be a trophy.

She didn't want to feel a shred of pride for anything that had happened this day. It would be a painful memory for the rest of her life – one she would live simply because Faunus wanted her to do so.

In the blink of an eye, Jabez disappeared – only to reappear seconds later next to the winged Demon. Then he placed his hand on its shoulder and they were both gone.

Even though he'd asked to take Faunus' skull before he so 'kindly' let her keep it, and maybe he'd truly wanted her to come with him, she couldn't help thinking he'd approached her just because he wanted to be an asshole and taunt her for obviously caring about him.

FORTY

"Who the hell was that?" Klaus asked when he sprinted over to Mayumi.

At Jabez's disappearance, the wooden vines holding them flat against the ground withered away and died. She was honestly surprised he let any of them live. Maybe it was because they were all humans and were seen as weak and insignificant to him.

Whatever the reason, she wasn't given time to linger on it when she was suddenly crowded.

"More like what the hell was that?" Yoshida said, while wiping his chest and shuddering. "Obviously wasn't a human. Those vines felt gross."

"Don't worry about it," Mayumi murmured before looking down at Faunus' skull, thankful she still had it in her arms. "There are a lot of unknown things in the world, and it is burdensome for the mind."

"Cut the crap," Klaus snapped. "You can't just expect us not to ask a bunch of questions after what happened here today."

Henry, who had been silent the entire time, lowered himself onto one knee and leaned to the side to look at her expression from below.

"Why are you holding that Duskwalker's skull like you just lost someone dear to you, Yumi?"

Her lips tightened, the desire to keep them shut strong. She relaxed them when she peeked at Henry as he removed his helmet. He appeared concerned, and the lack of judgement in his expression was enough for her to answer.

"Because he was my friend. I've been trying to save him."

"Was that why you came to us asking about glue?" Yoshida added, and she raised her gaze to him standing there.

"Yes."

"Why were the Demonslayers after you?" Klaus asked while removing his own helmet so he could brush back his long, matted orange hair.

"The Duskwalker gave me information about Demons and the Veil, and I was stupid for sharing it with the guild. I knew too much, so they needed me dead."

"Fuck's sake, Yumi," Henry rasped while shaking his head. "You're a bundle of chaos, no matter where you go and what you do."

She shrugged, wishing she had the strength to stand, but she couldn't move. She worried Faunus' skull would be too heavy for the weight of her heart to carry.

"Makes me interesting."

"What did you learn about Demons? It must have been serious for the guild to come after you," Klaus pressed. "And how did you even befriend a Duskwalker, anyway?"

Henry snapped his head to him. "Stop asking her questions. Just let it lie. She's obviously not doing too well. Let her deal with this."

"It's a Duskwalker!" Klaus yelled in outrage. He even threw his hands forward. "Who gives a shit about it? It's better for us that it's fucking dead, so I don't understand why she's upset about it."

Heat flared through her, but before she could get to her feet and confront him, Yoshida surprised them all when he suddenly went into motion. He grabbed Klaus by the shoulders of his armour and yanked him forward.

"Shut that loud mouth of yours before I shut it for you," he threatened, shocking Mayumi when she had been expecting him to take Klaus' side.

Klaus grabbed his leather shirt in return, his eyes turning hostile. "The hell you taking its side for?! They're nothing but monsters that deserve to die!"

"I would be dead if it wasn't for that Duskwalker. I had a

sword through my chest, and he healed me!" Then he nearly pressed his nose to Klaus' with his teeth gritted. "Talk shit like that about him, and I'll break your nose again."

Henry placed his hand on her shoulder, ignoring the men at each other's throats behind him. Emotions were high, and no one was thinking calmly – except for Henry, it seemed. He was always so damn calm and thoughtful, which could be irritating at times, but for once, she was thankful. She just needed someone to not be weirded out by all this right now, and Henry was being a wonderful rock.

"Get up, Yumi. We all need to clean up, eat, and drink some water."

"There must be something I can do," she mumbled in answer.

This isn't it. It can't be. She dug her fingertips into the hard bone. *But his whole body just... disappeared.*

"Is there?" Henry asked, causing her eyes to lift back to his gentle brown ones. "I know they're hard to kill, so they must heal, right?"

"Yeah, usually in a day, but that's only if their skull isn't broken. I don't think he can come back from this."

"Can you just put his face back together somehow?"

"I tried..."

If only it was that easy. She knew it was too late.

Or was it? Cordon's golden medallion glinting in the sun caught her attention. *A day...*

What if I put his skull back together before a day passes? Her heart, which had been drowning, beat faster to match her rapid thoughts. *What if that's all I need to do?*

Her eyes widened, and she frantically looked around as she stood while cradling Faunus' skull.

"Help me find it," she demanded, walking towards her home. "Help me find the rest of his face."

An idea had lit within her mind, and she firmly clutched onto the sliver of hope.

Henry was the one to find the other side of Faunus' skull since Yoshida and Klaus were rolling on the ground throwing punches. They'd likely tire themselves out, since it wasn't the first time they'd gone at each other.

Mayumi inspected the bone and horn fragment to find it was mostly intact. She took it inside and placed the two pieces of him on the dining table so she could open the hidden latch that was in the storage room. The coin sack within it was heavy, and she heaved it up and carelessly emptied it against the ground.

The specific gold coins she retrieved were few, but bigger than the others available. They were also purer of quality, and she took every piece she found and his skull outside to the back of her house.

After settling down, her friends had gone to the stream so they could fill the spring bath and wash themselves of the blood upon them.

She stole from the heating furnace to light her smithing furnace and then placed all her gold coins into a smelting cup. While it was heating, she wiped down Faunus' skull to make sure it was clean before using a file to roughen the edges of his crack so it would be easier to bond with.

She stood there for a long while, mentally preparing herself for the excruciating wait that would be the next twenty-four hours.

Her friends eventually coaxed her to enter the bath with them by reminding her of the human blood she was covered in. That was the only reason she stripped and quickly bathed – she had no issue being naked in front of men.

It was common for the guild, and if these men had any desires for her, that was their problem, not hers.

"You should all leave," she said while hopping out, water sluicing down her naked body and dripping into the spring bath. "Night will fall soon, and this place will become a Demon hunting ground before long. You need to get away."

"We can't leave you here by yourself," Henry said, gripping her arm when she was standing out of the tub. "Come back with us to Colt's Outpost. Let the Demons come and feed, then return when you know it's safer."

Her gaze flittered to the furnace and Faunus' skull lying on her smithing table.

"I can't. I need to stay here with him, just in case. I won't be able to bring him into the town if this works."

"Yumi..."

"No!" she shouted, ripping her arm from him and taking two steps back, so she was out of reach. The words that were about to fall from her mouth were rude, but she was in too much emotional anguish to care right then. "Thank you so much for coming here. I'm not so high-handed to admit that without you three... I probably would have died today. In saying that, I want to be alone, and you're all getting on my nerves. So, if you don't mind, kindly fuck off back to your walled prison and leave me to the forest."

Not another word was uttered to her until they were leaving, but she didn't respond to their attempts to change her mind – no matter how much all three of them begged.

By that point, she was too busy carefully trying to pour gold onto Faunus' skull without ruining it. She couldn't listen to a conversation that was unimportant in comparison to the task she was completing.

Things can be broken, Mayumi, the memory of her father echoed. *You can't apologise to a cup and have it fix itself, but you can work hard and pour value into it, making it better, stronger. It depends on what you've broken is worth to you.*

Resting on the smithing table was the teacup her grandfather had reworked after her father had broken it as a child. That same lesson had been instilled in Mayumi as a way to teach her the value of finding beauty in one's flaws. To celebrate missteps rather than disguising them.

The art of kintsugi had come from her family's homeland, and she had never been more thankful for her bloodline than in that moment.

She wouldn't have known what else to do.

However... she didn't have the specialised tree resin required. What her family had was nothing more than mixed resin they'd acquired from the tree sap they'd bought in their travels. She also didn't have golden dust – at least, if she did, she wouldn't know where to find it in the mess of her storage room.

These two ingredients combined were kintsugi, or golden joinery.

She was bastardising the art now in a desperate attempt to

return something that was lost. An attempt that could see all of what she had left disintegrating in black charcoal.

Human bone could only survive certain heats before it oxidised into charred powder. However, the bone she was working with was from a magical creature who was stronger than anything else in existence, one that should not exist but did. That had survived strikes to the face by swords and claws.

That was all she needed to have hope.

When it had cooled and was threatening to harden, Mayumi smeared a small droplet of molten gold against the top of the crack on one side just to make sure it didn't damage it. The remaining gold was put back in the furnace as she waited.

When the bone didn't splinter or begin to change in shape or colour, her heart swelled with hope.

She stuck Faunus' skull back together with molten gold by smearing it along the edge of the smaller piece she had. Then she strapped it together with leather. Once she was done, she watched the hot ore cooling against the bone.

The heat felt like it was burning her flesh. Sweat dripped down her arms, neck, and face as the glow of it reddened her.

It looked bumpy and ugly, she wasn't the greatest at fine arts, and she'd been shaking the entire time, but if this worked, she'd kiss every inch of that metal in appreciation.

Please... please come back.

FORTY-ONE

Mayumi spent one of the longest and most gruelling nights of her life holding Faunus' skull in her arms. Hiding behind the walls of her home and every incense canister she had available, she'd listened to the sounds of Demons entering her surrounding yard.

They were too distracted by the overwhelming scent of human blood and bodies to even think she was alive within her cottage.

She stayed quiet and barely moved as she waited for the sun to rise and scare them off.

Many would linger in the forest, not too close, as her family had thinned the trees here to make it sunny in parts, but she was sure they'd be able to watch her from a distance.

Her body was alert, the back of her neck prickling in awareness of at least one set of red eyes on her when she placed Faunus' skull in the snow of her clearing.

Mayumi was geared up from head to toe with everything from her bow, to a whip, and a coil of rope. She wasn't going to take any chances with the vermin outside, but she couldn't have Faunus come back to life in her home.

She didn't know what would happen, but noon had come just like it had the day before, and it was now quickly descending into late afternoon. *It's almost time.*

She stood there staring down at it, waiting.

"Come on," she whispered, bouncing on her legs in anxiety. "Come on. Start working."

The sun was warm on her back, winter finally beginning to

change as the shortest days of the year were growing longer. Human towns would soon begin celebrating that light.

Mayumi cared little for it. She'd always preferred the night. It's where her enemy lived, and it was when she felt as though she thrived. Would that change now?

She'd finally found a creature to hide and fight with her in the darkness. She didn't want that to end when it'd only just begun.

Her fingertips twitched when something glittered beneath the base of the skull. It was slow at first, but a swirling flurry of black, goopy sand formed.

Whenever she'd seen Faunus heal, it'd always been in a matter of seconds. This took far longer.

His skull began to lift as a body rose underneath it, and her lips parted as they curled.

"It worked," she gasped, her smile growing. She even laughed as she bounced on her feet with fists clenched. "It fucking worked! I can't believe it!"

Eventually, he towered over her as that familiar, soft, glossy fur grew. Claws tipped his human-like hands and feline-pawed feet just as his tail swished to the side.

Faunus turned his head down to her once the sands faded, showing her the process was nearing completion. Her heart was almost bashfully stammering in her chest.

Mayumi stepped forward with her hand reaching up, waiting for the last piece of him to form. She continued to smile at his empty, shadowed eye sockets.

"Show me those pretty yellow glowing orbs of yours."

He cocked his head, hearing her before he leaned forward while sniffing only inches from her fingertips. She could feel his warm breath dancing over them, could smell his mind-tingling lemongrass and lime scent.

I wonder if I'll be able to touch his face freely from now on.

The roar that followed his parting fangs was beastly, inhuman, and the wrongness of it sent her blood curdling.

His orbs never formed, even when he lowered himself onto all fours and sprinted for her. With her eyes wide, a gasp tore from her, and she dived to the side just in time to avoid being clawed.

She rolled before getting to her feet in a crouched position with one hand on the ground. Faunus turned, a constant snarl emitting from him. His body was tense, his fur and spikes puffing higher than she'd ever seen them go before.

Something's wrong.

He shot for her again, and Mayumi dived between his arms to avoid him and slid against the snow, having nowhere else to go. When she was back in her crouched position, she unhooked and pulled her whip into her free hand.

She started to back up, her hand rising from the ground. "Faunus, it's me."

His fangs clinked and clacked as he opened and closed them, his orbless head shaking one way and then the other. When he roared once more and sprinted in her direction, Mayumi ran.

Whatever she'd brought back, it was no longer her sweet, funny Duskwalker. And it was gaining on her.

When he was right behind her, she turned, flicked her whip forward, and caught it around his snout to close it. The horns on his head rammed into her when she jumped, and Mayumi found herself flipping through the air until she was behind him.

A wheeze tore from her when she hit the ground.

Then she was dragged as he ran around sporadically, trying to remove her whip from his face. With grunting groans coming from her, she climbed the line until she could grab a fistful of fur on his behind.

Faunus bucked to remove her.

She held strong, even when he bashed the side of his body against tree trunks. He turned his head so it was facing down his back, and she stayed out of reach of his quickly swiping claws.

There was only one thing she could do if she didn't want to die. She let go at the last second when he was close to one of the thickest trees surrounding her home and threw herself to the other side.

She slipped when he kept going forward but managed to coil the whip around itself and lock him to the tree.

It groaned and creaked against the strength of this mindless, crazed Duskwalker. She let the whip go with her hands, ready to grab it, assessing if it would hold long enough for her to do what she needed to next.

Her heart was racing and threatening to come up her throat. Her lungs were sawing in and out of her like she'd swallowed a hacksaw and was being severed by the very blade.

She waited with her hands out, and it held.

Mayumi unlooped her enchanted rope, braved the possibly Demon-filled forest, and threaded the rope around a tight collection of three trees, looping the rope together so it was stronger. She tied the other end into a lasso and waited for the opening she needed to catch it around his throat.

She failed the first three times, Faunus moving so wildly and erratically that it was nearly impossible to predict where he would go.

On the fourth try, she climbed up the side of one of the three trees. She only managed to get it around his neck because she jumped onto his back from a low-hanging branch and threaded it around him from behind. He reared back on his paws.

Thrown off since she was unbalanced standing on a living, thrashing creature by nothing more than her feet, she took the impact to her entire side. Her elbow crushed her ribs, and she choked out a cry.

The growl above her forced her to look up. Her eyes widened when a set of big, clawed hands were moments from coming down upon her. *Shit!*

She quickly rolled and narrowly missed being impaled.

Faunus leapt forward, only to be yanked back by the rope collared around his neck. His legs shot forward as they came out from under him while a choking noise punched out of him at the same time. He tried multiple times and let out a grunt every time he was pulled.

Like a restless wild animal, he paced at the very end of the line, his head turning to her often to growl and snarl.

He was trapped by both the enchanted rope and whip she had, keeping him there. But for how long? She'd seen Faunus lift a tree. She didn't know if three rooted deeply into the ground would be enough to hold him back forever.

On her arse and leaning back on the palms of her hands, she stared at him, huffing.

What's wrong with him? Why are his orbs missing? Only the physical parts of him seemed to have returned, his mind absent.

She couldn't believe she'd almost died because he'd attacked her. Had she been any other human, she couldn't have made it past the first leap.

A clacking sound in the distance had her head snapping to the side.

A Demon was nearby.

Both she and Faunus were in the sun, but night was only hours away.

I can't leave him like this. Not trapped with his fangs clamped shut. He'd be a sitting duck!

He's... he's gotta be in there somewhere... right? Her lips pressed into a tight line. *Maybe I just need to wait another day?*

If that were the case, then she would spend the whole night protecting this shell of Faunus. Her mind was scattered, shoving thoughts and ideas at her until she gave herself a splitting headache. She wasn't thinking clearly, hadn't been since he'd been obliterated into dust.

All she knew was that she needed to prepare the area as much as she could to keep him safe.

Backing away from him, keeping her eyes firmly on him in case looking away for too long could mean he'd disappear, she went up the side of her house. She finally took her gaze off of him so she could enter the shallow shed.

Hunting traps were piled into one corner, and she dragged three out at a time by their chains. She took them to where he was tied and began setting them up out of range of him – she didn't want him hurting himself.

The clamps she used had a corkscrew pin at the top, and they helped her to set the springs in place by herself. Faunus growled whenever she got too close and tried to swipe at her, but she ignored him – especially since one small mistake could see her own arm being crushed.

Once she set down all seven traps, she assessed them from far away. It wasn't much, but it was better than nothing.

Other than removing the whip from around his snout and laying on her roof with her bow and arrows, there was little else she could do. Nothing that wouldn't possibly cost Mayumi her own life, of course.

I don't know why I'm so worried. He can fight for himself.

She would just be around to make sure he damn well saw the sun rise... or rather felt it, since he lacked his orbs.

The emotional whiplash she was experiencing, had been experiencing for days, for weeks even, was beginning to take a toll on her. Eventually, this horrible up and down slide would end, but she worried about what would be left of her afterwards.

I don't think my heart can take much more of this.

FORTY-TWO

Curled in a ball in his monstrous form, Faunus lifted his head the following day when he heard Mayumi's approaching footsteps. From what she figured, he'd most likely been sleeping.

It was impossible to tell with his lack of eyes.

It was way past noon, and she stood before him, waiting as she had done the day before.

She'd learnt that being a distance away from him tended to leave him calm but alert. He was sensing her, whether that was by scent or sound, but it was nearness that made him frantic.

He didn't trust her, didn't know her, didn't remember her.

He couldn't see the way her eyes morphed into beseeching bows with the ends crinkling. He couldn't see the way her lips would tighten before loosening to tremble or how her teeth bit into the bottom one.

And when time passed, revealing no changes in him, he didn't see how she bit back her choke of emotions.

He was covered in claw marks she knew would fade twenty-four hours from when he'd obtained them, but she didn't know if they pained him or not. He'd roared and yelped throughout the night while he was attacked, and those sounds had been hollowing to listen to.

There were three dead Demons around him. Two who had eventually bled out and died by his claws or fangs. The other's death hadn't been so slow since it'd moved around with its legs crushed in a hunting trap until it crawled headfirst into a second one.

Mayumi had done what she could to protect him from the rooftop with her bow, only once coming to the ground when he encountered a particularly speedy Demon he couldn't get his claws into.

She had emerged from the night unscathed, thankfully, but she couldn't imagine doing this for the rest of her life.

Reality was settling in, and it was cold and lonely.

He's not coming back, she thought as she stared at his gold-struck, ethereal face. Those black eye sockets seemed like pools of emptiness, an emptiness she knew was within his mind. *He's gone.*

Her hands shook when she curled them into tight fists, feeling her nails digging into the plump flesh of her palms.

Just as liquid filled the waterline of her eyes, Mayumi reached down and grabbed a large handful of snow. She tossed it at Faunus, who twisted his head when it hit him in the shoulder. He made a thoughtful sound as he stood.

"This isn't what I wanted!" she screamed when a second snowball splattered against his shoulder. "I didn't want you to turn into some zombie freak of a fucking Duskwalker!"

The tooth-gritted screech that exploded from her as she started lobbing snowball after snowball at this zombie shell was accompanied by a heavy droplet running from her left eye. It didn't take long for both eyes to start crying, and she barely registered it.

Her loss and grief finally overflowed when she realised she had failed. That Faunus wasn't going to return, and she was going to be stuck by herself.

And now... now Mayumi was going to have to face the consequences of what her desperate hope had brought.

"I don't want to babysit a wild Duskwalker like it's nothing more than a dog on a chain!" she screamed.

She wanted Faunus back. The big, fluffy, arrogant Duskwalker that liked to tease her just as much as she did him. The one that wanted to protect her, not tear her to shreds. The one that chuckled at her and only growled or snarled when he was feeling frisky – and occasionally when she playfully irritated him.

I want my damn friend back!

Her sadness rode the waves of her fury as she finally let it all out after days of holding onto hope and denying this was the end. She'd spent her whole life containing her emotions because emotions were for fools, for people who thought the world was filled with potential sunshine and rainbows and fairies.

All she'd known was the hardness of steel, the blood of Demons and humans across her flesh, and the smell of death. All she'd seen was the terribleness in people and the world.

She hated life but had always been determined to live it – just alone, with the coolness of misery to keep her company or the throaty burn of alcohol to numb her.

Her anger couldn't be held in. Her tears couldn't be stemmed as they ran down her face and wet her lips for her to drink the bitter saltiness of them. Her trembling had nothing to do with the winter air and everything to do with the ache she felt deep within.

She was tired. Tired from being up for two nights straight because of him. Tired from holding everything in, not just for these past few days with him gone, or the weeks leading up to this, but for years.

Mayumi was exhausted.

"How dare you do this to me!" she screamed with every fibre of her being. "How dare you come here and let me fall in love with you, only to fucking die! How dare you save me as a child and start my infatuation with you! You probably ate my fucking cat, you carnivorous jerk!"

Mayumi didn't know how many snowballs she made and threw or what number it was that caused him to start rearing back at the onslaught in confusion.

She didn't stop.

"Why couldn't you just have remained as a creepy monster in the shadows and left me to live by myself?!" She knew her tears were falling faster, flinging off her flesh as she screamed and tossed. "Why couldn't you be just like the Demons and try to kill me rather than protect me? I never asked you to come here and be so amazing, to change my life and give me hope that I could actually be happy for once. So why?!"

She hated when he roared at her, knowing that she herself

would have to cut that sound permanently from the world. She couldn't leave him like this to be bait for Demons, nor could she set him free to terrorise the world.

This wasn't the image she wanted to leave of Faunus.

She'd have to kill him, cut off his head and then break his skull again. She didn't want to, but there were many things she'd done in her life that she'd never wanted to do.

The tiredness finally pulled her under, and Mayumi's knees eventually buckled. Her last snowball fell only a foot from her hands when it crashed into the ground.

She watched as her teardrops fell into the snow to crystalise while she knelt there on her hands and knees.

"Why did you have to be so damn funny and caring and so damn perfect for me, Faunus? Every day you pretended to be okay when I could tell you were just as broken on the inside as your stupid face, and I couldn't help falling for that part of you... because it was just like me. I hate you. I hate you so much for leaving me here like this. I hate your stupid, pretty face and your stupid, warm body and your stupid personality. I tried so hard to save you. I tried everything I could think of that wouldn't cause you pain."

She turned her head up so she could look at him, pacing at the end of his tether on all fours. Misty white breaths blew out of his nose hole in heavy bursts.

He didn't understand her, didn't recognise what she was saying or the sound of her voice.

"I've never lost someone who made me feel so whole. How am I supposed to find my place in a world I know for certain you're not in?" Snow, like soft, light dandelion puffs, fell around them both. "How am I to find someone who felt like they were the other half of me when I know it was you... in all your big, fluffy glory? I hate you so much for doing this to me." Then she whispered, "And I love you so damn much that it feels like my heart is burning."

Mayumi fisted the snow as she sniffled.

"I was fine being numb," she sobbed, her saliva so thick in her throat it stuck together. "I was fine being... alone."

She didn't want to get up, knowing that the next thing she did would be regrettably drawing her sword.

I don't want to do it, she thought as she clenched her eyes shut when it was too hard to look at him. *If I do, then I know for certain there's no way at all to save you.*

Her chest heaved with shuddering breaths; her nose dripped from her tears. The cold crept into her aching, trembling body while she was on her hands and knees only a few metres in front of him.

When it was too much for her fingers, the tips of them burning from the frost, she cupped them to her chest as she laid over her folded knees.

The only person Mayumi had ever cried this hard over losing was her mother. Her father had sent her a message, and she had been given a small leave of absence from the guild so she could be with her in the final days.

Holding her mother's frail hand, her face pale and sickly, Mayumi had watched her pass peacefully.

She'd shed not one tear, nor had her father, who didn't allow either of them the comfort of a hug.

Instead, Mayumi just helped him dig a hole in their family graveyard in the forest, an hour's journey from their home, so they could give her the respectful burial she deserved with a gravestone. Then, once they were done, Mayumi packed her bags and left – only to break down and cry half a day's journey from her home.

She'd also never seen her father again since he had disappeared when she was on duty, and she'd stopped receiving his letters. He'd most likely been eaten. She didn't cry then, instead pouring herself into her work with even more tenacity in his honour.

She thought no other death could be as painful as theirs, yet here she was... on her hands and knees, unable to stand, unable to breathe. She was moments away from choking on the heartache that was nearly tearing her apart.

Why does everyone I love leave me?

She shook her head, unable to bear this.

"So this is where you are," a masculine, impossibly deep voice uttered softly.

She'd heard no footsteps or the sound of someone huffing from walking through the snow as they approached. The suddenness of it shocked her so deeply she opened her tear-filled eyes to look upwards.

At first, she thought it was nothing but a shroud of black cloud that was taller than it was wide. Then, suddenly, a black face made almost of chalk coalesced, only to disperse seconds later. A black, chalky hand formed as it lifted to touch Faunus' face, which had turned to the voice that had spoken to him. The hand was gone before it made contact and a small black cloud wafted over his snout.

A chalky leg appeared, a hip, the part of a shoulder, all of which faded almost as quickly as they came – yet the cloud itself never faded.

"W-who are you?" she asked with a stuttering, coarse voice, when really... she should have asked *what* they were.

That face appeared out of thin air, with no neck, head, or body attached, to look in her direction. It tilted before fading.

Yet, that voice spoke once more.

"I didn't expect to see a human with him," the cloud said before it moved to the other side of Faunus. The face appeared at the top, close to Faunus' skull. "Are you the one that tried to stick his face back together?"

"Yes," she answered as she crawled to her feet so she could put herself into a defensive stance.

A normal human may have been weirded out by the cloud freak, but Mayumi thought she had seen enough of the strange things the world had to offer to no longer be surprised by it.

She was also too worn out to care anymore.

The face disappeared, only to coalesce while staring in her direction. "Why would you try to save him?"

"Because I cared about him," she answered with a hiccup. "He was my friend."

"And yet you have cursed him to a half-life," he stated as the face disappeared. His hand waved sideways in its place. "You have kept his body alive and, in doing so, have fractured his soul in two."

I knew it. I knew something was wrong.

"Why are you here?" Mayumi placed her hand on the pommel of her sword. "Don't think I didn't notice you never answered my original question. If... if you plan to hurt him, I will fight you."

Her plan was to kill him as painlessly as possible. Even if he was a zombie, she worried the sentient part of him was still there and would feel it if he were being tortured.

It was only in the silence that greeted her she realised the black cloud wasn't actually empty. Within the centre of it, there was a white flame that was hidden until the slow swirl of the creature's essence parted slightly.

Mayumi crept closer so she could intervene, but she had no idea how she was supposed to fight a being made of cloud.

"Hmm." His chalky hand appeared before only the lower part of his face, so he could cup his jaw. "I came because I felt this little one die, and yet his soul did not come to me as it should have. I came to collect it and find out why." The cloud stopped swirling and instead pulsated for a moment, almost like one's shoulders might lift and fall on a sigh. "But like I said, I didn't expect to see a human with him, nor one that has obviously been weeping. Are you sad he is gone? Your soul appears to be withered within you. I only see this in humans who are experiencing intense levels of sorrow and pain."

She could have lied, and perhaps if a human had asked her, she would have – but Mayumi saw no point in lying.

"Yes. I tried to save him because I wanted him to stay."

The chalky face appeared, and she didn't like the way he grinned. Not with the fact he had large, sharp fangs like that of the Demon King – almost curling inward and shark-like.

The cloud moved so swiftly that she didn't even get the chance to step back when he was right in front of her. He smelt like nothing, and the cloud that passed over her cheek for just a second had no feeling to it. It passed over her eye before it settled backwards.

"I did not answer your question. I am Weldir, *semidei Custos Tenebris.*" A hand waved downwards with a swish before puffing away into cloud. "Or, to a human, Weldir, Warden of the Darkness."

"Weldir? Why do I know that name?" she whispered with her

eyes narrowing in thought. Then it clicked. "Weldir? As in Faunus' father, the spirit of the void guy?"

The chuckle that came from him was warm. "Calling me the spirit of the void is the equivalent of me calling you the human of this clearing. It has no meaning. It is nothing more than a description."

Well... how the hell was I supposed to know that? It's all Faunus had really told her.

"But yes, in short, I am this Mavka's father. Lindiwe and I have been awaiting his return."

"Lindiwe... who?" Mayumi asked.

"Their mother. They call her the Witch Owl, which is a fitting title for her, although I call her my mate."

Two hands formed and went around her, and then yanked back as if he wanted to pull her forward. Nothing happened, and Mayumi didn't feel anything. Yet, as the cloud fluttered backwards, she had the desire to follow it and did so hesitantly.

When he floated too close to Faunus, who growled at her closeness, she halted.

"Like I said, his soul is fractured." A hand appeared, seeming to catch something in the air before a yellow flame glowed to life. It was of Faunus' skull and horns and nothing more. "This should appear as all of him, just as your soul appears like you. Yet the body half of him is stuck inside the physical form you have granted in cursing him."

"I didn't mean to," she sighed, rubbing at her face in confusion. Everything she'd learnt, all the pain she'd felt in the last few weeks and especially days... this was all far too overwhelming for just one person.

That's when she noticed the liquid covering her cheeks and wiped her face clean of her tears and snot.

"It's fine," he stated. "All I need to do is pull his soul from his physical form."

Mayumi's heart clenched tightly as she turned her eyes to the side to look away from Weldir and, more importantly, Faunus.

"Your soul has dimmed further. You do not want this? You want to leave him how he is?"

"Not at all. I hate that I've done this to him." Her lips

tightened when a thought crossed her mind. "I don't understand something. If you can do this, fuck with his soul, it means you must have power, right?" Mayumi turned her squinting eyes to Weldir's cloudy essence. "Faunus said you're some kind of demigod or some shit. If that's the case, why didn't you help him? He's your son."

Faunus' fiery skull evaporated.

She jumped back when a hand materialised and shoved straight into her forehead.

"Because my power is limited. I can't even create a physical form in this world, and I have stolen power that I shouldn't have just to be here. I am not supposed to intervene, and punishment awaits me if it is discovered I do so."

The cloud parted to show Mayumi his centre, and she realised the white glow she had seen earlier was a white-flamed soul.

"I have used this human's soul just so I could leave the mist I have created in the Veil. I'm allowed to collect the souls of my children, but their life is their own. The only place I have any real strength is Tenebris, and even then, I am not able to stay physical for long – even if I wish it. What ghostly parts you see of me now are the same control I have physically in my own realm, and the longer I am apart from it, the sooner I will fade."

"You really couldn't have stopped the Demon King from cracking his skull?" Her eyes crinkled in the sadness and pity that washed over her. "Why is he after them, anyway? The Duskwalkers just existing doesn't seem like a good enough reason to me."

"Any excuse is enough for a tyrant," Weldir stated. "But what you have asked is valid. The cause for Jabez's ire solely has to do with me."

Her brows drew together tightly. "What do you mean?"

His face appeared, and it turned in Faunus' direction to look at him. It faded, but she had a funny feeling his gaze was rooted to the Duskwalker.

"He seeks to weaken me, and so he has targeted my children to do so since I, myself, cannot be harmed, and all attempts on Lindiwe have proven ineffective due to her being a Phantom and returning to me upon her many deaths. I am not permitted to intervene, other than how I have tampered with his portal to the Elven realm." The chalky face materialised facing her and then his hand lifted as though he was shrugging with it. Both disappeared at the same time. "I have three tasks in this world. One is to make Jabez's portal a one-way journey, meaning any full-breed Demon that crosses over from the Elven realm into this one is stuck here. I am what stops his army from attacking. I am the Elvish people's line of defence here."

"And in doing so, you have cursed us humans," she stated, her teeth gritting in irritation.

"Which is unfortunate but necessary. This realm is bigger, has more people, and you breed so quickly that the hope was that your kind would not be eradicated by the time the Elvish people came up with a solution to remove the Demons from your world, as well as their own."

Mayumi folded her arms, tightening them across her chest in anger she knew couldn't be unleashed. Her snarkiness, however, was a weapon she wielded freely.

"What are your other tasks then, oh great demigod of darkness?"

"You remind me of Lindiwe. Quick to anger, and yet cold. Are you sure your soul was not cut from the same flame as hers?" Mayumi blew a cowlick strand of hair from her forehead, but before she could answer with a retort, he said, "Since the Demons have been forced here, I have been given the task of purifying the tainted souls that come from the Demons. Whether it be an animal or a human, what a Demon eats corrupts the flame of one's soul, and I must use what little power I have to heal them. Then my final task is to give those souls a place to live, otherwise, your world would be overrun by Ghosts. Even though they are human, they do not pass over to whichever gods harbour the dead souls from here. I give them a home, and in doing so, I gain power – which is why using one like I have today to give myself a temporary boost in ability also weakens me deeply."

It was only then that she realised Weldir's entire cloud seemed... smaller than when it had first appeared.

She turned to Faunus when she saw in her peripheral that he was scratching at the rope around his neck. A whimper of distress wheezed from him, and her eyes bowed at watching him doing so.

He was trapped. This was hardly a life for him to live, even if it was a half-life.

"Are you going to take him there then? To Tenebris, or whatever you called it. Will he be able to walk there, or would he be a flame, not actually conscious?"

"I may not have to," Weldir said, just as his cloud moved to be in front of her line of sight.

"What do you mean, you may not have to?"

"How deeply do you care for this Mavka?" A leg formed as he stepped closer to her. "Are you aware that they seek a bride in order to become stable in this world?"

"Stable?"

"They seek to eat flesh because they are soul eaters, and like a bride metamorphosing into a Phantom by the Mavka becoming their living anchor, that soul in return anchors them to the physical world, which strengthens them. It is why they no longer have hunger once the bond is formed." His face formed before it faded and showed itself again to be turned to Faunus. "You have given him a name, I am guessing. You said he is your friend. But is he more? You tried to save him, but would you be willing to risk your life if I could bring him back?"

Her right fist clenched, desperately wanting to grab at this thread of hope but utterly fearing to do so. "You said you couldn't interfere."

"I can't interfere with Demons, nor can I save a Mavka once their skull has been damaged." His face appeared in front of her, and it once more had a large, fang-filled grin. "But he is currently in the bounds of my control. He has died, which means his soul is mine to do with what I will. I also can't tamper with a living human unless granted permission. How else do you think I gained a mate? My interference with her was rendered null and void once she became mine, as would you if you became his."

That piqued her interest, and she raised a singular brow.

"What would you do?"

"I must warn you. This may not work. This could see me bringing both of your souls back to Tenebris. Since I can't bring anyone back from the dead, not even my children, I see no other option. But, in you keeping part of his soul alive and in this realm by fixing his skull before a day passed, it means it is not a full revival but a half-one – in which I can bend the rules, so to speak."

"Oh, just spit it out!" she yelled, spooking Faunus, who launched at her only to be yanked back by the rope. "If there is a way to save him, then of course I want to do it! I don't care what it will cost me."

"Your soul has brightened." Weldir chuckled. "I'm sure it'll be nicer for him to eat when hot."

"You're planning to feed it to him? Wouldn't that make me his bride, then?"

"You appear confused and hesitant," Weldir said, his face forming to frown like she was. "Why?"

"Well," Mayumi grumbled as she rubbed one of her elbows. "I already offered him my soul, and he said no because he didn't want to doom me."

"If he cares for you, as you do him, it will be fine." His hand formed, hovering a mere inch from her sternum. "You must make your choice, or I will have to take him instead. Like I said, my time here runs short."

By the time her gaze fell on Faunus, she'd already made her decision.

"Fine." Her cheeks grew warm, almost like a bashful blush – which was weird for someone who rarely did. "Just take it."

Without warning, the hand shot forward into her chest, sinking beneath her flesh like one reaching into water. She felt nothing other than the heat that burst from her just as her soul was forced out of her body in his chalky, black hand.

Then the cloud of Weldir moved to stand in front of Faunus, who sniffed at the air. Weldir had been scentless, so Mayumi figured he was smelling her soul.

Weldir directed it one way, like someone teasing a dog with a ball, and Faunus' skull followed it. It went the other way, Faunus following it again before Weldir tossed it at him.

His fangs opened and then clamped around it. He turned his head up and swallowed.

"While I am here, I might as well heal him of his wounds, so he does not have to bear them if this works," Weldir said, just as black, glittering sand came from within his cloud to wrap around Faunus.

"If it's like how Faunus heals me, won't that hurt you?" Mayumi asked while cocking her head slightly.

She was surprised Weldir would care so much when Faunus would likely heal this on his own.

Maybe because he's his father? Faunus had given her the impression that he'd rarely met him, if at all – which meant he'd been absent most his life. She wouldn't expect him to care so much then.

The way Weldir grinned when his face formed momentarily, his eyes crinkled with deep humour, showed an underline of something else.

"You can't hurt something that feels *nothing*."

So, that was it. There was no sacrifice in taking his wounds for himself.

Regardless of the reason, she watched the glittering sand fill his wounds to leave not even a scar. It also cleaned him, making his fur fluffy and glossy in the sunlight.

Watching it all happen, how unromantic it was to watch herself be bonded to Faunus this way rather than in some grand gesture, she couldn't help silently laughing. It was fitting that it would be this way for her.

It's too late to change my mind now.

Not that she had been planning to.

FORTY-THREE

Mayumi knew by the way Weldir's chalky face was forming and dispersing while pointed in Faunus' direction that he was waiting to see if it worked.

The wait was long, and her heart raced in anticipation.

Come on... she mentally pleaded as she bounced impatiently on her feet. A soft gust of wind threw loose snowflakes into the air to dance. *Come onnnnn.*

"If this fails, you'll have to take me as well?" she asked Weldir, filling the nerve-wracking silence.

"Your soul has been eaten, and it no longer belongs to you. With no living anchor, your body will turn incorporeal and remain that way. I would only be leaving you here to suffer as a Ghost, and eventually, you'd forget who you are or how you came to die."

Her bottom lip cringed to the side before she lifted her arm and rubbed at the back of her neck. "He died to save me. I don't think he would be happy if he learned I died giving him my soul."

"What he does not know will not hurt him," he answered with a blasé tone.

"What happens to the souls you purify and keep? What's Tenebris like?"

He was silent for a moment, but she watched as his lips thinned in thought. It was hard to figure out what he looked like since she was only getting glimpses of him. She thought he may be attractive, and his ears were pointed and poking through inch-long hair.

"Tenebris is... beautiful," he finally answered quietly, but with a depth to his voice that revealed his care. "I made it so to keep the souls happy. It is dark except for where a soul lingers, and then it is bright for them. I guide them so they do not have to wander through nothingness and instead find peace in the world I have created for them. Maintaining it is draining, but it is better than being forced to hear them weep in fear and confusion. It makes it easier for them to accept that they have passed, and sometimes they don't realise they have died at all – some forgetting what it was like to have lived."

"If it is so beautiful, I hope I never see it then."

"It appears you won't, for now." He turned his face to her with his lips curled upwards. "He has accepted your soul, and it has allowed the part of him that is here to strengthen through the bond so I could force the lost fragment back together in that powerful moment."

Her brows knitted together. "But his eyes are still gone."

"I'm sure they will appear, give it time," he said as his form hovered backwards, a leg forming only once. "Since I'm no longer needed here, I will leave while I still have power from the soul I have consumed. Spooking my mate in this realm tickles me rather deeply, especially since I can't do so very often."

"How can you be so certain he will return to normal?"

When she received no response, she looked back to see he hadn't been stepping away to give Faunus and her space, but to leave.

Whatever. Mayumi shrugged as she faced Faunus once more and even stepped a little closer, although warily.

After minutes of having the world silent other than the rustling of leaves and a random bird squawk in the distance, she finally noticed a change.

Two pinpricks of yellow light formed just as her soul crested through the centre of his bony forehead. But they weren't the only changes that happened.

The gold she'd used to stick him together began to melt, pouring down his cheek and from his nose hole. It flattened and forked throughout the bone like it was seeping into tiny fissures she hadn't been able to see.

The excess was dripping away from him like her soul was a heat source that was binding him together properly.

When her soul fully emerged, it threw out both its arms. Black strings, like goopy ink, shot from the top curl of his ram horns and threaded around her hands and forearms. Then her soul pulled, and pulled, like it was trying to force his skull back together itself until its arms were crossed over its chest.

Finally, it curled and folded its legs underneath itself and laid its head against the middle of its arms.

Once it was done, his orbs flashed into large rotating swirls of fiery vortex that started fast before gentling in velocity.

His body shunted forward like he was taking a proper breath for the first time in ages. He looked one way, then the other, before leaning back on his hind legs so he could lift his claws to stare at them – like he couldn't believe they were real or that he was alive.

Mayumi stepped forward while dipping her body to the side as she assessed him. "Faunus?"

He lowered his hands and twisted his head at her.

"Mayumi?" He ghosted his fingertips against the crack in his skull before braving touching it completely. *"I am not in pain. How is this possible? I know I died."*

"It's a long story," she lightly chuckled, the relief she felt forcing the laugh from her.

She gave him a moment to collect himself when his body shifted from monstrous to the form she hadn't seen in days. The human-formed one that could stand with ease.

"You are bonded to me. I can feel it."

He lifted his hand further and wrapped his hand around her soul. He pulled it until the strings stretched and eventually broke apart so he could hold it and then look upon it. When he let it go, it floated back up to be between his horns and re-assumed its prior positioning with new strings attaching as though he'd never touched it.

He's back... truly back.

Just when she was about to tackle him and hug the ever-living fuck out of him, nuzzle that soft fur, and take in his delicious lemongrass and lime scent that she already missed, he did something that had her paling.

He grabbed the horn on what had been the bad side of his face and then fucking yanked on it like an idiot!

"What are you doing?!" Mayumi yelled as she ran forward and tugged on his arm to stop him.

He pushed her away to the point she almost fell and continued to yank as hard as he could on his horn. His body repeatedly dipped under the force.

"It's not breaking," he uttered with awe in his voice. Then he turned to the very tree behind him, placed his hands upon it, and rammed his face against it. A joyful laugh exploded from him. "It's not breaking!"

He did it one more time and then swiftly turned to her.

His yellow orbs were brighter than usual, the glee in them obvious before they turned bright pink.

She had a split second to realise he'd moved before she found herself squealing. He tossed her in the air, her arms and legs cartwheeling as her stomach dropped before he caught her and laid her torso over his very face.

"I feel no pain, Mayumi. I don't feel like I'm slipping away anymore. My face is as strong as it was before." He nuzzled her entire damn body like he'd been waiting an eternity to do so. "I don't know how you did this, but I will be eternally grateful for the rest of my life – especially with you by my side."

She slipped back and fell onto his forearm. She was seated on it like it was a perch or a swing, and he wrapped his other arm around her middle to hold her steady. Her legs swayed underneath his forearm with her chest smooshed just above his, while her knees were bent and pressing against the hard and warm plane of his abdomen.

He nuzzled the end of his snout underneath her chin, until he leaned forward to rub the golden streak underneath it instead.

The intense, vibrating purr that followed tickled her senses with affection. "Do you know how long I've wanted to just rub my damn face against you? It was nearly unbearable to deny myself the urge."

Mayumi couldn't contain the laugh that burst from her.

"Are you usually this joyful, or are you just happy to see me?"

she teased, needing to tease him to know she could again.

"Both," he answered with his own chuckle. "I once believed my eyes were yellow because I am quick to be gleeful but also very curious." He licked at her neck as he added, "As you have discovered."

She wrapped her arms around his entire head and cuddled it, thankful she didn't have to worry about hurting him. Her chest throbbed with such a blissful tenderness that she knew she'd never experienced anything like its intensity. It even caused more tears to well in her eyes, but for a completely different reason.

He's back. He's alive.

When he pulled his head back to gaze at her with his orbs a bright pink, the smile that curled her lips was soft yet filled with adoration.

"I told you that you are not allowed to cry these kinds of tears for me," he rumbled as he dabbed the tip of his tongue against one of her wet cheeks. "The only tears I want to see are the ones you give me when you're lost in abandon, moaning that second name you have for me."

Mayumi, trusting that he wouldn't let her fall, lifted her hands so she could cup the corners of his jaw. "They're tears of relief, Faunus. I didn't think I would get to see you again, and I'm so happy you're alive."

"I don't care, my fierce bride." He bumped the end of his snout against her lips to steal a kiss. "Not when I can see you have been crying for a while. Your face is all puffy and red."

"Oh, just shut up and take me inside."

Since he wanted a kiss, she lathered little pecks against the gold streak on his face when he began walking in the direction of her cabin.

He made it about two steps before he let out a choke and lunged back. Then he did that creepy thing where he twisted his neck to look over his shoulder, discovering he was attached to the tree.

"Why am I leashed like a pet?"

"Sorry about that." She laughed as she untied the loop around his neck. "Here, let me free you."

He brought his head forward. "You will have to explain what

has happened."

"I will, but later," she whispered with her lips brushing over the top of his snout once he was freed and walking. "For now, I just want to feel you. I want to feel that you're really here and that you're stuck with me now."

She bounced on his forearm with each step he took, her legs swinging underneath his arm. There was no need for surprise that he could hold her like this; he was her Duskwalker, strong and magnificent.

"That sounds foreboding," he said with the warm chuckle she'd missed terribly. "I was going to promise you eternity, but if you wring me dry, perhaps we both will perish from your insatiable desire."

Her lips curled into a smirk as she tried to think of a witty retort.

Thankfully she'd been wise enough to remove her charms, so they didn't harm him just in case he came back to her. It gave them the unimpeded freedom to walk up the porch and through the doorway of her home.

"Faunus?" she asked once they were inside, and Faunus did nothing but hold her.

Faunus had one hand wrapped around her thigh while the other was wrapped around her middle, their chests compressed against each other. The warmth of her was soothing to the side of his skull as he nestled it against her neck, enveloped by her chin above it, her gently pulsing jugular to the side of it, and her shoulder beneath.

"I don't want to put you down," he admitted, squeezing her tighter like his existence in this world depended on it.

"You don't have to," she replied softly, turning her face down to press it against the top of his.

His eyes darkened in the sheer bliss of her going beyond just accepting his embrace but deepening it.

Her little cottage was warmed by the dying fireplace, and it smelled like pumpkin and sleep. He took in these sensations, as well as her, and an overwhelming sense of gratitude washed over him.

He knew nothing of what awaited him on the other side, but he'd always worried it would be lonely.

When he'd sacrificed his life in his attempt to save hers, he'd thought he wouldn't come back. He'd also feared it wouldn't have been enough and that he would have found her somehow in the afterworld, wandering around lost and by herself.

This alternative was far better than he could ever have hoped for.

She is alive. And he was with her. She was his bride, something he'd wanted all the way down to the very fibre of his entire being.

Her flame was warm within his chest. He could feel it there while knowing it also sat on top of his skull.

Mayumi pressed the sweetest, softest little fluttering kisses to his face, following some line he could feel was different. He had no idea what it was, but he'd discover that later. All he knew was that it brought no pain.

She lowered while pressing her fingertips to the underside of his chin to lift it. She kissed the front of his fangs, and he opened his sight to find her eyes were firmly on him.

She appeared a little paler than he remembered, and the underneath of her eyes were puffy and pink, but when she smiled with a wicked hint in her expression, his heart sped up suddenly. There was a tender warmth there as well, one he'd never seen from her before.

Mayumi had always been sensual towards him, but this seemed like pure affection. Could any Duskwalker, or even human, not be enthralled by her being like this?

I don't think I will be able to handle her being sweeter to me. Just her kissing his face while gazing at him had his sight turning bright pink. The fact he felt comfortable enough to allow her to see it made it all the better.

I like her cold. It makes it easier not to fall prey to her – which was an odd thought coming from a beast like him.

Then she did something that had his jaws parting slightly

from a deep expire.

Mayumi *licked* across his fangs.

By the third time, she demanded, "Open up, Faunus."

He parted his fangs properly and greeted her tongue by licking it with his own. She deepened the contact by swiping hers down his hard and fast. He met each of her delicious tastebuds personally with a thrill passing through him on each stroke. When she twisted her head and went the other way, he did the same until she bit the tip of his tongue.

His head darted back, not expecting her to do this, but she held firm, and his tongue stretched between them.

He read the 'got you' expression on her face.

Faunus let out a little heat-struck growl. He pushed his head forward, his fangs parting around her face as he shoved his tongue through her teeth and deep within her mouth.

He couldn't help groaning at the taste and texture of her while she gave a soft moan in response as she lapped at him.

When her hands fiddled between them, he fisted the hood of her jacket and slipped it off her once she was done with the buttons. She pulled her shirt off and let it fall as well. He needed her beautiful bare body against his own. He needed to feel that she was real, that he was here with her in the physical world.

His hand caressed from between her hips all the way up her spine until he cut her hair tie with his claw and was shoving his fingers into the wonderful strands. He admired every inch of her, from soft skin and hard vertebrae to her silky hair.

Every bit of her had his palm tingling.

A thud was followed by a second, one of her boots falling to the timber floor while the other fell on top of his foot as she kicked them off.

"I thought I'd never get to touch you again," she whispered, brushing her fingers through the fur of his chest until they were sliding over his shoulders and down his upper back. "Or smell you," she murmured after she planted her face against his neck and breathed him in deeply. "Or feel your warmth or hear your breaths."

A blaze was sent through him, ruffling all the inhuman parts of him, from his fur to the spikes covering him. Even his tail tip curled at her admissions.

Her scent was ripening from soothing to heated, her arousal growing to wrap his mind like an ache. He panted against it and fisted her hair and thigh tighter from the quick tension it brought forth.

She was being so ravenous and passionate that he was spiralling out of control. He would happily let her eat him alive as long as she didn't stop, adoring being pampered by her continuously moving hands and mouth.

He couldn't contain the purr that rumbled as he rubbed the side of his skull against her. She pressed her naked chest more firmly so she could get to the root of his fur and touch against his very flesh.

"I missed that purr and the way it tickles my damn nipples. I don't care how you do it but take my pants off and take me, Faunus. God, I've missed you inside me."

Her laugh was teasing when a growl mingled with his purr. He removed his hand from her hair so he could hold her torso, holding her up as he dropped his arm from underneath her backside. Her legs swung against him when he grabbed the back of her trousers, his claws stabbing through the material before he tore them from her body. The strap of cloth between her legs, a meagre, useless barrier, went along with them.

He then walked forward so he could place her perfect, firm, round arse on the edge of her dining table. He wasn't ready to put her down completely, not in a way that could have her escaping him.

It was almost a better height as it brought her towards his groin with her shapely thighs parted wide around his own. Faunus bent over her on a straightened arm to cage her in even further.

Mayumi leaned back on both her hands while keeping her gaze on his orbs. Holding her had kept them pink, but looking upon her lovely body bared to him, his sight morphed to purple.

How could it not when he watched her dab her tongue at the seam of her lips before she bit the inside of the bottom one in obvious interest? Or when his sight drifted down to see her cute brown nipples were stiff as though they were begging for his attention – he flicked the back of one his claws up and down against them.

His orbs deepened in colour when the thin, muscled plane of her stomach dipped as she tilted her hips forward so she could present more of herself for him to see.

All his other sounds were cut short when he groaned at her brown folds and pink slit, so wet and slick that it was easy to see as it glistened in the dim light that filtered into her home. And, now that her legs were spread, the tantalising smell of her was even more clogging to his mind.

He swore the air was teasing him with little tastes every time he breathed in.

"Look at how small you are inside now," he rasped as he drew his index claw down the side of her abdomen muscles, watching them dance with clenches. He sheathed his claws as he dipped just the tip of his thumb into her entrance and pulled it open like a curtain. "I will not fit inside you like this."

"I told you I didn't want you to undo the spell."

Just because of her snarky tone, Faunus shoved his thumb inside her knuckle deep. Her breath hitched, but he didn't expect her limbs to prickle with goosebumps in reaction. Then he removed it, using it while it was wet to rub her hardened needy clit while he slipped his middle finger inside. She was tight and *hot.*

"Not... your fingers," she moaned, her right hand snapping down to grab his wrist. "I'm already ready, Faunus. I need your cock inside me. I need to feel you like before you changed me back."

Mayumi wasn't usually this impatient for his cock. So long as she was feeling pleasure, she didn't mind Faunus taking his time with her – touching, tasting, feeling, pushing her to higher and higher heights.

Maybe because she was feeling clingy... she wanted to be clingy around his cock too?

Regardless, Faunus speared her with a second finger as he leaned forward so he could brush his snout against her cheek. She didn't realise that Faunus was just as desperate to join with her, that he needed to be inside her just as much as she needed him. Taking his time with her was almost unbearable.

From the moment she'd bit his tongue, his cock had been jerking frantically with excitement and anticipation until he was hard and barely able to contain it behind his seam. He wanted to become one with her, to claim his new bride in a frenzy and devour every part of her, her heart, her soul, her body all at once.

"I must mount you, even if it's only by a little, to do the spell." He withdrew his fingers until he almost lost her, before shoving back all the way in. "I am not interested in destroying this wonderful place, but I will gladly ruin it for anyone else."

When her head tilted back slightly to moan from his moving fingers, it exposed the column of her neck. He licked at it, causing her to shiver and loosen for him.

He spread her with his fingers so he could make room to add a third, finding, like before, it was with great difficulty.

What control his tentacles had was weakened by this desirous woman starting to buck her hips on his fingers.

I hope it is possible a second time... He wasn't sure if he could redo the spell since he'd already done it to her once. The immense pressure of his shaft slipped from his seam when he thought, *But I don't think I can survive this female if I cannot fuck her senseless.*

Because he knew her well enough that she would tease him, and tease him, and tease him to the point he'd ram his cock in and break her.

"Oh God, hurry up. I swear you're just trying to punish me." She moaned, her head lolling to the side as he continued to lick at her neck. "Take them out, or I'm going to come."

For someone who didn't sound like she wanted that, she kept trying to move on his three fingers and his thumb petting the hard nub of her clit. The more he moved all three, the deeper he could go, slowly stretching her so she could at least take the very tip of his large cock.

"But I thought you only wanted my cock," he purred against her. "Or will this pretty little cunt take whatever I give it and come?"

His fur puffed in delight at being able to tease her again, play with her, touch her knowing he was planning on mounting her.

A week ago, he didn't think this would ever be possible again, and yet here he was... with this tiny female beneath him and gyrating wantonly.

Just for that reason alone, he wanted to toy with her. The reason, and the main one, was because she was being demanding, and he didn't always like giving her what she wanted.

"Faunus..." she started before her lips parted when he deliberately grazed that tender spot inside her. He flicked it with his middle finger, the other two behind it helping to make it easier to find and grow plump when he pushed.

He pulled back to create space between them. "Grab my horns."

Just the fact he could tell her to hold his horns had his cock slipping to the ends of his tentacles, threatening to break free. He had to clench his groin to keep their hold.

She lifted one hand and grabbed the right while the other only fisted the fur of his shoulder. She was avoiding what was once the bad side of his face.

Her back bowed deeply when he felt the first ripple of her pussy.

"I'm going to come. I'm going to come," she whispered under her breath.

A long moan followed, and her toes curled against his outer thighs. Just as her pussy clenched, Faunus pulled his fingers from her just before her orgasm could finish releasing, to rob her of it.

She gasped and looked down in disbelief.

Her features softened when his tentacles released, and she spread her thighs in welcome for it. He placed the tip of his throbbing, hard cock against her spread entrance.

"I want you to hold *both* my horns, Mayumi," he croaked at the kiss of plush heat spreading over the slightly pointed head, and he couldn't help trying to dig deeper. She was so soft, so hot, so perfect here. "Hold them nice and tight."

With her eyes riveted to where they were barely joined, she lifted her other hand and latched on to his free horn, so she was grabbing both.

I cannot wait any longer.

He stabbed his claws into her abdomen and it clenched around the hard protrusions. Blood welled, and for the first time in his life, he didn't feel starved for it, didn't hunger for it.

Faunus quaked as he shoved, feeling her body pushing forward as he tried to mount her. The spell was slow to enact, and at first, he thought it wasn't going to.

He held his breath until finally her pussy made way for him, slowly but steadily. He knew he made it harder when his shaft swelled and released a drop of precum straight into her quivering, snug core.

The last time he'd done this, he'd been angry, jealous, and possessive. He'd been desperate to spear her insides, so he'd claimed them for himself.

This time was different. It was already his. He was just taking it back – and it felt phenomenal to do so, knowing she was his bride, that she would forever be connected to him.

His fangs parted, and he yelped at the tight pressure and the delicious pop of the sensitive head pushing through.

"Oh fuck," she rasped.

"Look at you," he groaned as he watched himself burrowing deeper and deeper, her thighs twitching the entire time. "Look at your little cunt taking me so well, making way for me again." The possessive growl that came from him was in triumph. "So tight. So pretty as I spread you."

He didn't need to pull back in order to wet her with his lubricant. It was seeping from him and making his entrance easier, but he did it just so he could feel the sensation.

What he didn't know was that Mayumi had been trying to hold it together as he changed her. His pull back and thrust forward, until he was at the point he'd already stretched her to, sent her over the edge – just like last time.

The moment she clenched him, Faunus' claws dug into the timber of her table and ruined it. He thrust what he had inside her, plunging into her with hungry slams.

It rammed a crescendo of cries from her.

She wasn't finished by the time he burrowed as deep as he could, so he removed his claws from her flesh and began fucking her as fast as he could into the table. It wobbled beneath them, threatening to break as it bashed against the wall. Each bang was loud, proving just how savagely he was taking her.

He was ready to catch her, but he wasn't going to stop until his female had finished coming apart. *Mine. She's mine. Mine to hold, to fuck, to touch.*

Waves of heat spread throughout him, starting from his groin, and it caused his fur and spikes to lift in following ripples as his skin tightened.

Before, there had been a slight throbbing in his skull whenever he was this hard, which would only grow to a nagging point whenever he started thrusting.

Now, all he experienced was euphoria while this horny woman took his cock like the good girl he needed her to be. While she gripped both horns and even lifted herself by them in her ecstasy. While her body dipped and bowed in waves as she cried out. While she wet his shaft, the scent of it so delicious his pants grew even more choked – his tongue desperate to taste it.

I should have licked her first. He groaned when she started relaxing. *I should have let her come around my tongue. She always tastes so damn wonderful.*

His sight landed on his hand wrapped around her thigh, smearing both blood and her slick over her flesh. His thrusts stopped only so he could safely lift his hand and lick over his palm, then fingers, taking in both essences.

Her dazed eyes watched him, and he saw nothing but lust in them as he coated his tongue.

"All of you tastes good," he rumbled. "Your pussy, your blood, your sweat. I have always wanted to bite you but couldn't before. I think I will remedy that today."

Her parted lips, huffing with shallow breaths, curled upwards into a haunting smile. "I. Bite. Back."

"I'm betting on that," he said as he stepped back with his tentacles keeping a hold of her hips. "We're not done here. Hold on to me tight."

Faunus wished he could hold her cute arse and the backs of her thighs while standing upright, but instead he was forced to kneel once they were away from the table.

She was seated on top of him with her legs wrapped around his thighs, her hands gripping his horns to keep herself upright.

Her chest brushed against his torso when he held her still and shoved his cock upwards into her tight channel.

Like always, her body was too small to contain something as big and tall as him. He could see the first few inches bulging her flesh from the inside, pushing it upwards.

"Yes, Faun," she moaned, hanging by her arms and drawing her knees back, so she was spread even further for him. "Just like that. Don't stop."

Her feet were pointed so she could press the tops of them and her shins against his moving hips. She used them, and her arms, to help bounce herself, forcing them to go faster, for his impacts to be deeper, harder.

"I missed you," he groaned as he swelled momentarily within her, the warmth and plumpness cuddling his aching cock. "I missed this. Those last few days were so hard for me, Mayumi. Wanting to touch you but being unable to. I craved you, just as I have always craved you."

"Oh, Faun," she whispered, her eyes bowing in what he thought might be pity for him – so he fucking rammed his cock faster just so that expression would disappear.

Her cries suddenly got louder, more broken and lost. Mayumi threw her head back, her chest bowed in his direction, as she worked her hips back and forth while he thrust in and out.

Their mixing movements caused her eyes to water, just as her nose and cheeks pinkened in deep arousal. Her gaze completely lost its focus as she stared at nothing on the ceiling.

And Faunus knew by the spasms rippling around his cock, that she was moments from breaking apart again. Mayumi was completely swallowed up by the dark entity that was her lust.

"You're so damn beautiful like this," he growled, gripping her thighs and hips tighter and using them to bounce her. "It's the only time you go soft. Where your snarky, dirty mouth can't do anything but moan and whimper. You can't even see what's fucking you properly, can you?" He slowed just for a few thrusts as he said, "But I bet you can feel it, can feel my cock inside you."

Before she could even get a chance to collect her thoughts at all, he started back up with his rapid pace.

Her watering eyes crinkled, causing her lust-filled tears to drip down her cheeks in quick strikes. Faunus had little idea why seeing her cry in ecstasy riled him up so damn much, but it always made him want to do anything he could to see those pathetic streams down her face.

Letting go of one arse cheek, he shoved his clawed fingers through her hair, fisted it tightly, and shoved her head forward, forcing her to watch his cock moving in and out of her. He parted his tentacles to make sure she could see how stretched the lips of her pussy were around the thick girth of cock.

Faunus liked fucking her in the mirror whenever he could. He occasionally peered into it behind her now, watching him taking her from the back while also being able to look down between them.

He also adored the way her insides fluttered whenever *she* watched them, clenching, spasming, rippling with tantalising little squeezes.

"Mine," he snarled, wishing he could bury his snout against her. When she tried to turn her head up, he didn't let her. "Look at us. Watch me take my little bride's pussy. You wanted my cock, so you can watch it make you come."

All she could do was chant that adorable nickname she gave him, the one that was reserved for only this, right before she screamed in abandon.

His sacs lifted into the base of his cock as he clenched from the snug spasms of her walls trying to milk him. Faunus groaned deeply, his lungs quaking.

"I told you what would happen if you gave me your soul, Mayumi." Faunus shuddered through her orgasm, the thrusts of his cock becoming slicker as her liquid pooled in his seam and around the base of his tentacles. "That I would do what I want with that womb of yours, and fill it, breed it, make it *mine.*"

He loosened his grip on her hair when she relaxed once more, and he let her turn her gaze up to him. She came face-to-face with his wildly panting skull, his orbs such a dark colour purple.

He didn't know what the expression on her face was, but she was rendered silent. His cock was still moving. He wasn't going to give her a break – not when he was close to finishing right where he wanted.

"I don't know the spell to prevent it. I never thought I'd need it, but I think a part of me didn't want to know it."

Faunus' tentacles tightened their grip on her, trying to force her down so she couldn't escape him.

"I want to spend inside you so badly, Mayumi. Just like this, how we are now, with you as my precious bride... your body ready and waiting for me. I ache for it."

He didn't know if she understood he was waiting for an answer from her, but she'd better give it soon, or he'd make the choice for her. She gave a little mewl when his shaft swelled just as his sacs lifted again, warning her of the impending flood he wouldn't be able to hold back.

"Mayumi..." he groaned when she was taking too long.

"Just do it," she whispered. "I want to feel your hot come inside me more than anything. I don't care what happens; I just need to feel it."

With a snarl of victory, he let go of her hair so he could grip her shoulders to support her and himself as he curled his spine and shoved his head forward. Without warning, Faunus did as he promised earlier and shoved his fangs around the side of her neck.

He bit her, hard enough to draw blood but not enough to rend her muscle, and shoved her down on him. Mayumi gasped, her hands letting go of his horns so she could grip the fur on the backs of his shoulders tightly and tug.

His tentacles locked around her just as his cock spikes hardened and latched. His roar was muffled by flesh, his breaths through his nose hole snorted, when the first burst of his seed splashed inside her.

"*Nhnn*," she groaned, the tension from his bite easing out of her as he filled her perfect pussy with every drop he had to give.

Faunus' sight turned black as he basked in it, feeling her beginning to overflow as the sweetness of her blood slowly dripped into his mouth. The warmth of her body around him was like heaven, just as it felt like dear *home* in his arms.

Her sleepy pumpkin scent on top of it all had his mind going blank as he was overcome with tenderness and pleasure. His roar turned into a shaken, mind-altered groan.

His cock left very little room inside of her to keep his seed, except for deep inside her womb, and the rest was forced out through their snugness. In the quiet of her home, heavy splatters could be heard as the rest hit the ground between his spread knees.

His tail remained curled in tension all throughout, while his body gave wild shudders and twitches – his inability to thrust through this was agony.

Gently, Faunus removed his fangs from her by widening his clamping jaw and pulled back. A few drops of crimson dripped onto her shoulder when she fell forward with her arms dropping. Her pulse was beating frantically, and he could not only hear it but feel it against him – just as he heard and felt her lungs working fast.

His own heart and breaths were even more rapid.

Mayumi nuzzled and snuggled his fur, so he danced his fingertips up and down her spine.

"Are you okay? Does my bite hurt? Do you wish for me to heal you?" He'd heal her if she wanted him to, but he liked having it on her for a little while longer – the first of many bites he hoped to give her.

He was particularly fond of the idea of biting at her thighs and arse if she let him. He'd nibble every bit of flesh with utter joy.

"That felt so good," she said, not caring about her wound. Then she gave a soft laugh. "But I have bad news for you, Duskwalker."

"Bad news?" he asked as he licked at his snout, trying to drink every bit of her he'd stolen. It was sweet and almost tangy like her scent but metallic and salty like all blood.

"I'm no longer in the fertile part of my cycle." He tilted his head when he didn't understand what that meant – considering he thought females were fertile all the time. Then, with her voice going soft, she whispered, "Better luck next month... if I let you."

"I don't understand," he answered.

It only made her snort with humour.

"Of course not." A few long but beautiful seconds passed. He combed her hair before brushing his hands down her body, happily holding his new bride – the only one he'd ever wanted. "Did you hear me?"

"Hear what, Mayumi?"

"Before you came back, I shouted at you. Did you hear what I said?"

Faunus cocked his head at that. "No, I did not."

He didn't know how long he'd been gone. The last thing he remembered was fighting the Demonslayers.

"Good," she mumbled against him. "I want to tell you properly."

"What did you–" before he could finish interrogating her, wanting to know the secret things she'd said to him, soft snores fell from her.

Since the entire front of her body was buried against him, including her face, he gently turned her head to find that she'd fallen asleep. Not just any kind of sleep either... but the one where the person was languid and deathly pale from exhaustion. Since her newest tears had come from physical tension rather than emotional distress, he could see the puffed darkness under her eyes.

She didn't sleep.

He'd never seen her this tired.

Faunus carefully shuffled them until he could place his back against the wall so they could rest together while still joined. He liked that she was comfortable enough to sleep on top of him like this, with his cock still nestled deep within her, so he could hear and feel her fragile yet strong heartbeat all around him.

He'd sit like this forever if it was what she needed.

Pressing the side of his bony snout against her hair, he pet her with it as his hand continued to play along her flesh everywhere he could touch.

She did not sleep while I was gone.

He didn't need to ask why she had chosen to have sex with him if she was so exhausted.

She speaks with her body. He knew this about her.

This was Mayumi's way of letting him know she missed him, cared for him, loved him, just as he did her. It was also her way of showing that she needed him, not just in body, but in life. That she'd been deeply hurting before he was returned to her.

He brushed the backs of his fingers against her cheek and even down the soft edge of her nose.

I will never leave you again. He brushed his knuckle up her nose this time and then over to the short hairs of her quirky, always expressive eyebrows. *I will follow you wherever you want to go, and help you achieve whatever it is you wish to achieve.*

If she wanted to go south to the sea again, he would take her there. If she wanted to bait and fight Demons, he would be more than happy to help her – especially since he would be much better at staying sane while doing so.

And if she wanted to do nothing but fuck him half to death, he'd be absolutely delighted.

He'd started his life lonely. Now he knew it would be filled with naughty, joyful, and teasing memories. All of them of this bossy, downright annoying female, he had cherished from the moment he first met her.

His sight found the mirror to properly look at his face, seeing the glint of gold reflecting in it, as well as her beautiful soul. His orbs turned the brightest pink he'd ever seen.

My face is made of her will to keep me by her side.

EPILOGUE

3 months later

Mayumi gently swayed side to side as she sat on Faunus' back in his monstrous form, the warming winds softly wisping across her face. The sun was balmy as it shone through the canopy of leaves while they travelled through the forest.

Birds chirped cheerily while wildflowers crested through the thinning blanket of snow to dance hello for the first time in months.

There were scents in the air, pleasant to most, but for Mayumi...

Her loud, deep sneeze caused the birds to scatter with fear. She rubbed at her itching, sniffling nose. *I fucking hate spring!*

"That was a big one," Faunus chuckled, being careful of where he stepped to make sure he didn't disturb the environment and cause a plume of pollen to lift in the air around them.

"Allergies... I swear." She continued to itch her face. "I wish I could peel my nose off."

They usually weren't too bad, but she'd never travelled relatively fast on a Duskwalker's back before. She lifted her scarf over her face, which had been a decent barrier up until about five minutes ago.

"You said there were no flowers in the Veil, right?" she asked on a pained wheeze.

He lifted his head in a random direction, hearing something she couldn't. "There are no flowers. Only the mist and trees."

"Good. Hurry up and get me away from the pollen-infested

surface world before I shoot my brain through my sinuses."

He twisted his neck in that damn creepy fashion to peer at her on his back. Mayumi leaned on a straightened arm behind her and raised a brow.

"Are you usually this..." He paused when he was trying to figure out the right word to use.

"Bitchy?" she answered for him. "It's like spiteful and irritated."

He clicked his tongue as he took the word in. "Are you usually this bitchy during spring?"

Mayumi suddenly wished she hadn't helped him. She pouted.

"No, but my allergies aren't usually this bad." Her eyes narrowed into a deep, spiteful glare. "I bet this is all *your* damn fault. My whole damn face is itchy, Faunus!"

He looked down her body and then rolled his head forward. She could almost picture him rolling his eyes if he had any! He shook his head while his shoulders bounced like he was laughing at her.

"I warned you I would be victorious, that you wouldn't be able to stop me."

She placed her hand over her swelling abdomen. "If you weren't carrying all my shit, I'd throw something at that big, fat, hard head of yours."

Currently, they were transferring a large number of items from her home to deep within the Veil. They were going the long way around, avoiding it as much as possible, so they could enter it from the southwest. They were still rather north and had been for most of the week.

It didn't take much for Mayumi to realise she was pregnant, not that it was a surprise considering he'd been honest with his intentions. She'd let it happen, knowing there was nothing she could have done to stop it.

His pull-out game was exceedingly poor, considering not only his tentacles but also his barbs. She tried to calculate her cycle, tried to avoid it, which had failed terribly.

For two whole days they avoided sex in the middle of her cycle, yet here she was, carrying this horny Duskwalker's baby.

Once she'd realised, after vomiting what he called darkness

from her stomach – which sucked horribly – they'd both discussed their options.

Mayumi had already been toying with the idea of going into the Veil, since Faunus had expressed that he was disappointed he couldn't see his brothers and their own brides. She also knew, without a doubt, he hated her home.

He doesn't fit in it.

It wasn't fair to make him live in it when he couldn't even stand upright.

What made her fast track her decision was this. For the first time in her life, Mayumi was a little... scared? Okay, really scared. What the hell was she supposed to do with a child *anything*? And taking care of one of his kind seemed hard, and he barely had any answers.

Magnar and Delora had one, and she planned to strangle them for answers if they wouldn't give them willingly. Faunus told her she wouldn't need to, but her anxiety was making her want to be violent – maybe her pregnancy hormones as well.

Faunus and Mayumi were going to find a section of the forest near their homes and build their own. Faunus planned to lay down his own protection ward to keep her safe and was hoping to strong-arm Magnar and Orpheus into helping him build a house that would be suitable for them. However many of *them* there would be.

Now that his skull is strong, he's no longer afraid of Jabez. Faunus had told her he'd love to ram his partially golden skull into his.

Mayumi let out a little sigh.

I really hope I can come back and collect all my family's stuff. Currently strapped across Faunus' back from neck to backside were bags upon bags of her things.

She'd left behind what she could bear to, with every intention of returning to bring it to her new home. What she had were her clothes, her board games, her kitchen supplies, and weapons upon weapons.

There was also an old-style military tent she'd paid Klaus, Henry, and Yoshida to steal from the old barracks of Colt's Outpost. They planned to use it as a temporary home. It wasn't very wide, but it was tall enough that even Faunus could stand in it – she hoped.

Those boys annoy me sometimes, but I'm glad I got to say goodbye to them.

She'd told them that Faunus was alive, surprised when Yoshida seemed to be the most relieved at the news. She also informed them she was leaving and didn't know when she'd be returning.

After a little while of travel, her sneezing fits calmed since they weren't travelling through a particularly bad section of trees, and she looked around at the warming world.

She was searching for something, waiting.

There wasn't much to do on the back of a Duskwalker but annoy him, and she currently had a game she enjoyed playing. She would have to say it was one of her favourites of all time now.

"Veer a little to the right," she demanded quietly.

When he did, he slowly took them past a fallen tree trunk that was roughly knee height for him. She shook her head and eventually told him to go to the left when she spotted something else.

A boulder. A nice, big one.

"This looks perfect," she purred, rubbing the underside of her boot against the back of his horn. "It's your hip height. Perfect for laying me across."

Faunus' body *violently* quaked between her thighs as he shuddered, one of his hands crossing in front of the other before he almost stumbled. He even let out a shaking groan.

He snapped his head back over his shoulder, his orbs purple. "Don't," he rasped. "I must reach a good distance today."

With her free hand, she ghosted her fingertips from her hips, over her stomach, and between her breasts. "But I want to. It's perfect, Faunus, and the ground is too snowy still for you to lay me against it."

"Mayumi," he pathetically whined, before another full-body shudder shot through him.

Ever since he'd learned she was carrying his child, the damn horny Duskwalker got heated at the drop of a leaf. The more noticeable her stomach became, which wasn't hard since she was thin, the worse he seemed to be.

Mayumi had taken that as a challenge.

She threw her head back and laughed, deeply and loudly, to the world. She knew he just wanted to get to the Veil, where it was safer, and she was under his ward. He was also worried the journey might take longer than her weird, speedy pregnancy.

She was almost certain that being pregnant was exasperating her damn fucking hay fever! Of course, she was going to pick on him in retaliation.

"Come on, Faunus. Don't you want to *ravish* me while you have your big hand over my belly again?"

He let out a strangled choke, and her laughter grew infinitely more conniving when he tried to hold down a branch, and it whacked him in the face because he wasn't paying attention. He snorted a huff of annoyance.

Oh my God! I love messing with him so much.

Her laugh softened into giggles that eventually turned into her just smiling brightly at the back of his white skull in adoration.

I'm so glad he's mine.

Also by Opal Reyne

DUSKWALKER BRIDES
A Soul to Keep
A Soul to Heal
A Soul to Touch
A Soul to Guide
A Soul to Revive *(TBA 2023)*
A Soul to Steal *(TBA 2024)*
(More titles coming soon)

WITCH BOUND
The WitchSlayer
The ShadowHunter
(More titles coming soon)

Completed Series

A PIRATE ROMANCE DUOLOGY
Sea of Roses
Storms of Paine

~~THE ADEUS CHRONICLES~~
This series has been **unpublished** as of
20th of June 2022

If you would like to keep up to date with all the novels I will be publishing in the future, please follow me on my social media platforms.

Website:
https://www.opalreyne.com
Facebook Page:
https://www.facebook.com/OpalReyne
Facebook Group:
https://www.facebook.com/groups/opals.nawty.book.realm
Instagram:
https://www.instagram.com/opalreyne
Twitter
https://www.twitter.com/opalreyne
Patreon:
https://www.patreon.com/OpalReyne
Discord:
https://discord.gg/opalites
TikTok:
@OpalReyneAuthor